T0182438

By John Wyndham

TECHNICAL SLIP

JOHN WYNDHAM

TECHNICAL SLIP

collected stories

Previously published as *Jizzle*

THE MODERN LIBRARY

NEW YORK

A Note on the Text

This book was published in 1954 and reflects the attitudes of its time. The publisher's decision to present it as it was originally published is not intended as endorsement of any offensive cultural representations or language.

2024 Modern Library Trade Paperback Edition

Published in the United States by The Modern Library, an imprint of Random House, a division of Penguin Random House LLC, New York.

The Modern Library and the Torchbearer colophon are registered trademarks of Penguin Random House LLC.

Originally published in slightly different form as *Jizzle* by Dobson, London, in 1954. This edition contains the novella *The Curse of the Burdens* by John Wyndham, written under his pseudonym John B. Harris in 1927.

ISBN 9780593733493
Ebook ISBN 9780593733509

Printed in the United States of America on acid-free paper

modernlibrary.com
randomhousebooks.com

1st Printing

To Hippolyta for saying "Well shone, moon!"

CONTENTS

TECHNICAL SLIP

TECHNICAL SLIP

"Prendergast," said the Departmental Director, briskly, "there'll be that Contract XB2S23 business arising today. Look after it, will you?"

"Very good, sir."

———

Robert Finnerson lay dying. Two or three times before he had been under the impression that he might be dying. He had been frightened, and blusterously opposed to the idea; but this time it was different: he did not bluster, for he had no doubt that the time had come. Even so, he was still opposed; it was under marked protest that he acknowledged the imminence of the nonsensical arrangement.

It was so absurd to die at sixty, anyway, and, as he saw it, it would be even more wasteful to die at eighty. A scheme of things in which the wisdom acquired in living was simply scrapped in this way was, to say the least, grossly inefficient. What did it mean? That somebody else would have to go through the process of learning all that life had already taken sixty years to teach him; and then be similarly scrapped in the end. No wonder the race was slow in getting anywhere—if, indeed, it were getting anywhere—with this cat-and-mouse, ten-forward-and-nine-back system.

Lying back on one's pillows and waiting for the end in the quiet, dim room, the whole ground plan of existence appeared to suffer from a basic futility of conception. It was a matter to which some of these illustrious scientists might well pay more attention—

only, of course, they were always too busy fiddling with less important matters; until they came to his present pass, when they would find it was too late to do anything about it.

Since his reflections had revolved thus purposelessly, and several times, upon somewhat elliptical orbits, it was not possible for him to determine at what stage of them he became aware that he was no longer alone in the room. The feeling simply grew that there was someone else there, and he turned his head on the pillow to see who it might be. The thin clerkly man whom he found himself regarding, was unknown to him, and yet, somehow, unsurprising.

"Who are you?" Robert Finnerson asked him.

The man did not reply immediately. He looked about Robert's own age, with a face, kindly but undistinguished, beneath hair that had thinned and grayed. His manner was diffident, but the eyes which regarded Robert through modest gold-rimmed spectacles were observant.

"Pray do not be alarmed, Mr. Finnerson," he requested.

"I'm not at all alarmed," Robert told him testily. "I simply asked who you are."

"My name is Prendergast—not, of course, that that matters——"

"Never heard of you. What do you want?"

Prendergast told him modestly: "My employers wish to lay a proposition before you, Mr. Finnerson."

"Too late now for propositions," Robert replied shortly.

"Ah, yes, for most propositions, of course, but I think this one may interest you."

"I don't see how—all right, what is it?"

"Well, Mr. Finnerson, we—that is, my employers—find that you are—er—scheduled for demise on April 20, 1963. That is, of course, tomorrow."

"Indeed," said Robert calmly, and with a feeling that he should have been more surprised than he felt. "I had come to much the same conclusion myself."

"Quite sir," agreed the other. "But our information also is that you are opposed to this—er—schedule."

"Indeed!" repeated Mr. Finnerson. "How subtle! If that's all you have to tell me, Mr. Pendlebuss——"

"Prendergast, sir. No, that is just by way of assuring you of our grasp of the situation. We are also aware that you are a man of considerable means; and, well, there's an old saying that 'you can't take it with you,' Mr. Finnerson."

Robert Finnerson looked at his visitor more closely.

"Just what are you getting at?" he said.

"Simply this, Mr. Finnerson. My firm is in a position to offer a revision of schedule—for a consideration."

Robert was already far enough from his normal for the improbable to have shed its improbability. It did not occur to him to question its possibility. He said, "What revision—and what consideration?"

"Well, there are several alternative forms," explained Prendergast, "but the one we recommend for your consideration is our Reversion Policy. It is quite our most comprehensive benefit—introduced originally on account of the large numbers of persons in positions similar to yours who were noticed to express the wish 'if only I had my life over again.'"

"I see," said Robert, and indeed he did. The fact that he had read somewhere or other of legendary bargains of the kind went a long way to disperse the unreality of the situation. "And the catch is?" he added.

Prendergast allowed a trace of disapproval to show.

"The *consideration*," he said, with some slight stress upon the word. "The consideration in respect of a Revision is a down-payment to us of seventy-five percent of your present capital."

"Seventy-five percent! What is this firm of yours?"

Prendergast shook his head.

"You would not recall it, but it is a very old-established concern. We have had—and do have—numbers of notable clients. In the old days we used to work on a basis of—well—I suppose you would call it barter. But with the rise of commerce we changed our methods. We have found it much more convenient to have investable capital than to accumulate souls—especially at their present depressed market value. It is a great improvement in all ways. We benefit considerably, and it costs you nothing but money you must lose anyway—and you are still entitled to call your soul your own: as far, that is, as the law of the land permits. Your heirs will be a trifle disappointed, that's all."

The last was not a consideration to distress Robert.

"My heirs are round the house like vultures now," he said. "I don't in the least mind their having a little shock. Let's get down to details, Mr. Snodgrass."

"Prendergast," said the visitor, patiently. "Well now, the usual method of payment is this . . ."

———

It was a whim, or what appeared to be a whim, which impelled Mr. Finnerson to visit Sands Square. Many years had passed since he had seen it, and though the thought of a visit had risen from time to time there had seemed never to be the leisure. But now in the convalescence following the remarkable, indeed, miraculous recovery which had given such disappointment to his relatives, he found himself for the first time in years with an abundance of spare hours on his hands.

He dismissed the taxi at the corner of the square, and stood for some minutes surveying the scene with mixed feelings. It was both smaller and shabbier than his memory of it. Smaller, partly because most things seem smaller when revisited after a stretch of years, and partly because the whole of the south side including the house which had been his home was now occupied by an overbearing block of offices: shabbier because the new block emphasized the decrepitude of those Georgian terraces which had survived the bombs and had therefore had to outlast their expected span by twenty or thirty years.

But if most things had shrunk, the plane trees now freshly in leaf had grown considerably, seeming to crowd the sky with their branches, though there were fewer of them. A change was the bright banks of tulips in well-tended beds which had grown nothing but tired-looking laurels before. Greatest change of all, the garden was no longer forbidden to all but residents, for the iron railing, so long employed in protecting the privilege, had gone for scrap in 1941, and never been replaced.

In a recollective mood and with a trace of melancholy, Mr. Finnerson crossed the road and began to stroll again along the once familiar paths. It pleased and yet saddened him to discover the semi-concealed gardener's shed looking just as it had looked fifty years ago. It displeased him to notice the absence of the circular seat which used to surround the trunk of a familiar tree. He wandered on, noting this and remembering that, but in general remembering too much, and beginning to regret that he had come. The garden was pleasant—better looked after than it had been—but, for him, too full of ghosts. Overall there was a sadness of glory lost, with shabbiness surrounding.

On the east side a well-remembered knoll survived. It was, he recalled as he walked slowly up it, improbably reputed to be a last fragment of the earthworks which London had prepared against the threat of Royalist attack.

In the circle of bushes which crowned it a hard, slatted chair rested in seclusion. The fancy took him to hide in this spot as he had been wont to hide there half a century before. With his handkerchief he dusted away the pigeon droppings and the lesser grime. The relief he found in the relaxation of sitting down made him wonder if he had not been overestimating his recuperation. He felt quite unusually weary....

Peace was splintered by a girl's insistent voice.

"Bobby!" she called. "Master Bobby, where are you?"

Mr. Finnerson was irritated. The voice jarred on him. He tried to disregard it as it called again.

Presently a head appeared among the surrounding bushes. The

face was a girl's; above it a bonnet of dark blue straw; around it navy ribbons, joining in a bow on the left cheek. It was a pretty face, though at the moment it wore a professional frown.

"Oh, there you are, you naughty boy. Why didn't you answer when I called?"

Mr. Finnerson looked behind him to find the child addressed. There was none. As he turned back he became aware that the chair had gone. He was sitting on the ground, and the bushes seemed taller than he had thought.

"Come along now. You'll be late for tea," added the girl. She seemed to be looking at Mr. Finnerson himself.

He lowered his eyes, and received a shock. His gaze, instead of encountering a length of neatly striped trouser, rested upon blue serge shorts, chubby knees, white socks, and childish shoes. He waggled his foot, and that in the childish shoe responded. Forgetting everything else in this discovery, he looked down his front at a fawn coat with large flat brass buttons. At the same moment he became aware that he was viewing everything from beneath the curving brim of a yellow straw hat.

The girl gave a sound of impatience. She pushed through the bushes and emerged as a slender figure in a long, navy blue cape. She bent down. A hand, formalized at the wrist by a stiff cuff, emerged from the folds of the cape and fastened upon his upper arm. He was dragged to his feet.

"Come along now," she repeated. "Don't know what's come over you this afternoon, I'm sure."

Clear of the bushes, she shifted her hold to his hand, and called again.

"Barbara. Come along."

Robert tried not to look. Something always cried out in him as if it had been hurt when he looked at Barbara. But in spite of his will his head turned. He saw the little figure in a white frock turn its head, then it came tearing across the grass looking like a large doll. He stared. He had almost forgotten that she had once been like that: as well able to run as any other child, and forgotten, too, what a pretty, happy little thing she had been.

It was quite the most vivid dream he had ever had. Nothing in it was distorted or absurd. The houses sat with an air of respectability round the quiet square. On all four sides they were of a pattern, with variety only in the colors of the spring painting that most of them had received. The composite sounds of life about him were in a pattern, too, that he had forgotten: no rising whine of gears, nor revving of engines, nor squeal of tires; instead, an utterly different cast blended from the clopping of innumerable hooves, light and heavy, and the creak and rattle of carts. Among it was the jingle of chains and bridles, and somewhere in a nearby street a hurdy-gurdy played a once-familiar tune. The beds of tulips had vanished, the wooden seat encircled the old tree as before, the spiked railings stood as he remembered them, stoutly preserving the garden's privacy. He would have liked to pause and taste the flavor of it all again, but that was not permissible.

"Don't *drag*," admonished the voice above him. "We're late for your tea now, and Cook won't half create."

There was a pause while she unlocked the gate and let them out, then with their hands in hers they crossed the road toward a familiar front door, magnificent with new, shiny green paint and brass knocker. It was a little disconcerting to find that their way in led by the basement steps and not through this impressive portal.

In the nursery everything was just as it had been, and he stared around him, remembering.

"No time for mooning, if you want your tea," said the voice above.

He went to the table, but continued to look around, recognizing old friends. The rocking horse with its lower lip missing. The tall fireguard, and the rug in front of it. The three bars across the window. The dado procession of farmyard animals. The gas lamp purring gently above the table. A calendar showing a group of three very woolly kittens, and below, in red and black, the month— May 1910; 1910, he reflected: that would mean he was just seven.

At the end of the meal—a somewhat dull meal, perhaps, but doubtless wholesome—Barbara asked, "Are we going to see Mummy now?"

Nurse shook her head.

"Not now. She's out; so's your daddy. I expect they'll look in at you when they get back—if you're good."

The whole thing was unnaturally clear and detailed: the bathing, the putting to bed. Forgotten things came back to him with an uncanny reality which bemused him. Nurse checked her operations once to look at him searchingly and say, "Well, you're a quiet one tonight, aren't you? I hope you're not sickening for something."

There was still no fading of the sharp impressions when he lay in bed with only the flickering night-light to show the familiar room. The dream was going on for a long time—but then dreams could do that, they could pack a whole sequence into a few seconds. Perhaps this was a special kind of dream, a sort of finale while he sat out there in the garden on that seat; it might be part of the process of dying—the kind of thing people meant when they said "his whole life flashed before him," only it was a precious slow flash. Quite likely he had overtired himself: after all he was still only convalescent. . . .

At that moment the thought of that clerkly little man, Pendl-something—no, Prendergast—recurred to him. It struck him with such abrupt force that he sat up in bed, looking wildly round. He pinched himself—people always did that to make sure they were awake, though he had never understood why they should not dream they were pinching themselves—it certainly felt as if he were awake. He got out of bed and stood looking about him. The floor was hard and solid under his feet, the chill in the air quite perceptible, the regular breathing of Barbara, asleep in her cot, perfectly audible. After a few moments of bewilderment he got slowly back into bed.

People who wish: "If only I had my life over again." That was what that fellow Prendergast had said. . . .

Ridiculous . . . utterly absurd, of course—and, anyway, life did not begin at seven years old—such a preposterous thing could not happen, it was all against the laws of nature—and yet suppose . . . just suppose . . . that once, by some multi-millionth chance . . .

Bobby Finnerson lay still, quietly contemplating an incredible vista of possibilities. He had done pretty well for himself last time merely by intelligent perception, but now, armed with foreknowledge, what might he not achieve! In on the ground floor with radio, plastics, synthetics of all kinds—with prescience of the coming wars, of the boom following the first—*and* of the 1929 slump. Aware of the trends. Knowing the weapons of the second war before it came, ready for the advent of the atomic age. Recalling endless oddments of useful information acquired haphazardly in fifty years—where was the catch? Uneasily, he felt sure that there must be a catch: something to stop him communicating his useful knowledge. You couldn't disorganize history, but what was it that could prevent him telling, say, the Americans about Pearl Harbor, or the French about the German plans? There must be something to stop that, but what was it?

There was a theory he had read somewhere—something about parallel universes . . . ?

No. There was just no explanation for it all; in spite of seeming reality; in spite of pinching himself, it was a dream—just a dream . . . or was it?

—

Some hours later a board creaked. The quietly opened door let in a wedge of brighter light from the passage, and then shut it off. Lying still and pretending sleep, he heard careful footsteps approach. He opened his eyes to see his mother bending over him. For some moments he stared unbelievingly at her. She looked lovely in evening dress, with her eyes shining. It was with astonishment that he realized she was still barely more than a girl. She gazed down at him steadily, a little smile around her mouth. He reached up one hand to touch her smooth cheek. Then, like a piercing bolt came the recollection of what was going to happen to her. He choked.

She leaned over and gathered him to her, speaking softly not to disturb Barbara:

"There, there, Bobby boy. There's nothing to cry about. Did I wake you suddenly? Was there a horrid dream?"

He snuffled, but said nothing.

"Never mind, darling. Dreams can't hurt, you know. Just you forget it now, and go to sleep."

She tucked him up, kissed him lightly, and turned to the cot where Barbara lay undisturbed. A minute later she had gone.

Bobby Finnerson lay quiet but awake, gazing up at the ceiling, puzzling, and tentatively, planning.

The following morning, being a Saturday, involved the formality of going to the morning-room to ask for one's pocket money. Bobby was a little shocked by the sight of his father. Not just by the absurd appearance of the tall choking collar and the high-buttoned jacket with mean lapels, but on account of his lack of distinction; he seemed a very much more ordinary young man than he had liked to remember. Uncle George was there, too, apparently as a weekend guest. He greeted Bobby heartily.

"Hullo, young man. By Jingo, you've grown since I last saw you. Won't be long before you'll be helping us with the business, at this rate. How'll you like that?"

Bobby did not answer. One could not say: "That won't happen because my father's going to be killed in the war, and you are going to ruin the business through your own stupidity." So he smiled back vaguely at Uncle George, and said nothing at all.

"Do you go to school now?" his uncle added.

Bobby wondered if he did. His father came to the rescue.

"Just a kindergarten in the mornings, so far," he explained.

"What do they teach you? Do you know the Kings of England?" Uncle George persisted.

"Draw it mild, George," protested Bobby's father. "Did you know 'em when you were just seven—do you now, for that matter?"

"Well, anyway, he knows who's king now, don't you, old man?" asked Uncle George.

Bobby hesitated. He had a nasty feeling that there was a trick about the question, but he had to take a chance.

"Edward the Seventh," he said, and promptly knew from their faces that it had been the wrong choice.

"I mean, George the Fifth," he amended hastily.

Uncle George nodded.

"Still sounds queer, doesn't it? I suppose they'll be putting G.R. on things soon instead of E.R."

Bobby got away from the room with his Saturday sixpence, and a feeling that it was going to be less easy than he had supposed to act his part correctly.

He had a self-protective determination not to reveal himself until he was pretty sure of his ground, particularly until he had some kind of answer to his chief perplexity: was the knowledge he had that of the things which *must* happen, or was it of those that *ought* to happen? If it were only the former, then he would appear to be restricted to a Cassandra-like role; but if it were the latter, the possibilities were—well, was there any limit?

In the afternoon they were to play in the Square garden. They left the house by the basement door, and he helped small Barbara with the laborious business of climbing the steps while Nurse turned back for a word with Cook. They walked across the pavement and stood waiting at the curb. The road was empty save for a high-wheeled butcher's trap bowling swiftly toward them. Bobby looked at it, and suddenly a whole horrifying scene jumped back into his memory like a vivid photograph.

He seized his little sister's arm, dragging her back toward the railings. At the same moment he saw the horse shy and begin to bolt. Barbara tripped and fell as it swerved toward them. With frightened strength he tugged her across the pavement. At the area gate he himself stumbled, but he did not let go of her arm. Somehow she fell through the gate after him, and together they rolled down the steps. A second later there was a clash of wild hooves just above. A hub ripped into the railings, and slender shiny spokes flew in all directions. A single despairing yell broke from the driver as he flew out of his seat, and then the horse was away with the wreckage bumping and banging behind it, and Sunday joints littering the road.

There was a certain amount of scolding which Bobby took philosophically and forgave because Nurse and the others were all somewhat frightened. His silence covered considerable thought. They did not know, as he did, what *ought* to have happened. He knew how little Barbara *ought* to have been lying on the pavement screaming from pain of a foot so badly mangled that it would cripple her, and so poison the rest of her life. But instead she was just howling healthily from surprise and a few bumps.

There was the answer to one of his questions, and he felt a little shaky as he recognized it. . . .

—

They put his ensuing "mooniness" down to shock after the narrow escape, and did their best to rally him out of the mood.

Nevertheless, it was still on him at bedtime, for the more he looked at the situation, the more fraught with perplexity it became.

It had, among other things, occurred to him that he could only interfere with another person's life once. Now for instance, by saving Barbara from that crippling injury he had entirely altered her future: there was no question of his knowledgeably interfering with fate's plans for her again, because he had no idea what her new future would be. . . .

That caused him to reconsider the problem of his father's future. If it were to be somehow contrived that he should not be in that particular spot in France, when a shell fell there, he might not be killed at all, and if he weren't, then the question of preventing his mother from making that disastrous second marriage would never arise. Nor would Uncle George be left single-handed to ruin the business, and if the business weren't ruined the whole family circumstances would be different. They'd probably send him to a more expensive school, and thus set him on an entirely new course . . . and so on . . . and so on.

Bobby turned restlessly in bed. This wasn't going to be as easy as he had thought . . . it wasn't going to be at all easy.

If his father were to remain alive there would be a difference at every point where it touched the lives of others, widening like a series of ripples. It might not affect the big things, the pieces of solid history—but something else might. Supposing, for instance, warning were to be given of a certain assassination due to be attempted later at Sarajevo . . . ?

Clearly one must keep well away from the big things. As much as possible one must flow with the previous course of events, taking advantage of them, but being careful always to disrupt them as little as possible. It would be tricky . . . very tricky indeed. . . .

—

"Prendergast, we have a complaint. A serious complaint over XB2823," announced the Departmental Director.

"I'm sorry to hear it, sir. I'm sure——"

"Not your fault. It's those Psychiatric fellows again. Get on to them, will you, and give them hell for not making a proper clearance. Tell them the fellow's dislocated one whole ganglion of lives already—and it's damned lucky it's only a minor ganglion. They'd better get busy, and quickly."

"Very good, sir, I'll get through at once."

—

Bobby Finnerson woke, yawned, and sat up in bed. At the back of his mind there was a feeling that this was some special kind of day, like a birthday, or Christmas—only it wasn't really either of those. But it was a day when he had particularly meant to do something—if only he could remember what it was. He looked round the room and at the sunlight pouring in through the window; nothing suggested any specialness. His eyes fell on the cot where Barbara still slept peacefully. He slipped silently out of bed and across the floor. Stealthily he reached out to give a tug at the little plait which lay on the pillow.

It seemed as good a way as any other of starting the day.

—

From time to time as he grew older that sense of specialness recurred, but he never could find any real explanation for it. In a way it seemed allied with a sensation that would come to him suddenly that he had been in a particular place before, that somehow he knew it already—even though that was not possible. As if life were a little less straightforward and obvious than it seemed. And there were similar sensations, too, flashes of familiarity over something he was doing, a sense felt sometimes, say during a conversation, that it was familiar, as though it had happened before....

It was not a phenomenon confined to his youthful years. During both his early and later middle age it would still unexpectedly occur at times. Just a trick of the mind, they told him. Not even uncommon, they said.

—

"Prendergast, I see Contract XB2823 is due for renewal again."

"Yes, sir."

"Last time, I recall, there was some little technical trouble. It might be as well to remind the Psychiatric Department in advance."

"Very good, sir."

—

Robert Finnerson lay dying. Two or three times before he had been under the impression that he might be dying. He had been frightened....

A PRESENT FROM BRUNSWICK

The Partland home is the big house on the left, about a hundred yards, maybe, beyond that sign that says:

> Welcome to
> PLEASANTGROVE
> Pop.: 3,226

and the board beneath it which adds:

> The Livest Little City
> In This or Any State
> WATCH IT GROW

In the big Partland living room Mrs. Claybert was explaining:

"My dears, I *must* apologize. Only this morning I said to myself: 'Ethel, this time you're going to be on schedule.' That's just what I said. And now I've kept all you girls waiting again. Am I mortified! Something always happens. I'm interruption-prone, I guess. It was the mailman came, right as I was starting. He had a package from my boy, Jem. You know my Jem's over in Europe, occupying those Nazis. Of course I couldn't leave it that way. I just *had* to take a peek. And I was so thrilled when I saw what it was, I just had to bring it right along with me. There, now, look, isn't that a cute present?"

Mrs. Claybert, with a conjuror's air, stripped the paper from the object she carried, and held it up. The ladies of the Pleasantgrove Cultural Club Musical Society, Recorder Section, gathered round, impressed. Among the modest instruments they were holding—and which they would have been playing by this time had Mrs. Claybert kept her schedule—it was a king. The whole length of its dark body was carved with an intricacy of vines and leaves in low relief. The sharpness of the pattern was softened as though by much handling. The polished wood, of darkest chestnut shade, gleamed like satin.

"Why, Ethel, that's real antique. Maybe a hundred years old—maybe even more," said Mrs. Muller. "Aren't you the lucky girl! I didn't know you'd a millionaire son. Must've set him back plenty."

"Oh, my Jem's a good boy. He'd never be a tightwad where his Mom was concerned," said Mrs. Claybert, a trifle smugly.

Mrs. Partland was somehow in the middle of the group when she was thought to be on the outside. It was a way Mrs. Partland had. She took the instrument from Mrs. Claybert's hands, and examined it.

"The workmanship's just elegant," she pronounced, though with an air of impugning any other quality it might possess. She slid her fingers over the smooth polished undulations. "Yes, it certainly was made by one of those old-time craftsmen. But," she added severely, "is the pitch right?"

"I wouldn't know," admitted Mrs. Claybert. "I didn't have time to try it. I simply said to myself: 'Ethel, the girls'll just *love* to see that,' and I brought it right along with me."

Mrs. Partland handed it back.

"We'd better find out before we begin. Barbara, will you give Mrs. Claybert the 'D'?" she directed.

Mrs. Cooper lifted her recorder, and obliged. It was a plaintive note.

Mrs. Claybert found the finger holes, and raised the ivory mouthpiece of her resplendent instrument to her lips. She blew gently.

A silence fell on the room, and hung there a moment.

"Well, I guess it *is* 'D,'" acknowledged Mrs. Muller. "But it's a very unusual tone, isn't it? It is more like—well, I don't know quite what it is like. But it certainly is a *very* remarkable tone indeed."

Mrs. Partland, satisfied on the technical side, moved over to the footstool which served her as a rostrum. Mrs. Claybert was still looking at her instrument with astonishment and admiration.

"You wouldn't expect it to sound like a modern one," she said. "I mean, we have machinery and things now. That must make a difference. I guess this is the way they all sounded in those olden times."

Mrs. Partland rapped with her baton.

"Girls!" she said, decisively, but for the moment she went unheard.

"You know," Mrs. Claybert was saying, in a visionary fashion, "you know, somehow I can just see one of those old strolling players using maybe this very instrument in one of those big medieval halls. There'd be great oak beams, and rushes on the floor, and——"

"Ladies!" commanded Mrs. Partland. Her arresting tone cut short Mrs. Claybert, and brought them all round facing her. She went on: "There's that little thing by Purcell that we played last time. If we start with that, it'll get our fingers limbered up nicely. Have you all got your sheets?"

The ladies disposed themselves, arranged their fingers on their recorders, and frowned at their parts. Mrs. Partland stood on her footstool, baton poised.

"Now, is everybody ready? Well, I'm afraid you'll just have to look over Mrs. Schultz's sheet, Mrs. Lubbock. Now. One—two—three. . . ."

From the first breath it was clear that something was not well. One by one the others faltered and stopped, leaving Mrs. Claybert with a long, sweet note proceeding from her instrument, and an astonished look about her eyes. Mrs. Partland drew an admonitory breath, but before she could speak Mrs. Claybert's white fingers began to skip delicately on the dark wood. A tune, light, lilting, and lovely as a May morning danced through the room. Mrs. Claybert's comfortable body began to sway lissomely as she played. She posed one foot forward. The air was enchanting, irresistible. She began to dance. Lightly as a ballerina she crossed the room, and whisked beyond the door. After her swept and swayed the ladies of the Pleasantgrove Cultural Club, like nymphs upon a sward. . . .

———

At the crossroads, the lights were against them. They stopped, and stood there, looking dazed. The cop was a man of notable self-control. All the same, his eyes were still bulging slightly as he came across. He approached Mrs. Claybert with a look somewhere between compassion and suspicion. The glance he gave her instrument was wholly suspicious, as if it might be some ornamental kind of nightstick.

"What would it be, lady? What goes on here?" he inquired.

Mrs. Claybert did not answer. Her eyes dwelt on him with the wondering look of one only half untranced. For a moment nobody else spoke, either. Mrs. Partland felt that it in some way devolved on her to clear things up.

"It's all right, Officer. We were just—well. Well, it was just a—a kind of—of—er—Corybantic fancy," she finished desperately.

The cop looked them over. His eyelids lowered in a slow blink, lifted again.

"I wouldn't know much about that," he admitted. "But, lady, if I was you, I'd go fancy it someplace else."

"Yes," said Mrs. Partland, with unusual meekness. "Girls——" she began. Then out of the corner of her eye she saw Mrs. Claybert's hands raising her instrument once more. She made a quick snatch.

"Oh, no, you don't," she said. "Not again!"

———

Mr. Claybert examined the recorder. He peered at it this way and that under the light. He might have attempted to blow it had the mouthpiece not been removed to rest safely in Mrs. Claybert's handbag.

"Yes," he said, judiciously. "It certainly is old. But is it old enough——"

"How old would it have to be?" Mrs. Claybert asked.

"I can't say for sure—'bout seven or eight hundred years I guess."

"Well—maybe it is that."

"Uh-huh. Maybe. I wouldn't know what seven hundred years looks like, anyway."

"If it *is*——" Mrs. Claybert began. But she cut off the remark, and lapsed into thought.

"You *can* find out," observed her husband, pointedly.

She made no response. Mrs. Claybert laid the recorder down carefully on the table. The silence that ensued was broken only by the rhythm of his fingernails on the arm of his chair. His wife moved irritably.

Mr. Claybert obediently stopped, but though he controlled his fingers the rhythm went on in his mind. Tum! Tum! Te-tutta, te-tutta, te-Tum! He found that his foot was beginning to tap it. Turn! Turn! Te-tutta, te-tutta, te-Tum! He checked that, too, but it still went on inside him. Soon his head was nodding to it and his lips were framing the words, though silently: Rats! Rats! We gotta get ridda the rats!

"Maybe there'd be enough rats even in Pleasantgrove for a test, Honey," he suggested, at length.

Mrs. Claybert shuddered.

"If you think I'm going to fool around with a lot of rats, Harold——"

"But it'd prove it, Honey."

"Maybe it would. But not rats. Not me."

Mr. Claybert sighed. "The trouble with women is they got imagination, but they don't *apply* it. I'm right out ahead of you, Honey. Look at it this way. If it works on rats, and it works on your friends, we've got something. Something big. Maybe we could get it really selective. Maybe we could get, say, all the smokers of Camels, or all the members of the After-Shave Club dancing in the streets. And would that be an ad! Oh, boy! And there'd be some nice political angles, too, I guess. Now, suppose you were to play it over a nationwide hookup——"

"Harold! If you want any peace in this home, you'll put that imagination of yours right back in its cage, and let me think," Mrs. Claybert declared.

"But Ethel, this thing can be big. We could figure out a movie angle, too. Kinda bandwagon for——"

"Harold! *Please! And* will you stop that drumming!"

——

Breakfast the following morning was an even quieter meal than usual. Both the Clayberts appeared introspective. By a costly effort Harold Claybert had restrained himself from making further reference to the recorder. As a result it seemed to dominate the room in some way. He found his eyes wandering toward it continually. But only as he was about to leave did his resolution break down. At the door he hesitated.

"Honey, I've not even heard you play it," he said. "Couldn't you——? Well, just a note or two maybe?"

His wife shook her head.

"I'm sorry, Harold, but the very last thing I said to myself before I went to sleep was: 'Ethel, don't you dare blow that thing again till you get it someplace where it can't do any harm!' And I guess I'd better stick to that."

After he had gone, Mrs. Claybert did her cleaning speedily, if absentmindedly. When she had set the house to rights she picked up the recorder, and polished it gently with a duster. She contemplated it in a thoughtful fashion for a moment, then she took the ivory mouthpiece from her bag and pushed it into place. She half lifted it to her mouth, and paused. Then she lowered it, and laid it on the table again. She went upstairs to fetch a coat. As she came down she picked up the recorder, and, with a slightly furtive air, hid it beneath the coat before she opened the front door.

Instead of getting out of the car in her usual way she kept on down the path to the road. There she turned to her left, and began walking away from the town and the houses. After less than a mile a track led off to the right across a field. She followed it over that field and the next, and into the woods beyond. It was quiet there, and peaceful. Among the trees she felt removed from the world, as well as hidden, and her own inner self stretched the creases out of its wings a little. A faint footpath slanted away from the track, and, following it for a short distance, she came to a small natural clearing. There, in the sun, she spread out her coat, laid the recorder carefully on it, and sat down.

In spite of the sunshine there was a tinge of gentle eighteenth-century melancholy. In her present mood Mrs. Claybert found that not unpleasant.

For a while she sat, pensive; dreaming a little, with a touch of nostalgia. Not that she was unhappy. There was Jem—and Harold, too, of course, and Harold was a good husband, as husbands come. But she missed Jem. Germany seemed a terrible long way away. There's a kind of wistful mood that can come on you when you stop to think that the only child God let you bear has somehow turned into a man who's halfway round the world—and you're over forty now. . . . You can't help wondering about it sometimes. Not kicking: just wondering what it might all have been like if, maybe, it had been some other way. . . .

After a bit Ethel Claybert picked up the recorder. She stroked the smooth wood with her fingertips because it was Jem who had sent it. She looked beyond it, beyond the trees, smiling a little. Then, still smiling, she put the ivory mouthpiece to her lips, and began to play. . . .

—

A meeting, on the front porch of Mayor Duncan's house by the crossroads, included several of Pleasantgrove's more influential citizens. Though it was informal, it was clearly aware of obligations; it had, perhaps, authority, too; but what it excelled in was bewilderment. The only face to wear an expression of decision was Mrs. Partland's, but that was habitual, and this time nothing was coming of it. The look of reliability which Jim Duncan's conception of office caused him to wear was a kind of drop-scene, deceiving nobody. Mrs. Muller was offering comment and suggestion at her usual high velocity, but they had an expendable, radio-background quality. Everybody present stood looking out on Main Street in perplexity. Everybody, that is, except Mrs. Claybert who sat in the rocker, weeping quietly.

The sight of the junction of Main Street and Lincoln Avenue at that moment was one that nobody was going to forget. Not only the crossing itself, but the entrances to the four streets were jammed with children. The girls for the most part wore flaxen plaits hanging in pairs from beneath white caps embroidered with colored flowers. Short sleeves puffed out at their shoulders above tight bodices, and their full, striped skirts were covered in front with bright aprons. The boys were in tunics of green or brown, and long tight pants. Their hats were colored, with the brims shaped to narrow peaks in front, and the high crowns each set with a feather. All the roadway looked as if it had been spread with a brilliant but restless carpet from which rose a hubbub of young voices mingled with the tockerty clatter of hundreds of small clogs.

Astonishment was not one-sidedly restricted to the citizens of Pleasantgrove. The children's faces reflected it. Most of them were still looking around them in bewilderment, and regarding the amenities of the town with cautious suspicion. Others were already discovering compensations. There was a group near the movie house stricken with delighted awe by the posters. Another had its noses flattened against the plate-glass windows of Louise Pallister's Candy Store. Over their heads Louise herself could be observed bobbing about stressfully behind her barricaded door, her hands clasped, and her mouth opening for alternate "Oh, dear!"—"Oh, my!" Across on the other corner there was a press where some juvenile instinct had already led to the discovery of a soda fountain in Tony's Drug Store. But these high spots of adventure were only local, on the fringes of the crowd. Within, it consisted of children who stared about them in puzzlement while little girls and boys clung, big-eyed and fearful, to their elder sisters' skirts.

Not one of the Pleasantgrove citizens showed the least joy in the situation.

"I don't get it," complained Al Deakin from the filling station. "Where the heck did they all come from?" he demanded. He turned aggressively on Mrs. Claybert. "How did they get here? Where *did* they come from?" he repeated.

Mrs. Claybert sniffed the unsympathetic atmosphere. Before she could answer Mrs. Partland said, decisively:

"We can leave that till later. What I want to know is now they *are* here, who is going to do something about it?" She looked pointedly at Mayor Duncan. "Something *has* to be done," she added, emphatically.

Jim Duncan maintained the air of a man detached, and thinking deeply. He was still keeping it up when Elmer Drew shuffled forward and plucked urgently at his sleeve. Elmer was a house-painter who doubled in the less spacious art of sign-writing, but both are professions which make a conscientious man finicky about details.

"How many do you reckon there'd be, Jim?" he asked.

Here was something a Mayor could try to answer. Jim relaxed slightly.

"H'm," he judged. "I'd say three thousand, Elmer. Not less. Maybe more."

"Uh-huh." Elmer nodded, and edged his way out of the group to get his brushes. The way he saw it, it'd be near enough to change the preliminary 3 of the population figure to a 6, just till someone made up the full count.

"Three thousand kids!" repeated Al Deakin. "Three *thousand*! Well, that fixes it, I guess. No community the size of ours can stand that."

"And how does that fix it?" asked Mrs. Partland, coolly.

"Why, makes it a State job. It's too big for us to handle."

"No!" said Mrs. Claybert, distinctly.

They looked at her.

"What do you mean, 'no'?" Al demanded. "What else? What can we do with three thousand kids? Come to that, why should we? Seems to me you've got a mighty lot of explaining to do, Ethel Claybert."

Mrs. Claybert cast a forlorn glance round the semicircle that enclosed her.

"Well, it's difficult to explain . . ." she said.

Mrs. Muller came generously to her rescue.

"I guess three thousand children are sometimes not much more difficult to explain than one," she said, sharply.

This reference to an obscure incident in Al Deakin's past had the effect of deflating him for the moment.

"Well, we can't just go on standing here and doing nothing," Mrs. Partland said. "Those children are going to have to be fed soon, and—er—looked after."

It was quite true. Wonder was giving way to fractiousness. Some of the larger girls had taken little ones up in their arms and were lulling them to and fro, golden plaits swinging. Mrs. Claybert ran down the steps and came back holding one pretty small thing close to her.

"That's right. We have to do *something*," agreed Mrs. Muller.

"There's that old army camp out by Rails Hill," said Mrs. Partland. "If we could feed them and take them out there——"

"And who's going to feed them?" demanded Al Deakin. "I hold that Ethel Claybert just ain't got the right to dump three thousand kids down here and expect . . ."

"I reckon Pleasantgrove folks will be able to find a meal or two for them," the Mayor put in. "But outside that—— Oh, there's Larry!" he broke off. Like a ship-wrecked mariner hailing a lifeboat he called across the street: "Hey, Larry."

The cop looked up, and waved his big hand. He started to come over, wading carefully through children, and looking not unlike a man picking his way across a flower bed.

"Who did it, anyway? Who brought 'em here?" he demanded, as he climbed the steps.

Everybody looked at Mrs. Claybert. So did the cop.

"Are you responsible—for all this lot?" he inquired.

"Well, yes—I suppose I am . . ." admitted Mrs. Claybert.

"Three doggone thousand of 'em," put in Al Deakin. "Fifteen hundred little Gretchens, and fifteen hundred little Hanses—and not one word of American between the lot."

The cop tilted his cap back, and scratched.

"From Europe?" he asked.

"Well, yes . . ." said Mrs. Claybert again.

"You got their immigration papers?" inquired the cop.

"Well, no . . ." Mrs. Claybert told him.

The cop turned and surveyed the vista of children. He turned back.

"Lady," he said, "someplace there's several freight cars of trouble marked 'Rush,' and they're all headed your way." He paused. "What are they? D.P. children?" he added.

Mrs. Claybert detached her gaze from his, and looked out over the street.

"Why—why, yes," she said. "Yes—I guess that's just what they are."

"They don't look a bit like the D.P. children in *Life*," said Mrs. Partland. "Too clean. And tidy. Besides, they all looked happy before they began to get hungry."

"Wouldn't you be happy, coming to a town like Pleasantgrove after all those ruins over in Europe?" Mrs. Muller asked.

"They've got a right to look happy," said Mrs. Claybert, with a sudden firmness. "And Pleasantgrove has a duty to see that they *are* happy."

"Hey——!" began Al Deakin.

Mrs. Claybert clutched the little doll of a girl that she was holding more firmly to her breast.

"Aren't they lovely children? Did you ever see lovelier children?" she demanded.

"Sure they are, but——"

"And is there anything more valuable to a community than its children—and its children's happiness?" she went on, fiercely.

"Well, no, but——"

"Then I guess that makes Pleasantgrove the richest community in this state," concluded Mrs. Claybert, triumphantly.

There was a difficult silence.

"Er—sure. That's mighty true," agreed Mayor Duncan. "But right now we got to be practical." He turned an appealing eye on the cop.

The fascination of novelty was fast wearing thinner with the children. More of the little ones had begun to cry, few of the older ones still smiled. A girl in a brightly striped skirt with an embroidered blouse frothing out of her laced velvet bodice climbed up onto a box near the front of the dry-goods store. Her mouth opened, and she began to sway with her arms. At first nothing was audible from the porch. Then voices round her took up the song. It spread outwards across the crowd until it drowned the crying. The children began to sway together as they sang, rippling like a field of barley in the wind. Mrs. Claybert swung the one she held in time with the rest. She listened to the unfamiliar words with a smile on her lips and tears in her eyes.

"What we gotta do," said the cop, cutting through the lilt of massed trebles, "what we gotta do is to get on to the State Orphanage and tell 'em to start in sending trucks right away. Then we got to see about feedin' the kids till the trucks pull in."

Mrs. Claybert stiffened.

"Orphanage!" she exclaimed, in a thrusting voice.

She put down the little girl, and advanced.

"We gotta be practical——" began the cop, but she stopped him with a gesture.

"For the first time in my life I'm ashamed to be a citizen of Pleasantgrove," she proclaimed, bitterly. "You could send all these lovely children off to be orphans?"

"But, Mrs. Claybert, they *are* orphans——"

Mrs. Claybert swept that aside.

"They come away from that dreadful Europe; they come here to the land of liberty and opportunity; they ask you for love—and you give them orphanages. Just what do you think they're going to say about the American way of life when they grow up?"

Mayor Duncan looked at her helplessly.

"But, Mrs. Claybert, you got to be reasonable——"

"Is this, or is this not, a Christian community?" demanded Mrs. Claybert. "I've lived in Pleasantgrove all my life. I thought Pleasantgrove folks were great-hearted folks. Now the test comes I find they haven't got hearts or Christian charity."

"Listen, lady," said the cop, in a placatory tone. "We got hearts *and* we got Christian charity—but the little thing we can't fix is Christian miracles."

Mrs. Claybert glared at him, and then at the rest. Without comment she picked up the recorder from the floor beside the rocker. Looking out across the singing children, she settled her fingers on the holes.

"You just don't *deserve* to have lovely children," she said.

She lifted the pipe. Then she paused.

"I guess——" she said, wistfully—"I guess the only thing that's wrong with children is that they grow up to be people like you."

And she put the pipe to her lips.

As the long mellow note floated out across Main Street the children began to turn and look at Mayor Duncan's porch. The singing faded away. The little ones ceased to cry, and smiled as their sisters put them on their feet. There was no sound but the single note, trembling a little. . . . Mrs. Claybert put one foot forward. Her fingers flittered up and down the pipe stem. The air came, light and gay, tripping brightly as sunbeams on broken water. Hundreds of small clogs began to patter with a click-clocketty noise to its rhythm.

Down the steps danced Mrs. Claybert, and off across Main

Street, through a lane that opened among the children. They closed in behind her as she went, golden plaits and bright skirts swirling, red stockings flashing, feet tat-tattering.

There was a scuffle inside the Mayor's house and his two children bounded out across the porch to join the dancing crowd beyond.

"Hey! Stop them!" Jim Duncan called, but somehow neither he nor anyone else could move to do it.

Mrs. Claybert turned down Lincoln Avenue with the children streaming like a bouncing, bubbling, colored flood behind her. Down the front yards the American children came tumbling to join the rest. Out of the school poured another stream skipping and dancing to flow into the passing crowd and whirl away with them up the street.

"Hey! Mrs. Claybert! Come back!" bawled Mayor Duncan, but his hail was lost in the children's voices.

The only sound that could top the laughing and the singing and the clatter of clogs was the tune of Mrs. Claybert's pipe as she danced along ahead, across the fields, and away to the woods beyond. . . .

—

By the time that conscientious citizen Elmer Drew had finished turning the 3 into a 6, hotter news had reached him. So when the first carloads of reporters, detectives, and F.B.I. passed him as they came tearing into Pleasantgrove he was already painting out the population figure altogether, pending a revised estimate. After he had done that, he considered the lower board for a moment. Then he came to a decision, unscrewed it, and tucked it under his arm.

On his way back into town he met Mrs. Partland. Her children were walking sedately, one on either side of her. Elmer stopped and stared. Mrs. Partland beamed.

"The American children chose to come back to their own folks," she told him proudly.

"Yes," agreed Mortimer Partland, Junior, with a nod. "They

didn't have any ice cream, or movies, or gum—nothing but *dancing*! Was it corny!"

"And Mrs. Claybert?" asked Elmer.

"Oh, well, I guess she just *likes* dancing," said the young Mortimer Partland.

Elmer turned and walked back up the road. On the board he rewrote "Pop.: 3,226," and then thoughtfully changed the last figure to a 5. Underneath, with a deep feeling of civic satisfaction, he refixed the board which said:

WATCH IT GROW

CHINESE PUZZLE

The parcel, waiting provocatively on the dresser, was the first thing that Hwyl noticed when he got in from work.

"From Dai, is it?" he inquired of his wife.

"Yes, indeed. Japanese the stamps are," she told him.

He went across to examine it. It was the shape a small hatbox might be, about ten inches each way, perhaps. The address: *Mr. & Mrs. Hwyl Hughes, Ty Derwen, Llynllawn, Llangolwgcoch, Brecknockshire, S. Wales,* was lettered carefully, for the clear understanding of foreigners. The other label, also hand-lettered, but in red, was quite clear, too. It said: *EGGS—Fragile—With great CARE.*

"There is funny to send eggs so far," Hwyl said. "Plenty of eggs we are having. Might be chocolate eggs, I think?"

"Come you to your tea, man," Bronwen told him. "All day I have been looking at that old parcel, and a little longer it can wait now."

Hwyl sat down at the table and began his meal. From time to time, however, his eyes strayed again to the parcel.

"If it is real eggs they are, careful you should be," he remarked. "Reading in a book I was once how in China they keep eggs for years. Bury them in the earth, they do, for a delicacy. There is strange for you, now. Queer they are in China, and not like Wales, at all."

Bronwen contented herself with saying that perhaps Japan was not like China, either.

When the meal had been finished and cleared, the parcel was transferred to the table. Hwyl snipped the string and pulled off the brown paper. Within was a tin box which, when the sticky tape holding its lid had been removed, proved to be full to the brim with sawdust. Mrs. Hughes fetched a sheet of newspaper, and prudently covered the tabletop. Hwyl dug his fingers into the sawdust.

"Something there, there is," he announced.

"There is stupid you are. Of course there is something there," Bronwen said, slapping his hand out of the way.

She trickled some of the sawdust out onto the newspaper, and then felt inside the box herself. Whatever it was, it felt much too large for an egg. She poured out more sawdust and felt again. This time, her fingers encountered a piece of paper. She pulled it out and laid it on the table; a letter in Dafydd's handwriting. Then she put in her hand once more, got her fingers under the object, and lifted it gently out.

"Well, indeed! Look at that now! Did you ever?" she exclaimed. "Eggs, he was saying, is it?"

They both regarded it with astonishment for some moments.

"So big it is. Queer, too," said Hwyl, at last.

"What kind of bird to lay such an egg?" said Bronwen.

"Ostrich, perhaps?" suggested Hwyl.

But Bronwen shook her head. She had once seen an ostrich's egg in a museum, and remembered it well enough to know that it had little in common with this. The ostrich's egg had been a little smaller, with a dull, sallow-looking, slightly dimpled surface. This was smooth and shiny, and by no means had the same dead look: it had a lustre to it, a nacreous kind of beauty.

"A pearl, could it be?" she said, in an awed voice.

"There is silly you are," said her husband. "From an oyster as big as Llangolwgcoch Town Hall, you are thinking?"

He burrowed into the tin again, but "Eggs," it seemed, had been a manner of speaking: there was no other, nor room for one.

Bronwen put some of the sawdust into one of her best vegetable dishes, and bedded the egg carefully on top of it. Then they sat down to read their son's letter:

S.S. *Tudor Maid,*
Kobe.

Dear Mam and Dad,
I expect you will be surprised about the enclosed I was too. It is a funny looking thing I expect they have funny birds in China after all they have Pandas so why not. We found a small sampan about a hundred miles off the China coast that had bust its mast and should never have tried and all except two of them were dead they are all dead now. But one of them that wasn't dead then was holding this egg-thing all wrapped up in a padded coat like it was a baby only I didn't know it was an egg then not till later. One of them died coming aboard but this other one lasted two days longer in spite of all I could do for him which was my best. I was sorry nobody here can speak Chinese because he was a nice little chap and lonely and knew he was a goner but there it is. And when he saw it was nearly all up he gave me this egg and talked very faint but I'd not have understood anyway. All I could do was take it and hold it careful the way he had and tell him I'd look after it which he couldn't understand either. Then he said something else and looked very worried and died poor chap.
So here it is. I know it is an egg because I took him a boiled egg once he pointed to both of them to show me but nobody on board knows what kind of egg. But seeing I promised him I'd keep it safe I am sending it to you to keep for me as this ship is no place to keep anything safe anyway and hope it doesn't get cracked on the way too.
Hoping this finds you as it leaves me and love to all and you special.

Dai.

"Well, there is strange for you, now," said Mrs. Hughes, as she finished reading. "And *looking* like an egg it is, indeed—the shape of it," she conceded. "But the colors are not. There is pretty they are. Like you see when oil is on the road in the rain. But never an egg like that have I seen in my life. Flat the color is on eggs, and not to shine."

Hwyl went on looking at it thoughtfully.

"Yes. There is beautiful," he agreed, "but what use?"

"Use, is it, indeed!" said his wife. "A trust, it is, and sacred, too. Dying the poor man was, and our Dai gave him his word. I am thinking of how we will keep it safe for him till he will be back, now."

They both contemplated the egg awhile.

"Very far away, China is," Bronwen remarked, obscurely.

———

Several days passed, however, before the egg was removed from display on the dresser. Word quickly went round the valley about it, and the callers would have felt slighted had they been unable to see it. Bronwen felt that continually getting it out and putting it away again would be more hazardous than leaving it on exhibition.

Almost everyone found the sight of it rewarding. Idris Bowen who lived three houses away was practically alone in his divergent view.

"The shape of an egg, it has," he allowed. "But careful you should be, Mrs. Hughes. A fertility symbol it is, I am thinking, and stolen, too, likely."

"Mr. Bowen———" began Bronwen, indignantly.

"Oh, by the men in that boat, Mrs. Hughes. Refugees from China they would be, see. Traitors to the Chinese people. And running away with all they could carry, before the glorious army of the workers and peasants could catch them, too. Always the same, it is, as you will be seeing when the revolution comes to Wales."

"Oh, dear, dear! There is funny you are, Mr. Bowen. Propaganda you will make out of an old boot, I think," said Bronwen.

Idris Bowen frowned.

"Funny, I am not, Mrs. Hughes. And propaganda there is in an honest boot, too," he told her as he left with dignity.

By the end of a week practically everyone in the village had seen the egg and been told no, Mrs. Hughes did not know what kind of a creature had laid it, and the time seemed to have come to store it away safely against Dafydd's return. There were not many places in the house where she could feel sure that it would rest undisturbed, but, on consideration, the airing-cupboard seemed as likely as any, so she put it back on what sawdust was left in the tin, and stowed it in there.

It remained there for a month, out of sight, and pretty much out of mind until a day when Hwyl returning from work discovered his wife sitting at the table with a disconsolate expression on her face, and a bandage on her finger. She looked relieved to see him.

"Hatched, it is," she observed.

The blankness of Hwyl's expression was irritating to one who had had a single subject on her mind all day.

"Dai's egg," she explained. "Hatched out, it is, I am telling you."

"Well, there is a thing for you, now!" said Hwyl. "A nice little chicken, is it?"

"A chicken it is not, at all. A monster, indeed, and biting me it is, too." She held out her bandaged finger.

She explained that this morning she had gone to the airing-cupboard to take out a clean towel, and as she put her hand in, something had nipped her finger, painfully. At first she had thought that it might be a rat that had somehow got in from the yard, but then she had noticed that the lid was off the tin, and the shell of the egg there was all broken to pieces.

"How is it to see?" Hwyl asked.

Bronwen admitted that she had not seen it well. She had had a glimpse of a long, greeny-blue tail protruding from behind a pile of sheets, and then it had looked at her over the top of them, glaring at her from red eyes. On that, it had seemed to her more the kind of a job a man should deal with, so she had slammed the door, and gone to bandage her finger.

"Still there, then, is it?" said Hwyl.

She nodded.

"Right now. Have a look at it, we will, now then," he said, decisively.

He started to leave the room, but on second thoughts turned back to collect a pair of heavy working-gloves. Bronwen did not offer to accompany him.

Presently there was a scuffle of his feet, an exclamation or two, then his tread descending the stairs. He came in, shutting the door behind him with his foot. He set the creature he was carrying down on the table, and for some seconds it crouched there, blinking, but otherwise unmoving.

"Scared, he was, I think," Hwyl remarked.

In the body, the creature bore some resemblance to a lizard— a large lizard, over a foot long. The scales of its skin, however, were much bigger, and some of them curled up and stood out here and there, in a fin-like manner. And the head was quite unlike a lizard's, being much rounder, with a wide mouth, broad nostrils, and, overall, a slightly pushed-in effect, in which were set a pair of goggling red eyes. About the neck, and also making a kind of mane, were curious, streamer-like attachments with the suggestion of locks of hair which had permanently cohered. The color was mainly green, shot with blue, and having a metallic shine to it, but there were brilliant red markings about the head and in the lower parts of the locks. There were touches of red, too, where the legs joined the body, and on the feet, where the toes finished in sharp yellow claws. Altogether, a surprisingly vivid and exotic creature.

It eyed Bronwen Hughes for a moment, turned a baleful look on Hwyl, and then started to run about the tabletop, looking for a way off. The Hugheses watched it for a moment or two, and then regarded one another.

"Well, there is nasty for you, indeed," observed Bronwen.

"Nasty it may be. But beautiful it is, too, look," said Hwyl.

"Ugly old face to have," Bronwen remarked.

"Yes, indeed. But fine colors, too, see. Glorious, they are, like technicolor, I am thinking," Hwyl said.

The creature appeared to have half a mind to leap from the table. Hwyl leaned forward and caught hold of it. It wriggled, and tried to get its head round to bite him, but discovered he was holding it too near the neck for that. It paused in its struggles. Then, suddenly, it snorted. Two jets of flame and a puff of smoke came from its nostrils. Hwyl dropped it abruptly, partly from alarm, but more from surprise. Bronwen gave a squeal, and climbed hastily onto her chair.

The creature itself seemed a trifle astonished. For a few seconds it stood turning its head and waving the sinuous tail that was quite as long as its body. Then it scuttled across to the hearthrug, and curled itself up in front of the fire.

"By dammo! There was a thing for you!" Hwyl exclaimed, regarding it a trifle nervously. "Fire there was with it, I think. I will like to understand that, now."

"Fire indeed, and smoke, too," Bronwen agreed. "There is shocking it was, and not natural, at all."

She looked uncertainly at the creature. It had so obviously settled itself for a nap that she risked stepping down from the chair, but she kept on watching it, ready to jump again if it should move. Then:

"Never did I think I will see one of those. And not sure it is right to have in the house, either," she said.

"What is it you are meaning, now?" Hwyl asked, puzzled.

"Why, a dragon, indeed," Bronwen told him.

Hwyl stared at her.

"Dragon!" he exclaimed. "There is foolish——" Then he stopped. He looked at it again, and then down at the place where the flame had scorched his glove. "No, by dammo!" he said. "Right, you. A dragon it is, I believe."

They both regarded it with some apprehension.

"Glad, I am, not to live in China," observed Bronwen.

———

Those who were privileged to see the creature during the next day or two supported almost to a man the theory that it was a dragon. This, they established by poking sticks through the wire netting of the hutch that Hwyl had made for it until it obliged with a resentful huff of flame. Even Mr. Jones, the Chapel, did not doubt its authenticity, though on the propriety of its presence in his community he preferred to reserve judgment for the present.

After a short time, however, Bronwen Hughes put an end to the practice of poking it. For one thing, she felt responsible to Dai for its well-being; for another, it was beginning to develop an irritable disposition, and a liability to emit flame without cause; for yet another, and although Mr. Jones's decision on whether it could be considered as one of God's creatures or not was still pending, she felt that in the meantime it deserved equal rights with other dumb animals. So she put a card on the hutch saying: PLEASE NOT TO TEASE, and most of the time was there to see that it was heeded.

Almost all Llynllawn, and quite a few people from Llangolwg-coch, too, came to see it. Sometimes they would stand for an hour or more, hoping to see it huff. If it did, they went off satisfied that it was a dragon; but if it maintained a contented, non-fire-breathing mood, they went and told their friends that it was really no more than a little old lizard, though big, mind you.

Idris Bowen was an exception to both categories. It was not until his third visit that he was privileged to see it snort, but even then he remained unconvinced.

"Unusual, it is, yes," he admitted. "But a dragon it is not. Look you at the dragon of Wales, or the dragon of St. George, now. To huff fire is something, I grant you, but wings, too, a dragon must be having, or a dragon he is not."

But that was the kind of caviling that could be expected from Idris, and disregarded.

After ten days or so of crowded evenings, however, interest slackened. Once one had seen the dragon and exclaimed over the brilliance of its coloring, there was little to add, beyond being glad that it was in the Hugheses' house rather than one's own, and wondering how big it would eventually grow. For, really, it did not do much but sit and blink, and perhaps give a little huff of flame if you were lucky. So, presently, the Hugheses' home became more their own again.

And, no longer pestered by visitors, the dragon showed an equable disposition. It never huffed at Bronwen, and seldom at Hwyl. Bronwen's first feeling of antagonism passed quickly, and she found herself growing attached to it. She fed it, and looked after it, and found that on a diet consisting chiefly of minced horseflesh and dog biscuits it grew with astonishing speed. Most of the time, she let it run free in the room. To quieten the misgivings of callers she would explain:

"Friendly, he is, and pretty ways he has with him, if there is not teasing. Sorry for him, I am, too, for bad it is to be an only child, and an orphan worse still. And less than an orphan, he is, see. Nothing of his own sort he is knowing, nor likely, either. So very lonely he is being, poor thing, I think."

But, inevitably, there came an evening when Hwyl, looking thoughtfully at the dragon, remarked:

"Outside you, son. There is too big for the house you are getting, see."

Bronwen was surprised to find how unwilling she felt about that.

"Very good and quiet, he is," she said. "There is clever he is to tuck his tail away not to trip people, too. And clean with the house he is, also, and no trouble. Always out to the yard at proper times. Right as clockwork."

"Behaving well, he is, indeed," Hwyl agreed. "But growing so fast, now. More room he will be needing, see. A fine hutch for him in the yard, and with a run to it, I think."

The advisability of that was demonstrated a week later when

Bronwen came down one morning to find the end of the wooden hutch charred away, the carpet and rug smoldering, and the dragon comfortably curled up in Hwyl's easy chair.

"Settled, it is, and lucky indeed not to burn in our bed. Out you," Hwyl told the dragon. "A fine thing to burn a man's house for him, and not grateful, either. For shame, I am telling you."

The insurance man who came to inspect the damage thought similarly.

"Notified, you should have," he told Bronwen. "A fire-risk, he is, you see."

Bronwen protested that the policy made no mention of dragons.

"No, indeed," the man admitted, "but a normal hazard he is not, either. Inquire, I will, from Head Office how it is, see. But better to turn him out before more trouble, and thankful, too."

So, a couple of days later, the dragon was occupying a larger hutch, constructed of asbestos sheets, in the yard. There was a wire-netted run in front of it, but most of the time Bronwen locked the gate, and left the back door of the house open so that he could come and go as he liked. In the morning he would trot in, and help Bronwen by huffing the kitchen fire into a blaze, but apart from that he had learnt not to huff in the house. The only times he was any bother to anyone were the occasions when he set his straw on fire in the night so that the neighbors got up to see if the house was burning, and were somewhat short about it the next day.

Hwyl kept a careful account of the cost of feeding him, and hoped that it was not running into more than Dai would be willing to pay. Otherwise, his only worries were his failure to find a cheap, non-inflammable bedding-stuff, and speculation on how big the dragon was likely to grow before Dai should return to take him off his hands. Very likely all would have gone smoothly until that happened, but for the unpleasantness with Idris Bowen.

The trouble which blew up unexpectedly one evening was really of Idris's own finding. Hwyl had finished his meal, and was peacefully enjoying the last of the day beside his door, when Idris happened along, leading his whippet on a string.

"Oh, hullo you, Idris," Hwyl greeted him, amiably.

"Hullo you, Hwyl," said Idris. "And how is that phony dragon of yours, now then?"

"Phony, is it, you are saying?" repeated Hwyl, indignantly.

"Wings, a dragon is wanting, to be a dragon," Idris insisted, firmly.

"Wings to hell, man! Come you and look at him now then, and please to tell me what he is if he is no dragon."

He waved Idris into the house, and led him through into the yard. The dragon, reclining in its wired run, opened an eye at them, and closed it again.

Idris had not seen it since it was lately out of the egg. Its growth impressed him.

"There is big he is now," he conceded. "Fine the colors of him, and fancy, too. But still no wings to him; so a dragon he is not."

"What then is it he is?" demanded Hwyl. "Tell me that."

How Idris would have replied to this difficult question was never to be known, for at that moment the whippet jerked its string free from his fingers, and dashed, barking, at the wire netting. The dragon was startled out of its snooze. It sat up suddenly, and snorted with surprise. There was a yelp from the whippet which bounded into the air, and then set off round and round the yard, howling. At last Idris managed to corner it and pick it up. All down the right side its hair had been scorched off, making it look very peculiar. Idris's eyebrows lowered.

"Trouble you want, is it? And trouble you will be having, by God!" he said.

He put the whippet down again, and began to take off his coat.

It was not clear whether he had addressed, and meant to fight, Hwyl or the dragon, but either intention was forestalled by Mrs. Hughes coming to investigate the yelping.

"Oh! Teasing the dragon, is it!" she said. "There is shameful, indeed. A lamb the dragon is, as people know well. But not to tease. It is wicked you are, Idris Bowen, and to fight does not make right, either. Go you from here, now then."

Idris began to protest, but Bronwen shook her head and set her mouth.

"Not listening to you, I am, see. A fine brave man, to tease a helpless dragon. Not for weeks now has the dragon huffed. So you go, and quick."

Idris glowered. He hesitated, and pulled on his jacket again. He collected his whippet, and held it in his arms. After a final disparaging glance at the dragon, he turned.

"Law I will have of you," he announced ominously, as he left.

———

Nothing more, however, was heard of legal action. It seemed as if Idris had either changed his mind or been advised against it, and that the whole thing would blow over. But three weeks later was the night of the Union Branch Meeting.

It had been a dull meeting, devoted chiefly to passing a number of resolutions suggested to it by its headquarters, as a matter of course. Then, just at the end, when there did not seem to be any other business, Idris Bowen rose.

"Stay you!" said the chairman to those who were preparing to leave, and he invited Idris to speak.

Idris waited for persons who were half-in and half-out of their overcoats to subside, then:

"Comrades——" he began.

There was immediate uproar. Through the mingled approbation and cries of "Order" and "Withdraw" the chairman smote energetically with his gavel until quiet was restored.

"Tendentious, that is," he reproved Idris. "Please to speak halfway, and in good order."

Idris began again:

"Fellow workers. Sorry indeed, I am, to have to tell you of a discovery I am making. A matter of disloyalty, I am telling you: grave disloyalty to good friends and com—and fellow workers, see." He paused, and went on:

"Now, every one of you is knowing of Hwyl Hughes's dragon, is it? Seen him for yourselves you have likely, too. Seen him myself, I have, and saying he was no dragon. But now then, I am telling you, wrong I was, wrong, indeed. A dragon he is, and not to doubt, though no wings.

"I am reading in the encyclopedia in Merthyr Public Library about two kinds of dragons, see. Wings the European dragon has, indeed. But wings the Oriental dragon has not. So apologizing now to Mr. Hughes, I am, and sorry."

A certain restiveness becoming apparent in the audience was quelled by a change in his tone.

"*But*——" he went on, "but another thing, too, I am reading there, and troubled inside myself with it, I am. I will tell you. Have you looked at the feet of this dragon, is it? Claws there is, yes, and nasty, too. But how many, I am asking you? And five, I am telling you. Five with each foot." He paused dramatically, and shook his head. "Bad, is that, bad, indeed. For, look you, Chinese a five-toed dragon is, yes—but five-toed is not a Republican dragon, five-toed is not a People's dragon; five-toed is an *Imperial* dragon, see. A symbol, it is, of the oppression of Chinese workers and peasants. And shocking to think that in our village we are keeping such an emblem. What is it that the free people of China will be saying of Llynllawn when they will hear of this, I am asking? What is it Mao Tse Tung, a glorious leader of the heroic Chinese people in their magnificent fight for peace, will be thinking of South Wales and this imperialist dragon——?" he was continuing, when difference of view in the audience submerged his voice.

Again the chairman called the meeting to order. He offered Hwyl the opportunity to reply, and after the situation had been briefly explained, the dragon was, on a show of hands, acquitted of political implication by all but Idris's doctrinaire faction, and the meeting broke up.

Hwyl told Bronwen about it when he got home.

"No surprise there," she said. "Jones the Post is telling me, telegraphing Idris has been."

"Telegraphing?" inquired Hwyl.

"Yes, indeed. Asking the *Daily Worker*, in London, how is the party line on imperialist dragons, he was. But no answer yet, though."

———

A few mornings later the Hugheses were awakened by a hammering on their door. Hwyl went to the window and found Idris below. He asked what the matter was.

"Come you down here, and I will show you," Idris told him.

After some argument, Hwyl descended. Idris led the way round to the back of his own house, and pointed.

"Look you there, now," he said.

The door of Idris's henhouse was hanging by one hinge. The remains of two chickens lay close by. A large quantity of feathers was blowing about the yard.

Hwyl looked at the henhouse more closely. Several deep-raked scores stood out white on the creosoted wood. In other places there were darker smears where the wood seemed to have been scorched. Silently Idris pointed to the ground. There were marks of sharp claws, but no imprint of a whole foot.

"There is bad. Foxes is it?" inquired Hwyl.

Idris choked slightly.

"Foxes, you are saying. Foxes, indeed! What will it be but your dragon? And the police to know it, too."

Hwyl shook his head.

"No," he said.

"Oh," said Idris. "A liar, I am, is it? I will have the guts from you, Hwyl Hughes, smoking hot, too, and glad to do it."

"You talk too easy, man," Hwyl told him. "Only how the dragon is still fast in his hutch, I am saying. Come you now, and see."

They went back to Hwyl's house. The dragon was in his hutch, sure enough, and the door of it was fastened with a peg. Furthermore, as Hwyl pointed out, even if he had left it during the night, he could not have reached Idris's yard without leaving scratches and traces on the way, and there were none to be found.

They finally parted in a state of armistice. Idris was by no means convinced, but he was unable to get round the facts, and not at all impressed with Hwyl's suggestion that a practical joker could have produced the effect on the henhouse with a strong nail and a blowtorch.

Hwyl went upstairs again to finish dressing.

"There is funny it is, all the same," he observed to Bronwen. "Not seeing, that Idris was, but scorched the peg is, on the *outside* of the hutch. And how should that be, I wonder?"

"Huffed four times in the night the dragon has, five, perhaps," Bronwen said. "Growling, he is, too, and banging that old hutch about. Never have I heard him like that before."

"There is queer," Hwyl said, frowning. "But never out of his hutch, and that to swear to."

Two nights later Hwyl was awakened by Bronwen shaking his shoulder.

"Listen, now then," she told him.

"Huffing, he is, see," said Bronwen, unnecessarily.

There was a crash of something thrown with force, and the sound of a neighbor's voice cursing. Hwyl reluctantly decided that he had better get up and investigate.

Everything in the yard looked as usual, except for the presence of a large tin can which was clearly the object thrown. There was, however, a strong smell of burning, and a thudding noise, recognizable as the sound of the dragon tramping round and round in his hutch to stamp out the bedding caught alight again. Hwyl went across and opened the door. He raked out the smoldering straw, fetched some fresh, and threw it in.

"Quiet, you," he told the dragon. "More of this, and the hide I will have off you, slow and painful, too. Bed, now then, and sleep."

He went back to bed himself, but it seemed as if he had only just laid his head on the pillow when it was daylight, and there was Idris Bowen hammering on the front door again.

Idris was more than a little incoherent, but Hwyl gathered that something further had taken place at his house, so he slipped on jacket and trousers, and went down. Idris led the way down beside his own house, and threw open the yard door with the air of a conjuror. Hwyl stared for some moments without speaking.

In front of Idris's henhouse stood a kind of trap, roughly contrived of angle-iron and wire netting. In it, surrounded by chicken feathers, and glaring at them from eyes like live topazes, sat a creature, blood-red all over.

"Now, there is a dragon for you, indeed," Idris said. "Not to have colors like you see on a merry-go-round at a circus, either. A serious dragon, that one, and proper—wings, too, see?"

Hwyl went on looking at the dragon without a word. The wings were folded at present, and the cage did not give room to stretch them. The red, he saw now, was darker on the back, and brighter beneath, giving it the rather ominous effect of being lit from below by a blast furnace. It certainly had a more practical aspect than his own dragon, and a fiercer look about it, altogether. He stepped forward to examine it more closely.

"Careful, man," Idris warned him, laying a hand on his arm.

The dragon curled back its lips, and snorted. Twin flames a yard long shot out of its nostrils. It was a far better huff than the other dragon had ever achieved. The air was filled with a strong smell of burnt feathers.

"A fine dragon, that is," Idris said again. "A real Welsh dragon for you. Angry he is, see, and no wonder. A shocking thing for an imperialist dragon to be in his country. Come to throw him out, he has, and mincemeat he will be making of your namby-pamby, best-parlor dragon, too."

"Better for him not to try," said Hwyl, stouter in word than heart.

"And another thing, too. Red this dragon is, and so a real people's dragon, see."

"Now then. Now then. Propaganda with dragons again, is it? Red the Welsh dragon has been two thousand years, and a fighter, too, I grant you. But a fighter for Wales, look; not just a loud-mouth talker of fighting for peace, see. If it is a good red Welsh dragon he is, then out of some kind of egg laid by your Uncle Joe, he is not; and thankful, too, I think," Hwyl told him. "And look you," he added as an afterthought, "this one it is who is stealing your chickens, not mine, at all."

"Oh, let him have the old chickens, and glad," Idris said. "Here he is come to chase a foreign imperialist dragon out of his rightful territory, and a proper thing it is, too. None of your D.P. dragons are we wanting round Llynllawn, or South Wales, either."

"Get you to hell, man," Hwyl told him. "Sweet dispositioned my dragon is, no bother to anyone, and no robber of henhouses, either. If there is trouble at all, the law I will be having of you and your dragon for disturbing of the peace, see. So I am telling you. And goodbye, now."

He exchanged another glance with the angry-looking, topaz eyes of the red dragon, and then stalked away, back to his own house.

—

That evening, just as Hwyl was sitting down to his meal, there was a knock at the front door. Bronwen went to answer it, and came back.

"Ivor Thomas and Dafydd Ellis wanting you. Something about the Union," she told him.

He went to see them. They had a long and involved story about dues that seemed not to have been fully paid. Hwyl was certain that he was paid-up to date, but they remained unconvinced. The argument went on for some time before, with head-shaking and reluctance, they consented to leave. Hwyl returned to the kitchen. Bronwen was waiting, standing by the table.

"Taken the dragon off, they have," she said, flatly.

Hwyl stared at her. The reason why he had been kept at the front door in pointless argument suddenly came to him. He crossed to the window, and looked out. The back fence had been pushed flat, and a crowd of men carrying the dragon's hutch on their shoulders was already a hundred yards beyond it. Turning round, he saw Bronwen standing resolutely against the back door.

"Stealing, it is, and you not calling," he said accusingly.

"Knocked you down, they would, and got the dragon just the same," she said. "Idris Bowen and his lot, it is."

Hwyl looked out of the window again.

"What to do with him, now then?" he asked.

"Dragon fight, it is," she told him. "Betting, they were. Five to one on the Welsh dragon, and sounding very sure, too."

Hwyl shook his head.

"Not to wonder, either. There is not fair, at all. Wings, that Welsh dragon has, so air attacks he can make. Unsporting, there is, and shameful indeed."

He looked out of the window again. More men were joining the party as it marched its burden across the waste-ground, toward the slag heap. He sighed.

"There is sorry I am for our dragon. Murder it will be, I think. But go and see it, I will. So no tricks from that Idris to make a dirty fight dirtier."

Bronwen hesitated.

"No fighting for you? You promise me?" she said.

"Is it a fool I am, girl, to be fighting fifty men, and more. Please to grant me some brains, now."

She moved doubtfully out of his way, and let him open the door. Then she snatched up a scarf, and ran after him, tying it over her head as she went.

The crowd that was gathering on a piece of flat ground near the foot of the slag heap already consisted of something more like a hundred men than fifty, and there were more hurrying to join it. Several self-constituted stewards were herding people back to clear an oval space. At one end of it was the cage in which the red dragon crouched huddled, with a bad-tempered look. At the other, the asbestos hutch was set down, and its bearers withdrew. Idris noticed Hwyl and Bronwen as they came up.

"And how much is it you are putting on your dragon?" he inquired, with a grin.

Bronwen said, before Hwyl could reply:

"Wicked, it is, and shamed you should be, Idris Bowen. Clip your dragon's wings to fight fair, and we will see. But betting against a horseshoe in the glove, we are not." And she dragged Hwyl away.

All about the oval the laying of bets went on, with the Welsh dragon gaining favor all the time. Presently, Idris stepped out into the open, and held up his hands for quiet.

"Sport it is for you tonight. Super colossal attractions, as they are saying on the movies, and never again, likely. So put you your money, now. When the English law is hearing of this, no more dragon-fighting, it will be—like no more to cockfight." A boo went up, mingled with the laughter of those who knew a thing or two about cockfighting that the English law did not. Idris went on: "So now the dragon championship, I am giving you. On my right, the Red Dragon of Wales, on his home ground. A people's dragon, see. For more than a coincidence, it is, that the color of the Welsh dragon——" His voice was lost for some moments in controversial shouts. It re-emerged, saying: "—left, the decadent dragon of the imperialist exploiters of the suffering Chinese people who, in their glorious fight for peace under the heroic leadership——" But the rest of his introduction was also lost among the catcalls and cheers that were still continuing when he beckoned forward attendants from the ends of the oval, and withdrew.

At one end, two men reached up with a hooked pole, pulled over the contraption that enclosed the red dragon, and ran back hurriedly. At the far end, a man knocked the peg from the asbestos door, pulled it open, scuttled round behind the hutch, and no less speedily out of harm's way.

The red dragon looked round, uncertainly. It tentatively tried unfurling its wings. Finding that possible, it reared up on its hind legs, supporting itself on its tail, and flapped them energetically, as though to dispel the creases.

The other dragon ambled out of its hutch, advanced a few feet, and stood blinking. Against the background of the waste-ground and the slag heap it looked more than usually exotic. It yawned largely, with a fine display of fangs, rolled its eyes hither and thither, and then caught sight of the red dragon.

Simultaneously, the red dragon noticed the other. It stopped flapping, and dropped to all four feet. The two regarded one another. A hush came over the crowd. Both dragons remained motionless, except for a slight waving of the last foot or so of their tails.

The oriental dragon turned its head a little on one side. It snorted slightly, and shriveled up a patch of weeds.

The red dragon stiffened. It suddenly adopted a passant guardant, one forefoot uplifted with claws extended, wings raised. It huffed with vigor, vaporized a puddle, and disappeared momentarily in a cloud of steam. There was an anticipatory murmur from the crowd.

The red dragon began to pace round, circling the other, giving a slight flap of its wings now and then.

The crowd watched it intently. So did the other dragon. It did not move from its position, but turned as the red dragon circled, keeping its head and gaze steadily toward it.

With the circle almost completed, the red dragon halted. It extended its wings widely, and gave a full-throated roar. Simultaneously, it gushed two streams of fire, and belched a small cloud of black smoke. The part of the crowd nearest to it moved back, apprehensively.

At this tense moment Bronwen Hughes began suddenly to laugh. Hwyl shook her by the arm.

"Hush, you! There is not funny, at all," he said, but she did not stop at once.

The oriental dragon did nothing for a moment. It appeared to be thinking the matter over. Then it turned swiftly round, and began to run. The crowd behind it raised a jeer, those in front waved their arms to shoo it back. But the dragon was unimpressed by arm-waving. It came on, with now and then a short spurt of flame from its nostrils. The people wavered, and then scattered out of its way. Half a dozen men started to chase after it with sticks, but soon gave up. It was traveling at twice the pace they could run.

With a roar, the red dragon leapt into the air, and came across the field, spitting flames like a strafing aircraft. The crowd scattered still more swiftly, tumbling over itself as it cleared a way.

The running dragon disappeared round the foot of the slag heap, with the other hovering above it. Shouts of disappointment rose from the crowd, and a good part of it started to follow, to be in at the death.

But in a minute or two the running dragon came into view again. It was making a fine pace up the mountainside, with the red dragon still flying a little behind it. Everybody stood watching it wind its way up and up until, finally, it disappeared over the shoulder. For a moment the flying dragon still showed as a black silhouette above the skyline, then, with a final whiff of flame, it, too, disappeared—and the arguments about paying up began.

Idris left the wrangling to come across to the Hugheses.

"So there is a coward your imperialist dragon is, then. And not one good huff, or a bite to him, either," he said.

Bronwen looked at him, and smiled.

"So foolish, you are, Idris Bowen, with your head full of propaganda and fighting. Other things than to fight, there is, even for dragons. Such a brave show your red dragon was making, such a fine show, oh, yes—and very like a peacock, I am thinking. Very like the boys in their Sunday suits in Llangolwgcoch High Street, too—all dressed up to kill, but not to fight."

Idris stared at her.

"And our dragon," she went on. "Well, there is not a very new trick, either. Done a bit of it before now, I have, myself." She cast a sidelong glance at Hwyl.

Light began to dawn on Idris.

"But—but it is *he* you were always calling your dragon," he protested.

Bronwen shrugged.

"Oh, yes, indeed. But how to tell with dragons?" she asked.

She turned to look up the mountain.

"There is lonely, lonely the red dragon must have been these two thousand years—so not much bothering with your politics, he is, just now. More single with his mind, see. And interesting it will be, indeed, to be having a lot of baby dragons in Wales before long, I am thinking."

ESMERALDA

Esmeralda was far and away the best performer I ever had in my show. I'd never seen another to touch her then, and I haven't since.

I got her off a Russian—for fifty cents. The Russians always seemed to have the best in those days; maybe they still do, but it's kind of hard to find Russians now. And fifty cents was a mighty big price, even though it was winter and prices were up. All the same, once I'd seen her, I had to have her. Big, she was, and strong. The Russky knew what he'd got, and he was pretty proud of her. I dickered a bit, but he wasn't taking less than the fifty.

I was glad to see her, too. The stock quality hadn't been so good lately. I'd had to change the card that I hung on my van whenever we stopped over at any place so that it read:

SUITABLE FLEAS
BOUGHT FOR CASH

with the *suitable* underlined, on account of folks were forever bringing me dog fleas, cat fleas, and chicken fleas, and then getting mad at me when I wouldn't buy. They still did, but the *suitable* let me out easier. They couldn't seem to get it into their heads that you gotta have sound, strong human fleas. Those others are too small, and they ain't lively enough. Like as not they'll lay down on the job, or else they'll go and die just when you got 'em trained. They can't take it like human fleas. One look at Esmeralda, and I knew she'd got the right makings, and being Russian put her in the top class, like I said.

I was ready to take a lot of trouble over her. Not just on account of the fifty cents, either—I've given seventy-five cents in winter for a poorer performer since then; there's times when you got to nowadays, seems like they're getting rarer, or something. No, it was because right away I could see the word *star* in Esmeralda's future like it was in lights, if she was properly handled.

Molly Doherty came into the van just when I was getting her fixed up, and stood watching while I tied the red silk thread I always use round that groove they have between the head and body. When I'd fixed that, I tied the thread to a strip of card, put a pin through the other end of the strip into the table, and then set Esmeralda down. Of course she tried to jump first, like they all do. And what a jumper! But for the pin she'd have taken the card with her. It pulled her down quick, but she tried a few more jumps.

"Gee!" Molly said. "This one's sure got what it takes."

That was one of the things I liked most about Molly. She'd got the professional angle. Mostly, women don't take a serious interest. They'll giggle and squeak, and most likely wriggle a bit when the show's on, but they ain't got what you could call appreciation, even then. Molly was different. She could tell an artist when she saw one, almost like she was in show business herself. She wasn't, though. Old Dan Doherty, her pop, used to run the hot-dog interest that had the concession near the gate, and she and her mom took turns helping him out there.

She was pretty, Molly was, in that dark-haired, fresh-colored Irish way. About nineteen she'd be then, and me twenty-four. The Dohertys had been traveling with the show a couple of years and more. I used to get on fine with her old man, and not too badly with her mom—though the old lady would never take to the performers, and sometimes just the sight of me around could start her scratching, just absentminded like. Kind of sensitive, she was. But Molly—well, I've never been to Ireland, though, knowing her, I sometimes thought I had. When she was quiet or sad there'd be mist in her eyes, and I'd think that was, maybe, like the slow, blue peat smoke. And other times, they'd look dark and deep, the way pools in heather do. Sometimes I'd wonder whether the curves of her weren't the curves of the Irish hills. And her voice was gentle like it might be made for singing those songs about wanting to go back to Ireland. But there was the other side of her, too—when you looked at her and saw, all of a sudden, why it is the Irish like to dance jigs. . . .

Molly and me got along fine most of the time. Going places and doing things together had come to be a habit with us. Not more than that. She'd have other dates. I'd make dates with other girls in the outfit, too, for a bit—though sooner or later I'd find them leading round to a grouch against the performers, and they couldn't seem to understand that a guy has professional pride that can be hurt. So they would kind of fade out without making any difference to anything—until Helga Liefsen showed up. . . .

But, like I said, Molly had the slant. We stood there watching Esmeralda for quite a while. She'd begun to learn that trying to jump wasn't getting her anyplace. The thread and card brought her down every time, so she'd walk a bit until she reckoned she'd got clear, and then have another shot. You could almost see her looking surprised that it had misfired some way, and trying to figure out what was screwy. Then she'd walk on a bit till she calculated she *must* be clear this time. There's some in the profession claim you can train them better by putting them in a small glass box on a spindle so that when they start jumping they bang their nuts on the other side, and the whole thing spins round. After this has got 'em rattled they start stepping cagey. And nowadays there's some kind of electric gimmick, too, but I've always stuck to the way I used with Esmeralda. It works. Before long they get to dragging the card round and round in a circle with the pin for a pivot. They keep it up for hours, and seemingly forget about jumping, except now and then.

Esmeralda was learning fast. As near a natural as they come. As a rule it takes a couple of weeks training before they're ready for the show, but I could see that if I'd not been going to star Esmeralda she'd have made good in a lot less.

"What's she going to do? And you needn't tell me bicycle," Molly said.

That was on account of I had an idea a performer could be trained to ride a bicycle—nobody had ever done it, and I wanted to be first. Matter of fact, nobody *has* done it yet, though I still try when I get a likely one—'s funny, they can't seem to get the idea of balance, somehow.

"I'll try her at that," I told Molly, "and if she can't, well, I reckon she could pull the coach by herself."

"Donkey work," said Molly. "She's got more future in her than that. We'll have to think up something special for her."

She was right, at that. The way Esmeralda was pulling that card round was something to see. Mighty strong, fleas are. The best performer I'd had up to then could drag near two hundred and fifty times his own weight when he got mad enough at it, and I could see Esmeralda was going to beat that a long way. I was just going to tell Molly how I reckoned it would be worthwhile taking real trouble over her and not hurry to get her into the show, when she quit looking at Esmeralda and turned to look at me.

"Joey," she said, "what about you and me going down to the beach tomorrow morning? They say it's a swell beach here—got huts, an' canoes, an' everything."

"Why, I'd like to, Molly," I said. "But just tomorrow I got a date."

Molly looked back at Esmeralda still making circles.

"A blonde date?" she asked, speaking sort of quiet.

There was no reason why I shouldn't have a blonde date, a ginger date, or a tortoiseshell date if I could get one, but you know how it is—there's something in the tone of voice, or maybe it's something that isn't in the tone of voice. Anyway:

"As a matter of fact it's a man," I told her. "Guy in town said he could get me a couple of dozen good stock if I'd call in and collect."

It was just my luck that Helga showed up then. She opened the van door without knocking, and put her head inside. Molly looked up once, and then back at Esmeralda. Helga gave Molly one glance, and then wrinkled her nose at Esmeralda.

Helga could do that and still not lose by it. Lovely, she was; not just her face, but all over. She'd wide blue eyes, hair like sunshine, and a figure to make a sculptor give up. You couldn't wonder at the hands she got every show. When she was up on the wire or swinging on the bar with all the lights turned on her she looked like she was floating in the sky. I used to reckon an angel might look just that way—'cept, maybe, for the tights. I'll always remember her calm and lovely up there, though I never watched her do her act more than a couple of times on account of it made me sweat so. Right now she was wearing a red jumper and blue slacks, but she still looked lovely.

"Oh, Joey," she said to me, "I guess we'll have to call it off. They just told me they got a practice fixed for eleven o'clock tomorrow. I didn't know. Sorry."

And then she'd gone again.

I looked at Molly, but she didn't say a thing. You'd think she'd not heard it, the way she kept on watching Esmeralda going round and round and round. . . .

—

Well, I didn't see a lot of Molly for a while after that. I was sorry not to have her looking into the van to see the way things were going. Specially the first couple of weeks. Esmeralda was shaping up nicely, and Molly'd likely have had some good ideas about her. Still, that's the way it was. She reckoned she'd got a right to feel sore, though I didn't see it—it wasn't like we were engaged or anything. But they do get that way. Seems to me when you reckon you've staked a claim, you notify . . . but they just act that anybody ought to know they got a lease without the asking or telling. So she'd got to going around like she'd wrapped herself up in cellophane.

It didn't worry me a lot. Mostly when I wasn't busy with the performers—and quite a bit of the time when I was—I'd got Helga on my mind. I was thinking of when I'd last seen her, or when I'd see her again, what I'd forgotten to say, and what I'd say next time, and things of that sort, the way you do. Maybe I was a bit light-headed about her. It wasn't just the way she looked, but every-thing. How she moved, for instance—so *sure*. There's something about wire artists, you can always tell 'em by the way they move. She had class, too. She was big-top, and in those days big-top didn't mix overmuch with the shows as a rule.

I'd see her as much as I could, and hang around on the chance quite a bit when I couldn't. On the mornings that she'd got a prac-tice or a rehearsal we'd meet and go out someplace, and most eve-nings I'd see her for a while after the ground was closed down.

It wasn't at all easy. If I'd been on the Ride of Death, or the River of Romance, or the Hall of Horrors it'd have been simpler, I guess. As it was, the performers were always kind of in the back-ground. We'd be talking, maybe, and I'd notice a little frown and see that she was looking down at the backs of my hands. She'd give a sort of wriggle, and I'd know the way she was thinking. But hell, performers have to be fed, same as anyone else; the best I could do about that was to put them further up my arm where the marks would be hidden by my sleeve. But she wasn't reasonable about it, like women aren't.

"Honey," I'd tell her, "you want to see this thing right. If it was lions now, or seals, or elephants, you'd not be feeling that way. The performers ain't big, I grant you, but they're God's creatures, like the rest of us."

"I know," she said, "all the same, I'd sooner it was lions."

"Great clumsy brutes," I told her. "All they can do is to jump onto things, and stand there snarling while the crowd hopes for the worst. Now, with the performers you can really put on a show. . . .

But it wasn't any use. When I was through, she'd still be saying she'd sooner it was lions.

And there was another thing, too. No matter what your business is, some gals ain't got no standard of affection except how much you neglect it for 'em. Seems they just got to back themselves against it—and they got it all nicely fixed so they win both ways. If you don't neglect it, you ain't lovin' them enough; if you do, they reckon you were that kind of sap, anyway. I can see now that Helga was getting around to that—though at the time I thought it was just the performers being what they were that was the trouble.

Maybe I did let up on the job a bit, too—but you couldn't call it neglect. I gave the shows, and I still went on getting Esmeralda groomed up for a good *première*. It was disappointing that she couldn't seem to get a line on that bicycle any more than the rest had, still, I'd some other ideas for her—but I'll allow I was missing the suggestions Molly would have put up. It wasn't till then that I came to see how many of her ideas had been getting into the show lately, and I could have done with more of them right then. All the same, Esmeralda and me were making out. She certainly was strong. She could shift that coach with six performers in it, and keep it moving, but Molly had been right about her being wasted on heavy draught work.

It took all of three weeks before I reckoned she was set for her big night. Then I put up a special bill for her outside the tent. It went:

HERE TONITE
ESMERALDA
FIRST PERFORMANCE OF
THE WORLD'S MOST ACCOMPLISHED
PULEX
OR
FLEA

SEE HER
HERE TONITE

And maybe it did help to fetch them in. Anyway, there was a full house around the ring.

I led off in the usual way, with switching the light on over the empty ring. Then I pulled back the curtain so they could see the orchestra. A ten-piece combination it was all tied in their seats, and an instrument fastened on one leg. The crooner made an eleventh; he was a bit out in front, hitched to his mike stand. They were all sitting there quiet till I put the phonograph on underneath them. Once the motor gets going it vibrates their platform, and that kind of sends them excited; they start waving their instruments and everything else like they was swinging it fit to bust. I let them have the record out, then I announced:

"Ladies and gentlemen. Tonight we present for the first time in any show the world's most talented flea—the flea with a college education. Ladies and gentlemen, we bring you *Esmeralda!*"

I put on another record, and loosed Esmeralda off into the ring. Just for the first second I thought she was going to fluff, but then she was away. No bicyclist maybe, but, boy, those long, kangaroo jumping-legs of hers could shift the tricycle along like nobody's business. She made one lightning spurt right across the ring, and capsized in front of the orchestra. But I got her set up again quick and away she went, beating it round and round the ring at the end of her wire like she was out for a championship. Great, she was, and they gave her a real hand, too. Everything was dandy—'cept that maybe I ought to have given her a brighter dress than pink, but I changed that later.

While I got her ready for her next act we had a boxing interlude. Nowadays they keep the performers lively with compressed air, but the way I did it there was clockwork under their platform to make it tremble a bit. The two performers had gloves on their upper legs, and they were hitched together by a wire you couldn't properly see. Once I put 'em down on the platform they got het up, and looked near enough to the real thing. They went on slugging it out while I fixed Esmeralda right for the chariot race.

We got along fine. The finale went okay, too. What I used to have there was a Grand Gladiators' Combat. I'd get eight performers rigged with a sword on one front leg, and a shield on the other, and put them in a little ring inside the big one. There was a small hutch on one side of it, and when you lifted the gate and tapped the back, the old bug used to come out. Performers ain't got no kind of use for bugs, and they'd go for him whenever he got near, and the old bug'd get pretty riled with 'em. But I'd given that up. I used to get folks saying it was cruelty to bugs, and threatening me with the Watch Committee. They wouldn't believe it didn't do no more than make the old bug tearing mad. Looked too realistic, I guess—it's funny the way folks are.

Anyway, I'd taken to putting on a wedding instead. Mighty fine wedding it was, too. There was the orchestra swinging it like crazy to "Here Comes the Bride" on one side, and the choir waving their little music sheets like just as crazy on the other, and the parson bobbing about in between, with the happy couple in front of him. I had to have Esmeralda play the bridegroom instead of bride, partly on account of she was bigger and so looked better that way, and partly on account of she was kind of allergic to veils—but I reckoned nobody except me was likely to notice that.

It went over huge. The audience was still laughing when I let down the curtain, and showed 'em out. And the three other performances that evening were as good.

Then I closed down pretty fast on account of I had a date with Helga. . . .

———

Next morning when I went to the tent to feed the troupe I had a nasty shock. A dozen of the performers were missing, and one of them was Esmeralda. Well, I'd lost performers before—no matter how careful you are, there's times when you slip up—but never a dozen at once. But there it was: the lids of their little glass-topped boxes were loose, and they'd beat it. I'd almost have thought someone had let them out, if there'd been any reason why they'd want to. But as folk in general would sooner know that they're in their boxes, I had to reckon that it had come of my being in too big a hurry to keep that date with Helga—she always got sort of sharp if she thought it was the performers that had kept her waiting.

Well, I scouted round. I reckoned they'd not have gone far, but I couldn't find one of them. It looked like they'd beat it fast, and got clean away. Of course, you can't expect a performer not to walk out on the show if he gets his chance. All the same, I felt sore about Esmeralda—she'd got the makings of a real trouper. . . .

I had to switch the acts that night, and do the best I could with what I had, but the show didn't go well. The crowd were kind of interested, and giggled a bit, but I couldn't get 'em really laughing like the night before. I was still sore about it when I met Helga afterward—though I didn't tell her about Esmeralda and the rest making their getaway. I knew she wouldn't see it the way I did—the only one that would was Molly. . . . But what thoughts I'd got were on Helga right then. . . .

All the same, she knew there was something wrong.

"What's on your mind tonight, Joey?" she asked, when we were walking in the wood behind the ground.

"Why, nothing," I told her. "That is, 'cept being in love, maybe."

"Maybe——?" she repeated, looking aside at me.

I stopped walking, and caught both her arms.

"No," I said, "not maybe. Helga, honey, I'm crazy about you. You know that. I love you like I never knew I could love anyone. Honest I do. . . . Don't you love me a little . . . ? Give me a break, honey—ain't you got no heart?"

She stood still, with her blue eyes looking right back into mine, and they were softer than I'd ever seen them.

"I got a heart, Joey—maybe too much heart. . . . But I guess what you need is a one-track heart, Joey boy—and that's what I *ain't* got. . . ."

I wasn't giving much attention to what she was saying so much as to the way she looked.

"Just give it a chance, honey. We could make out—me loving you the way I do . . ." I said.

She was looking at me, sort of wondering. Then she put her arm in mine, and we went on without talking.

When we got back to her van I put my arms round her and kissed her.

"Honey," I whispered. "Oh, honey, can't I come in—just for a while. . . . ?"

For a bit she didn't say anything. She didn't move, either. Then: "Yes, Joey—I guess you can come in," she said. . . .

—

They talk about a woman scorned—I wonder if they ever seen a woman bitten?

Helga whipped that sheet back off us so sudden it made me jump. She stared; then she kind of squawked.

"Look!" she said.

I looked.

There were half a dozen of them. And they were mine, all right, too—I could see the red silk round their necks.

"So it was you that took them!" I said. "What would you be wanting them for?"

There was a sound like she could be choking. "Me!" she bawled. "Me!" She took a breath. "You get out of here! Go on, get right out! And take *them* with you!"

I stared at the performers. Seeing the way she felt about them, I couldn't see why she would have been wanting to steal them in the first place. I looked back at her, kind of baffled.

She'd got her face twisted up at me—the first time I'd seen how she might have looked if she'd missed being lovely the way she regularly was. She brought her arm round in an open-handed smack—with all that trapeze-trained muscle behind it.

"Get out!" she said again. "Beat it! Get the hell out of here!" she told me, close to spitting it.

When the lights in my head had stopped flashing enough for me to see straight, I got—and the heck with the performers.

—

A knocking at my van door woke me the next morning, with the clock showing an hour over my regular time.

"Okay! Come in!" I called.

It was old man Doherty. He was wearing a steady, responsible look which didn't fit quite right. He was careful about the way he shut the door and then sat himself down on my stool, looking me over.

"Layin' in, huh?" he said. "Kinda late last night?"

There was something about the way he said it—besides it wasn't quite his style for opening up.

"Uh-huh," I said, not giving a lot.

"I knew you were late. I was around here 'bout half after one. Wanted to know what there is to this talk of raising the concession rate—and you weren't home." He held on there a bit, still looking me over. "Care to tell me where you were so late?" he added.

I faced right back at him. That wasn't like his way, either—and it wasn't like my way to answer it to anybody. His being Molly's father made it just that more difficult.

"I reckon that's my business," I told him.

"Maybe mine, too," he said.

I could see then by the look of him that he'd gotten hold of something. Well, even if he had . . . ? Half the place knew I was sweet on Helga, anyway. I'd concede it was tough on Molly, but sometimes life's like that—you can't help it. . . .

"*Your* business?" I asked, looking like I was puzzled.

"Yeh!" he said.

He brought out a hand he'd been keeping in his pocket.

I had a nasty moment thinking it was going to be a gun. But it wasn't. It was just a small glass bottle, and he handed it to me. Inside the bottle was Esmeralda, looking pretty bright and chippy. I took her.

"Gee! That's great, Dan," I said. "Where'd you find her?"

"I didn't," he said, slowly. "It was the old lady found her. Kinda happened across her this morning—she was making Molly's bed for her at the time."

I stared at him, and I guess I looked no dumber than I felt.

He spoke still slower, sort of tired it sounded:

"So right now, son, I'd be mighty interested to know just what you're aimin' to do about it . . . ?"

———

Well, there's some things it's better to let ride. One way and another neither Molly nor me said a lot about just what happened that night Esmeralda missed the show.

But I put Esmeralda back on the job, and she played to big hands. For the next ten months she was the best performer I've ever had. Then one night she died. Died still sitting right there on her tricycle, like a regular trouper. A big loss to the show, she was. They don't come like her anymore, and I reckon Molly missed her as much as I did.

All the same, when Molly gave me a present on our first wedding anniversary there was a funny look in her eye. Just for a minute I thought she was laughing . . . though there wasn't anything to laugh about.

A mighty fine present, it was. A stick-pin, like we used to wear in those days, made of real, solid, fourteen-carat gold. There was an oval bit of glass set at the head of it, and, nicely mounted inside the glass, was Esmeralda. . . .

HOW DO I DO?

Frances paused to look into the showcase that was fastened to the wall between the pastrycook's and the hairdresser's. It was not a novelty. Passing it a hundred times, she could not fail to be aware of it, or of the open door beside it, but until now it had not really impinged. There had been no reason for it to impinge. Hers was a future that seemed, in its main outlines at least, and in so far as any woman's is, pretty well charted.

Nor did the carefully worded leaflets behind the glass refer to the future directly. They offered Character Delineation, Scientific Palmistry, Psychological Prognosis, Semasiological Estimates, and other feats just beyond the scope of the Witchcraft Act or the practical interests of the police, but the idea of the future somehow showed through. And now, for the first time, Frances found herself interested—for it is not every day that one sends her ring back, and then looks out upon a suddenly futureless world.

All the same, and unlikely though it seemed at the moment, there must be a future of *some* kind lying ahead of her. . . .

She read about Mastery of one's Fate, Development of one's Personality, Guidance of one's Potentialities, and through a number of testimonials from persons who had been greatly helped, valuably guided, spiritually strengthened, and generally rendered more capable of managing themselves by the sympathetic counsels of Señora Rosa.

It was the word "guidance" occurring several times that set up the most responsive echo. Frances did not exactly imagine that she could go to this perfect stranger and extract a plan for living a neatly readjusted life, but the world, ever since she had handed that small, registered package across the post office counter, had become a place for which she had no plans of her own, and she felt that an improved acquaintance with one's potentialities might give some kind of a lead. . . .

She turned. She glanced along the street both ways, with an air of noticing and approving the freshness of the early-summer day. Then, having observed no one whom she knew, she edged into the doorway, and climbed the dusty stairs. . . .

——

"Marriage, of course," said Señora Rosa, with the slightest trace of a hiccup. "Marriage! That's what they all want to know about. Want to know what he looks like—'s if that mattered. Don't want to know if he'll beat 'em, or leave 'em, or murder 'em. Jus' what he looks like—so they'll know where to throw the lash—the lasso." She took a drink from the glass beside her, and went on: "Same with babies. Not interested to know if they'll turn out to be gangsters or film-shtarsh. Jus' want to know how many. No 'riginality. No 'magination. Jus' like a lot of sheep—'cept, of course, they want a ram each." She hiccupped discreetly again.

Frances started to get up. "I think, perhaps——" she began.

"No. Sit down," the Señora told her. Then, while Frances hesitated, she repeated not loudly, but quite firmly: *"Sit down!"*

Against her inclinations, and rather to the front of the chair, Frances sat down.

She regarded the Señora across the small table which held a crystal and a lamp, and knew that she had been a fool to come into the place at all. The Señora, with her swarthy skin, glittering dark eyes, and glaringly unnatural red hair, was difficult to visualize in the role of sympathetic counselor at the best of times: slightly drunk, with the high comb which supported her mantilla listing to the right, an artificial rose sagging down over her left ear, and her heavy eyelids half lowered against the trickle of her cigarette's smoke, she became more than displeasing. It was, in fact, absurd not to have turned back at the very first sight of her, but somehow Frances had lacked the resolution then, and not been able to gain it since.

"Fair return. That's my rule, an' no one's going to say I break it," announced the Señora. "Fee in advance, an' fair return. Mind you, there's nothing against a bit more for special satisfaction given, but fair return you *shall* have."

She switched on a small, heavily pink-shaded lamp close to the crystal, crossed the room a trifle uncertainly to draw the window curtains, and returned to her chair.

"Cozier," she explained. "'S easier to conshentrate, too."

She stubbed out her cigarette, drank off most of the remaining contents of her glass, gave her comb a push toward the vertical, and prepared to get to work.

"'S *on* me today," she observed. "Some days it's *on* you; some days it's not—never can tell till you start. But I can feel it now. Tell you pretty near anything today, I could—wouldn't, of course; doesn't do, but could. Something special you'd be wanting to know, beyond husband, babies, an' the usual?"

The low lighting worked quite a change in the Señora. It modified the redness of her hair, made the lines of her face more decisive; it glinted fascinatingly on her long brass earrings swinging like bell-clappers, and glistened even more brightly in her dark eyes.

"Er—no," said Frances. "As a matter of fact, I think I've changed my mind. So if you——"

"Nonsense," the Señora told her, shortly. "You'll only be back in a day or two if you do, and then it might not be *on* me the way it is today. We'll start on your future husband."

"No. I'd rather not——" began Frances.

"Nonsense," said the Señora again. "They all want that. Jus' you keep quiet now. Got to conshentrate."

She leaned forward, shading the crystal with one hand from the direct light while she gazed into it. Frances watched uncomfortably. For a time nothing happened, except that the earrings swung slowly to a stop. Then:

"H'm," said the Señora, with a suddenness that made Frances jump. "Nice-looking young fellow, too."

Frances had a vague feeling that such pronouncements, whatever their worth, were usually made in a more impressive tone and form, but the Señora went on:

"Nice tie. Dark blue an' old gold, with a thin red stripe in the blue."

Frances sat quite still. The Señora leaned closer to the crystal.

"Couple of inches taller than you, I'd say. 'Bout five foot ten. Smooth fair hair. Nice mouth. Good chin. Straight nose. Eyes sort of dark gray with a touch of blue. Got a small, crescent-shaped scar over his left eyebrow, an old one. He——"

"Stop it!" Frances snapped.

The Señora looked up at her for a moment, and then back to the crystal.

"Now, as to children——" she went on.

"Stop it, I tell you!" Frances told her again. "I don't know how you found out about him, but you're *wrong*. Yesterday I'd have believed you, but now you're quite *wrong*!" The recollection of putting the ring with its five winking diamonds into its nest of cotton wool, and closing the box on it became unbearably vivid. She was exasperatedly aware of tears starting to well up.

"There's often jus' a bit of a tiff——" began the Señora.

"How dare you! It's not just a tiff, at all. It's finished. I'm never going to see him again. So you might as well stop this farce now," Frances said.

The Señora stared. "Farce!" she exclaimed, incredulously. "You call my work farce! Why, you— I'd have you know——"

Frances was angry enough for tears to wait.

"Farce!" she repeated. "Farce, and cheating! I don't know how you find out about people, but this time it hasn't worked. Your information's out of date. You—you—you're just a drunken old

cheat, taking advantage of people who are unhappy. That's what you are."

She stood up to get herself out of the room before the tears should come.

The Señora glared back at her. She snatched across the table, and caught her wrist in a grip like a steel claw.

"Cheat!" she shouted. "Cheat! Why, you—you silly ignorant little ninny! Sit down!"

"Let me go," Frances told her. "You're hurting my wrist."

The Señora leaned closer. Her brows were lowered angrily over her eyes that glittered more than ever. *"Sit down there!"* she ordered again.

Frances suddenly found herself more scared than angry. She stood for a moment, trying to outstare the Señora; then her eyes dropped. She sat down, partly because the grip on her wrist was urging her, but more from sheer nervousness.

Señora Rosa sat down again, too, but she continued to hold Frances's wrist across the table.

"Cheat!" she muttered. "*You* called *me* a cheat!"

Frances avoided meeting her gaze.

"Somebody must have told you about me and Edward," she said stubbornly.

"*That* told me," said the Señora, pointing her free hand at the crystal. "That, an' nothing else. Tells me a lot, that does. But you don't believe it, do you?"

"I didn't really mean——" Frances began.

"Don't give me that. 'Course you meant it. No respec'. No respec' at all. Ninnies like you need a lesson to teach 'em respec'." Sh'll I tell you when you're going to die, and how? Or when your Edward's going to die?"

"No—no, please!" said Frances.

"Ha! Don't believe me—but you're afraid to hear," observed the Señora.

"I'm sorry, really I am. I was upset. Please let me——"

Frances began, but the Señora was not to be easily mollified.

"Farce! Cheat!" she muttered again. *"Ninny!"* she added again forcibly, and then fell silent.

The silence lengthened, but the grip on Frances's wrist did not relax. Presently, curiosity drove her to a swift upward glance. She had a glimpse of a quite different expression on the Señora's face—more alarming in some indefinite way, than her former anger. She appeared to have had some kind of inspiration. Her hand clutched Frances's wrists more tightly.

"*Show* you, that's what," she said, decisively. "Sick of ninnies. Jus' *show* you. Look in the crysh—crystal!"

"Look in the crystal!" commanded the Señora.

Unwillingly Frances lifted her head a little, and looked at it. It was a quite uninteresting lump of glass, showing a number of complicated and distorted reflections.

"This is silly," she said. "I can't see anything there. You've no right to——"

"Be quiet! Jus' *look!*" snapped the Señora.

Frances went on looking, wondering at the same time how she was going to get herself out of this. Even if she were able to pull herself free, it was impossible in the small room for her to reach the door without coming within reach of the Señora's grasp again—and there'd be delay in getting the door open, too. If— Then her thoughts broke off as she noticed that the crystal was no longer clear. It seemed to have become fogged, rather as if it had been breathed upon. But the foggy look grew thicker as she watched until it was like smoke wreathing inside it. Queer! Some trick of the old woman's, of course. . . . Some kind of hypnotic effect which made it seem to grow bigger and bigger. . . . It appeared to widen out as she watched it until there was nothing at all anywhere but convolving whorls of fog. . . .

Then, like a flash, it was gone, and she was sitting in her chair, looking at the clear crystal.

The grip on her arm was gone, too; and so, when she looked up, was the Señora. . . .

Frances snatched up her bag and made for the door. No sound came from the inner room as she tiptoed across. She opened the door carefully, closed it quietly behind her, and skipped swiftly away down the stairs.

—

A very unpleasant experience, Frances told herself, walking briskly away. In fact, being held there like that against her will was the sort of thing one ought to tell a policeman about; probably it ranked as assault, or something quite serious, really. . . . Still not quite certain whether she was wanting to see a policeman or not, she emerged from her thoughts, and looked about her.

In the very first glance she made a discovery which drove such frivolous subjects as policemen right out of her mind. It was that everyone else in sight who had decided that the time for cotton had arrived was clad in a frock very much shorter and very much narrower than her own. She stared at them, bewildered. She must have had an inconceivable preoccupation with her own affairs not to have realized that there had been such a radical change of line. She paused for a moment in front of a shop window to observe the reflection of the blue-and-white striped cotton frock that she had thought good for another summer. It looked terrible; just as if she had been unholstered. Another glance from it to the other frocks made her go hot with embarrassment: they must all be thinking she had come out wrapped in a bedspread. . . .

Clearly, there was one thing to be done about that, and done at once. . . .

She started to walk hurriedly in the direction of Weilberg's Modes. . . .

—

Frances re-emerged into the street half an hour later, feeling considerably soothed. The congenial occupation of shopping, and the complete clearing of mental decks required for concentration on the choice of a creation in an amusing pattern of palm trees and pineapples, had helped to put Señora Rosa into proper perspective. Considered calmly, over an ice-cream soda, the affair dwindled quite a lot—and her own part in it came to seem curiously spineless. Her intention of informing the police faded. If there were a charge, and she had to give evidence, she would scarcely be able to help exhibiting herself first as a fool for having gone into the place at all, and then as a nitwit for staying when she did not want to. Moreover, it would very likely be reported in the papers, and she would hate that—so would Edward. . . .

Which brought one back to thinking of Edward. . . . And to wondering whether one had perhaps behaved like a silly little fool there, too. After all, he had known Mildred for years and years—and just two or three dances. . . . People said one ought to be careful about not feeling *too* possessive. . . . All the same, just a few days after he had become engaged. . . . No, it didn't do to look cheap, or easygoing, either. . . . And yet . . . Really, life could be very difficult. . . .

—

Though Frances decided that she would walk home, she did not consciously choose her route. That is to say, she did not tell herself: "I'll go by St. James's Avenue, past that house that we decided would just suit us." It simply was that her feet happened to carry her that way.

Coming nearer to the house, she walked more slowly. There was a moment when she almost decided to turn back and go round by another way. But she squashed that. One could not go about forever avoiding every reminder: a person had to get used to things, sooner or later. She walked resolutely on. Presently she was able to see the upper floor of the house above the hedges. A comfortable, sensible-looking, friendly house; not new, but modern, and without being *moderne*. It gave her a little knot high in her chest to see it again now. Then, as more of it came into view, the knot gave way to a feeling of dismay. There were curtains in the windows that had been blank, the hedges had been trimmed, the board which had announced "For Sale" was gone.

She paused at the front gate. An astonishing amount had been done to the place in the few days since she had last seen it. It looked altogether fresher. The flower beds in the front garden were bright with tulips, the fig tree against the side wall had been cut and tied back, the windows shone. The doors of the garage were open, and a comfortable-looking car stood on the concrete apron in front. The lawn had been closely mown. On it, a little girl of four or so, dressed in a blue frock, was conducting a tea party with earnest admonitions to the guests who consisted of three sizes of teddy bear and a golliwog.

Frances was filled with a sharp indignation. The house had been almost hers: she had quite decided that it was the one her father was going to give them for a wedding present—and now it had been snatched away without a word of warning. It might not have been so bad if it had not somehow contrived already to look so aggressively *settled*. . . . not that it actually mattered, of course, now that she had finished with Edward. . . . All the same, there *was* a feeling of having been cheated in some way that one did not quite understand. . . .

The little girl on the lawn became aware of someone at the gate. She broke off scolding the golliwog to look up. She dropped the miniature cup and saucer that she was holding, and started to run toward Frances.

"Mummy!" she called.

Frances looked around and behind her. There was no one there. Then she bent down instinctively as the small figure hurtled itself toward her. The little girl flung her arms round her neck.

"Mummy," she said, with breathy intensity. "Mummy, you *must* come and tell Golly not to. He *will* talk with his mouth full."

"Er——" said Frances, out of the sudden stranglehold. "I—er—you—I mean——"

The little girl relaxed the clinch, and tugged at her arm.

"Oh, *do* come along, Mummy," she said. "He's 'veloping bad habits."

Dazedly, Frances allowed herself to be led across the lawn to the tea party. The little girl improved the dissolute-looking golliwog by propping him into a sitting position.

"There," she told him. "Now Mummy's here you'll have to behave. Tell him, Mummy." She looked at Frances expectantly.

"I—er—um—you——" Frances began, confusedly.

The child looked up at her, puzzled.

"What's the matter, Mummy?" she asked.

Frances stared back at her, recollecting photographs of herself at about the same age. A peculiar feeling began to come over her. The small earnest face seemed to swim slightly as she looked at it. Its expression grew concerned.

"Aren't you feeling well, Mummy?"

Frances pulled herself together.

"I'm—I'm all right—er—darling," she said, unsteadily.

"Then *do* tell Golly he mustn't. It's awfly rude."

Frances went down on her knees. She was glad to: the ground felt more solid that way. She leaned toward the offending golliwog who promptly fell flat on his face and was hastily propped up again by his mistress.

"Er—Golly," Frances told him. "Golly, I'm very shocked indeed to hear this about you. People who are invited to parties . . ."

———

So real . . . ! All of it . . . !

Now that the lump in her chest which wasn't quite panic or scare, but a bit like both, had subsided, Frances found herself able to regard the situation a little more calmly. The classic certificate was to be obtained by pinching oneself; she had done that, sharply, but without changing any of it a bit. She looked at her hand, flexed it; it was her perfectly familiar hand. She plucked a little grass from the lawn beside her; real grass, beyond doubt. She listened to the sounds about her; they had an authentic quality difficult to deny. She picked up the nearest teddy bear, and examined it; no dream ever finished anything with that amount of detail. She sat back on her heels, looking up at the house, noticing the striped chairs on the porch, the patterns of the curtains, the recent painting.... One had always thought that hallucinations must be vague, misty experiences.... All this had a solidity that was rather frightening....

"Mummy," said the little girl, turning away from her tea party, and standing up.

Frances's heart jumped slightly.

"Yes, dear?" she said.

"'Mportant business. Will you see that Golly behaves himself?"

"I—I think he understands now, dear," Frances told her.

The small face in its frame of fair hair looked doubtful.

"P'raps. He's rather wicked, though. Back soon. "'Mportant.'"

Frances watched the blue frock vanish as the child scampered away round the corner of the house on her mysterious errand. She felt suddenly forlorn. For some moments she remained on her knees, returning the boot-button stare of the teddy bear in her hands. Then the absurdity of the whole thing flooded over her. She dropped the bear, and got to her feet. At just that moment a man emerged from the front of the house onto the porch.

And he wasn't Edward.... He wasn't a bit like him.

... He wasn't anybody she'd ever seen before in her life.

He was tall, rather thin, but broad in the shoulders. His dark hair curled a little, and there were slight flecks of gray over his ears. He had been making toward the car, but at the sight of her he stopped. His eyes crinkled at the corners, and seemed to light up.

"Back so early!" he said. "New frock, too! And looking like a schoolgirl in it. How do you manage it?"

"Uh!" gasped Frances, caught in a strong, and entirely unexpected embrace.

"Look, darling," he continued, without loosening his hold. "I simply must tear off now and see old Fanshawe. I won't be more than an hour."

His hug brought the rest of Frances's breath out in another involuntary "Uh!" He kissed her soundly, slapped her behind affectionately, and dashed for the car. A moment later it carried him out of her sight.

Frances stood getting her breath back, and staring after him. She found that she was shaking, and filled with a most odd sensation of weakness, particularly in the knees. She staggered over to one of the chairs on the porch, and subsided there. For a space she sat motionless, her eyes set glazedly on nothing. Then, not quite accountably, she burst into tears.

——

When emotion had declined to a sniff-and-dab stage, it was succeeded by misgivings about the orthodoxy of her situation. In whatever peculiar way it had come about, the fact remained that she had been "Mummy" to someone else's child, warmly embraced by someone else's husband, and was now sitting sniveling on someone else's porch. A convincing explanation of all this to the someone else looked like being so difficult that the best way out would be to get clear as soon as possible, and avoid it.

Frances gave a final dab, and got up with decision. She retrieved her bag from the medley of teddy bears and teacups, and glanced at the mirror in the flap. She frowned at it, and burrowed for her compact. In the act of a preparatory scrub on the sieve, the sound of a step caused her to look up. A woman was coming in through the gateway. A moderately tall, nicely built woman, dressed in a light-green linen suit, and carrying it well; a woman who was a few years older than herself but still ... At that moment the woman turned so that Frances could see her face, and all coherent thought expired. Frances's jaw sagged. She gaped. . . .

The other woman noticed her. She looked hard at her, but showed no great surprise. She turned off the path and approached across the grass. There was nothing alarming about her; indeed, she was wearing the trace of a smile.

"Hullo!" she said. "I was thinking this morning that you must be due somewhere about now."

Frances's bag slipped out of her fingers, and spilled at her feet, but her eyes never left the other's face.

The woman's eyes were a little deeper and wiser than those she was wont to see in the mirror. There were the very faintest touches of shadows at their corners, and at the corners of the mouth. The lips favored a shade of color just a trace darker. . . . Something as indescribable as the touch of dew had been exchanged for a breath of sophistication. But otherwise . . . otherwise . . .

Frances tried to speak, but all that came was a croak, strangled in rising panic.

"It's all right," said the other. "Nothing to be scared about." She linked her arm into Frances's, and led her back to the porch. "Now sit down there and just relax. You don't need to worry a bit."

Frances sank unresistingly into the chair, and stared dumbly at her. Presently, the other opened her bag.

"Cigarette?" she suggested. "Oh, no. Of course. I didn't then." She took one for herself, and lit it. For what seemed a long time they surveyed one another through the smoke. It was the other who broke the silence. She said:

"How pretty—and charming! If I had only understood more— still, I suppose one could scarcely have had innocence *and* experience." She sighed, with a touch of wistfulness. Then she shook her head. "But no. No. Being young is very exhausting and unsatisfactory, really—although it looks so nice."

"Er——" said Frances. She swallowed, with difficulty. "Er— I think I must be going mad."

The other shook her head. "Oh, no you're not. Nothing like it. Just take it easy, and try to relax."

"But this? I mean, you—me—as if—oh, I *am* going mad! I must be. It's impossible!" Frances protested wildly. "Nobody can possibly be in two places at once. I mean, nobody can be twice in the same place at once. I mean, one person can't be two people, not at the same——"

The other leaned across, and patted her hand.

"There, there now. Calm down. I know it's terribly bewildering at first, but it comes all right. I remember."

"Y—you *remember*?" stammered Frances.

"Yes. From when it happened to me, of course. From when I was where you are now."

Frances stared at her, with a sensation of slowly and helplessly drowning.

"Look," said the other. "I think I'd better get you a drink. Yes, I know you don't take it, but this *is* rather exceptional. I remember how much better I felt for it. Just a minute." She got up, and went indoors.

Frances leaned back, holding hard to both arms of her chair for reassurance. She felt as if she were falling over and over, a long way down.

The other came back holding a glass, and gave it to her. She drank, spluttering a little over the strange taste of it. But the other had been right: she did immediately begin to feel somewhat better.

"Of course, it's a bit of a shock," said the other. "And I fancy you're right about one person not being in two places—up to a point. But the way I think it must happen is that you just *seem* to yourself to go on being the same person. But you never can be, not really. I mean, as the cells that make you are always gradually being replaced, you can't really be *all* the same person at any two times, can you?"

Frances tried to follow that, without success, but:

"Well—well, I suppose not *quite*," she conceded, doubtfully.

The other went on talking, giving her time to recover herself.

"Well, then, when *all* the cells have been replaced by new ones, over seven years or so, then you can't *any* of you be the same person any longer, although you still think you are. So that means that the cells that make up you and me are two different sets of cells—so they aren't really having to be in two different places at once, although it does look like it, don't you see?"

"I—er—perhaps," said Frances, on a slightly hysterical note.

"So that sets a sort of natural limit," the other went on. "There obviously has to be a kind of minimum gap of seven years or so in which it is quite impossible for this to happen at all—until all your present cells have been replaced by others, you see."

"I—I suppose so," said Frances, faintly.

"Just take another drink of that. It'll do you good," the other advised.

Frances did, and leaned back again in the chair. She wished her head would stop whirling. She did not understand a word that the woman—her other self—whoever it was—had said. All she knew was that none of it could possibly make sense. She kept on hanging on to the arms of the chair until, presently, she began to feel herself growing a little calmer.

"Better? You've more color now," the other said.

Frances nodded. She could feel the tears of a reaction not far away. The other came over and put an arm round her.

"Poor dear! What a time you're having! All this confusion, and then falling in love on top of it—as if that weren't confusing enough by itself."

"F-falling in love?" said Frances.

"Why, yes. He kissed you, and patted your behind—and you fell in love. I remember so well."

"Oh, dear—is it like that? I didn't——" Frances broke off. "But how did you know about——? Oh, I see, of course——"

"And he's a dear. You'll adore him. And little Betty's a love, too, bless her," the other told her. She paused, and added: "I'm afraid you've rather a lot to go through first, but it's worth it. You'll remember it's worth it all?"

"Yes-s-s," Frances told her vaguely.

She thought for a moment of the man who had come out of the house and gone off in the car. He would be——

"Yes," she said, more stoutly. She pondered for some seconds and then turned to look at the other.

"I suppose one does have to grow old—er, older, I mean," she amended. "Somehow, I've never thought——"

The other laughed. "Of course you haven't. But it's really very nice, I assure you. Such a much less anxious state than being young—though, naturally, you won't believe that."

Frances let her eyes wander round the porch and across the garden. They came to rest on the teddy bears and the delinquent golliwog. She smiled.

"I think I do," she said.

The other smiled, too; her eyes a little shiny.

"I really was rather a sweet thing," she said.

She got up abruptly.

"Time you were going, my dear. You've got to get back to that horrid old woman."

Frances got up obediently, too. The other seemed to have an idea of what she was talking about, and what was necessary. Frances herself had little enough.

"Back to the Señora?" she asked.

The other nodded without speaking. She put her arms round Frances, and held her close to her. She kissed her gently. "Oh, my dear!" she said, unsteadily, and turned her head away.

Frances walked down the short drive. At the gate she turned and looked back, taking it all in.

The other, on the porch, kissed her hand to her. Then she put it over her eyes, and ran into the house.

Frances turned to the right and walked back by the way she had come, toward the town, and the Señora. . . .

—

The cloudiness cleared. The crystal became just a glass ball again. Beyond it sat Señora Rosa, with her comb awry. Her left hand held Frances's wrist. Frances stared at her for some moments, then:

"You *are* a cheat," she burst out. "*And* you've been telling lies, too. You described Edward, but the man you showed me wasn't Edward—he wasn't even a bit like Edward." She pulled her arm free with a sudden wrench. "Cheat!" she repeated. "You told me Edward, and you showed me somebody else. It's all cruel, silly lies and cheating. All of it."

Her vehemence was enough to take the Señora a little aback.

"There *was* jus' a little mistake," she admitted. "By 'n'unfortunate——"

"Mistake!" shouted Frances. "The mistake was my ever coming here at all. You've just made a fool of me, and I hate you! *I hate you!*"

The Señora recoiled, and then rallied slightly. With a touch of dignity, she said:

"Th'xplanation's really quite simple. It was——"

"No!" Frances shouted. "I don't want to hear any more about it."

She pushed the table with all her force. The far edge of it took the Señora in the middle. Her chair teetered backward, then she, table, crystal, and lamp, went down all in a heap. Frances sprang for the door.

The Señora grunted, and rolled over. She struggled stertorously to her feet, leaving comb and mantilla in the debris. She made determinedly through the door in Frances's wake. On the landing, she leaned over the banisters.

"You damned little duffer," she shouted. "That was your *shecond* marriage—an' I say the hell with *both* of 'em."

But Frances was already out in the street, beyond earshot.

——

"A very unpleasant experience—humiliating, too," thought Frances, as she pegged along, with the jolting step of the incensed. Humiliating because she had nearly—no, she'd be honest; for a time she *had* fallen for it. It had all seemed so convincingly, so really real. Even now she could scarcely believe that she hadn't walked up that drive, sat on that porch, talked to . . . but what a ridiculous thing to think. . . . As if it could possibly be . . . !

All the same, to find oneself facing that horrible Señora again, and realize that it had all been some kind of trick. . . . If she were not in the public street, she could have kicked herself, and wept with mortification. . . .

Presently, however, as the first flush of her anger began to cool, she became more aware of her surroundings. It was borne in upon her attention that a number of the people she met were looking at her with curiosity—not quite the right kind of curiosity. . . .

She glanced down at her frock, and stopped dead. Instead of her familiar blue-and-white striped cotton, she was wearing an affair covered with an absurd, niggly pattern of palm trees and pineapples. She raised her eyes again, and looked round. Every other cotton frock in sight was inches longer and far fuller than hers.

Frances blushed. She walked on, trying to look as if she were not blushing; trying, too, to pretend that the skimpy frock did not make her feel as if she had come out dressed in a rather inadequate bath towel.

Clearly, there was one thing to be done about that; and done at once. . . .

She made hastily toward Weilberg's Modes. . . .

UNA

The first thing I knew of the Dixon affair was when a deputation came from the village of Membury to ask us if we would investigate the alleged curious goings-on there.

But before that, perhaps, I had better explain the word "us."

I happen to hold a post as Inspector for the S.S.M.A.—in full, the Society for the Suppression of the Maltreatment of Animals— in the district that includes Membury. Now, please don't assume that I am wobble-minded on the subject of animals. I needed a job. A friend of mine who has influence with the Society got it for me; and I do it, I think, conscientiously. As for the animals themselves, well, as with humans, I like some of them. In that, I differ from my co-Inspector, Alfred Weston; he likes—liked?—them all; on principle, and indiscriminately.

It could be that, at the salaries they pay, the S.S.M.A. has doubts of its personnel—though there is the point that where legal action is to be taken two witnesses are desirable; but, whatever the reason, there is a practice of appointing their inspectors as pairs to each district; one result of which was my daily and close association with Alfred.

Now, one might describe Alfred as the animal-lover *par excellence*. Between him and all animals there was complete affinity—at least, on Alfred's side. It wasn't his fault if the animals didn't quite understand it; he tried hard enough. The very thought of four feet or feathers seemed to do something to him. He cherished them one and all, and was apt to talk of them, and to them, as if they were his dear, dear friends temporarily embarrassed by a diminished I.Q.

Alfred himself was a well-built man, though not tall, who peered through heavily rimmed glasses with an earnestness that seldom lightened. The difference between us was that while I was doing a job, he was following a vocation—pursuing it wholeheartedly, and with a powerful imagination to energize him.

It didn't make him a restful companion. Under the powerful magnifier of Alfred's imagination the commonplace became lurid. At a run-of-the-mill allegation of horse-thrashing, phrases about fiends, barbarians, and brutes in human form would leap into his mind with such vividness that he would be bitterly disappointed when we discovered, as we invariably did, (a) that the thing had been much exaggerated, anyway, and (b) that the perpetrator had either had a drink too many, or briefly lost his temper.

It so happened that we were in the office together on the morning that the Membury deputation arrived. They were a more numerous body that we usually received, and as they filed in I could see Alfred's eyes begin to widen in anticipation of something really good—or horrific, depending on which way you were looking at it. Even I felt that this ought to produce something a cut above cans tied to cats' tails, and that kind of thing.

Our premonitions turned out rightly. There was a certain confusion in the telling, but when we had it sorted out, it seemed to amount to this:

Early the previous morning, one Tim Darrell, while engaged in his usual task of taking the milk to the station, had encountered a phenomenon in the village street. The sight had so surprised him that while stamping on his brakes he had let out a yell which brought the whole place to its windows or doors. The men had gaped, and most of the women had set up screaming when they, too, saw the pair of creatures that were standing in the middle of their street.

The best picture of these creatures that we could get out of our visitors suggested that they must have looked more like turtles than anything else—though a very improbable kind of turtle that walked upright upon its hind legs.

The overall height of the apparitions would seem to have been about five foot six. Their bodies were covered with oval carapaces, not only at the back, but in front, too. The heads were about the size of normal human heads, but without hair, and having a horny-looking surface. Their large, bright black eyes were set above a hard, shiny projection, debatably a beak or a nose.

But this description, while unlikely enough, did not cover the most troublesome characteristic—and the one upon which all were agreed despite other variations. This was that from the ridges at the sides, where the back and front carapaces joined, there protruded, some two-thirds of the way up, a pair of human arms and hands!

Well, about that point I suggested what anyone else would: that it was a hoax, a couple of fellows dressed up for a scare.

The deputation was indignant. For one thing, it convincingly said, no one was going to keep up that kind of hoax in the face of gunfire—which was what old Halliday who kept the saddler's had given them. He had let them have half a dozen rounds out of a twelve-bore; it hadn't worried them a bit, and the pellets had just bounced off.

But when people had got around to emerging cautiously from their doors to take a closer look, they had seemed upset. They had squawked harshly at one another, and then set off down the street at a kind of waddling run. Half the village, feeling braver now, had followed them. The creatures had not seemed to have any idea of where they were going, and had run out over Baker's Marsh. There they had soon struck one of the soft spots, and finally they had sunk out of sight into it, with a great deal of floundering and squawking.

The village, after talking it over, had decided to come to us rather than to the police. It was well meant, no doubt, but, as I said:

"I really don't see what you can expect us to do if the creatures have vanished without trace."

"Moreover," put in Alfred, never strong on tact, "it sounds to me that we should have to report that the villagers of Membury simply hounded these unfortunate creatures—whatever they were—to their deaths, and made no attempt to save them."

They looked somewhat offended at that, but it turned out that they had not finished. The tracks of the creatures had been followed back as far as possible, and the consensus was that they could not have had their source anywhere but in Membury Grange.

"Who lives there?" I asked.

It was a Doctor Dixon, they told me. He had been there these last three or four years.

And that led us on to Bill Parsons's contribution. He was a little hesitant about making it at first.

"This'll be confidential like?" he asked.

Everyone for miles around knows that Bill's chief concern is other people's rabbits. I reassured him.

"Well, it was this way," he said. "'Bout three months ago it'd be——"

Pruned of its circumstantial detail, Bill's story amounted to this: finding himself, so to speak, in the grounds of the Grange one night, he had taken a fancy to investigate the nature of the new wing that Doctor Dixon had caused to be built on soon after he came. There had been considerable local speculation about it, and, seeing a chink of light between the curtains there, Bill had taken his opportunity.

"I'm telling you, there's things that's not right there," he said. "The very first thing I seen, back against the far wall was a line of cages, with great thick bars to 'em—the way the light hung I couldn't see what was inside: but why'd anybody be wanting them in his house?

"And then when I shoved myself up higher to get a better view, there in the middle of the room I saw a norrible sight—a norrible sight it was!" He paused for a dramatic shudder.

"Well, what was it?" I asked, patiently.

"It was—well, 'tis kind of hard to tell. Lying on a table, it was, though. Lookin' more like a white bolster than anything—'cept that it was moving a bit. Kind of inching, with a sort of ripple in it—if you understand me."

I didn't much. I said:

"Is that all?"

"That it's not," Bill told me, approaching his climax with relish. "Most of it didn't 'ave no real shape, but there was a part of it as did—a pair of hands, human hands, a-stickin' out from the sides of it. . . ."

———

In the end I got rid of the deputation with the assurance we would look into the matter. When I turned back from closing the door behind the last of them I perceived that all was not well with Alfred. His eyes were gleaming widely behind his glasses, and he was trembling.

"Sit down," I advised him. "You don't want to go shaking parts of yourself off."

I could see that there was a dissertation coming: probably something to beat what we had just heard. But, for once, he wanted my opinion first, while manfully contriving to hold his own down for a time. I obliged:

"It has to turn out simpler than it sounds," I told him. "Either somebody *was* playing a joke on the village—or there are some very unusual animals which they've distorted by talking it over too much."

"They were unanimous about the carapaces and arms—two structures as thoroughly incompatible as can be," Alfred said, tiresomely.

I had to grant that. And arms—or, at least, hands—had been the only describable feature of the bolster-like object that Bill had seen at the Grange. . . .

Alfred gave me several other reasons why I was wrong, and then paused meaningly.

"I, too, have heard rumors about Membury Grange," he told me.

"Such as?" I asked.

"Nothing very definite," he admitted. "But when one puts them all together . . . After all, there's no smoke without——"

"All right, let's have it," I invited him.

"I think," he said, with impressive earnestness, "I think we are on the track of something *big* here. Very likely something that will at last stir people's consciences to the iniquities which are practiced under the cloak of scientific research. Do you know what I think is happening on our very doorstep?"

"I'll buy it," I told him, patiently.

"I think we have to deal with a super-vivisectionist!" he said, wagging a dramatic finger at me.

I frowned. "I don't get that," I told him. "A thing is either vivi- or it isn't. Super-vivi- just doesn't——"

"Tcha!" said Alfred. At least, it was that kind of noise. "What I mean is that we are up against a man who is outraging nature, abusing God's creatures, wantonly distorting the forms of animals until they are no longer recognizable or only in parts, as what they were before he started distorting them," he announced, involvedly.

At this point I began to get a line on the truly Alfredian theory that was being propounded this time. His imagination had got its teeth well in, and, though later events were to show that it was not biting quite deeply enough, I laughed:

"I see it," I said. "I've read *The Island of Doctor Moreau,* too. You expect to go up to the Grange and be greeted by a horse walking on its hind legs and discussing the weather; or perhaps you hope a super-dog will open the door to you, and inquire your name?

"A thrilling idea, Alfred. But this is real life, you know. Since there has been a complaint, we must try to investigate it, but I'm afraid you're going to be dreadfully disappointed, old man, if you're looking forward to going into a house filled with the sickly fumes of ether and hideous with the cries of tortured animals. Just come off it a bit, Alfred. Come down to earth."

But Alfred was not to be deflated so easily. His fantasies were an important part of his life, and, while he was a little irritated by my discerning the source of his inspiration, he was not quenched. Instead, he went on turning the thing over in his mind, and adding a few extra touches to it here and there.

"Why turtles?" I heard him mutter. "It only seems to make it more complicated, to choose reptiles."

He contemplated that for some moments, then he added:

"Arms. Arms and hands! Now where on earth would he get a pair of arms from?"

His eyes grew still larger and more excited as he thought about that.

"Now, now! Keep a hold on it!" I advised him.

All the same, it was an awkward, uneasy kind of question....

—

The following afternoon Alfred and I presented ourselves at the lodge of Membury Grange, and gave our names to the suspicious-looking man who lived there to guard the entrance. He shook his head to indicate that we hadn't a hope of approaching more closely, but he did pick up the telephone.

I had a somewhat unworthy hope that his discouraging attitude might be confirmed. The thing ought, of course, to be followed up, if only to pacify the villagers, but I could have wished that Alfred had had longer to go off the boil. At present, his agitation and ex-pectation were, if anything, increased. The fancies of Poe and Zola are mild compared with the products of Alfred's imagination powered by suitable fuel. All night long, it seemed, the most hor-rid nightmares had galloped through his sleep, and he was now in a vein where such phrases as the "wanton torturing of our dumb friends" by "the fiendish wielders of the knife," and "the shudder-ing cries of a million quivering victims ascending to high heaven" came tripping off his tongue automatically. It was awkward. If I had not agreed to accompany him, he would certainly have gone alone, in which case he would be likely to come to some kind of harm on account of the generalized accusations of mayhem, mu-tilation, and sadism with which he would undoubtedly open the conversation.

In the end I had persuaded him that his course would be to keep his eyes cunningly open for more evidence while I conducted the interview. Later, if he was not satisfied, he would be able to say his piece. I just had to hope that he would be able to withstand the internal pressure.

The guardian turned back to us from the telephone, wearing a surprised expression.

"He says as he'll see you!" he told us, though not quite certain he had heard aright. "You'll find him in the new wing—that redbrick part, there."

The new wing, into which the poaching Bill had spied, turned out to be much bigger than I had expected. It covered a ground-area quite as large as that of the original house, but was only one story high. A door in the end of it opened as we drove up, and a tall, loosely clad figure with an untidy beard stood waiting for us there.

"Good Lord!" I said, as we approached. "So that was why we got in so easily! I'd no idea you were *that* Dixon. Who'd have thought it?"

"Come to that," he retorted, "you seem to be in a surprising occupation for a man of intelligence, yourself."

I remembered my companion.

"Alfred," I said, "I'd like to introduce you to Doctor Dixon— once a poor usher who tried to teach me something about biology at school, but later, by popular repute, the inheritor of millions, or thereabouts."

Alfred looked suspicious. This was obviously wrong: a move toward fraternization with the enemy at the very outset! He nodded ungraciously, and did not offer to shake hands.

"Come in!" Dixon invited.

He showed us into a comfortable study-cum-office which tended to confirm the rumors of his inheritance. I sat down in a magnificent easy chair.

"You'll very likely have gathered from your watchman that we're here in an official way," I said. "So perhaps it would be better to get the business over before we celebrate the reunion. It'd be a kindness to relieve the strain on my friend Alfred."

Doctor Dixon nodded, and cast a speculative glance at Alfred who had no intention of compromising himself by sitting down.

"I'll give you the report just as we had it," I told him, and proceeded to do so. When I reached a description of the turtle-like creatures he looked somewhat relieved.

"Oh, so that's what happened to them," he said.

"Ah!" cried Alfred, his voice going up into a squeak with excitement. "So you admit it! You admit that you are responsible for those two unhappy creatures!"

Dixon looked at him, wonderingly.

"I *was* responsible for them—but I didn't know they were unhappy: how did you?"

Alfred disregarded the question.

"That's what we want," he squeaked. "He admits that he——"

"Alfred," I told him coldly. "Do be quiet, and stop dancing about. Let me get on with it."

I got on with it for a few more sentences, but Alfred was building up too much pressure to hold. He cut right in:

"Where—where did you get the arms? Just tell me where *they* came from?" he demanded, with deadly meaning.

"Your friend seems a little over—er, a little dramatic," remarked Doctor Dixon.

"Look, Alfred," I said severely, "just let me get finished, will you? You can introduce your note of ghoulery later on."

When I ended, it was with an excuse that seemed necessary. I said to Dixon: "I'm sorry to intrude on you with all this, but you see how we stand. When supported allegations are laid before us, we have no choice but to investigate. Obviously this is something quite out of the usual run, but I'm sure you'll be able to clear it up satisfactorily for us. And now, Alfred," I added, turning to him, "I believe you have a question or two to ask, but do try to remember that our host's name is Dixon, and not Moreau."

Alfred leapt, as from a slipped leash.

"What I want to know is the meaning, the reason, and the method of these outrages against nature. I demand to be told by what right this man considers himself justified in turning normal creatures into unnatural mockeries of natural forms."

Doctor Dixon nodded gently.

"A comprehensive inquiry—though not too comprehensibly expressed," he said. "I deplore the loose, recurrent use of the word 'nature'—and would point out that the word 'unnatural' is a vulgarism which does not even make sense. Obviously, if a thing has been done at all it was in someone's nature to do it, and in the nature of the material to accept whatever was done. One can act only within the limits of one's nature: that is an axiom."

"A lot of hairsplitting isn't going to——" began Alfred, but Dixon continued smoothly:

"Nevertheless, I think I understand you to mean that my nature has prompted me to use certain material in a manner which your prejudices do not approve. Would that be right?"

"There may be lots of ways of putting it, but I call it vivisection—*vivisection!*" said Alfred, relishing the word like a good curse. "You may have a license. But there have been things going on here that will require a very convincing explanation indeed to stop us taking the matter to the police."

Doctor Dixon nodded.

"I rather thought you might have some such idea: and I'd prefer you did not. Before long, the whole thing will be announced by me, and become public knowledge. Meanwhile, I want at least two, possibly three, months to get my findings ready for publication. When I have explained, I think you will understand my position better."

He paused, thoughtfully eyeing Alfred who did not look like a man intending to understand anything. He went on: "The crux of this is that I have not, as you are suspecting, either grafted, or readjusted, nor in any way distorted living forms. I have *built* them."

For a moment, neither of us grasped the significance of that—though Alfred thought he had it.

"Ha! You can quibble," he said, "but there had to be a basis. You must have had some kind of living animal to start with—and one which you wickedly mutilated to produce these horrors."

But Dixon shook his head.

"No, I mean what I said. I have *built*—and then I have induced a kind of life into what I have built."

We gaped. I said, uncertainly: "Are you really claiming that you can create a living creature?"

"Pooh!" he said. "Of course I can, so can you. Even Alfred here can do that, with the help of a female of the species. What I am telling you is that I can animate the inert because I have found how to induce the—or, at any rate, a—life-force."

The lengthy pause that followed was broken at last by Alfred.

"I don't believe it," he said, loudly. "It isn't possible that you, here in this one-eyed village, should have solved the mystery of life. You're just trying to hoax us because you're afraid of what we shall do."

Dixon smiled calmly.

"I said that I had found *a* life-force. There may be dozens of other kinds for all I know. I can understand that it's difficult for you to believe; but, after all, why not? Someone was bound to find one of them somewhere sooner or later. What's more surprising to me is that this one wasn't discovered before."

But Alfred was not to be soothed.

"I don't believe it," he repeated. "Nor will anybody else unless you can produce proofs—if you can."

"Of course," agreed Dixon. "Who would take it on trust? Though I'm afraid that when you examine my present specimens you may find the construction a little crude at first. Your friend, Nature, puts in such a lot of unnecessary work that can be simplified out.

"Of course, in the matter of arms, that seems to worry you so much, if I could have obtained real arms immediately after the death of the owner I might have been able to use them—I'm not sure whether it wouldn't have been more trouble though. However, such things are not usually handy, and the building of simplified parts is not really difficult—a mixture of engineering, chemistry, and common sense. Indeed, it has been quite possible for some time, but without the means of animating them it was scarcely worth doing. One day they may be made finely enough to replace a lost limb, but a very complicated technique will have to be evolved before that can be done.

"As for your suspicion that my specimens suffer, Mr. Weston, I assure you that they are coddled—they have cost me a great deal of money and work. And, in any case, it would be difficult for you to prosecute me for cruelty to an animal hitherto unheard of, with habits unknown."

"I am not convinced," said Alfred, stoutly.

The poor fellow was, I think, too upset by the threat to his theory for the true magnitude of Dixon's claim to reach him.

"Then, perhaps a demonstration . . . ?" Dixon suggested. "If you will follow me . . ."

———

Bill's peeping exploit had prepared us for the sight of the steel-barred cages in the laboratory, but not for many of the other things we found there—one of them was the smell.

Doctor Dixon apologized as we choked and gasped.

"I forgot to warn you about the preservatives."

"It's reassuring to know that that's all they are," I said, between coughs.

The room must have been getting on for a hundred feet in length, and about thirty high. Bill had certainly seen precious little through his chink in the curtain, and I stared in amazement at the quantities of apparatus gathered there. There was a rough division into sections: chemistry in one corner, bench and lathes in another, electrical apparatus grouped at one end, and so on. In one of several bays stood an operating table, with cases of instruments to hand; Alfred's eyes widened at the sight of it, and an expression of triumph began to enliven his face. In another bay there was more the suggestion of a sculptor's studio, with molds and casts lying about on tables. Further on were large presses, and sizable electric furnaces, but most of the gear other than the simplest conveyed little to me.

"No cyclotron, no electron-microscope; otherwise, a bit of everything," I remarked.

"You're wrong there. There's the electron— Hullo! Your friend's off."

Alfred had kind of homed at the operating table. He was peering intently all around and under it, presumably in the hope of bloodstains. We walked after him.

"Here's one of the chief primers of that ghastly imagination of yours," Dixon said. He opened a drawer, took out an arm, and laid it on the operating table. "Take a look at that."

The thing was a waxy yellow, and without other coloring. In shape, it did have a close resemblance to a human arm, but when I looked closely at the hand, I saw that it was smooth, unmarked by whorls or lines: nor did it have fingernails.

"Not worth bothering about at this stage," said Dixon, watching me.

Nor was it a whole arm: it was cut off short between the elbow and the shoulder.

"What's that?" Alfred inquired, pointing to a protruding metal rod.

"Stainless steel," Dixon told him. "Much quicker and less expensive than making matrices for pressing bone forms. When I get standardized I'll probably go to plastic bones: one ought to be able to save weight there."

Alfred was looking worriedly disappointed again; that arm was convincingly non-vivisectional.

"But why an arm? Why any of this?" he demanded, with a wave that largely included the whole room.

"In the order of askings: an arm—or, rather, a hand—because it is the most useful tool ever evolved, and I certainly could not think of a better. And 'any of this' because once I had hit upon the basic secret I took a fancy to build as my proof the perfect creature—or as near that as one's finite mind can reach.

"The turtle-like creatures were an early step. They had enough brain to live, and produce reflexes, but not enough for constructive thought. It wasn't necessary."

"You mean that your 'perfect creature' does have constructive thought?" I asked.

"She has a brain as good as ours, and slightly larger," he said. "Though, of course, she needs experience—education. Still, as the brain is already fully developed, it learns much more quickly than a child's would."

"May we see it—her?" I asked.

He sighed regretfully.

"Everyone always wants to jump straight at the finished product. All right then. But first we will have a little demonstration— I'm afraid your friend is still unconvinced."

He led across toward the surgical instruments cases and opened a preserving cupboard there. From it he took a shapeless white mass which he laid on the operating table. Then he wheeled it toward the electrical apparatus further up the room. Beneath the pallid, sagging object I saw a hand protruding.

"Good heavens!" I exclaimed. "Bill's 'bolster with hands'!"

"Yes—he wasn't entirely wrong, though from your account he laid it on a bit. The little fellow is really my chief assistant. He's got all the essential parts; alimentary, vascular, nervous, respiratory. He can, in fact, live. But it isn't a very exciting existence for him—he's a kind of testing motor for trying out newly made appendages."

While he busied himself with some electrical connections he added:

"If you, Mr. Weston, would care to examine the specimen in any way, short of harming it to convince yourself that it is not alive at present, please do."

Alfred approached the white mass. He peered through his

glasses at it closely, and with distaste. He prodded it with a tentative forefinger.

"So the basis is electrical?" I said to Dixon.

He picked up a bottle of some gray concoction and measured a little into a beaker.

"It may be. On the other hand, it may be chemical. You don't think I am going to let you into *all* my secrets, do you?"

When he had finished his preparations he said:

"Satisfied, Mr. Weston? I'd rather not be accused later on of having shown you a conjuring trick."

"It doesn't seem to be alive," Alfred admitted, cautiously.

We watched Dixon attach several electrodes to it. Then he carefully chose three spots on its surface and injected at each from a syringe containing a pale-blue liquid. Next, he sprayed the whole form twice from different atomizers. Finally, he closed four or five switches in rapid succession.

"Now," he said, with a slight smile, "we wait for five minutes—which you may spend, if you like, in deciding which, or how many, of my actions were critical."

After three minutes the flaccid mass began to pulsate feebly. Gradually the movement increased until gentle, rhythmic undulations were running through it. Presently it half sagged or rolled to one side, exposing the hand that had been hidden beneath it. I saw the fingers of the hand tense, and try to clutch at the smooth tabletop.

I think I cried out. Until it actually happened, I had been unable to believe that it would. Now some part of the meaning of the thing came flooding in on me. I grabbed Dixon's arm.

"Man!" I said. "If you were to do that to a dead body . . . !"

But he shook his head.

"No. It doesn't work. I've tried. One is justified in calling this life—I think. . . . But in some way it's a different kind of life. I don't at all understand why . . ."

Different kind or not, I knew that I must be looking at the seed of a revolution, with potentialities beyond imagination. . . .

And all the time that fool Alfred kept on poking around the thing as if it were a sideshow at a circus, and he was out to make sure that no one was putting anything across him with mirrors, or working it with bits of string.

It served him right when he got a couple of hundred volts through his fingers. . . .

—

"And now," said Alfred, when he had satisfied himself that at least the grosser forms of deception were ruled out, "now we'd like to see this 'perfect creature' you spoke about."

He still seemed as far as ever from realizing the marvel he had witnessed. He was convinced that an offense of some kind was being committed, and he intended to find the evidence that would assign it to its proper category.

"Very well," agreed Dixon. "By the way, I call her Una. No name I could think of seemed quite adequate, but she is certainly the first of her kind, so Una she is."

He led us along the room to the last and largest of the row of cages. Standing a little back from the bars, he called the occupant forward.

I don't know what I expected to see—nor quite what Alfred was hoping for. But neither of us had breath for comment when we did see what lumbered toward us.

Dixon's "Perfect Creature" was a more horrible grotesquerie than I had ever imagined in life or dreams.

Picture, if you can, a dark, conical carapace of some slightly glossy material. The rounded-off peak of the cone stood well over six feet from the ground: the base was four foot six or more in diameter; and the whole thing supported on three short, cylindrical legs. There were four arms, parodies of human arms, projecting from joints about halfway up. Eyes, set some six inches below the apex, were regarding us steadily from beneath horny lids. For a moment I felt close to hysterics.

Dixon looked at the thing with pride.

"Visitors to see you, Una," he told it.

The eyes turned to me, and then back to Alfred. One of them blinked, with a click from its lid as it closed. A deep, reverberant voice emerged from no obvious source.

"At last! I've been asking you long enough," it said.

"Good God!" said Alfred. "That appalling thing can talk?"

The steady gaze dwelt upon him.

"That one will do. I like his glass eyes," rumbled the voice.

"Be quiet, Una. This isn't what you think," Dixon interposed. "I must ask you," he added to us, but looking at Alfred, "to be careful in your comments. Una naturally lacks the ordinary background of experience, but she is aware of her distinction—and of her several physical superiorities. She has a somewhat short temper, and nothing is going to be gained by offending her. It is natural that you should find her appearance a little surprising at first, but I will explain."

A lecturing note crept into his voice.

"After I had discovered my method of animation, my first inclination was to construct an approximately anthropoid form as a convincing demonstration. On second thoughts, however, I decided against mere imitation. I resolved to proceed functionally and logically, remedying certain features which seemed to me poorly or weakly designed in man and other existing creatures. It also proved necessary later to make a few modifications for technical and constructional reasons. However, in general, Una is the result of my resolve." He paused, looking fondly at the monstrosity.

"I—er—you did say 'logically'?" I inquired.

Alfred paused for some time before making his comment. He went on staring at the creature which still kept its eyes fixed on him. One could almost see him causing what he likes to think of as his better nature to override mere prejudice. He now rose nobly above his earlier, unsympathetic remark.

"I do not consider it proper to confine so large an animal in such restricted quarters," he announced.

One of the horny eyelids clicked again as it blinked.

"I like him. He means well. He will do," the great voice rumbled.

Alfred wilted a little. After a long experience of patronizing dumb friends, he found it disconcerting to be confronted by a creature that not only spoke, but patronized him as it did so. He returned its steady stare uneasily.

Dixon, disregarding the interruption, resumed:

"Probably the first thing that will strike you is that Una has no distinct head. That was one of my earliest rearrangements; the normal head is too exposed and vulnerable. The eyes should be carried high, of course, but there is no need whatever for a semi-detached head.

"But in eliminating the head, there was sight to be considered. I therefore gave her three eyes, two of which you can see now, and one which is round the back—though, properly speaking, she has no back. Thus she is easily able to look and focus in any direction without the complicated device of a semi-rotatory head.

"Her general shape also ensures that any falling or projected object would glance off the reinforced plastic carapace, but it seemed wise to me to insulate the brain from shock as much as possible by putting it where you might expect the stomach. I was thus able to put the stomach higher and allow for a more convenient disposition of the intestines."

"How does it eat?" I put in.

"Her mouth is round the other side," he said shortly. "Now, I have to admit that at first glance the provision of four arms might give an impression of frivolity. However, as I said before, the hand is the perfect tool—*if* it is the right size. So you will see that Una's upper pair are delicate and finely molded, while the lower are heavily muscular.

"Her respiration may interest you, too. I have used a flow principle. She inhales here, exhales there. An improvement, you must admit, on our own rather disgusting system.

"As regards the general design, she unfortunately turned out to be considerably heavier than I had expected—slightly over one ton, in fact—and to support that I had to modify my original plan somewhat. I redesigned the legs and feet rather after the pattern of the elephant's so as to spread the weight, but I'm afraid it is not altogether satisfactory; something will have to be done in the later models to reduce the overall weight.

"The three-legged principle was adopted because it is obvious that the biped must waste quite a lot of muscular energy in merely keeping its balance, and a tripod is not only efficient, but more easily adaptable to uneven surfaces than a four-legged support.

"As regards the reproductory system——"

"Excuse me interrupting," I said, "but with a plastic carapace, and stainless steel bones I don't—er—quite see——"

"A matter of glandular balance: regulation of the personality. Something had to be done there, though I admit that I'm not quite satisfied that I have done it the best way. I suspect that an approach on parthenogenetic lines would have been . . . However, there it is. And I have promised her a mate. I must say I find it a fascinating speculation. . . ."

"He will do," interrupted the rumbling voice, while the creature continued to gaze fixedly at Alfred.

"Of course," Dixon went on to us, a little hurriedly, "Una has never seen herself to know what she looks like. She probably thinks she——"

"I know what I want," said the deep voice, firmly and loudly, "I want——"

"Yes, yes," Dixon interposed, also loudly. "I'll explain to you about that later."

"But I want——" the voice repeated.

"Will you be quiet!" Dixon shouted fiercely.

The creature gave a slight rumbling protest, but desisted.

Alfred drew himself up with the air of one who after communing seriously with his principles is forced into speech.

"I cannot approve of this," he announced. "I will concede that this creature may be your own creation—nevertheless, once created it becomes, in my opinion, entitled to the same safeguards as any other dumb—er, as any other creature.

"I say nothing whatever about your application of your discovery—except to say that it seems to me that you have behaved like an irresponsible child let loose with modeling clay, and that you have produced an unholy—and I use that word advisedly—unholy mess; a monstrosity, a perversion. However, I say nothing about that.

"What I do say is that in law this creature can be regarded simply as an unfamiliar species of animal. I intend to report that in my professional opinion it is being confined in too small a cage, and clearly without proper opportunities for exercise. I am not able to judge whether it is being adequately nourished, but it is easy to perceive that it has needs that are not being met. Twice already when it has attempted to express them to us you have intimidated it."

"Alfred," I put in, "don't you think that perhaps——" but I was cut short by the creature thrumming like a double bass.

"I think he's wonderful! The way his glass eyes flash! I want him!" It sighed in a kind of deep vibrato that ran along the floor. The sound certainly was extremely mournful, and Alfred's one-track mind pounced on it as additional evidence.

"If that is not the plaint of an unhappy creature," he said, stepping closer to the cage, "then I have never——"

"Look out!" shouted Dixon, jumping forward.

One of the creature's hands made a darting snatch through the bars. Simultaneously Dixon caught him by the shoulders, and pulled him back. There was a rending of cloth, and three buttons pattered onto the linoleum.

"Phew!" said Dixon.

For the first time, Alfred looked a little alarmed.

"What——?" he began.

A deep, threatening sound from the cage obliterated the rest of it.

"Give him to me! I want him!" rumbled the voice, angrily.

All four arms caught hold of the bars. Two of them rattled the gate violently. The two visible eyes were fixed unwaveringly on Alfred. He began to show signs of reorientating his outlook. His own eyes opened a little more widely behind his glasses.

"Er—it—it doesn't mean——?" he started, incredulously.

"Gimme!" bellowed Una, stamping from one foot to another, and shaking the building as she did so.

Dixon was regarding his achievement with some concern.

"I wonder—I wonder, could I have overdone the hormones a bit?" he speculated, thoughtfully.

Alfred had begun to get to grips with the idea now. He backed a little further away from the cage. The move did not have a good effect on Una.

"Gimme!" she cried, like a kind of sepulchral public-address system. "Gimme! Gimme!"

It was an intimidating sound.

"Mightn't it be better if we——?" I suggested.

"Perhaps, in the circumstances——" Dixon agreed.

"Yes!" said Alfred, quite decisively.

The pitch on which Una operated made it difficult to be certain of the finer shades of feelings; the window-rattling sound that occurred behind us as we moved off might have expressed anger, or anguish, or both. We increased our pace a little.

"Alfred!" called a voice like a disconsolate foghorn. "I want Alfred!"

Alfred cast a backward glance, and stepped out a trifle more smartly.

There was a thump which rattled the bars and shook the building.

I looked round to see Una in the act of retiring to the back of her cage with the obvious intention of making another onslaught. We beat it for the door. Alfred was first through.

A thunderous crash sounded at the other end of the room. As

Dixon was closing the door behind us I had a glimpse of Una carrying bars and furnishings before her like a runaway bus.

"I think we shall need some help with her," Dixon said.

Small sparkles of perspiration were standing on Alfred's brow.

"You—you don't think it might be better if we were to——?" he began.

"No," said Dixon. "She'd see you through the windows."

"Oh," said Alfred, unhappily.

Dixon led the way into a large sitting room, and made for the telephone. He gave urgent messages to the fire brigade and the police.

"I don't think there's anything we can do till they get here," he said, as he put the receiver down. "The lab wing will probably hold her all right if she isn't tantalized anymore."

"Tantalized! I like that——!" Alfred started to protest, but Dixon went on:

"Luckily, being where she is, she couldn't see the door; so the odds are that she can have no idea of the purpose or nature of doors. What's worrying me most is the damage she's doing in there. Just listen!"

We did listen for some moments to the muffled sounds of smashing, splintering, and rending. Amongst it there was occasionally a mournful disyllabic boom which might, or might not, have been the word "Alfred."

Dixon's expression became more anguished as the noise continued unabated.

"All my records! All the work of years is in there," he said, bitterly. "Your Society's going to have to pay plenty for this, I warn you—but that won't give me back my records. She was always perfectly docile until your friend excited her—never a moment's trouble with her."

Alfred began to protest again, but was interrupted by the sound of something massive being overturned with a thunderous crash, followed by a noise like a waterfall of broken glass.

"Gimme Alfred! I want Alfred!" demanded the stentorian voice.

Alfred half rose, and then sat down agitatedly on the edge of his chair. His eyes flicked nervously hither and thither. He displayed a tendency to bite his fingernails.

"Ah!" said Dixon, with a suddenness which startled both of us. "Ah, that must have been it! I must have calculated the hormone requirement on the overall weight—*including* the carapace. Of course! What a ridiculous slip to make! Tch-tch! I should've done much better to keep to the original parthenogen— Good heavens!"

The crash which caused his exclamation brought us all to our feet, and across to the door.

Una had discovered the way out of the wing, all right, and come through it like a bulldozer. Door, frame, and part of the brickwork had come with her. At the moment she was stumbling about amid the resulting mess. Dixon didn't hesitate.

"Quick! Upstairs—that'll beat her," he said.

At the same instant Una spotted us, and let out a boom. We sprinted across the hall for the staircase. Initial mobility was our advantage; a freight like Una's takes appreciable time to get under way. I fled up the flight with Dixon just ahead of me and, I imagined, Alfred just behind. However, I was not quite right there. I don't know whether Alfred had been momentarily transfixed, or had fumbled his takeoff, but when I was at the top I looked back to see him still only a few steps up, with Una thundering in pursuit like a rocket-assisted car of Juggernaut.

Alfred kept on coming, though. But so did Una. She may not have been familiar with stairs, nor designed to use them. But she tackled them, for all that. She even got about five or six steps before they collapsed under her. Alfred, by then more than halfway up, felt them fall away beneath his feet. He gave a shout as he lost his balance. Then, clawing wildly at the air, he fell backward.

Una put in as neat a four-armed catch as you could hope to see.

"What coordination!" Dixon, behind me, murmured admiringly.

"Help!" bleated Alfred. "Help! Help!"

"Aah!" boomed Una, in a kind of deep diapason of satisfaction. She backed off a little, with a crunching of timbers.

"Keep calm!" Dixon advised Alfred. "Don't do anything that might startle her."

Alfred, embraced by three arms, and patted affectionately by the fourth, made no immediate reply.

There was a pause for assessment of the situation.

"Well," I said, "we ought to do something. Can't we entice her somehow?"

"It's difficult to know what will distract the triumphant female in her moment of success," observed Dixon.

Una set up a sort of—of—well, if you can imagine an elephant contentedly crooning. . . .

"Help!" Alfred bleated again. "She's—*ow!*"

"Calm, calm!" repeated Dixon. "There's probably no real danger. After all, she's a mammal—mostly, that is. Now if she were a quite different kind like, say, a female spider——"

"I don't think I'd let her overhear about female spiders just now," I suggested. "Isn't there a favorite food, or something, we could tempt her with?"

Una was swaying Alfred back and forth in three arms, and prodding him inquisitively with the forefinger of the fourth. Alfred struggled.

"Damn it. Can't you *do* something?" he demanded.

"Oh, Alfred! Alfred!" she reproved him, in a kind of besotted rumble.

"Well," Dixon said, doubtfully, "perhaps if we had some ice cream . . ."

There was a sound of brakes, and vehicles pulling up outside. Dixon ran swiftly along the landing, and I heard him trying to explain the situation through the window to the men outside. Presently he came back, accompanied by a fireman and his officer. When they looked down into the hall their eyes bulged.

"What we have to do is surround her without scaring her," Dixon was explaining.

"Surround *that?*" said the officer, dubiously. "What in hell is it, anyway?"

"Never mind about that now," Dixon told him, impatiently. "If we can just get a few ropes onto her from different directions——"

"Help!" shouted Alfred again. He flailed about violently. Una clasped him more closely to her carapace, and chuckled dotingly. A peculiarly ghastly sound, I thought: it shook the firemen, too.

"For crysake——!" one of them began.

"Hurry up," Dixon told him. "We can drop the first rope over her from here."

They both went back. The officer started shouting instructions to those below: he seemed to be having some difficulty in making himself clear. However, they both returned shortly with a coil of rope. And that fireman was good. He spun his noose gently, and dropped it as neatly as you like. When he pulled in, it was round the carapace, below the arms so that it could not slip up. He belayed to the newel-post at the top of the flight.

Una was still taken up with Alfred to the exclusion of everything else around her. If a hippopotamus could purr, with a kind of maudlin slant to it, I guess that's just about the sort of noise she'd make.

The front door opened quietly, and the faces of a number of assorted firemen and police appeared, all with their eyes popping and their jaws dropping. A moment later there was another bunch gaping into the hall from the sitting room door. One fireman stepped forward nervously, and began to spin his rope. Unfortunately his cast touched a hanging light, and it fell short.

In that moment Una suddenly became aware of what went on.

"No!" she thundered. "He's mine! I want him!"

The terrified ropeman hurled himself back through the door on top of his companions, and it shut behind him. Without turning, Una started off in the same direction. Our rope tightened, and we jumped back. The newel-post was snapped away like a stick, and the rest of the rope went trailing after it. There was a forlorn cry from Alfred, still firmly clasped, but, luckily for him, on the side away from the line of progress. Una took the front door like a cruiser-tank. There was an almighty crash, a shower of wood and plaster, and then a screen of dust through which came sounds of consternation, topped by a voice rumbling:

"He's mine! You shan't have him! He's mine!"

By the time we were able to reach the front windows Una was already clear of obstructions. We had an excellent view of her galloping down the drive at some ten miles an hour, towing, without apparent inconvenience, half a dozen or more firemen and police who clung grimly to the trailing rope.

Down at the lodge, the guardian had had the presence of mind to close the gates. He dived for personal cover into the bushes while she was still some yards away. Gates, however, meant nothing to Una; she kept on going. True, she staggered slightly at the impact, but they crumbled and went down before her. Alfred was waving his arms, and kicking out wildly; a faint wail for help floated back to us. The collection of police and firemen was towed into the jumbled ironwork, and tangled there. When Una passed out of sight round the corner there were only two dark figures left clinging heroically to the rope behind her.

There was a sound of engines starting-up below. Dixon called to them to wait. We pelted down the back stairs, and were able to fling ourselves upon the fire engine just as it moved off.

There was a pause to shift the obstructing ironwork in the gateway, then we were away down the lane in pursuit.

After a quarter mile the trail led off down a steep, still narrower lane to one side. We had to abandon the fire engine, and follow on foot.

At the bottom, there is—was—an old packhorse bridge across the river. It sufficed, I believe, for several centuries of packhorses, but nothing like Una at full gallop had entered into its builders' calculations. By the time we reached it, the central span was missing, and a fireman was helping a dripping policeman carry the limp form of Alfred up the bank.

"Where is she?" Dixon inquired, anxiously.

The fireman looked at him, and then pointed silently to the middle of the river.

"A crane. Send for a crane, at once!" Dixon demanded. But everyone was more interested in emptying the water out of Alfred, and getting to work on him.

—

The experience has, I'm afraid, permanently altered that air of bonhomie which used to exist between Alfred and all dumb friends. In the forthcoming welter of claims, counterclaims, cross-claims, and civil and criminal charges in great variety, I shall be figuring only as a witness. But Alfred, who will, of course, appear in several capacities, says that when his charges of assault, abduction, attempted—well, there are several more on the list; when they have been met, he intends to change his profession as he now finds it difficult to look a cow, or indeed, any female animal, in the eye without a bias that tends to impair his judgment.

AFFAIR OF THE HEART

Eliot suddenly left what he was saying in midair. From the other side of the D'Avignon restaurant the headwaiter, Jules, was goggling at him. Concern transfigured every line of the big man's expressive face; the effect was dramatic, and somewhat startling.

Jean followed her escort's line of sight.

"What's wrong with him?" she asked.

"Search me," said Eliot.

They watched Jules's black bulk come weaving between the glistening tables like a skillfully handled dirigible until it swayed to anchor beside them. The look of controlled horror on the man's face fascinated Eliot.

"Poison in the soup?" he inquired, amiably.

Jules, unsmiling, continued to radiate distress.

"Excuse me, m'sieur. I am very sorry. A mistake has been made," he said, intensely.

Eliot heard him the way he usually heard people until he was well-accustomed to them. One of the troubles of a practicing phonetician's life is that wherever he goes, his work goes right along with him. Every chance-heard stranger speaks in a double language—behind the words he is telling where he comes from, where he was educated, where he lives now. The sounds he makes are analyzed as he utters them; his lips, tongue, and teeth are watched to see how he forms them. All this is likely to be so professionally interesting that intended purpose of the sounds is frequently overlooked.

It was so now. Eliot could have told any interested person right off that one of Jules's parents—most likely his mother—had come from the Midi; that Jules himself had been brought up in England; that he could have spoken perfectly normal English if he had liked, but that he had sustained his maternal accent, with Soho variations, for professional purposes until it had become a habit; also that his articulation revealed him as a man thoughtful of detail. Which was quite a lot for a few words. What he could not have told was what Jules had actually said.

Jules had made his own modest deduction, too. He had observed that the patron was an American—from New York, of course, because in England all Americans are supposed to be from New York, except a few in the movie business. He had also realized that contact was imperfect. He amplified:

"An unfortunate mistake, m'sieur. This table. It is reserved."

"Sure it is. I reserved it yesterday—by telephone."

"But that is the mistake, m'sieur. If m'sieur and mam'selle would not mind moving——? There are other good tables——"

"That seems a good reason for letting me keep to the one I booked."

"But it was not right, m'sieur. It was a mistake to make the booking. Every year this table is reserved on May 28. Every year."

Jean leaned forward, her eyes on Jules's troubled face.

"Every year, on May 28?" she repeated.

"Yes, mam'selle. For eight-thirty. It is a standing order."

"Well, this year——" Eliot began, but the girl broke in.

"That sounds romantic. Is it?"

"Mam'selle has guessed. It is an affair of the heart," Jules admitted with a sigh.

"I too am here upon an affair of the heart," Eliot observed, pointedly.

"That," Jules said, allowing concern to be replaced momentarily by appreciation as he looked at the girl, "is very easy to understand, and a matter for congratulation. But——" He turned his eyes back from Jean's becoming blush. "But it is very clear m'sieur cannot have had the same affair of the heart for more than thirty years."

"I'll admit that," agreed Eliot. "Do you mean to say——?"

"That is how it is, m'sieur. Every May 28, for more than thirty years."

Jean drew her beaded handbag toward her.

"In the face of that, Eliot, we can scarcely refuse, can we?"

Eliot nodded and rose. Jules beamed.

"M'sieur is very kind—and mam'selle she understands the heart," he observed. He led the way to another table and saw to their seating there with great attention.

"I am so sorry to have troubled m'sieur. If I had been here there would not have been the mistake."

"As a compensation you might tell us something about this Darby and Joan," Eliot suggested. "Wedding anniversary?"

"Oh, no." Jules leaned a little closer. "They are Lord Solby and Mrs. Blayne." From his expression that should have been important, but Eliot shook his head.

"Means nothing to me, but then I'm from Chicago," he said.

Jules revealed himself as more English than his accent.

"I would never have known that, m'sieur," he said, sympathetically. "But here it is a famous affair, very romantic, very sad. Mrs. Blayne was once Lily Morveen."

"I don't——" Eliot began. Then something came back to him. "Yes, I do, though. My old man used to speak of her. He was over here in the war—the other war. She was in vaudeville, wasn't she?"

Jules inclined his head.

"Everybody's old man used to speak of her then, m'sieur. All the young men of those days, they were crazy about her."

"I've heard of her," Jean put in. "What they used to call a 'Toast of the Town.' Champagne out of slippers, and all that."

"That is so, mam'selle—though champagne out of slippers was just a little old-fashioned in 1918. But there were parties. All the young officers on leave went to hear her sing at the Coliseum or the Empire, and every night there were parties where she would make them forget that they had to go back to France. They all loved her—but there was nothing else, you understand. They loved her because she made them laugh and feel happy for a time. And when they went back they took the picture postcards she had signed, and pinned them up in dugouts, and went on loving her without feeling sad about it. But some did feel sad about it. Two of the serious ones were Lord Solby—Captain Solby then—and Captain Charles Blayne.

"She was a star, so very little was private. Everybody knew about those two young men. They were great rivals, and they were of the same regiment. When one came on leave everybody said he was the one; when the other came, they said he was. The younger people saw that Captain Blayne was gay and good-looking; the older ones said that Captain Solby had a lot more money, and the title. It was very difficult for Miss Morveen.

"Captain Solby brought her here to the D'Avignon on May 28, 1918. It was the last night of his leave—and he asked her to marry him. Then she told him she could not. She had married secretly two months before, and was already Mrs. Blayne. . . .

"Gaston, who was here then, has told me that Lord Solby looked like a man kicked stupid. He even forgot to pay his bill, and they had to send it to him. It was very tragic.

"Lord Solby went back to France, and they said he did not seem to care whether he was killed or not. But it was Captain Blayne who was killed a few weeks later.

"On the next May 28 the war was over, and Lord Solby brought Mrs. Blayne here again. All evening Lord Solby pleaded with her, but she would shake her head. They were the last to leave. Gaston said that Lord Solby looked worse than the time before—perhaps he had been more sure, now that Captain Blayne was dead.

"So there it was. Lord Solby was twenty-four, and ladies with marriageable daughters admired him very much. But he was not interested in their daughters. He had no social life. Soon everybody perceived that he was interested only in Mrs. Blayne—and it was very well known that she was devoted to the memory of her husband. Even now, they say, her house is crowded with pictures and mementos of him.

"Lord Solby has become an important man in some big companies, and he speaks in the House of Lords. But he has never married. Every year he brings Mrs. Blayne here on May 28—but it is always the same. She is still faithful to the memory of that young husband who died in France all those years ago. It is very romantic, very sad, you see."

"It must be dreadful to love somebody as much as that," murmured Jean.

"Which?" inquired Eliot.

She gave him a cooling glance.

"Both," she said, shortly. Of Jules she inquired: "Is it quite hopeless? Will they never marry?"

Jules shrugged. "Ladies' minds change—but when one has said 'no' for more than thirty years——" then he broke off.

"Excuse me, mam'selle, m'sieur——"

His eyes, which had made alert sweeps over the restaurant while he talked, now caught a movement beyond the door, and he slid off on a sinuous course toward it.

Presently he reappeared, his face all gratification as he led a couple toward the table Eliot had vacated. Several of the diners looked up to watch the progress with interest. The man was tall and slender, with an ascetic face looking older than the late fifties beneath hair of silvery distinction. The woman was carefully tended. Her face was smooth, her fair hair looked natural. She carried, perhaps, a little more weight than she wished, but it was easy to re-create her former prettiness, and she might still have passed for little over forty.

Jules bowed them into their seats, and summoned the table waiter with an imperious flourish.

Jean studied them.

"You can see he's had a sad life," she said.

She watched Mrs. Blayne arrange herself with calm assurance

as though unaware of the eyes upon her, and smile at her escort. His attempt to return the smile was bleak.

"Poor man," said Jean. "It's not fair. No woman has the right to keep any man dangling after her like that for years. After she said 'no' she should have cut it clean—if she meant it."

"She seems to have meant it," said Eliot. "Maybe he's the kind of guy that just doesn't know the word."

He was not greatly interested in the couple. First they had taken his table, now they were taking Jean's attention.

"Do you suppose he really proposes properly to her every time?" she asked.

"I wouldn't know. It'd become a bit stagy after a while, wouldn't it?" he suggested.

"She'd still like it."

"Well, maybe he does, then."

Jean looked at him.

"What I hate about men is the way they spoil things," she announced.

"Uh-huh. You don't think this is a bit—uh—corny?" he said, tilting his head to indicate the couple.

It took him quite a while to repair the conversation after that. Even when he did get it on the rails he was aware that her attention was divided. She kept on jerking little glances across the room to see how the couple was doing, and responding with a bright inappropriateness to some of his remarks. She cut right across one to say:

"Look! I think they've got to it. I'm sure he's proposing now."

Eliot looked over irritably. The pair were facing one another earnestly. He watched the man's lips for a moment.

"If you'd really like to know——" he began. Then he stopped. He always had the feeling that knowledge which reached him through his professional abilities was in the nature of a confidence or a trust. Luckily Jean had not heard him. Her attention was all on the couple. The man had finished speaking and was awaiting the woman's reply with anxious attention. She looked up thoughtfully. She shook her head ever so slightly, her lips moved.

"No," Jean murmured. "She said 'No.'"

The woman spoke a little more, slowly and deliberately.

A gray, pinched look came over the man's face. For several seconds he looked back at her without moving. Then he rose to his feet, bowed slightly to her, and walked out of the room as if he saw nothing of it.

Jean's hand clenched on the table.

"It's too bad, too bad! All because of a man who's been dead, thirty years. It's wrong of her. He looked simply dreadful, poor man."

"It's not our affair," said Eliot, and did his best to change the subject.

From somewhere outside came a sound like a door slamming. Jules, disapproval all over his face, removed himself to investigate. A minute or two later he returned, his expression too bland to be true. Unhurriedly he made his way to the corner and spoke to Mrs. Blayne. Composedly she collected her belongings, and followed him out.

When he reappeared, Eliot beckoned him over.

"Lord Solby?" he inquired, in a tone not to be heard at the next table.

"A slight accident, m'sieur," Jules assured him.

"I know the sound of a pistol when I hear one. Is he dead?"

Jules leaned closer. "Yes, m'sieur, but please———"

"Okay. We'll keep it under our hats."

"Thank you, m'sieur. Not good for business, you understand." He moved away, leaving Jean staring at Eliot.

"Oh, dear," she said, inadequately. Eliot poured her some wine. She drank it gratefully, and set the glass down with a shaky hand.

"It makes me feel rather small somehow," she said. "I didn't know men could love women as much as that. Thirty years of hoping. . . . Thirty years—and then this! It was her fault. If she couldn't love him she should have sent him away."

"Uh-huh," said Eliot.

Had he been in any other profession than the one he was, he might have achieved more competent comment. But the last thing his trained observation had understood Mrs. Blayne's lips to say was:

"No, John. I feel like settling down now. It'll probably cost you a lot less, too, when you do marry me. Remember, I still have only to tell them what really happened to Charles in France. . . ."

CONFIDENCE TRICK

"Never again," Henry Baider said to himself, once he had been condensed enough for the doors to close, "never again will I allow myself to be caught up in this."

It was a decision he had expressed before, and would probably, in spite of its face-value, express another day. But, in between, he did do his best to assure that his infrequent visits to the City should not involve him in the rush hour. Today, however, already delayed by his business, he faced the alternatives of vexing his wife by delaying still further, or of allowing himself to be drawn into the flood that was being sucked down the Bank Station entrances. After looking unhappily at the moving mass and then at the unmoving bus queues he had squared his shoulders. "After all, they do it twice a day, and survive. Who am I——?" he said, and stepped stoutly forward.

The funny thing was that nobody else looked as if he or she thought it a sub-human, stockyard business. They just waited blank-eyed, and with more patience than you would find in a stockyard. They didn't complain, either.

Nobody got out at St. Paul's, though the increased pressure suggested that somebody had inexplicably got in. The doors attempted to close, drew back, presumably because some part of somebody was inexpertly stowed, tried again, and made it. The train drew heavily on. The girl in the green mackintosh on Henry's right said to the girl in the blue mackintosh who was jammed against her:

"D'you think you actually *know* when your ribs crack?" but on a philosophical note of fair comment rather than complaint.

Nobody got out at Chancery Lane, either. A lot of exhortation, shoving, and staggering achieved the impossible: somebody more was aboard. The train picked up speed slowly. It rattled on for a few seconds. Then there was a jolt, and all the lights went out.

Henry swore at his luck as the train drew up, but then, almost the instant it had stopped, it started to pull again. Abruptly, he discovered that he was no longer supported by the people round him, and flung out an arm to save himself. It struck something yielding. At that moment the lights came on again, to reveal that the object struck had been the girl in the green mackintosh.

"Who do you think you're——?" she began. Then her mouth stayed open, her voice failed, and her eyes grew rounder and wider.

At the same moment Henry had started to apologize, but his voice, too, cut out, and his eyes also bulged.

He looked up and down the coach that a moment ago had been jammed solid with people to the last inch. It now contained three others besides themselves. A middle-aged man who was opening his newspaper with an air of having been given his due at last; opposite him a woman, also middle-aged, and lost in contemplation; right away at the other end of the coach, in the last seat, sat a younger-looking man, apparently asleep.

"Well, really!" said the girl. "That Milly! Just wait till I see her in the morning. She knows I have to change at Holborn, too. Getting off and leaving me without a word!" She paused. "It *was* Holborn, wasn't it?" she added.

Henry was still looking dazedly about him. She took hold of his arm, and shook it.

"It *was* Holborn, wasn't it?" she repeated, uncertainly.

Henry turned to look at her, but still with a vagueness in his manner.

"Er—what was Holborn?" he asked.

"That last stop—where they all got out. It *must*'ve been Holborn, mustn't it?"

"I—er—I'm afraid I don't know this line well," Henry told her.

"I do. Like the back of my hand. Couldn't be anywhere but Holborn," she said, with self-convincing firmness.

Henry looked up the swaying coach, past the rows of strap-handles emptily swaying.

"I—er—didn't see any station," he said.

Her head in its red knitted cap tilted further back to look up at him. Her blue eyes were troubled, though not alarmed.

"Of course there was a station—or where would they all go to?"

"Yes——" said Henry. "Yes, of course."

There was a pause. The train continued to speed along, swaying more and jerking more now on its lightly loaded springs.

"The next'll be Tottenham Court Road," said the girl, though with a touch of uneasiness.

The train rattled. She stared at the black windows, growing more pensive.

"Funny," she said, after a while. "Funny-peculiar, I mean."

"Look here," said Henry. "Suppose we go and have a word with those people up there. They might know something."

The girl glanced along. Her expression showed no great hopes of them, but: "All right," she said, and turned to lead the way.

Henry stopped opposite the middle-aged woman. She was dressed in a well-cut coat surmounted by a fur cape. An inch or two of veil fringed the round hat on her carefully dressed dark hair; her shoes, on the end of almost invisible nylon stockings, were black patent-leather with elegant heels; both her gloved hands rested on the black leather bag on her lap as she sat in absent contemplation.

"I beg your pardon," said Henry, "but could you tell us the name of the last station—the one where all the other people got out?"

The lids rose slowly. The eyes regarded him through the fringe of veil. There was a pause during which she appeared to consider the several reasons which could have led such a person as Henry to address her, and to select the most becoming. Henry decided that no-longer-young was perhaps more apposite than middle-aged.

"No," she said, with a slight smile which did not touch the matter. "I'm afraid I didn't notice."

"It didn't strike you that there was anything—er—odd about it?" Henry suggested.

The lady's well-marked eyebrows rose slightly. The eyes pondered him on two or three levels.

"Odd?" she inquired.

"The way they all went so very quickly," he explained.

"Oh, was that unusual?" said the lady. "It seemed to me a very good thing; there were far too many of them."

"Quite," agreed Henry, "but what is puzzling us is how it happened."

The eyebrows rose a little higher.

"Really. I don't think I can be expected to——"

There was a harrumph noise, and a rustling of newspaper behind Henry. A voice said:

"Young man. It doesn't seem to me to be necessary for you to bother this lady with the matter. If you have any complaints, there are proper channels for them."

Henry turned. The speaker was a man with graying hair, and a well-trimmed mustache set on a pinkly healthy face. He was aged perhaps fifty-five and dressed City–*comme il faut* from black Homburg to dispatch-case. At the moment he was glancing interrogatively toward the lady, and receiving a small, grateful smile in return. Then his eyes met Henry's. His manner changed slightly; evidently Henry was not quite the type that his back view had suggested.

"I am sorry," Henry told him, "but this young lady may have missed her station—besides, it does seem rather odd."

"I noticed Chancery Lane, so the rest must have got out at Holborn—that is obvious, surely," said the man.

"But they went so quickly."

"A good thing too. The people in charge must have found some new method of handling the traffic. They're always developing new ideas and techniques, you know—even under public owner-ship."

"But we've been going on for nearly ten minutes, nonstop, since then, and we've certainly not passed a station," Henry objected.

"Probably been re-routed. Technical reasons, I expect," said the man.

"Re-routed! On the Underground!" protested Henry.

"My dear fellow, it's not my job to know how these things work—nor yours, I take it. We have to leave it to those who do. That's what they're there for, after all. Take it from me, they know what they're up to, even though it may seem 'odd,' as you call it, to us. God bless me, if we don't have faith in our expert authorities, where are we?"

Henry looked at the girl in the green mackintosh. She looked back at him. She shrugged slightly. They went and sat down, fur-ther up the coach. Henry glanced at his watch, offered her a ciga-rette, and they both lit up.

The train rattled along to a steady rhythm. Both of them watched the windows for the sight of a lighted platform, but they could see no more than their own reflections against outside blackness. When there was no more of the cigarette to hold, Henry dropped the remains on the floor, and ground it out. He looked at his watch again, and then at the girl.

"More than twenty minutes," he said. "That's impossibility, raised several powers."

"It's going faster now, too," the girl observed. "And look at the way it's tilted."

Henry regarded the hanging straps. There could be no doubt that they were running down an appreciable incline. Glancing forward, he saw that the other couple were now in quite animated conversation.

"Shall we try 'em again?" he suggested.

"—never more than fifteen minutes, even in the rush hour. Absolutely never," the lady was saying as they came up. I'm afraid my husband will be so worried about me."

"Well?" inquired Henry, of the man.

"Certainly very unusual," the other conceded.

"Unusual! Nearly half an hour at full bat, without a station? It's absolutely impossible," said Henry.

The other regarded him coldly.

"It is clearly *not* impossible because it is being demonstrated now. Very likely this is some underground escape route from London that they constructed during the war, and we have been switched on to it in error. I have no doubt that the authorities will presently discover the mistake, and bring us back."

"Taking them a long time," said the girl. "Due home before this, I am. And I got a date at the Pallay this evening."

"We'd better stop the train," said the lady. Her eyes were on the handle, with its notice that threatened five pounds for improper use.

Henry and the other man looked at one another.

"Well, if this isn't an emergency, what is?" demanded the lady.

"Er——" said Henry.

"The authorities——" the other began.

"All right," she announced. "If you men are afraid to touch it, I'm not." She reached up, took a firm hold of the handle, and yanked it down.

Henry dropped into a seat quickly, pulling the girl down too, before the brakes should go on.

The brakes did not go on.

They sat waiting. Presently it became a fair bet that the brakes were not going to go on. The lady pushed the handle up impatiently, and pulled it down again. Nothing happened. She expressed her opinion of it.

"Cor! Listen to her! Did you ever?" said the girl beside Henry.

"Fluent. Have another cigarette," said Henry.

The train clattered and swayed along, the straps still hanging with a forward slant.

"Well," said the girl, after a time, "this properly dishes my date at the Pallay all right. Now that Doris'll get him. D'you think I could sue them?"

"I'm afraid not," Henry told her.

"You a lawyer?"

"Well, as a matter of fact, yes. Suppose we introduce ourselves. It looks as if we shall have to spend some time here, whatever they do. I'm Henry Baider."

"Mine's Norma Palmer," said the girl.

The City man said: "Robert Forkett," and nodded slightly to them.

"Barbara Branton—Mrs., of course," said the lady.

"What about him?" asked Norma, pointing to the man at the far end of the coach. "D'you think we ought to wake him, and tell him?"

"I don't fancy it would help much," said Mr. Forkett. He turned to Henry. "I understood you to say you were a legal man, sir. Perhaps you can tell us just what our position is in this matter?"

"Well, speaking without my references," Henry told him, "I should say that in the matter of delay, no claim by us would lie. I think we shall find that the Company only undertakes to provide——"

Half an hour later he became aware of a weight pressing lightly against him. Looking round, he found that Norma had gone to sleep with her head on his shoulder. Mrs. Branton, on the other side, had also dozed off. Mr. Forkett yawned, and apologized.

"Might as well all have a nap to pass the time, though," he suggested.

Henry looked at his watch once more. Practically an hour and a half now: Unless they had been going in a closed circle, they must have passed beneath several counties by this time. The thing remained incomprehensible.

To reach a cigarette he would have had to disturb the girl, so he remained as he was, looking at the blackness outside, swaying slightly to the train's motion, listening to the ti-tocketty-tock, ti-tocketty-tock, ti-tocketty-tock, of the hurrying wheels until his head drooped sideways and rested on the knitted cap on his shoulder.

—

The change of rhythm, the slight shuddering from the brakes brought Henry awake; the rest stirred a moment later. Mr. Forkett yawned audibly. Norma opened her eyes, blinked at the unexpected scene, and discovered the situation of her head. She sat up. "Well, I never," she said, regarding Henry. He assured her it had been a pleasure. She began to pat her hair and correct herself according to her reflection in the still dark window opposite. Mrs. Branton reached under her cape, and consulted a small fob-watch.

"Nearly midnight. My husband'll be quite frantic about me," she observed.

The sounds of slowing continued to descend the scale. Presently the windows ceased to be altogether black; a light, rather pinkish compared with the lamps inside, started to show, and gradually to grow stronger.

"That's better," said Norma. "I always hate it when it stops in the tunnel."

The light grew brighter still, the speed dwindled, and presently they were running into a station. They leaned forward to catch the name, but could see no plate on the wall. Mrs. Branton, on the other side, suddenly craned across.

"There!" she said. They turned quickly, but not soon enough.

"It was something Avenue, or Avenue something," she said.

"Well, we'll soon find out now," Mr. Forkett reassured them.

The train drew up, with a sigh from the braking system, but the doors did not open at once. There was a sound of echoing commotion further along the platform out of which voices presently distinguished themselves calling: "All change!"—"End of the line!"—"All out here!"

"All very well—all change, indeed!" murmured Norma, getting up, and moving toward the doors.

The others followed her. Quite suddenly the doors ran back. Norma gave one look at the figure standing on the platform.

"Ee-ow!" she yelped, and backed violently into Henry.

The figure wore little clothing. What there was seemed to be chiefly straps holding appurtenances, so that it was revealed as angularly male, in a rich mahogany red. Ethnologically, perhaps, the face might have been North-American Indian, only instead of feathers it wore a pair of horns. Its right hand carried a trident; its left dangled a net.

"All out!" it said, moving a little aside.

Norma hesitated, and then scuttled past it. The others followed warily but more sedately, and joined her on the platform. The creature leaned into the open doorway, and they were able to observe his back view. The tail was waving with a slow, absent-minded kind of motion. The barb at the end of it looked viciously sharp.

"Er——" began Mr. Forkett. Then he changed his mind. He cast a speculative eye on each of his companions in turn, and pondered.

The creature caught sight of the sleeper at the other end of the car. He walked down, and prodded him with his trident. There was some inaudible altercation. The creature prodded a few more times, and presently the man came out to join them, with the sleep not yet out of his eyes.

There was a shout higher up the platform, followed by a sound of running feet. A tough-looking young man came sprinting toward them. A net whistled after him and entangled him so that he fell and rolled over and over. A hearty shout of laughter came from the other end of the platform.

Henry glanced about. The dim rosy light was strong enough for him to see and read the station's nameplate.

"Something Avenue!" he repeated under his breath. "Tch-tch!"

Mrs. Branton overheard him, and looked at it.

"Well, if that doesn't spell 'Avenues,' what does it spell?" she demanded.

Before he could reply a voice began to call: "This way out! This way out!" and the creature motioned them on, with its trident at the ready. The young man from the other end of the coach walked next to Henry. He was a large, forceful, intellectual-looking young man, but still not quite clear of the mists of sleep.

"What is all this nonsense about?" he said. "Collecting for the hospitals, or something? No excuse for it now we've got the Health Scheme."

"I don't think so," Henry told him, "in fact, I'm afraid it doesn't look too good." He indicated the station nameplate. "Besides," he added, "those tails—I don't see how it could be done."

The young man studied the sinuous movements of one of the tails.

"But really——!" he protested.

"What else?" inquired Henry.

Altogether, and exclusive of the staff, there were about a dozen people collected at the barrier. They were passed through one by one while an elderly demon in a small hutch checked them off on a list. Henry learnt that the large young man was entered as Christopher Watts, physicist.

Beyond the barrier was an escalator of a somewhat antiquated type. It moved slowly enough for one to read the advertisements at the sides: preponderantly they offered specifics for burns, cuts, abrasions, and bruises, with here and there the recommendation of a particular tonic or pick-me-up.

At the top stood an ill-used-looking demon with a tray of tin boxes suspended against his chest. He was saying monotonously: "All guaranteed. Best quality." Mr. Forkett who was in front of

Henry caught sight of the card on the tray, and stopped abruptly. The lettering ran:

FIRST-AID KITS COMPLETE
each
£1 or $1.50 (U.S.)

"That's an insult to the pound," Mr. Forkett announced indignantly.

The demon looked at Mr. Forkett. He thrust his face forward aggressively. "So what?" he demanded.

Pressure of those behind pushed Mr. Forkett on, but he moved reluctantly, murmuring about the necessity for confidence, stability, and faith in sterling

After crossing a hall, they passed into the open. There was a faint tang of sulfur in the air. Norma pulled on the hood of her mackintosh against the light drizzle of cinders. Trident-bearers shepherded them round to the right, into a wire-netted enclosure. Three or four demons followed in with them. The last paused to speak to the guard on the gate.

"Heaven's harps, is that celestial bus behind time again?" he asked resentfully.

"Is it ever *on* time nowadays?" the gate-demon asked.

"Never used to have these hold-ups when the old man was running his ferry," grumbled the guard.

"Individual enterprise, that was," said the gate-demon, with a shrug.

Henry joined the others who were surveying the scene. The view to the right was rugged and extensive, though smoky. Far away, at the end of a long valley, could be seen a brightly glowing area in which large bubbles formed, rose slowly, and took tantalizingly long to burst. To the left of it a geyser of flame whooshed up intermittently. At the back right a volcano smoked steadily while little streams of red-hot lava trickled down from its rim. In the middle distance the valley walls narrowed in two towering crags. The one on the left bore the illuminated sign: TRY HOOPER'S HIDE-HARD. The other proclaimed: UNBURN IS THE ANSWER.

A little short of the right-hand crag, on the level valley floor, was a square encampment surrounded by several fences of barbed wire, and overlooked by a guard tower at each corner. Every now and then a string of flaming arrows would fly tracer-like into the compound from one of the towers, and the sound of howls mixed with demonic laughter would be borne faintly on the sulfurous breeze. From that point one was able to follow the road as it wound up and past them to the station entrance. A building opposite the station appeared to be a barracks where demons were queueing up to sharpen their tridents and touch up their tail-barbs on a grindstone in the yard. The whole thing struck Henry as somewhat conventional.

Almost opposite their netted enclosure was a kind of gibbet. It was occupied at the moment by a lady with nothing on who was hanging suspended upside down from chains round her ankles while a couple of junior demons swung on her hair. Mrs. Branton searched in her bag, and found a pair of spectacles.

"Dear me! Surely not——?" she murmured. She looked more carefully. "So difficult to tell that way up, and with the tears running into her hair. I'm afraid it is, though. Such a nice woman, I always thought, too."

She turned to the nearest demon. "Did she commit a murder or something dreadful?" she asked.

He shook his head. "No," he said. "She just nagged at her husband so that he would find another woman and she would be able to divorce him for the alimony."

"Oh," said Mrs. Branton a little flatly. "Is that all? I mean, there must have been something more serious, surely?"

"No," said the guard.

Mrs. Branton remained thoughtful. "Does she have to do a lot of that?" she asked, with a trace of uneasiness.

"Wednesdays," said the guard. "She does other things other days."

"Pss-t!" a voice hissed suddenly in Henry's ear. One of the guard demons beckoned him aside.

"Want to buy a bit of the real stuff?" inquired the demon.

"What stuff?" Henry asked.

The demon brought his hand out of his pouch. He opened it and showed a metal tube which looked as if it might contain toothpaste. He leaned closer.

"The goods, this is. Best analgesic cream on the white-market. Just rub it on every time before tortures—you'll not feel a thing."

"No, thank you. As a matter of fact, I think they'll probably find there's been a mistake in my case," Henry told him.

"Come off it, chum," said the demon. "Look. I'll take a couple of pounds—special to you, that is."

"No thanks," said Henry.

The demon frowned. "You'd better," he advised, shifting his tail into a threatening position.

"Well—one pound," said Henry.

The demon looked a little surprised. "Okay. It's yours," he said, and handed it over.

When Henry rejoined the group he found most of them watching three demons exuberantly chasing an extensive, pink middle-aged man up the opposite mountainside. Mr. Forkett, however, was reviewing the situation.

"The accident," he said, raising his voice a little to contend with the increased lowing of sinners in the concentration camp, "the accident must have occurred between Chancery Lane and Holborn stations, that's fairly clear, I think. What is not at all clear to me, however, is why *I* am *here*. Undoubtedly there has been a departmental error in my case, which I hope will be rectified soon." He looked speculatively at the rest. Everyone became thoughtful.

"It'd have to be a *big* thing, wouldn't it?" asked Norma. "I mean they wouldn't send a person here for a little thing like a pair of nylons, would they?"

"Well, if it was only *one* pair of nylons——" Henry was beginning, but he was cut short by an exclamation from Mrs. Branton. Following her gaze, he saw a woman coming down the street in a magnificent fur coat.

"Perhaps this place has another side to it that we've not seen yet," she suggested, hopefully. "After all, where there are mink coats——"

"She doesn't look very pleased with it, though," Norma remarked, as the woman came closer.

"Live minks. Very sharp teeth," observed one of the demons, helpfully.

There was a sudden, startling yelp behind them. They turned to observe the dark young man, Christopher Watts, in the act of twisting a demon's tail. The demon yelped again, and dropped the tube of analgesic cream it had been offering him. . . . It attempted a stab with its trident.

"Oh, no, you don't!" said Mr. Watts, skillfully avoiding the thrust.

He caught the trident by the shaft, and wrenched it out of the demon's hand. "Now!" he said, with satisfaction. He dropped the trident, and laid hold of the tail with both hands. He swung the demon twice round his head, and let go. The demon flew over the wire-netting fence, and landed in the road with a yell and a bump. The other demons deployed, and began to advance upon Mr. Watts, tridents leveled, nets swinging in their left hands.

Christopher Watts squared up to them, grimly watching them come on. Then, suddenly his expression changed. His frown gave place to a smile. He unclenched his fists, and dropped his hands to his sides.

"Dear me, what nonsense all this is!" he said, and turned his back on the demons.

They stopped abruptly, and looked confused.

A surprising sense of revelation came over Henry. He saw quite clearly that the young man was right. It *was* nonsense. He laughed at the bewildered look on the demons' faces, and heard Norma beside him laughing too. Presently, all the party was laughing at the discomforted demons who looked first apprehensive, and then sheepish.

Mr. Christopher Watts strode across to the side of the enclosure which faced up the valley. For some moments he regarded the smoky, luridly somber view. Then:

"I don't believe it!" he said, quietly.

An enormous bubble rose and burst in the fiery lake. There was a *woomph!* as the volcano sent up a mushroom cloud of smoke and cinders, and spilled better, brighter streams of lava down its sides. The ground trembled a little under their feet. Mr. Watts drew a deep breath.

"I don't believe it!" he said, loudly.

There was a loud crack. The dizzy crag which bore the recommendation for UNBURN split off, and toppled slowly into the valley. Demons on the mountainside dropped their hunting, and started to lope homeward with cries of panic. The ground shook violently. The fiery lake began to empty into a huge split which had opened in the valley floor. A tremendous gush of flame burst from the geyser. The mighty crag on the other side heeled over. There was a roaring and a crashing and a hissing of steam all around them, and through it Mr. Watts's voice bawled again:

"I DON'T BELIEVE IT!"

———

Suddenly, all was quiet, as if it had been switched off. All was black, too, with nothing whatever to be seen but the lighted windows of the train where it stood on the embankment behind them.

"Well," said Mr. Watts, on a note of cheerful satisfaction. "Well, that's that. Now let's go home again, shall we?" And, by the light from the train windows, he began to scramble up the embankment.

Henry and Norma moved to follow him. Mr. Forkett hesitated.

"What's the matter?" Henry asked him, looking back.

"I'm not sure. I feel it's not quite—not quite——"

"You can't very well stay here now," Henry pointed out.

"No—no, I suppose not," Mr. Forkett admitted, and, half reluctantly, he too began to climb the embankment.

———

Without any spoken agreement the five who had previously traveled together again chose a coach to themselves. They had scarcely got aboard when the doors closed, and the train began to move. Norma sighed with relief, and pushed her hood back as she sat down.

"Like being halfway home already," she said. "Thank you ever so, Mr. Watts. It's been a real lesson to me, it has, though. I'll never go near a stocking counter again, never—except when I'm going to buy some."

"I'll second that—the thanks part, I mean," said Henry. "I still feel that there was very likely some confusion between the legal and the common view in my particular case, but I'm extremely obliged to you for—er—cutting the red tape."

Mrs. Branton held out a gloved hand to Mr. Watts.

"Of course, you'll realize that it was all a stupid mistake that I should be there, but I expect you've saved me hours and hours of dealing with ridiculous officials. I do hope you may be able to come and dine with us sometime. I'm sure my husband will want to thank you."

There was a pause. It lengthened. Gradually the realization that Mr. Forkett was not taking his cue drew all their eyes upon him. He himself was gazing in a pensive way at the floor. Presently he looked up, first at them, and then at Christopher Watts.

"No," he said. "I am sorry, but I cannot agree. I am afraid I must continue to regard your action as anti-social, if not actually subversive."

Mr. Watts, who had been looking rather pleased with himself, showed first surprise, and then a frown.

"I beg your pardon?" he said, with genuine puzzlement.

"You've done a very serious thing," Mr. Forkett told him. "There simply cannot be any stability if we do not respect our institutions. You, young man, have destroyed one. We all had confidence in this affair—even you, to begin with—then you suddenly go and break it all up, an institution of considerable standing, too. No, I really cannot be expected to approve of that."

The rest of them stared at him.

"But Mr. Forkett," said Norma, "surely you wouldn't rather be back there, with all those demons and things?"

"My dear young lady, that is scarcely the point," Mr. Forkett reproved her. "As a responsible citizen I must strongly oppose anything that threatens to undermine public confidence. Therefore I must regard this young man's action as dangerous; verging, I repeat, upon the subversive."

"But if an institution is phony——" began Mr. Watts.

"That, too, sir, is beside the point If enough people believe in an institution, then it is important to those people—whether it is what you call phony, or not."

"You prefer faith to truth?" said Mr. Watts, scornfully.

"You must have confidence, and if you have that, truth follows," said Mr. Forkett.

"As a scientist, I consider you quite immoral," said Mr. Watts.

"As a citizen, I consider you unscrupulous," said Mr. Forkett.

"Oh, dear!" said Norma.

Mr. Forkett pondered. Mr. Watts frowned.

"Something that is *real* isn't going to fall to bits just because I disbelieve in it," observed Mr. Watts.

"How can you tell? The Roman Empire was real enough once—as long as people believed in it," replied Mr. Forkett.

The argument continued for some little time, with Mr. Forkett growing more monumental, and Mr. Watts more fundamental. Finally Mr. Forkett summed up his opinion:

"Frankly, your iconoclastic, revolutionary views seem to me to differ only in name from bolshevism."

Mr. Watts rose to his feet.

"The consolidation of society on faith, irrespective of scientific truth, is the method of a Stalin," he observed, and withdrew to the other end of the car.

"Really," said Norma. "I don't know how you can be so rude and ungrateful to him. When I think of them all with the toasting forks, and that poor woman hanging there without a stitch on, and upside-down, too——"

"It was all quite appropriate to the time and place. He's a very dangerous young man," said Mr. Forkett, firmly.

Henry thought it time to change the conversation. The four of them chatted more generally as the train rattled on at a good speed, though not as fast as it had descended, but after a time the talk began to wilt. Glancing up the coach, Henry noticed that Mr. Watts had already gone to sleep again, and felt that there was no better way of spending the time.

——

He awoke to hear voices shouting: "Stand clear of the doors!" and to find that the carriage was full of people again. Almost as his eyes opened, Norma's elbow stuck into his ribs.

"Look!" she said.

The straphanger in front of them was interested in the racing part of his paper so that the front page faced them with the head-line: RUSH-HOUR TUBE SMASH: 12 DEAD. Under it was a column of names. Henry leaned forward to read them. The holder of the paper lowered it to glare indignantly, but not before Henry had noticed his own name and those of the others.

Norma looked troubled.

"Don't know *how* I'm going to explain that at home," she said.

"You get my point?" inquired Mr. Forkett on Henry's other side. "Just think of the trouble there's going to be straightening this out—newspapers, coroners, heaven knows what. Not a safe fellow to have about. Quite anti-social."

"I don't know what my husband is going to think. He's such a jealous man," remarked Mrs. Branton, not without satisfaction.

The train stopped at St. Paul's, thinned somewhat, and then went on. Mr. Forkett and Norma prepared to get out. It occurred to Henry that he might as well get out, too. The train slowed.

"Don't know what they're going to say in the office, seeing me walk in. Still, it's been ever so int'resting, really. Ta-ta for now, everyone," said Norma, and wriggled into the departing crowd, with the skill of long practice.

A hand grasped Henry's arm as they stepped onto the platform.

"There he is," said Mr. Forkett. He nodded ahead. Henry saw the back view of Mr. Watts preceding them up the platform. "Can you spare a few minutes? Don't trust the fellow at all."

They followed up the escalator and round to the steps which brought them to the surface in front of the Royal Exchange.

There, Mr. Watts paused, and looked around him, seeming to consider. Then his attention fixed itself on the Bank of England. He strode forward in a forceful manner, and came to a stop facing the Bank, looking up at it. His lips moved.

The ground shook slightly underfoot. Three windows fell out of one of the Bank's upper stories. One statue, two urns, and a piece of balustrading swayed and toppled. Several people screamed.

Mr. Watts squared his shoulders, and took a deep breath.

"Good heavens! He's——" began Mr. Forkett, but the rest was lost as he sped from Henry's side.

"I——" announced Mr. Watts, at the top of his voice.

"DON'T——" he went on, to the accompaniment of an ominous trembling of the ground.

"BE——" but at that moment a strong push between his shoulder blades thrust him full in the path of a hurtling bus.

There was a shriek of brakes applied too late.

"That's 'im! I sore 'im do it!" screamed a woman, pointing at Mr. Forkett.

Henry caught up with him just as a policeman came running.

Mr. Forkett was regarding the facade of the Bank with pride.

"No telling what might have happened. A menace to society, that young man," he said. "They ought to give me a medal, but I'm afraid they're more likely to hang me—after all, tradition must be observed."

THE WHEEL

The old man sat on his stool and leaned back against the whitened wall. He had upholstered the stool elegantly with a hare skin because there didn't seem to be much between his own skin and his bones these days. It was exclusively his stool, and recognized in the farmstead as such. The strands of a whip that he was supposed to be plaiting drooped between his bent fingers, but, because the stool was comfortable and the sun was warm, his fingers had stopped moving, and his head was nodding.

The yard was empty save for a few hens that pecked more inquisitively than hopefully in the dust, but there were sounds that told of others who had not the old man's leisure for siesta. From round the corner of the house came the occasional plonk of an empty bucket as it hit the water, and its scrape on the sides of the well as it came up full. In the shack across the yard a dull pounding went on rhythmically and soporifically. The old man's head fell further forward as he drowsed.

Presently, from beyond the rough, enclosing wall there came another sound, slowly approaching. A rumbling and a rattling, with an intermittent squeaking. The old man's ears were no longer sharp, and for some minutes it failed to disturb him. Then he opened his eyes and, locating the sound, sat staring incredulously toward the gateway. The sound drew closer and a boy's head showed above the wall. He grinned at the old man, an expression of excitement in his eyes. He did not call out, but moved a little faster until he came to the gate. There he turned into the yard proudly towing behind him a box mounted on four wooden wheels.

The old man got up suddenly from his seat, alarm in every line. He waved both arms at the boy as though he would push him back. The boy stopped. His expression of gleeful pride faded into astonishment. He stared at the old man who was waving him away so urgently. While he still hesitated the old man continued to shoo him off with one hand while he placed the other on his own lips, and started to walk toward him. Reluctantly and bewilderedly the boy turned, but too late. The pounding in the shed stopped. A middle-aged woman appeared in the doorway. Her mouth was open to call, but the words did not come. Her jaw dropped slackly, her eyes seemed to bulge, then she crossed herself, and screamed. . . .

The sound split the afternoon peace. Behind the house the bucket fell with a clatter, and a young woman's head showed round the corner. Her eyes widened. She crammed the back of one hand across her mouth, and crossed herself with the other. A young man appeared in the stable doorway, and stood there transfixed. Another girl came pelting out of the house with a little girl behind her. She stopped as suddenly as if she had run into something. The little girl stopped too, vaguely alarmed by the tableau, and clinging to her skirt.

The boy stood quite still with all their gaze upon him. His bewilderment began to give way to fright at the expression in their eyes. He looked from one horrified face to another until his gaze met the old man's. What he saw there seemed to reassure him a little—or to frighten him less. He swallowed. Tears were not far away as he spoke:

"Gran, what's the matter? What are they all looking at me like that for?"

As if the sound of his voice had released a spell the middle-aged woman came to life. She reached for a hayfork which leaned against the shack wall. Raising its points toward the boy she walked slowly in between him and the gate. In a hard voice she said:

"Go on! Get in the shed!"

"But, Ma——" the boy began.

"Don't you dare call me that now," she told him.

In the tense lines of her face the boy could see something that was almost hatred. His own face screwed up, and he began to cry.

"Go on," she repeated harshly. "Get in there."

The boy backed away, a picture of bewildered misery. Then, suddenly, he turned and ran into the shed. She shut the door on him, and fastened it with a peg. She looked round at the rest as though defying them to speak. The young man withdrew silently into the gloom of the stable. The two young women crept away, taking the little girl with them. The woman and the old man were left alone.

Neither of them spoke. The old man stood motionless, regarding the box where it stood on its wheels. The woman suddenly put her hands up to her face. She made little moaning noises as she swayed, and the tears came trickling out between her fingers. The old man turned. His face was devoid of all expression. Presently she recovered herself a little.

"I never would have believed it. My own little David . . . !" she said.

"If you'd not screamed, nobody need have known," said the old man.

His words took some seconds to sink in. When they did, her expression hardened again.

"Did you show him how?" she asked, suspiciously.

He shook his head.

"I'm old, but I'm not crazy," he told her. "And I'm fond of Davie," he added.

"You're wicked, though. That was a wicked thing you just said."

"It was true."

"I'm a God-fearing woman. I'll not have evil in my house—whatever shape it comes in. And when I see it I know my duty."

The old man drew breath for a reply, but checked it. He shook his head. He turned, and went back to his stool, looking, somehow, older than before.

———

There was a tap on the door. A whispered "Sh!" For a moment Davie saw a square of night sky with a dark shape against it. Then the door closed again.

"You had your supper, Davie?" a voice asked.

"No, Gran. Nobody's been."

The old man grunted.

"Thought not. Scared of you, all of 'em. Here, take this. Cold chicken, it is."

Davie's hand sought and found what the other held out to him. He gnawed on a leg while the other man moved about in the dark, searching for somewhere to sit. He found it, and let himself down with a sigh.

"This is a bad business, Davie, boy. They've sent for the priest. He'll be along tomorrow."

"But I don't understand, Gran. Why do they all act like I've done something wrong?"

"Oh, Davie!" said his grandfather, reproachfully.

"Honest, I don't, Gran."

"Come now, Davie. Every Sunday you go to church, and every time you go, you pray. What do you pray?"

The boy gabbled a prayer. After a few moments the old man stopped him.

"There," he said. "That last bit."

"Preserve us from the Wheel?" Davie repeated, wonderingly. "What *is* the Wheel, Gran? It must be something terrible bad, I know, 'cos when I ask them they just say it's wicked, and not to talk of it. But they don't say what it is."

The old man paused before he replied, then he said:

"That box you got out there. Who told you to fix it that way?"

"Why, nobody, Gran. I just reckoned it'd move easier that way. It does, too."

"Listen, Davie. Those things you put on the side of it—they're *wheels.*"

It was some time before the boy's voice came back out of the darkness. When it did, it sounded bewildered. "What, those round bits of wood? But they can't be, Gran. That's all they are—just round bits of wood. But the Wheel—that's something awful, terrible, something everybody's holy scared of."

"All the same, that's what they are." The old man ruminated awhile. "I'll tell you what's going to happen tomorrow, Davie. In the morning the priest will come here and see your box. It'll be still there because nobody dares to touch it. He'll sprinkle some water on it and say a prayer just to make it safe to handle. Then they'll take it into the field and make a fire under it, and they'll stand round singing hymns while it burns.

"Then they'll come back, and take you down to the village, and ask you questions. They'll ask you what the Devil looked like when he came to you, and what he offered to give you if you'd use the Wheel."

"But there wasn't any Devil, Gran."

"That don't matter. If they think there was, then sooner or later you'll be telling them there was, *and* just how he looked when you saw him. They've got ways. . . . Now what you got to do is act innocent. You got to say you found that box just the way it is now. You didn't know what it was, but you just brought it along on account of it would make good firewood. That's your story, and you've got to stick to it. 'F you stick to it, no matter what they do, *maybe* you'll get through okay."

"But Gran what is there that's so bad about the Wheel. I just can't understand."

The old man paused more lengthily than before.

"Well, it's a long story, Davie—and it all began a long, long while ago. Seems like in those days everybody was happy and good and suchlike. Then one day the Devil came along and met a man and told him that he could give him something to make him as strong as a hundred men, an' make him to run faster than the wind, an' fly higher than the birds. Well, the man said that'd be mighty fine, an' what did the Devil want for it? And the Devil said he didn't want a thing—not just then. And so he gave the man the Wheel.

"By and by, after the man had played around with the Wheel awhile he found out a whole lot of things about it; how it would make other Wheels, and still more Wheels, and do all the things the Devil had said, with a whole heap more."

"What, it'd fly, 'n everything?" said the boy.

"Sure. It did all those things. And it began to kill people, too— one way and another. Folks put more and more Wheels together the way the Devil told them, and they found they could do a whole lot bigger things, and kill more people, too. And they couldn't stop using the Wheel then on account of they would have starved if they had.

"Well, that was just what the Devil wanted. He'd got 'em cinched, you see. Pretty near everything in the world was depending on Wheels, and things got worse and worse, and the old Devil just lay back an' laughed to see what his Wheel was doing. Then things got terrible bad. I don't know quite the way it happened, but things got so terrible worse that there wasn't scarcely anybody left alive—only just a few, like it had been after the Flood. An' they was near finished."

"And all that was on account of the Wheel?"

"Uh-huh— Leastways, it couldn't have happened without it. Still, somehow they made out. They built shacks, an' planted corn, and by an' by the Devil met a man, and started talking about his Wheel again. Now this man was very old and very wise and very God-fearing, so he said to the Devil: 'No. You go right back to Hell,' and then he went all around warning everybody about the Devil and his Wheel, and got 'em all plumb scared.

"But the old Devil don't give up that easy. He's mighty tricky, too—there's times when a man gets an idea that turns out to be pretty nearly a Wheel—maybe like rollers, or screws, or somethin'—but it'll just pass so long as it ain't fixed in the middle. Yes, he keeps along trying, an' now and then he does tempt a man into making a Wheel. Then the priest comes and they burn the Wheel. And they take the man away. And to stop him making any more Wheels, and to discourage any other folk, they burn him, too."

"They b-burn him?" stammered the boy.

"That's what they do. So you see why you got to say you *found* it, and stick to that."

"Maybe if I promised never to make another——?"

"That wouldn't be no good, Davie. They're all scared of the Wheel, and when men are scared they get angry and cruel. No, you gotta keep to it."

The boy thought for some moments, then he said:

"What about Ma? She'll know. I had that box off her yesterday. Does it matter?"

The old man grunted. He said, heavily:

"Yes, it does matter. Women do a lot of pretending to be scared—but once they do scare, they scare more horribly than men. And your Ma's dead scared."

There was a long silence in the darkness of the shed. When the old man spoke again, it was in a calm, quiet voice:

"Listen, Davie, lad. I'm going to tell you something. And you're going to keep it to yourself—not tell a soul till maybe you're an old man like me?"

"Sure, Gran, 'f you say."

"I'm tellin' you because you found out about the Wheel for yourself. There'll always be boys like you who do. There've got to be. You can't kill an idea the way they try to. You can keep it down awhile, but sooner or later it'll come out. Now what you've got to understand is that the Wheel's *not* evil. Never mind what the scared men all tell you. No discovery is good or evil until men make it that way. Think about that, Davie, boy. One day they'll start to use the Wheel again. I hoped it would be in my time, but—well, maybe it'll be in yours. When it does come, don't you be one of the scared ones; be one of the ones that's going to show 'em how to use it better than they did last time. It's not the Wheel—it's fear that's evil, Davie. Remember that."

He stirred in the darkness. His feet clumped on the hard earth floor.

"Reckon it's time I was gettin' along. Where are you, boy?"

His groping hand found Davie's shoulder, and then rested a moment on his head.

"God bless you, Davie. And don't worry anymore. It's goin' to be all right. You trust me?"

"Yes, Gran."

"There you go to sleep. There's some hay in the corner, there."

The glimpse of dark sky showed briefly again. Then the sound of the old man's feet shuffled across the yard into silence.

—

When the priest arrived he found a horror-stricken knot of people collected in the yard. They were gazing at an old man who worked away with a mallet and pegs on a wooden box. The priest stood, scandalized.

"Stop!" he cried. "In the name of God, stop!"

The old man turned his head toward him. There was a grin of crafty senility on his face.

"Yesterday," he said, "I was a fool. I only made four wheels for it. Today I am a wise man—I am making two more wheels so that it will run half as easily again."

—

They burnt the box, as he said they would. Then they took him away.

In the afternoon a small boy whom everyone had forgotten turned his eyes from a column of smoke that rose in the direction of the village, and hid his face in his hands.

"I'll remember, Gran. I'll remember. It's only fear that's evil," he said, and his voice choked in his tears.

LOOK NATURAL, PLEASE!

The photographer stepped forward. There was a touch of the acrobat in his alert pose, a suspicion of the conjuror in the way he carried his left hand to the lens cap.

"Watch the birdie!" murmured Ralph.

"Shush!" his bride reproved him.

The photographer held his pose till it should dominate. There has to be a sedative for all the archness, facetiousness, and nervous jocularity that comes to the top in a studio. Experience had taught the photographer that a showman's drama reinforced by an undertaker's gravity will work in time. He waited for the notes of frivolity to settle. Then he said:

"Smile, please!" And tightened his fingers on the cap.

"Why?" asked Ralph, conversationally.

The photographer looked coldly at him, and checked his intended movement.

"It is customary," he said.

"I know," said Ralph. "That is why I was asking why."

If the photographer sighed, it was inaudibly. They all have their pictures taken—the large, the small, the illustrious, the dumb, the brilliant, the crazy—so there has to be a technique to deal with them. An air of professional knowledgeability is frequently effective:

"The effect is considered more pleasing, sir. That is just right, madam. Keep it just like that. Now, sir, for a moment, please. Quite still."

Troublesomely, Ralph returned to the subject while Letty was putting on her coat and arranging her hat.

"Do you think the effect really is more pleasing?" he asked.

"Of course it is," said the photographer, irritably. "People don't want glum faces all over the house. You wouldn't yourself."

"All the same," Ralph said, "old family portraits don't seem to need to grin down on their descendants like a row of mixed chorus. Why should taste have changed so much—if it has?"

The photographer pushed the slide over the plate, and took the holder out.

"The way I make my living is by giving people what they want and what they will pay for," he said shortly.

The invitation to drop the subject was plain enough, but Ralph ignored it.

"What I can't understand, is why you don't take people the way they *really* look," he said. "I mean, surely that's what they actually want—a record of how anyone actually appeared at the time, not just a string of standardized grins?"

Mr. and Mrs. Plattin were the last customers at the end of a tiring day. The photographer put the plateholder carefully into a numbered pigeonhole before he replied. Then he said:

"Young man, if you are trying to tell me how to run my business, let me tell you that I've learned it from the bottom up. I was making portraits before you were born. Over thirty years now I've been in the trade—so I ought to know what I'm doing. I don't know what your trade is, and I don't want to, but I'll thank you to leave mine to me." And he held the door open for them with cold politeness.

Outside, Letty put her arm in her husband's as he turned to look in the window.

"One day," he told her, "we'll have a good laugh over that picture."

It was in Letty's mind that a picture taken on a honeymoon should be material for a wistful smile rather than a good laugh, but the remark did not demand any reply, so she let it pass.

Ralph was still looking in the window whence faces, large, small, tough, delicate, intelligent, imbecile, in units, pairs, and families, smiled back at him.

"My God!" he said. "See where Lewis Carroll got the idea? He's taken away practically everything but the grin."

"Well——" Letty began. But he went on.

"And look at the technique of the portraits. Ears fuzzy-edged, tip of nose fuzzy—just the eyes in focus every time. And those groups! Take your place by numbers! How do they tell which wedding is which?"

"Some of them look quite nice, though," Letty murmured.

Ralph stepped back and surveyed the whole display.

"You know," he said, "there's scope here. If the old boy can go on making a living out of this sort of junk . . ."

"Darling," ventured Letty, "it's his trade. He must know the kind of thing people want, surely."

"No 'must' about it. The people in this place have to take the stuff people like him give them, or none at all, don't they?"

"Well, yes . . ." Letty admitted, doubtfully.

"Then there's scope. . . . It wouldn't take a lot of capital, either. Damn it, I could turn out a lot better stuff than that right now, and give them *real* portraits of themselves."

Letty looked up at him.

"Darling, you don't think it's because they want to think they look like that? I mean, because they see their real selves as happy and smiling people underneath?"

"No," said her husband. "It's a sheer convention, and pretty near hypocrisy, too. They aren't *true* pictures of the people at all—has one of them any character as they look there, I ask you?"

Letty looked at the rows of harmlessly amiable faces.

"I——" she began. Then she checked herself.

In the profession of wifehood the exams begin at the church door—and there is never a final degree.

"I expect you're right, dear," she said.

—

Within the firm of Ralph Plattin Portrayals Ltd., its success was attributed to the gifts of its protagonist. Elsewhere, there was a tendency to assign it to the lucky success of a single picture. Truth was probably in the usual intermediate position.

The business had been in existence about a year before *the* picture made its public appearance. Ralph was pleased when it and three others out of the half-dozen that he had submitted to the Annual Exhibition were accepted and hung, but, whatever may have been said later, neither he nor anyone else goes on record as having described it as a "masterpiece" at that stage. This quality was left to the Press and public to discover, and point out to the judges who had only conceded it second prize in its class.

It was a portrait, taken from a low angle, of a young bride—and, to some extent, of her husband. The girl, in her white satin gown, was in the foreground. Close behind her and slightly to her right stood the young man. He made an excellent dark background roughly contoured to her gleaming white. The sky behind their heads was filtered dark, too. Against it the wind had twitched her veil in a misty caprice. To the top left of the picture, for composition's sake, floated part of a summer cloud—it was something not quite right about the angle of light on this cloud that had made the difference between the first and second prize.

The bride stood with her chin raised, and her head tilted a little back. She was lovely, and natural; one could all but feel the freshness of the wind on her cheeks. The lips of a mouth that scarcely smiled were slightly parted. Her eyes looked on something far, far away. There was a serene happiness in her whole face—and more than that, too: a delicate gleam of radiance miraculously held, something so fragile and fugitive that one looked again with a wistful, glad-sad feeling that life was meant to bring a few such moments to everyone.

The status of the picture was established at the preview when the staff writer from *View* said to his photographer companion:

"Bill, I never thought to see the day, but there's a pic upstairs that's got Frosty Florence from *Woman's Ways* all dewy-eyed. And if that doesn't spell heart-appeal in neon, I quit."

The editors of a dozen illustrated papers agreed, and *View*, in betting a full page on it, also managed to produce the most torn-out and pinned-up page of the year.

A framed enlargement, three feet by four and a half, appeared in Ralph Plattin's then modest window. It was set off by black velvet curtains. A cushion to the left supported a bride's bouquet, one to the right, a simple gold ring. Beneath the picture, lettered on a gilt panel was the title: "Figurehead for Happiness." And, indeed, the angle, the breeze, the underlying suggestion of outset, all helped to enhance the notion of an adventurous prow pointed bravely to the future.

It was a display not to be passed without at least a pause—and, for many, a long, dreamy kind of pause. The telephone began to ring frequently. Advertising agents put in bids. Talent scouts came inquiring for the name and address of the model. But most important were the girls who slipped quietly into the shop, and said shyly:

"Well, it's—well, I'm getting married soon, you see. And I wondered if . . . Yes, something like that, if you could . . ." And then, wistfully: "I think it's the loveliest picture I've ever seen. . . . Oh, if you could . . ." And then went out, a little shaky, shiny-eyed, and smiling confidentially.

Ralph Plattin himself always maintained that much was lost in the enlargements to poster sizes, and disapproved of the style of type chosen to announce: "All this . . . and the Ring by Baker, too," which had been the outcome of the final contest between Baker and Rosyhealth Nightfood, but it prominently announced that the photograph was by Plattin and so, far from harming him, enabled him in a few months to move to new premises off Bond Street.

"What did I tell you?" he asked a little smugly of Letty. "That's what they want, a real picture that sells you something about the sitter, not just this toothpaste-grin rubbish. That's a *real* portrait of a *real* person."

Letty looked at the original prize-winning print in its place of honor above the fireplace.

"It has quite taken on as a style, hasn't it?" she observed.

"Of course it has. That's what I've been saying all along. People want individuality and character, not standardization."

"Er——" said Letty, hesitantly.

"Well, haven't I proved it?" asked her husband.

Letty cleared the faint shadow off her brow.

"Yes, of course, dear. You were perfectly right."

The fortunes of the firm were laid; its name established. The outburst of plagiarism in the trade did it little harm, for Ralph undoubtedly had a touch—had some of his competitors had it, too, many more brides of the ensuing year would have looked like proud figureheads, and far fewer like reeling statues.

But it quickly became clear to Ralph that with every hack photographer in the country figureheading brides he could not rest on his success. The idea would soon be done to death, and something must be found to follow it. An evening in the very first month of the new studio's existence saw the answer emerge.

The subject lay on a divan. Her face filled an opening in a white-velvet-covered board across which an assistant combed her hair. Ralph sprawled on an overhanging gantry to observe the vertical effect and direct operations.

"It has to *radiate*. All that hair must concentrate attention on the center. That's right, but keep the spread *even*—like a fan. No, bring those strands *under* the others, together under her chin, and then straight down. Keep it regular. What I'm after is a kind of sunburst effect, with her face quite serene and beautiful in the middle of it. . . . Now, lights! Oh, hell, no! It's got to be *soft* on the face, *dramatic* on the hair. . . . All right, then, we'll use a red furniture-filter with a clear center; that'll bring the hair up sharp. And you know, we shan't be able to go through all this pantomime with every client—besides, there's going to be some hair that just won't stand for it. Better get a few boards made up with different shades of hair ready stuck on 'em. . . ."

Thus was evolved the famous "Sunburst Medallion" style that quickly came to ornament many an expensive wall. And when that declined in favor, there was the "Water Lily" conception ready to follow it. In this, the sitter's head appeared vertically through the board, cupped in a calyx, and with her hair arranged in careful ripples over a dull mirror surface, as though floating. Its rather Burne-Jones quality had an appeal which easily outweighed professionally jealous references to Plattin's "Woman Overboard" technique.

"It is God who makes woman a thing of beauty," observed Mr. Plattin modestly. "I simply preserve her as a joy forever."

In less public circles he was fond of saying:

"What you have to do is to find out first how your sitter appears to herself, then how she would like to appear; these two you do your best to synthesize with the way she looks to you. It frequently isn't easy—sometimes it's damned near impossible, but you can usually produce a result which she will feel expresses at least one side of her personality. And there's fashion, too—the current climate of taste, sometimes frilly, sometimes austere—so you give her the opportunity of expressing herself with a certain limit of style—just as her hairdresser and her milliner do. When taste changes, you change your manner of presentation. There's tremendous scope there, any amount of scope...."

The years that followed seemed to bear him out, and whether it was the theory or a flair made little difference; the important thing was that the firm throve into the status of an institution. A visit to Plattin's was part of being a debutante.

In an astonishingly short time, as it seemed to Ralph, there were girls saying to him: "I suppose it's very sentimental of me, but you did such a beautiful picture of my mother when *she* was a bride, and I'd rather like..." Then, presently, there were awed little girls finding it hard to believe that anyone old enough to have taken pictures of their grandmothers as young women could still exist. And then, quite suddenly, there came a day when Ralph found himself wondering whether he wouldn't retire in a year or two more.

On his sixtieth birthday, however, he was still giving his personal supervision to the work, inspecting and making the final adjustments before the exposures were permitted. "Figurehead," "Sunburst," and other motifs had waxed and waned in public favor several times, and the date fell when the cycle had brought a revived demand for "Flowerpiece"; a type which required the careful close-packing of expensive blooms to set off a pretty face. It was one of his favorite styles, for it could never be completely a repeat. Every time there was a new problem in harmony between the face and the flowers, and to solve it again always gave him pleasure. Yet, that evening, Letty could tell from the very sound of his footsteps as they crossed the threshold that he had come home in a poor temper.

"A trying day at business, dear?" she inquired solicitously as they sat at dinner.

"Business is fine," Ralph told her. "The only thing wrong is some of the customers. I've always done my best to be tactful, as you know, but really, sometimes . . . !" He broke off expressively.

"You shouldn't let them worry you, dear. Not after all this time, and with your reputation."

"I know. As a rule I take no notice, of course. But today there was one young fellow . . . Came along with his fiancée, and looked on. Afterward he started off on a whole string of questions. Wanted to know why I didn't take people the way they *really* look—was sure that was what they *really* wanted. Thought there was great scope for the realistic portrait instead of my *artificial* stuff! Damned impudence! I let the tact go hang. 'Look here, young man,' I told him. 'Thirty years I've been in this trade, so do you think you're likely to know more about it than I do? Why, I was taking prize photographs before you were born. I think I may be allowed to know my own business best.' But even then he still went on chattering about *real* portraits. Damned puppy!"

Letty's eye wandered to the mantelshelf and a small photograph of a handsome young couple smiling. A slight, responsive smile touched her own mouth.

"Do you remember——?" she began. Then she stopped. In over thirty years she had not yet flunked an exam. She started again:

"What a ridiculous young man! How can he possibly imagine that with all your experience you don't know best, dear?"

PERFORCE TO DREAM

"But, my dear Miss Kursey," said the man behind the desk, speaking with patient clarity, "it is *not* that we have changed our minds about the quality of your book. Our readers were enthusiastic. We stand by our opinion that it is a charming light romance. But you must see that we are now in an impossible position. We simply cannot publish two books that are almost identical—and now that we know that two exist, we can't even publish one of them. Very understandably either you or the other author would feel like making trouble. Equally understandably we don't want trouble of that kind."

Jane looked at him steadily, with hurt reproach.

"But mine was first," she objected.

"By three days," he pointed out.

She dropped her eyes, and sat playing with the silver bracelet on her wrist. He watched her uncomfortably. He was not a man who enjoyed saying no to personable young women at any time; also, he was afraid she was going to cry.

"I'm terribly sorry," he said earnestly.

Jane sighed. "I suppose it was just too good to be true—I might have known." Then she looked up. "Who wrote the other one?" she added.

He hesitated. "I don't know that we can——" he began.

Jane broke in: "Oh, but you must! It wouldn't be fair not to tell me. You simply must give me—us—a chance to clear this up."

His instinct was to steer safely out of the whole thing. If he had

had the least doubt about her sincerity he would have done so. As it was, his sense of justice won. She did have a right to know, and the chance to sort the whole thing out; if she could.

"Her name is Leila Mortridge," he admitted.

"That's her real name?"

"I believe so."

Jane shook her head. "I've never heard it. It's so queer," she went on. "Nobody can have seen my manuscript. I don't believe anyone knew I was writing it. I just can't understand it at all."

The publisher had no comment to make on that. Coincidences, he knew, do occur. It seems sometimes as though an idea were afloat in the ether and settles in two independent minds simultaneously. But this was something beyond that. Save for the last two chapters, Miss Kursey's *Amaryllis in Arcady* had not only the same story as Miss Mortridge's *Strephon Take My Heart,* but the settings, as well as much of the conversation, were identical. There could not be any question of chance about it.

Curiously, he asked:

"Where did it come from? How did you get the idea of it in the first place, I mean?"

Jane saw that he was looking at her with a peculiar intensity. She looked back at him uncertainly, miserably aware of tears not far behind her eyes.

"I—I dreamt it—at least, I think I dreamt it," she told him.

She was not able to see the puzzled astonishment that came over his face, for suddenly, and to her intense exasperation, tears from a source deeper than mere disappointment about the book overwhelmed her.

He groaned inwardly, and sat regarding her with helpless embarrassment.

Out in the street again, conscious of looking far from her best although considerably recovered, Jane made her way to a café in a mood of deep self-disgust. The exhibition she had put up was the kind of thing she heartily despised: a thing, in fact, that she would have thought herself quite incapable of a year ago.

But the truth of the matter, which she scarcely admitted to herself, was that she was no longer the same person as she had been a year ago. Though a careful observer might have said that her manner was a little altered, her assurance more individual, yet superficially she was the same Jane Kursey doing the same job in the same way. Only she knew how much more tedious the job had gradually become.

It is galling for a young woman of literary leanings to keep on day after day for what seems several lifetimes writing with a kind of standardized verve and coded excitement about such subjects as diagonal tucks, slashed necklines, swing backs, and double peplums; frustrating for her to have to season her work with the adjectives *heavenly, tiny, captivating, enchanting, divine, delicious,* marching round and round like an operatic army when she yearns to put her soul on paper. When, in fact, something has happened to her so that she feels that a spirit such as hers should be mounting skylark-like to the empyrean, that her heart is no less tender than that of Elaine the Lovable, that, should the occasion arise, she would be found not incompetent among the hetaerae.

The publisher's letter, therefore, had, despite her attempts to retain a level sensibleness, given her a choky, heart-thumping excitement. It did more than disclose the first rungs of a new and greatly preferable career for which many of her associates also struggled: it petted and pleased her secret self. The publisher had spoken of literary merit as if drawing a line between her and those others who worked with three-quarters of their attention on the film rights.

Her novel, he told her frankly, he found charming. An idyllic romance which could not fail to delight a large number of readers. There were, perhaps, a few passages where the feeling was a little Elizabethan for these prudish times, but they could be toned down with scarcely perceptible loss. . . .

The only qualification of her delight was a faint suspicion of her own undeserving—but, after all, was a dream any more of a gift than a talent? It was just a matter of the way your mind worked really, and if hers happened to work better when she slept than when she was awake, what of it? Nobody had ever been heard to think the worse of Coleridge for dreaming Kubla Khan rather than thinking it up. And anyway, she would not be taken literally even though she admitted frankly to dreaming it. . . .

And now there came this blow. Something so like her own story that the publisher would not touch it! She did not see how that could possibly have happened. She had not told anyone anything about it, not even that she was working on a book. . . .

She gazed moodily into her coffee. Then, as she raised the cup, she became aware of the other person who had come to her table almost unnoticed. The woman was looking her over with careful speculation. Jane paused with her cup a few inches from her mouth, returning the scrutiny. She was about her own age, quietly dressed, but wearing a fur coat that was beyond Jane's means, and a becoming small fur cap on her fair hair. But for the difference in dress she was not unlike Jane herself; the same build and size, much the same coloring, hair, too, that was a similar shade, though differently worn. Jane lowered her cup. As she put it down she noticed a wedding-ring on the other woman's hand. The woman spoke first:

"You are Jane Kursey," she said, in a tone that was more state-ment than question.

Jane had a curious sense of tenseness.

"Yes," she admitted.

"My name," said the woman, "is Leila Mortridge."

"Oh," said Jane. She could not find anything to add to that at the moment.

The other woman sipped her coffee, with Jane's eyes following every movement. She set her cup very precisely in the saucer, and looked up again.

"It seemed likely that they would be wanting to see you, too," she said. "So I waited outside the publisher's to see." She paused. "There is something here that requires an explanation," she added.

"Yes," Jane agreed again.

For some seconds they regarded one another levelly without speaking.

"Nobody knew I was writing it," the woman observed.

"Nobody knew *I* was writing it," said Jane.

She looked back at the woman, unhappily, resentfully, bitterly. Even if it had been only a dream—and it was hard to believe it was only that, for she had never heard of a dream that went on in installments night by night so vividly that one seemed to be living two alternating lives—but, even if it were, it was *her* dream, her *private* dream, save for such parts of it as she had chosen to write down—and even those parts should remain private until they were published.

"I don't see——" she began, and then broke off, feeling none too certain of herself.

The other woman's self-control was none too good, either; the corners of her mouth were unsteady. Jane went on:

"We can't talk in this place. My flat's quite near."

They walked the few hundred yards there immersed in thought. Not until they were in Jane's small sitting room did the woman speak again. When she did she looked at Jane as though she were hating her.

"How did you find out?" she demanded.

"Find out what?" Jane countered.

"What I was writing."

Jane regarded her coldly.

"Attack is sometimes the best form of defense, but not in this case. The first I knew of your existence was in the publisher's office about one hour ago. I gather that you found out about me in the same way, just a little earlier. That makes us practically even. I *know* you can't have read my manuscript. I know I've not read yours. It's a waste of time starting with accusations. What we have to find out is what has really happened. I—I——" But there she floundered to a stop without any idea how she had intended to continue.

"Perhaps you have a copy of your manuscript here?" suggested Mrs. Mortridge.

Jane hesitated, then without a word she went to her desk, unlocked a lower drawer, and took out a pile of carbon copy. Still without speaking, she handed it over. The other took it without hesitation. She read a page, and stared at it for a little, then she turned on and started to read another page. Jane went into her bedroom, and stood there awhile, staring listlessly out of the window. When she went back the pile of pages was lying on the floor, and Leila Mortridge was hunched forward, crying uncontrollably into a scrap of a handkerchief.

Jane sat down, looking moodily at the script and the weeping girl. For the moment she was feeling cold and dead inside, as if with a numbness which would turn to pain as it passed. Her dream was being killed, and now she was terribly afraid of life without it. . . .

The dream had begun about a year ago. When and where it was placed she neither knew, nor cared to know. A never, never land perhaps, for it seemed always to be spring or early summer there in a sweet, unwithering Arcady. She was lying on a bank where the grass grew close like green velvet. It ran down to a small stream of clear water chuckling over smooth white stones. Her bare feet were dabbling in the fresh coolness. The sunshine was warm on her bare arms. Her dress was a simple white cotton frock patterned with small flowers and little amorets.

There were small flowers set among the grass, too: she could not name them, but she could describe them minutely. A bird no larger than a blue-tit came down close to her, and drank. It turned a sparkling eye on her, drank again, and then flew away, unafraid. A light breeze rustled the taller grasses beside her and shimmered the trees beyond. Her whole body drank in the warmth of the sunshine as though it were an elixir.

Dimly she could remember another kind of life full of work and bustle, but it did not interest her: *it* was the dream, and this the reality. She could feel the ripples against her feet, the grass under her fingertips, the glow of the sun. She was intensely aware of the colors, the sounds, the scents in the air; aware as she had never been before, not merely of being alive, but of being part of the whole flow of life.

She had a glimpse of a figure approaching in the distance. A quickening excitement ran through every vein, and her heart sang. But she did not move. She lay with her head turned to one side on her arm. A tress of hair rested on her other cheek, heavy and soft as a silk tassel. She let her eyes close, but more than ever she was aware of the world about her.

She heard the soft approaching footsteps and felt the faint tremor of them in the ground. Something light and cool rested on her breast and the scent of flowers filled her nostrils. Still she did not move. She opened her eyes. A head with short dark curls was just above her own. Brown eyes were watching her from a suntanned face. Lips smiling slightly. She reached up with both arms, and clasped them round his neck. . . .

That was how it had begun. The sentimental dream of a schoolgirl, but preciously sweet for all that, and with a bright might-have-been quality which dulled still further the following dull day. She could remember waking with a radiance which was gradually drained away by the dimness of ordinary things and people. She was left, too, with a sense of loss, of having been robbed of what she should have been, and should have felt. It was as though in the dream she had been her rightful, essential self while by day she was forced to carry out a drab mechanical part, an animated lay figure—something at any rate that was not properly alive in a world that was not properly alive.

The following night the dream came again. It did not repeat; it continued. She had never heard of a dream that did that, but there it was. It was the same countryside, the same people, the same particular person, and herself. A world in which she felt quite familiar, and with people whom she seemed always to have known. There was a cottage which she could describe to the smallest detail, where she seemed to have spent all her life, in a village where she knew everyone. There was her work at which her fingers flickered surely among innumerable bobbins and produced exquisite lace upon a black pillow. The neighbors she talked to, the girls she had grown up with, the young men who smiled at her, were all of them quite real. They became even more real than the world of offices, dress shows, and editors demanding copy. In her waking world she came gradually to feel a drab among drabs: in her village world she was alive, perceptive—and in love. . . .

For the first week or two she had opened her eyes on the workaday world with painful reluctance, afraid that the dream would slip from her. But it was not finished. It went on, becoming all the time less elusive and more solid, until tentatively she allowed herself the hope that it had come to stay. She scarcely dared to believe that at first for fear of the blankness that would follow if it should stop when she had allowed herself really to live in it. Yet as the weeks went on she could only admit it fully, and cherish it more. Once she had allowed that, it began curiously to illuminate her daily life and pierce the dullness with unexpected glimpses. She found pleasure in noticing details which she had never observed before. Things and people changed in value and importance. She had more sense of detachment, and less of struggle. It came to her one day with a shock to find how her interests had altered and her impatience had declined.

The dream had caused that. Now that she had begun to feel that there was not the likelihood of it fading away any moment she could risk feeling happy in it—and the more tolerant of things outside it. The world looked altogether a different place when you knew that you had only to close your eyes at night to come alive as your true self in Arcady.

And why, she wondered, could real life not be like that? Or, perhaps, for some people, it was—sometimes, in glimpses. . . .

There had been that wonderful night when they had gone along the green path which led up the little hill to the pavilion. She had been excited, happy, a little tremulous. They had lain on cushions, looking out between the square oak pillars while the sun sank smoky red, and the thin bank of cloud lost its tinge to become dark lines across a sky that had turned almost green. All the sounds had been soft. A faint susurring of insects, the constant whisper of leaves, and, far away, a nightingale singing. . . . His muscles were firm and brave; she was soft as a sun-warmed peach. Does a rose, she had wondered, feel like this when it is about to open . . . ?

And then she had rested content, looking up at the stars, listening to the nightingale still singing, and to all nature gently breathing. . . .

In the morning when her eyes were open to her familiar small room and her ears to the sound of traffic in the street below, she had lain for a while in happy lassitude. It was then that she had decided to write the book—not, at first, for others to read, but for herself, so that she would never forget.

Unashamedly it was a sentimental book—one such as she had never thought herself capable of writing. But she enjoyed writing it, and reliving in it. And then it had occurred to her that perhaps she was not the only person who was tired of carrying a tough, unsentimental carapace. So she had produced a second version of the book, somewhat pruned—though not quite enough, apparently, for the publisher's taste—and added an ending of her own invention.

And here, now, was the inexplicable result. . . .

———

The first pressure of Leila Mortridge's flood of tears subsided. She dabbed at her eyes, giving little sniffs.

With the air of one accepting the necessity of somebody being practical, Jane said:

"It seems to me it's quite clear that one of two things has happened: either there is some kind of telepathy between us—and I don't see that that fits very well—or we are both having the same dream."

Mrs. Mortridge sniffed again.

"That's impossible," she said, decidedly.

"The whole situation's impossible," Jane told her shortly, "but it's happened—and we have to find the least impossible explanation. Anyway, is two people having the same dream so much more unlikely than anybody having a dream which goes on and on, like a serial?"

Mrs. Mortridge dabbed again, and regarded her thoughtfully.

"I don't see," she said, a trifle primly, "how an unmarried girl like you could be having a dream like that at all."

Jane stared.

"Come off it," she advised, briefly. "Besides," she added, after a moment's reflection, "it seems to me every bit as unsuitable for a respectably married woman."

Mrs. Mortridge looked forlorn.

"It's ruined my marriage," she said, a little plaintively.

Jane nodded understandingly.

"I was engaged—and it wrecked that," she told her. "How could one? I mean, after——" She let the sentence trail away.

"Quite," said Mrs. Mortridge.

They fell into abstract contemplation for some moments. Mrs. Mortridge broke the silence to say:

"And now *you*'re spoiling *it*, too."

"Spoiling your marriage?" said Jane amazedly.

"No, spoiling the dream."

Jane said, firmly:

"Now, don't let's be silly about this. We're both in the same boat. Do you think I want you muscling in on my dream?"

"*My* dream."

Jane disregarded that, and thought for a while. At last:

"Perhaps it won't make any difference," she suggested. "After all, if we were both dreaming we were her, and didn't know anything about one another then, why shouldn't we go on without knowing anything about one another?"

"But we do."

"No, when we are *there*, I mean. If that's so, it won't really matter, will it? At least, perhaps it won't."

Mrs. Mortridge looked unconsoled.

"It'll m-matter when I wake up and know you've b-been sharing——" she mumbled, tearfully.

"Do you think I like the idea of that any more than you do?" Jane said, coldly.

It took her a further twenty minutes to get rid of her visitor. Only then did she feel at liberty to sit down and have a good cry about it all.

———

The dream did not stop, as Jane had half feared it might. Neither was it spoiled. Only for a few succeeding mornings was Jane troubled on waking by the thought that Leila Mortridge must be aware of every detail of the night's experiences—and though there should have been some compensation to be found in the fact that she was equally aware of what had happened to Leila Mortridge, it did not, for some reason, seem to work quite that way.

That the girl in the dream was in no way affected for either of them by their knowledge of one another they established over the telephone the following morning with a thankfulness which was almost amiability. That settled, the besetting fear lost something of its edge, and antagonism began to dwindle. Indeed, so thoroughly did it decline, that the end of the month saw it replaced by a certain air of sorority, expressed largely in telephone calls that were almost schoolgirlish in manner, if not in content. For after all, Jane said to herself, if a secret had to be shared, why not make the best of the sharing . . . ?

———

It was on an evening some three months after their first meeting that Leila Mortridge came through on the telephone with an unusual, almost panicky note in her voice.

"My dear," she demanded, "have you seen this evening's *Gazette*?"

Jane said that she had just glanced at it.

"If you have it there, look at page four. It's in *Theatre Chat*. The thing in the second column, headed 'Dual Role'—no, don't ring off. . . ."

Jane laid down the receiver. She found the newspaper, and the paragraph:

DUAL ROLE

The production due to open shortly at the Countess Theatre is described as a romantic play with music. In it Miss Rosalie Marbank will have the unique distinction of being both the Leading Lady and the Authoress. This work, which is her first venture into authorship, is, she explains, neither a musical comedy, nor a miniature opera, but a play with music, that has been specially composed by Alan Cleat. It is the rustic love story of a girl lacemaker. . . .

Jane read on to the end of the paragraph and sat quite still, clutching the paper. A tinny chattering from the neglected telephone recalled her. She picked it up.

"You've read it?" Leila Mortridge's voice inquired.

"Yes," said Jane, slowly. "Yes . . . I— You don't happen to know her, do you?"

"I don't remember ever hearing of her. But it looks, well, I mean, what else can it be . . . ?"

"It *must* be." Jane thought for a moment, then: "All right. We'll find out," she said, decisively. "I'll get on to our critic and push him into wangling us a couple of seats for the first night. Will you be free?"

"I'm certainly going to be."

—

The dream went on. That night there was some kind of fair in the village. Her little stall looked lovely. Her lace was as delicate as if large snowflake patterns had been spun from the finest spider-thread. It was true that nobody was buying, but that did not seem to matter. When he came he found her sitting on the ground beside the stall telling stories to two adorable, wide-eyed children. Later on, they closed up the stall. She hung her hat over her arm by its ribbons, and they danced. When the moon came up they drifted away from the crowd. On a little rise they turned and looked back at the bonfire and the flares and the people still dancing. Then they went away along a path through the woods, and forgot all about everything and everybody but each other. . . .

——

One of the reasons why Jane was able to get her tickets with no great difficulty was the clash of the opening night of *Idyll* with that of a better publicized and more ambitious production. As a result, few of the regular first-night ornaments were to be seen, and the critics were second-flight. Nevertheless, the house was full.

She and Leila Mortridge found their seats a few minutes before the lights were lowered. The orchestra began an overture of some light, pretty music, but she could pay little attention to it for her empty, sick feeling of excitement. She put out an unsteady hand. Leila's grasped it, and she could feel that it, too, was trembling. She found herself wishing very much that she had not come, and guessed that Leila was feeling the same, but they had *had* to come: it would have been still worse not to. . . .

The orchestra wove its way from one simple, happy tune to another, and finished. There were five seconds of expectancy, and then the curtain rose. A sound that was half sigh and half gasp rustled through the theater and shrank into a velvet silence.

A girl lay on a green bank set with star-like flowers. She wore a simple dress of white, patterned with small flowers and amorets. Her bare feet dabbled in the edge of a pool.

Somewhere in the audience a woman gave a giggling sob, and was hushed.

The girl on the bank stirred in lazy bliss. She raised her head and looked beyond the bank. She smiled, and then lowered her head, lying as if asleep, with a tress of hair across her cheek.

From the audience there was no sound. It seemed not to breathe. A clarinet in the orchestra began a plaintive little theme. Every eye in the house left the girl, and dwelt upon the o.p. side of the stage.

A man in a green shirt and russet trousers came out of the bushes. He was carrying a bunch of flowers, and treading softly.

At the sight of him a sigh, as of huge, composite relief breathed through the house. Jane's hand relaxed its unconscious pressure upon Leila's. He was not *the* man.

He approached the girl on the bank, bent over, looking down at her for a moment, then gently laid the flowers on her breast. He sat down beside her, leaning over on one elbow to gaze into her face....

It was at that moment that something impelled Jane to take her attention from the stage. She turned her head slowly, as if drawn invisibly. Then she froze. Her heart gave a jump that was physically painful. She clutched Leila's arm.

"Look!" she whispered. "In that box up there!"

There could not be a moment's doubt. She knew the face better than she knew her own: every curl of his hair, every plane of his features, every lash around the brown eyes. She knew the tender smile with which he was leaning forward to watch the stage so well that she ached. She knew—everything about him....

Then, suddenly, she was aware that the eyes of almost every woman in the audience had left the stage and turned the same way as her own. The expressions on the rows of faces made her shiver and hold more tightly to Leila's arm.

For some minutes the man continued to watch, appearing oblivious of anything but the lighted scene. Then something, perhaps the intense stillness of the audience, caused him to turn his head.

Before the hundreds of eyes that were watching, his smile faded.

Abruptly the silence was broken by hysterics in half a dozen parts of the house at once.

He stood up uncertainly, his expression became tinged with alarm. Then, decisively, he turned toward the back of the box. What happened there was invisible from the floor, but in a moment Jane was aware that he had not left. He came into view again, backing away from the door toward the rail of the box. Beyond him the heads of several women came into sight. The look on their faces caused Jane to shudder. When the man turned she could see that he was afraid. He was cornered, and the women came on toward him like outraged furies.

With a merely momentary hesitation he swung one leg over the rail of the box, and clambered outside. Quite evidently he intended to escape by climbing to the neighboring box. With a foot on one of the light brackets, he reached for its edge. Simultaneously two of the women in the box he was leaving clutched at his other arm. They broke his hold upon the rail. For a fearful, prolonged moment he teetered there, arms waving to regain his balance. Then he went, turning as he fell backward, and crashed headfirst into the aisle below. . . .

Jane clutched Leila to her, and bit her lip to keep from screaming. She need not have made the effort: practically everyone else screamed. . . .

———

Back in her own room, Jane sat looking at the telephone for a long time before she could bring herself to use it. At last she lifted the receiver, and got through to the office. She gave a desk number, then:

"Oh Don. It's about that man at the Countess Theatre tonight. Do you know anything?" she asked, in a voice flatly unlike her own.

"Sure. Just doing the obit now," said a cheerful voice. "What do you want to know?"

"Just——" she said, unsteadily. "Oh, just who he was—and things."

"Fellow called Desmond Haley. Age thirty-five. Quite a show of letters after his name, medical mostly. Practiced as a psychiatrist. Seems to have written quite a flock of things. Best known is a standard work: *Crowd Psychology and the Communication of Hysteria*. Latest listed publication is a paper which appears to be generally considered pretty high-flown bunk called *The Inducement of Collective Hallucination*. He lived at— Hullo there, what's wrong?"

"Nothing," Jane told him, leveling her voice with an effort.

"Thought you sounded— I say, you didn't know him or anything, did you?"

"No," said Jane, as steadily as she could. "No, I didn't know him."

Very precisely she returned the telephone to its rest. Very carefully she walked into the next room. Very deliberately and sadly she drooped on her bed, and let the tears flow as they would.

———

And who shall say how many tears flowed upon how many pillows for the dream that did not come that night, nor ever again . . . ?

RESERVATION DEFERRED

Dying at seventeen, and provided the circumstances allow it to be decorous, can be terribly romantic. The picture one makes: pretty, though a little pale, spiritual-eyed, displayed, as it were, against a pile of pillows, with the frills of the nylon nightie showing beneath the lacy wool bed jacket; the lights in one's hair glistened by the bedside lamp, the slender hand so delicately ivory on the pink silk eiderdown.

The bud scarce unfurled, the dew still undried, the heart not yet hardened.

Character, too: patience, sweetness, gratitude for the little things people do, kindly forgiveness to the doctors one has defeated, sympathy for those who are weepy about one, resignation, quiet fortitude. It can all be very beautiful and sad-romantic, and not nearly so distressing as people think—particularly if one is quite sure of heaven, as Amanda was.

Search as she might, she could find no more than a few featherweight reproaches to lay upon herself. The one or two peccadilloes she had managed to dredge up from earliest childhood, matters concerning an ownerless penny spent on sweets, an apple that had fallen from a barrow, one's failure to own up to putting the drawing pin on Daphne Deakin's chair, would, the Rev. Mr. Willis assured her, be unlikely to have any appreciable effect upon the granting of her entry permit. So, in a way, she had an advantage over other people who would have to go on living longer lives, and probably earning black marks in the course of them. There was a lot of compensation in being assured of heaven.

At the same time, she would have liked to be a little surer of what to expect there. Mr. Willis was positive enough about the place, but in such a general way, so difficult to pin down to details. He tended, too, to evade the more piercing questions with unsatisfactory observations on the possibility of something happening which would make the exact nature of heaven a less urgent question for her. In fact, nobody seemed either to know much about heaven, or to be willing to discuss its organization with her. Dr. Frobisher, after admitting his ignorance, always steered the conversation to what he called a less morbid topic—though how heaven, of all places, could be classified as morbid Amanda failed to understand. It was much the same with her mother. Mrs. Day's expression would cloud; she would answer awkwardly once or twice, and then say: "Darling, let's talk about something more cheerful, shall we?" So Amanda, though she did not in the least understand how heaven could be heaven if it weren't cheerful, would, in the sweetness of her disposition, talk about something quite uninteresting, instead.

Still, it was very nice to know that one was qualified for heaven, and that everyone was agreed about it. Rather like winning a scholarship and becoming self-supporting at an early age, and carrying something of an obligation to be kind and thoughtful toward those who had not such advantages.

A slow decline, someone had called it—a funny idea, that: the Present, the Imperfect, the Perfect—but it was prettier to think of petals falling, fluttering softly down until one day they would all be gone, and people would cry a little and say how brave she had been, and how happy she must be in heaven now.

And possibly it would have gone off tidily like that but for the ghost.

Just at first, Amanda did not realize it was a ghost. When she woke up and saw her standing inside the door, she thought for a moment that perhaps they had now got a night nurse who was looking in to see how she was doing. Then it occurred to her that a nurse would very likely be wearing more than just silk panties and vest, and also that she oughtn't to be visible at all, because the room was dark. The ghost, seeing her there, showed a trace of surprise.

"Oh, sorry to intrude," she said. "I thought you would have gone by now." And she turned as if to leave.

She was a very unalarming-looking ghost. A friendly-seeming girl, with slightly red hair, rather wide eyes, an enviable figure, and charming hands and feet. Amanda guessed her at about seven or eight years older than herself.

"No. Please don't go," she told her, on impulse.

The ghost turned back, a little surprised.

"You're sure you don't mind?" she said gratefully. "I mean, people are so touchy. Usually they scream."

"I don't see why," said Amanda. "Anyhow, I'll probably be a ghost or something myself soon."

"Oh, I shouldn't think so," said the ghost, in a social-polite voice.

"Come and sit down. You can put the eiderdown round you if you feel cold," invited Amanda.

"Luckily that's not one of my troubles," said the ghost, sitting down and crossing one elegant leg over the other.

"Er—my name's Amanda," Amanda told her.

"Mine's Virginia," said the ghost. "I can't imagine why."

There was a pause during which Amanda's curiosity mounted. She hesitated, then she said:

"I hope it's not something I shouldn't ask, but how do you happen to be a ghost? I mean, I thought people just went to one place or the other, if you see what I mean."

"One place or the other?" repeated Virginia. "Oh, I see. No, it isn't quite as simple as that. But anyway, I'm a special case—a sort of D.P. at the moment. The whole thing is *sub judice*, so I just have to wander round until they've made up their minds."

Amanda was puzzled. "How do you mean?" she asked.

"Well," exclaimed Virginia, "when my husband strangled me it looked just like an ordinary murder, really, but then someone raised a question about the degree of provocation. If they decide I went above a particular reading they can bring it in as suicide, which would be bad. Of course, I should appeal on grounds of prior counter-provocation. He's that tame sort who would provoke a saint into provoking him. I suppose I did overdo it a bit—but if you knew him, you'd understand."

"What's it like? Being strangled, I mean?" Amanda asked, interestedly.

"Horrid, really," said Virginia. "And I'd have been more careful if I'd known it was going to lead to all this hanging around while they argue about it."

"It's disappointing," said Amanda. "I was hoping you might be able to tell me something about heaven."

"Heaven? Why?"

"Well," said Amanda, "nobody here seems to be able to tell me, and I expect to be going there soon, so I thought it'd be nice to know what it's like."

"Good gracious!" exclaimed Virginia, opening her wide eyes wider.

Amanda did not see that there was any "Good gracious!" about it: expecting to go to heaven seemed to her a very reasonable ambition. She said so.

"Dear, dear. Poor thing," observed Virginia, compassionately.

In anyone less sweet than Amanda, her faint moue might have been called sulkiness.

"I don't see what's wrong with that," she said.

"From personal observation, I wouldn't——" began Virginia.

"Oh, you do know about it, then?"

"I've looked it over. Parts of it, anyway," Virginia admitted.

"Oh, please tell me about it, please!" she said, eagerly.

Virginia considered. "Well," she said, "the first district I saw was the oriental section. It's all very gorgeous and technicolored, and you wear lots of jewels and a veil and transparent trousers. The men wear beards and turbans, and you have to cluster them in groups of not less than twenty to each. It looks a bit like autograph-hunting, only it isn't, of course. Then after a time he beckons one out of the mob, and it always turns out to be somebody else, and so you have to go and find another place to cluster, and everybody simply loathes you for crashing in on their lot. It's all terribly frustrating."

"Is that all?" asked Amanda, unhappily.

"Pretty much. You can eat Turkish delight in the intervals, of course, and I suppose by the law of averages——"

"I mean, it doesn't sound a bit like I thought."

"Oh, it's different in different sections. The Nordic part isn't a bit like that. There you spend nearly all your time washing and bandaging great gashes in heroes, and making broth for them in between whiles. I suppose it's all right for people who happen to have had a hospital training, but it seemed frightfully gory and messy to me. Besides, the heroes are such types. Never take a scrap of notice of you. They're either bragging, or flat out, or just off to get some more gashes. All terribly tedious, I thought."

"That doesn't sound quite the kind——" Amanda began, but Virginia went on:

"Still, I must say for high-octane tediousness you want to take a look at the Nirvana district. Talk about highbrow! You can only see it if you peep over the wall, because there's a notice saying 'No Women Allowed,' and——"

"What I was meaning," Amanda interrupted firmly, "is the ordinary kind of heaven. You know, the one they tell us about when we're children, but never seem to explain properly."

"Oh, that one," said Virginia. "Oh, my dear! So prim. I wouldn't advise it, really. So much choral singing and poetry reading all the time. Good, you know, high quality and all that, but sort of serious—and the music being all trumpets and harps gets kind of monotonous. So much white's awfully tiring, too. The whole thing's frightfully—what's the word, antiseptic?—no, ascetic, that's it. They've got a no-marriage law there. Imagine it! The result is nobody dares even ask you out for a cup of coffee after the music for fear of being arrested. Mind you, I daresay saints like it quite a lot———" She broke off. "You're not a saint, are you?"

"I—I don't think so," admitted Amanda, uncertainly.

"Well, unless you are, I simply wouldn't recommend it." Virginia went on to give a more detailed account. Amanda listened to her with growing dismay. At last she broke in:

"But it just *can't* be like that. You're simply spoiling everything for me. I was so happy knowing I was going to heaven, too. I think you're just being cruel and beastly." Tears came into her eyes.

Virginia stared at her. Then she said:

"But my poor dear, don't you understand. They're all men's heavens, and that's hell for women. Seems as if nobody ever got around to designing a heaven for women, don't ask me why. But, honest, I'd keep well clear of these men's heavens if I were you. Speaking as one woman to another———"

But at that point Amanda's tears overflowed. The sound of her own unhappy sobs prevented her from hearing any more, and when she looked up again Virginia had gone. So she laid her head on her pillow and cried herself to sleep.

In fact, Amanda was so disappointed that she was irritable and surprised everyone by starting to get better.

And when she was quite well she married an accountant who seemed to think of heaven as the perfect cybernetics machine, and that wasn't very interesting to a girl, either.

HEAVEN SCENT

Although she had been expecting it any minute in this last half hour, Miss Mallison started slightly as the door opened. But she kept her eyes intently, if not intelligently, upon the open letter on her desk.

"Good morning, Miss Mallison," said the expected voice, cheerfully enough, but somehow as if it had been saying, "Hullo, housewives."

"Good morning, Mr. Alton," she responded, carefully.

By the time he had hung up his coat and hat she had left her desk, and was rootling about in the filing cabinet with her back his way.

"Anything in the mail?" he inquired.

"Nothing much, Mr. Alton. It's on your desk," she told him.

She went on rootling, waiting exasperatedly for the fluttery feeling inside and the flush that was burning her face up to wear off. Experience told her that once it was over she would probably get through the rest of the day all right: what experience seemed unable to tell her, and she resented that, was how to stop it happening afresh each morning.

Presently she felt able to turn round. She looked at Mr. Alton sifting through the letters with his slight frown of concentration. Then, carrying a file which she did not need, she went back to her desk, and finished pulling herself together.

"Nothing much here," he agreed, a few minutes later. "I'd better go over this Simon and Smith thing. It'll do tomorrow. Think you can manage the rest?"

Michael Alton was a pleasing young man, not over tall, but well built. Beneath his curling dark hair, he had a friendly, somewhat ingenuous look on a rather chunky face. Miss Mallison seldom noticed the chunks: her attention usually seemed to fix on his eyes, or his mouth.

"Yes, Mr. Alton," she said.

"Good. No fixtures for today, except Mr. Grosburger, are there?"

She glanced down.

"No, Mr. Alton. Only lunch with Mr. Grosburger."

"It's more than only, Miss Mallison. Mr. Grosburger is going to make our fortune."

Her reply was a nod.

"You don't believe that?" he asked.

Miss Mallison fiddled a little with her handkerchief, and then looked up.

"Something always happens," she said, unhappily.

He shook his head. "Not this time," he told her. "And Grosburger's only the first shot—there are plenty more if he won't play. The first time I have been sensible. No more head-on collisions with vested interests. I've learnt the big lesson. I see now that the thing to do is not to invent something new, but simply to improve an *already existing* article. You make it a bit more efficient than whatever your competitors are trying to sell, advertise it, and there you are."

"I hope so, Mr. Alton," said Miss Mallison.

"Amplified faith is what you require, Miss Mallison. Well, this time you'll see. I'll get along to the lab now. Put through any call that sounds important, and ring me if there's anything you're not sure of in that mail." At the door, he paused. "And," he added, "please, Miss Mallison, do try to remember that it's 'i' before 'e' except after 'c,' there's a dear."

It was only the last word that really registered with Miss Mallison.

"Yes, Mr. Alton," she said faintly, and blushed.

Miss Mallison studied the mirror in her bag-flap carefully. It was, without any self-deception, a pretty face that looked back at her. Heart-shaped, fitted out with nice hazel eyes, smooth at the corners, neat narrow brows, wide clear forehead, brown hair with red glints, a satisfactory nose, mouth not too small, pearly teeth, peachy complexion. There really didn't seem to be anything more one could do with it. The main trouble seemed to be competition. Nowadays, what with modern science and things, there were so many pretty girls that everybody expected all girls to be pretty, and only started noticing them when they weren't; and there didn't seem to be anything practical one could do about that, either.

She sighed, and shut up her bag. In a businesslike way she fed paper into the machine, and typed the date. And then, somehow, she was thinking about Mr. Alton.

There were two or three keys in which it was possible to think of Mr. Alton: this was the one in which she grew warm with indignation at the world's lack of appreciation.

It was not that anyone denied that Mr. Alton was a brilliant young man. They admitted that he had clever ideas, something to give to the world. She had even heard him called a genius. The trouble was that the world didn't seem to want genius, or the things that it could give.

In the old days of Edison and people like that, Miss Mallison thought, it had all been so different. An inventor was welcomed and respected, almost a national hero—which was what Mr. Alton ought to be. Instead, people nowadays seemed to think he was just a nuisance who had to be paid for *not* inventing things.

First, and, Mr. Alton still said, most importantly, there had been his fluorescent paint. You just coated the ceiling which then glowed so brilliantly in the illumination from one ten-watt lamp that quite a big room could be adequately lit. All that had happened about it was that several people had got together and paid quite a lot of money to have the paint and its formula securely locked away.

Then there had been the project for impregnating seeds, and consequently the resulting crop, with synthetic flavors. Alarm at the thought of potatoes tasting of chocolate, turnips masquerading as pineapple, tapioca supplanting caviar, and worse horrors, had caused similar steps to be taken with that.

Even a simple product like plasticized silk had arrived before it was welcome.

The record over four years had certainly shown that lucrative opportunities for young men exist in the not-inventing business, and that they may even achieve a position of influence where the mere threat to invent will secure them a comfortable income, free from the nuisance of outlay on research and experiment. Nevertheless, an inventor is a creator, and no more than any other creative artist does he want to see his brainchildren refrigerated. Money, Miss Mallison appreciated, is nice, but it is not everything.

The last time it had happened—over the matter of a cheap, incombustible paper which had pleased neither the timber nor the insurance interests—the laboratory staff had all but walked out. Indeed, they might have done so had Mr. Alton himself not felt as frustrated and ready to walk out as any of the rest of them. There had been a discussion, terminating in the unanimous resolution that next time, come all the cartels of hell and the myrmidons of mammon in arms against them, there should be no surrender, no suppression, and, whatever it might be, they would give it to a world that should benefit from it.

And—well, thought Miss Mallison, here was next time; and here was she, feeling no better about it than when it had been last time. Admittedly, the region of cosmetics was not one of those where he had done battle before, but she saw no least reason why its methods should not be just the same as those of the others; in fact, she suspected that under the elegant packaging there might be even more wheedle, wangle, fiddle, and threat than in some others.

Learnt his lesson, he *said*. And ready to go off, just as he had the other times, like a lamb to the slaughter—well, not *quite* like, perhaps, because he always managed somehow to sell his surrenders for a very good price in the end—but he would be disappointed again, and they would all have a terrible week or two.

The thing was, really, that he had no one to back him up. He was the sort of man who really did need someone to look after him and see that——

But it was at this point that Miss Mallison's thoughts slipped from the key of warm indignation into one of the other keys in which she sometimes considered Mr. Alton, and into which it might be impertinent to follow them.

Some little time later she happened to notice the clock. She stared at it in disbelief, and then attacked her typewriter furiously. . . .

At twelve-thirty Mr. Alton reappeared. He signed the letters ready for him, and then got up to take his coat from the stand.

"Aren't you going to wish me luck, Miss Mallison?" he asked, as he put it on.

"Oh, yes. Yes, of course, Mr. Alton," she said.

"But that doesn't stop you looking as if you thought I oughtn't to be let out alone?" he observed.

He was close enough to Miss Mallison's thoughts to raise her color a little.

"Oh, no, Mr. Alton. It's only——"

"You can rest easy this time," he reassured her. "I'm upsetting no applecarts. All I'm doing is to say: 'Put one drop of this in each bottle, and you'll outsell all your competitors.'" He drew a small vial of colorless liquid from his pocket, and held it up for her to see. "You can't tell me *that* isn't done every day. They usually call it 'Ingredient X,' or something of the kind. Nothing revolutionary at all."

"Yes, Mr. Alton," said Miss Mallison, trying to add conviction to her tone.

Mr. Alton restored the bottle to his waistcoat pocket. In doing so, his fingers encountered something else there. He drew out an envelope.

"Oh, Lord, I'd better not carry that about so casually. It's the formula. Put it away in the safe for me, will you?" he said, laying it on her desk.

"Yes, Mr. Alton," she said, watching him reach for his hat—he ought to have a new hat instead of that old thing. "And I—I *do* wish you the very best of luck. I do, really."

He regarded her gravely.

"I'm sure you do, Miss Mallison—and thank you very much. I'll be back before you leave," he added, and then the door closed behind him.

Miss Mallison went on sitting for some seconds with her eyes on the door. Then, as she dropped them, she caught sight of the envelope he had left lying on the desk. Written clearly on it were the words:

PERFUME IMPROVER:
Formula 68 (Adopted)

She pondered them idly . . . then interestedly . . . then intently. . . . For some minutes she sat perfectly still, deep in thought. Then she came to a decision.

She slipped the envelope under her blotting paper, rose purposefully, and made her way to the laboratory.

She found Mr. Dirks in there alone. All the others had apparently gone to lunch. He paused, test tube tilted in his hand, at the sight of her.

"Why, Miss Mallison!" he said. "Now, how did you know? Not

another soul in sight, and won't be for an hour or so yet. Miss Mallison, often in my dreams——"

Miss Mallison told him severely that that would be enough of that. "What I've come for," she said, "is the stock of the Formula 68 stuff. Mr. Alton says it's got to be locked up in the safe."

"And very wise, too," agreed Mr. Dirks. He placed his test tube in a rack, and stepped back. He ran his eye along a shelf, and paused when he came to one of the large bottles that the lab people called winchesters. This winchester had a sixty-eight penciled on its label, and was nearly full. He reached it down and handed it to her.

"Be careful now," he advised. "I know it looks like mere gin; but it's far more dangerous, and much more expensive."

"Thank you, Mr. Dirks," she said, politely.

"Not at all, Miss Mallison. A pleasure to see you here. How often have I said to myself: 'Now if only Miss Mallison were a chemist instead of a secretary——'"

"Now, please, Mr. Dirks——"

"Ah, well!" sighed Mr. Dirks sadly, and picked up his test tube.

Back in the office. Miss Mallison set the winchester on her desk and regarded it thoughtfully. She pulled the envelope from under the blotting paper, hesitated over it a moment, then decisively tore it open. The single slip of paper that was inside bore a line of letters and figures which conveyed nothing whatever to her. Once more she hesitated, then she laid it in the ashtray. It burnt much more quickly than a boat would, but the principle was the same.

She emptied the ashtray neatly into the wastepaper basket and reached her mackintosh off its hook. Presently, with the mackintosh bulging somewhat oddly from the presence of the big bottle beneath it, she took herself out for her lunch hour.

———

Mr. Grosburger was undoubtedly more widely known under his professional name of Diana Marmion, for it was in this guise that he ran the ubiquitous line of "*Sweet* 16" preparations. He was not one of the loudest noises in his profession, but, by and large, he had done very comfortably by concentrating on the pure-fragrance-of-dainty-youth angle which is less crowded than the enticement-of-dangerous-glamour side.

The nicety of gradation within the profession was unknown to Michael Alton, and since this ignorance extended even to the distinctions between scents, perfumes, and parfums, it was not surprising that, back in Mr. Grosburger's office after a good lunch, he should get away on the wrong foot. He led off with a well-considered but, in the circumstances, inappropriate piece about irresistibility, exoticism, ecstasy, captivation, passion, and points slightly west.

Mr. Grosburger explained a little shortly that his interest—his professional interest, that was—lay rather in charm, freshness, radiance, innocence, and dew.

Once launched, Michael was not easily stalled. He had planned his approach, and he continued to plan, impercipient of the width of the gulf yawning between them.

After a while Mr. Grosburger checked him with a raised hand.

"Listen, young man," he said. "The type of customer who comes to me is looking for delicacy, not delinquency—you'd better try one of the French firms."

A shadow of disappointment fell over Michael. He pointed out that he was offering the chance of a lifetime.

Mr. Grosburger was unimpressed. He was accustomed to sniffing a score of times a day at little bottles, each of which professed to contain the chance of a lifetime. Nevertheless, he would not have it thought that he was one who would throw away a chance blindly. Besides, there might be some commission arrangement.

"Just what is it you have?" he ventured, cautiously. "Possibly I could advise——"

Michael took the small vial out of his pocket. He stood it on Mr. Grosburger's desk and regarded its colorless innocence with the beam of a proud father. Mr. Grosburger picked it up, withdrew the stopper, and sniffed at the glass rod attached to it. He frowned. He looked at it hard, and sniffed again. Then he looked at Michael equally hard.

"Is this some kind of joke, young man?" he inquired.

Michael reassured him. It was not, he explained, a scent in itself. It was a new factor; a fresh element to be added to the ancient art of perfumery. For its proper activation it required the right conditions, just as, you might say, a fine brandy needs warmth. Mr. Grosburger listened, mingling the skepticism of experience with appreciation of a new angle in salesmanship.

"—And, well, just let me have a bottle of one of your scents—any kind will do," Michael finished.

"H'm," said Mr. Grosburger, reservedly, but from a drawer he produced a bottle of "*Sweet* 16" *Dawn Petals*, and handed it across. He watched while Michael carefully added to it a single drop of his essence, recorked the bottle, and shook it.

"Now, if you wouldn't mind asking your secretary to come in for a moment?" he suggested.

Mr. Grosburger flipped a switch, and requested the presence of Miss Boyle. He observed with curiosity that his visitor was thrusting cotton wool into his nostrils. Michael explained, through a thick cold in the head, that his work on the essence had left him a trifle oversensitive to it.

Almost the first thing one noticed about Miss Boyle was that nature had treated her with some hostility, but, since the alternative for any secretary to Mr. Grosburger was to incur the even fiercer hostility of Mrs. Grosburger, he had learned to look upon her with resignation. Michael smiled at her, and received a kind of nervous spasm of the mouth in return. With a bashful wriggle she consented to try a sample of the scent on her handkerchief. He poured a drop or two onto it, and then handed it back to her. She put it to her nose and inhaled.

"Why, it's just like our *Dawn Petals*," she said, flourishing the handkerchief, and sending a waft of its perfume across the room. I thought it was going to be———" She broke off, suddenly aware of the strange expression on her employer's face. "Oh, Mr. Grosburger, what on earth's the matter?"

Her surprise was understandable. Mr. Grosburger had the appearance of a man wrestling with his spirit, no holds barred. He choked. When he spoke, it was with difficulty.

"Miss Boyle!" he said hoarsely. "Hermione! Oh, how blind I've been! Can you ever forgive me?"

Miss Boyle blenched and withdrew a step.

"Wh—why, Mr. Grosburger!" she said, uncertainly.

"No!" said Mr. Grosburger. "Not that anymore. Call me Solly, Hermione, *your* Solly. Oh, Hermione, how can I have been so blind! How could I have failed to see that paradise was just beside me? Why did I not know before that you, my sweet Hermione, you are the center, the whole meaning of my life? Come to me, Hermione! Come!"

"Really, Mr. Grosburger!" said Miss Boyle, nervously.

"I could not help my blindness—you must not be cruel, Hermione. Coldness from you would twist like a knife in my heart." Mr. Grosburger stood up. He advanced, his arms spread wide.

Miss Boyle, with plaintive protests, edged tactically round a table.

"Coy!" exclaimed Mr. Grosburger. "This is no time for coyness. This is your moment of triumph. Let your torrid, sultry fires leap in ecstasy. Let your———"

"Help!" bleated Miss Boyle, dodging round the table. "Keep him off! Help!"

Michael felt that perhaps the time had come when he should break a sachet of ammonia under Mr. Grosburger's nose. He did so. Miss Boyle seized her opportunity, and broke away briskly for the outer office. A minute or so went by before the perfumer became coherent, then:

"Good gracious!" he muttered, mopping his forehead. "What an experience! And Miss Boyle, too! Good heavens!"

Michael removed his protective cotton wool. He apologized for the somewhat high concentration. One drop to a pint had been his estimate of a reasonable safety factor, he explained. It had been rather a small bottle of *Dawn Petals,* but Mr. Grosburger would get the general idea. Mr. Grosburger said yes, he had got the general idea. He had, and, as he gradually recovered, business instinct rolled uppermost. He was not the man to neglect the chance of a lifetime when one really did show up—and this was *it.* The full-page ads come to life; the thing that all the really big boys in the game would give their ears for. To hell with *Dawn Petals, Spring Zephyrs,* and *Englysshe Mayde.* . . .

A vision rose before him, a scene of Homeric debacle where the fragrant towers in the scented empires of Doty, Orden, Helenstein, Charbon, Cordley, Yarday, Mactor, Value, Munhill, and the rest swayed, reeled, and collapsed, leaving Diana Marmion standing alone, magnificently supreme.

"We must put it," he said, dreamily, "in a kind of sultry perfume—something that smolders. Maybe we could get Steuben to design a special flask for it. It is fame and fortune, young man: it is genius!" Then he frowned. "Of course, there'll be marketing problems. And a name for it. We must have a name for it— Ah! I've got it—*Séduction.*"

"Wouldn't that be a bit—well, er——?" Michael suggested.

"Not at all. Perfectly all right—as long as you insist on the accent and pronounce it Frenchly. I know this business, young man, you can leave all that side of it to me. Now, tell me, is it possible to make this stuff in a dry form so that we can put it into face powder, too?"

They got down to business. Once Mr. Grosburger started, he moved.

An hour later a well-satisfied Michael Alton parted temporarily from an elated Mr. Grosburger. Passing through the outer office he turned a benevolent beam on his involuntary assistant, Miss Boyle, while remembering to hold his breath in her vicinity. Miss Boyle, however, failed to notice him: she was having an exacting, but not unenjoyable time controlling the several young men who surrounded her in a sappy cluster of devotion.

—

The exuberant mood was still lasting when Michael reached his own office. It irked him a little that Miss Mallison did not look up eagerly for news, but continued furiously to type. He threw his hat at the hatstand.

"Hey!" he said. "Take notice, there! I've done it. No buying-up. No vested interest is going to suppress this one. The stuff is going to be *used*—and, boy, is it going to be used! What's more, we shall be moving into the big money. How about that, Miss Mallison?"

Miss Mallison looked up uncertainly.

"Oh, I—I'm so glad, Mr. Alton," she said.

He paused. "You don't *look* all that glad, you know. What's wrong?"

"N-nothing, Mr. Alton. I'm just glad you're glad, I think."

He came closer. "But one doesn't start to cry because——" He paused again. "That's a nice scent you're wearing. What is it?"

Miss Mallison dabbed her handkerchief at her nose.

"I th-think it's c-called *D-Dawn P-Petals*," she said, in a small voice. "I——" She broke off. There was a look in Mr. Alton's eye that she had never seen there before. "Oh——!" she said, tremulously.

Michael Alton continued to stare at her. Her eyes shone back at him. In fact, in some inexplicable way she seemed to be shining all over. He had never seen her, or anyone else, look quite like that before. It was an overwhelming sort of discovery. He reached out for her hands, and pulled her to her feet.

"Oh, Miss Mallison! Jill, darling! How can I have been so blind? Oh, my dear, my beautiful Jill. . . ."

"Huh!" gasped Miss Mallison involuntarily.

. . . Of course, it was going to take an awful lot of explaining later on. But there ought to be enough in that big bottle to last just a single user more than her lifetime.

So, for the present; and, very likely, for the future:

"Oh, darling, *darling* Mr. Alton . . ." said Miss Mallison.

MORE SPINNED AGAINST

One of the things about her husband that displeased Lydia Charters more as the years went by was the shape of him: another was his hobby. There were other displeasures, of course, but it was these in particular that rankled her with a sense of failure.

True, he had been much the same shape when she had married him, but she had looked for improvement. She had envisioned the development, under her domestic influence, of a more handsome, suaver, better-filled type. Yet, after nearly twelve years of her care and feeding there was scarcely any demonstrable improvement. The torso, the main man, looked a little more solid, and the scales endorsed that it was so, but, unfortunately, this simply seemed to have the result of emphasizing the knobbly, gangling, loosely hinged effect of the rest.

Once, in a mood of more than usual dissatisfaction, Lydia had taken a pair of his trousers, and measured them carefully. Inert, and empty, they seemed all right—long in the leg, naturally, but not abnormally so, and the usual width that people wore—but, put to use, they immediately achieved the effect of being too narrow and full of knobs, just as his sleeves did. After the failure of several ideas to soften this appearance, she had realized that she would have to put up with it. Reluctantly, she had told herself: "Well, I suppose it can't be helped. It must be just one of those things—like horsey women getting to look more like horses, I mean," and thereby managed to dig at the hobby, as well.

Hobbies are convenient in the child, but irritant in the adult;

which is why women are careful never to have them, but simply to be interested in this or that. It is perfectly natural for a woman— and Lydia was a comely demonstration of the art of being one—to take an interest in semi-precious and, when she can afford them, precious stones: Edward's hobby, on the other hand, was not really natural to anyone.

Lydia had known about the hobby before they were married, of course. No one could know Edward for long without being aware of the way his eyes hopefully roved the corners of any room he chanced to be in, or how, when he was out of doors, his attention would be suddenly snatched away from any matter in hand by the sight of a pile of dead leaves, or a piece of loose bark. It had been irritating at times, but she had not allowed it to weigh too much with her, since it would naturally wither from neglect later. For Lydia held the not uncommon opinion that though, of course, a married man should spend a certain amount of his time assuring an income, beyond that there ought to be only one interest in life—from which it followed that the existence of any other must be slightly insulting to his wife, since everybody knows that a hobby is really just a form of sublimation.

The withering, however, had not taken place.

Disappointing as this was in itself, it would have been a lot more tolerable if Edward's hobby had been the collection of ob- jects of standing—say, old prints, or first editions, or oriental po- etry. That kind of thing could not only be displayed for envy, it had value; and the collector himself had status. But no one achieved the status of being more than a crank for having even a very extensive collection of spiders.

Even over butterflies or moths, Lydia felt without actually put- ting the matter to the test, one could perhaps have summoned up the appearance of some enthusiasm. There was a kind of nature's- living-jewel's line that one could take if they were nicely mounted. But for spiders—a lot of nasty, creepy-crawly, leggy horrors, all getting gradually more pallid in tubes of alcohol—she could find nothing to be said at all.

In the early days of their marriage Edward had tried to give her some of his own enthusiasm, and Lydia had listened as tactfully as possible to his explanations of the complicated lives, customs, and mating habits of spiders, most of which seemed either disgusting, or very short on morals, or frequently both, and to his expatiations on the beauties of coloration and marking which her eye lacked the affection to detect. Luckily, however, it had gradually become apparent from some of her comments and questions that Edward was not awakening the sympathetic understanding he had hoped for, and when the attempt lapsed Lydia had been able to retreat gratefully to her former viewpoint from which all spiders were undesirable, and the dead only slightly less horrible than the living.

Realizing that frontal opposition to spiders would be poor tactics, she had attempted a quiet and painless weaning. It had taken her two or three years to appreciate that this was not going to work; after that, the spiders had settled down to being one of those bits of the rough that the wise take with the smooth and leave unmentioned except on those occasions of extreme provocation when the whole catalogue of one's dissatisfactions is reviewed.

Lydia entered Edward's spider room about once a week, partly to tidy and dust it, and partly to enjoy detesting its inhabitants in a pleasantly masochistic fashion. This she could do on at least two levels. There was the kind of generalized satisfaction that anyone might feel in looking along the rows of test tubes that, at any rate, here were a whole lot of displeasing creepies that would creep no more. And then there was the more personal sense of compensation in the reflection that though they had to some extent succeeded in diverting a married man's attention from its only proper target, they had had to die to do it.

There was an astonishing number of test tubes ranged in the racks along the walls; so many that at one time she had hopefully inquired whether there could be many more kinds of spiders. His first answer of five hundred and sixty in the British Isles had been quite encouraging, but then he had gone on to speak of twenty thousand or so different kinds in the world, not to mention the allied orders, whatever they might be, in a way that was depressing.

There were other things in the room beside the test tubes: a shelf of reference books, a card index, a table holding his carefully hooded microscope. There was also a long bench against one wall supporting a variety of bottles, packets of slides, boxes of new test tubes, as well as a number of glass-topped boxes in which specimens were preserved for study alive before they went into the alcohol.

Lydia could never resist peeping into these condemned cells with a satisfaction which she would scarcely have cared to admit, or, indeed, even have felt in the case of other creatures, but somehow with spiders it just served them right for being spiders. As a rule there would be five or six of them in similar boxes, and it was with surprise one morning that she noticed a large bell jar ranged neatly in the line. After she had done the rest of the dusting, curiosity took her over to the bench. It should, of course, have been much easier to observe the occupant of the bell jar than those of the boxes, but in fact it was not because the inside, for fully two-thirds of its height, was obscured by web. A web so thickly woven as to hide the occupant entirely from the sides. It hung in folds, almost like a drapery, and on examining it more closely, Lydia was impressed by the ingenuity of the work; it looked surprisingly like a set of Nottingham-lace curtains—though reduced greatly in scale, of course, and perhaps not quite in the top flight of design. Lydia went closer to look over the top edge of the web, and down upon the occupant. "Good gracious!" she said.

The spider, squatting in the center of its web-screened circle, was quite the largest she had ever seen. She stared at it. She recalled that Edward had been in a state of some excitement the previous evening, but she had paid little attention except to tell him, as on several previous occasions, that she was much too busy to go and look at a horrible spider: she also recalled that he had been somewhat hurt about her lack of interest. Now, seeing the spider, she could understand that: she could even understand for once how it was possible to talk of a beautifully colored spider, for there could be no doubt at all that this specimen deserved a place in the nature's-living-jewels class.

The ground color was a pale green with a darker stippling, which faded away toward the underside. Down the center of the back ran a pattern of blue arrowheads, bright in the center and merging almost into the green at the points. At either side of the abdomen were bracket-shaped squiggles of scarlet. Touches of the same scarlet showed at the joints of the green legs, and there were small markings of it, too, on the upper part of what Edward resoundingly called the cephalothorax, but which Lydia thought of as the part where the legs were fastened on.

Lydia leaned closer. Strangely, the spider had not frozen into immobility in the usual spiderish manner. Its attention seemed to be wholly taken up by something held out between its front pair of legs, something that flashed as it moved. Lydia thought that the object was an aquamarine, cut and polished. As she moved her head to make sure, her shadow fell across the bell jar. The spider stopped twiddling the stone, and froze. Presently, a small, muffled voice said:

"Hullo! Who are you?" with a slight foreign accent.

Lydia looked round. The room was as empty as before.

"No. Here!" said the muffled voice.

She looked down again at the jar, and saw the spider pointing to itself with its number two leg on the right.

"My name," said the voice, sociably, "is Arachne. What's yours?"

"Er—Lydia," said Lydia, uncertainly.

"Oh, dear! Why?" asked the voice.

Lydia felt a trifle nettled. "What do you mean, why?" she asked.

"Well, as I recall it, Lydia was sent to hell as a punishment for doing very nasty things to her lover. I suppose you aren't given to———?"

"Certainly not," Lydia said, cutting her voice short.

"Oh," said the voice, doubtfully. "Still, they can't have given you the name for nothing. And, mind you, I never really blamed Lydia. Lovers, in my experience, usually deserve——" Lydia lost the rest as she looked around the room uncertainly.

"I don't understand," she said. "I mean, is it really——?"

"Oh, it's me, all right," said the spider. And to make sure, it indicated itself again, this time with the third leg on the left.

"But—but spiders can't——"

"Of course not. Not real spiders, but I'm Arachne—I told you that."

A hazy memory stirred at the back of Lydia's mind.

"You mean *the* Arachne?" she inquired.

"Did you ever hear of another?" the voice asked coldly.

"I mean, the one who annoyed Athene—though I can't remember just how?" said Lydia.

"Certainly. I was technically a spinster, and Athene was jealous and——"

"I should have thought it would be the other way—oh, I see, you mean you spun?"

"That's what I said. I was *the* best spinner and weaver, and when I won the all-Greece open competition and beat Athene she couldn't take it; she was furiously jealous and so she turned me into a spider. It's very unfair to let gods and goddesses go in for competitions at all, I always say. They're spitefully bad losers, and then they go telling lies about you to justify the bad-tempered things they do in revenge. You've probably heard it differently?" the voice added, on a slightly challenging note.

"No, I think it was pretty much like that," Lydia told her, tactfully. "You must have been a spider a very long time now," she added.

"Yes, I suppose so, but you give up counting after a bit." The voice paused, then it went on: "I say, would you mind taking this glass thing off? It's stuffy in here; besides, I shouldn't have to shout."

Lydia hesitated.

"I never interfere with anything in this room. My husband gets so annoyed if I do."

"Oh, you needn't be afraid I shall run away. I'll give you my word on that, if you like."

But Lydia was still doubtful.

"You're in a pretty desperate position, you know," she said, with an involuntary glance at the alcohol bottle.

"Not really," said the voice in a tone that suggested a shrug. "I've often been caught before. Something always turns up—it *has* to. That's one of the few advantages of having a really permanent curse on you. It makes it impossible for anything really fatal to happen."

Lydia looked round. The window was shut, the door, too, and the fireplace was blocked up.

"Well, perhaps for a few minutes, if you promise," she allowed.

She lifted the jar, and put it down to one side. As she did so the curtains of web trailed out, and tore.

"Never mind about them. Phew! That's better," said the voice, still small, but now quite clear and distinct.

The spider did not move. It still held the aquamarine catching the light and shining, between its front legs.

On a sudden thought, Lydia leaned down, and looked at the stone more closely. She was relieved to see that it was not one of her own.

"Pretty, isn't it?" said Arachne. "Not really my color, though. I rather kill it, I think. One of the emeralds would have been more suitable—even though they were smaller."

"Where did you get it?" Lydia asked.

"Oh, a house just near here. Next door but one, I think it was."

"Mrs. Ferris's—yes, of course, that would be one of hers."

"Possibly," agreed Arachne. "Anyway, it was in a cabinet with a lot of others, so I took it, and I was just coming through the hedge out of the garden, looking for a comfortable hole to enjoy it, when I got caught. It was the stone shining that made him see me. A funny sort of man, rather like a spider himself, if he had had more legs."

Lydia said, somewhat coldly:

"He was smarter than you were."

"H'm," said Arachne, noncommittally.

She laid the stone down, and started to move about, trailing several threads from her spinnerets. Lydia drew away a little. For a moment she watched Arachne who appeared to be engaged in a kind of doodling, then her eyes returned to the aquamarine.

"I have a little collection of stones myself. Not as good as Mrs. Ferris's, of course, but one or two nice ones amongst them," she remarked.

"Oh," said Arachne, absentminded as she worked out her pattern.

"I—I should rather like a nice aquamarine," said Lydia. "Suppose the door happened to have been left open just a little . . ."

"There!" said Arachne, with satisfaction. "Isn't that the prettiest doily you ever saw?"

She paused to admire her work.

Lydia looked at it, too. The pattern seemed to her to show a lack of subtlety, but she agreed tactfully. "It's delightful! Absolutely charming! I wish I could—I mean, I don't know how you do it."

"One has just a little talent, you know," said Arachne, with undeceiving modesty. "You were saying something?" she added.

Lydia repeated her remark.

"Not really worth my while," said Arachne. "I told you something *has* to happen, so why should I bother?"

She began to doodle again. Rapidly, though with a slightly abstracted air, she constructed another small lace mat suitable for the lower-income-bracket trade, and pondered over it for a moment. Presently she said:

"Of course, if it were to be *made* worth my while . . ."

"I couldn't afford very much——" began Lydia, with caution.

"Not money," said Arachne. "What on earth would I do with money? But I am a bit overdue for a holiday."

"Holiday?" Lydia repeated, blankly.

"There's a sort of alleviation clause," Arachne explained, "lots of good curses have them. It's often something like being uncursed by a prince's kiss—you know, something so improbable that it's a real outside chance, but gets the god a reputation for not being such a Shylock after all. Mine is that I'm allowed twenty-four hours holiday in the year—but I've scarcely ever had it." She paused, doodling an inch or two of lace edging. "You see," she added, "the difficult thing is to find someone willing to change places for twenty-four hours."

"Er—yes, I can see it would be," said Lydia, detachedly.

Arachne put out one foreleg and spun the aquamarine round so that it glittered.

"Someone willing to change places," she repeated.

"Well—er—I—er—I don't think——" Lydia tried.

"It's not at all difficult to get in and out of Mrs. Ferris's house—not when you're my size," Arachne observed.

Lydia looked at the aquamarine. It wasn't possible to stop having a mental picture of the other stones that were lying bedded on black velvet in Mrs. Ferris's cabinet.

"Suppose one got caught?" she suggested.

"One need not bother about that—except as an inconvenience. I should have to take over in twenty-four hours again, in any case," Arachne told her.

"Well—I don't know——" said Lydia, unwillingly.

Arachne spoke in a ruminative manner:

"I remember thinking how easy it would be to carry them out one by one, and hide them in a convenient hole," she said.

Lydia was never able to recall in detail the succeeding stages of the conversation, only that at some point where she was still intending to be tentative and hypothetical Arachne must have thought she was more definite. Anyway, one moment she was standing beside the bench, and the next, it seemed, she was on it, and the thing had happened.

She didn't really feel any different, either. Six eyes did not seem any more difficult to manage than two, though everything looked exceedingly large, and the opposite wall very far away. The eight legs seemed capable of managing themselves without getting tangled, too.

"How do you? Oh, I see," she said.

"Steady on," said a voice from above. "That's more than enough for a pair of curtains you've wasted there. Take it gently, now. Always keep the word 'dainty' in mind. Yes, that's much better— a little finer still. That's it. You'll soon get the idea. Now all you have to do is walk over the edge, and let yourself down on it."

"Er—yes," said Lydia, dubiously. The edge of the bench seemed a long way from the floor.

"Oh, there's just one thing," she said. "About men?"

"Men?" said Lydia.

"Well, male spiders. I mean, I don't want to come back and find that——"

"No, of course not," agreed Lydia. "I shall be pretty busy, I expect. And I don't—er—think I feel much interested in male spiders, as a matter of fact."

"Well, I don't know. There's this business of like calling to like."

"I think it sort of probably depends on how long you have been like," suggested Lydia.

"Good. Anyway, it's not very difficult. He'll only be about a sixteenth of your size, so you can easily brush him off. Or you can eat him, if you like."

"*Eat* him!" exclaimed Lydia. "Oh, yes, I remember my husband said something—— No, I think I'll just brush him off, as you said."

"Just as you like. There's one thing about spiders, they're much better arranged to the female advantage. You don't have to go on being cumbered up with a useless male just because. You simply find a new one when you want him. It simplifies things a lot, really."

"I suppose so," said Lydia. "Still, in only twenty-four hours——"

"Quite," said Arachne. "Well, I'll be off. I mustn't waste my holiday. You'll find you'll be quite all right once you get the hang of it. Goodbye till tomorrow." And she went out, leaving the door slightly ajar.

Lydia practiced her spinning a little more until she could be sure of keeping a fairly even thread. Then she went to the edge of the bench. After a slight hesitation she let herself over. It turned out to be quite easy, really.

Indeed, the whole thing turned out to be far easier than she had expected. She found her way to Mrs. Ferris's drawing-room, where the door of the cabinet had been carelessly left unlatched, and selected a nice fire opal. There was no difficulty in discovering a small hole on the roadside of the front bank in which the booty could be deposited for collection later. On the next trip she chose a small ruby; and the next time an excellently cut square zircon, and the operation settled down to an industrious routine which was interrupted by nothing more than the advances of a couple of male spiders who were easily bowled over with a flip of the front leg, and became discouraged.

By the late afternoon Lydia had accumulated quite a nice little hoard in the hole in the bank. She was in the act of adding a small topaz, and wondering whether she would make just one more trip, when a shadow fell across her. She froze quite still, looking up at a tall gangling form with knobbly joints, which really did look surprisingly spidery from that angle.

"Well, I'm damned," said Edward's voice, speaking to itself. "Another of them! Two in two days. Most extraordinary."

Then, before Lydia could make up her mind what to do, a sudden darkness descended over her, and presently she found herself being joggled along in a box.

A few minutes later she was under the bell jar that she had lifted off Arachne, with Edward bending over her, looking partly annoyed at finding that his specimen had escaped, and partly elated that he had recaptured it.

After that, there didn't seem to be much to do but doodle a few lace curtains for privacy, in the way Arachne had. It was a consoling thought that the stones were safely cached away, and that any time after the next twelve or thirteen hours she would be able to collect them at her leisure. . . .

———

No one came near the spider room during the evening. Lydia could distinguish various domestic sounds taking place in more or less their usual succession, and culminating in two pairs of footfalls ascending the stairs. And but for physical handicaps, she might have frowned slightly at this point. The ethics of the situation were somewhat obscure. Was Arachne really entitled . . . ? Oh, well, there was nothing one could do about it, anyway. . . .

Presently the sound of movement ceased, and the house settled down for the night.

She had half expected that Edward would look in to assure himself of her safety before he went to work in the morning. She remembered that he had done so in the case of other and far less spectacular spiders, and she was a trifle piqued that when at last the door did open, it was simply to admit Arachne. She noticed, also, that Arachne had not succeeded in doing her hair with just that touch that suited Lydia's face.

Arachne gave a little yawn, and came across to the bench.

"Hullo," she said, lifting the jar, "had an interesting time?"

"Not this part of it," Lydia said. "Yesterday was very satisfactory, though. I hope you enjoyed your holiday."

"Yes," said Arachne. "Yes, I had a nice time—though it did somehow seem less of a change than I'd hoped." She looked at the watch on her wrist. "Well, time's nearly up. If I don't get back, I'll have that Athene on my tail. You ready?"

"Certainly," said Lydia, feeling more than ready.

"Well, here we are again," said Arachne's small voice. She stretched her legs in pairs, starting at the front, and working astern. Then she doodled a capital "A" in a debased Gothic script to assure herself that her spinning faculties were unimpaired.

"You know," she said, "habit is a curious thing. I'm not sure that by now I'm not more comfortable like this, after all. Less inhibited, really."

She scuttered over to the side of the bench and let herself down, looking like a ball of brilliant feathers sinking to the floor. As she reached it, she unfolded her legs, and ran across to the open door. On the threshold she paused.

"Well, goodbye, and thanks a lot," she said. "I'm sorry about your husband. I'm afraid I rather forgot myself for the moment."

Then she scooted away down the passage as if she were a ball of colored wools blowing away in the draught.

"Goodbye," said Lydia, by no means sorry to see her go.

The intention of Arachne's parting remark was lost on her: in fact, she forgot it altogether until she discovered the collection of extraordinary knobbly bones that someone had recently put in the dustbin.

JIZZLE

The first thing that Ted Torby saw, when his reluctant eyelids had gathered enough strength to raise themselves, seemed to be a monkey, perched on the top of the cupboard, watching him. He sat bolt upright with a jerk that joggled Rosie awake and shook the whole trailer.

"Oh, God!" he said. It was a tone which held more of depressed realization than surprise.

He closed his eyes, and then looked again, hard. The monkey was still there, staring from round, dark eyes.

"What's the matter?" Rosie asked sleepily. Then she saw the direction of his gaze. "Oh, that! Serves you right."

"It's real?" said Ted.

"Of course it's real. And lie down. You've pulled all the bed-clothes off me."

Ted leaned back, keeping his eyes fixed warily on the monkey. Slowly, and hindered by a painful throbbing in his head, memories of the evening began to reassemble.

"I'd forgotten," he said.

"I don't wonder—seeing the way you came home," said Rosie, dispassionately. "I expect you've got a lovely head," she added, with a slightly sadistic shading.

Ted did not answer. He was remembering about the monkey.

"How much did you give for that?" asked Rosie, nodding at it.

"Couple o' quid," said Ted.

"Two pounds for *that*," she said with disgust. "And you call your customers mugs!"

Ted made no response. In point of fact, it had been ten pounds, but he did not feel equal to meeting the storm that the admission would arouse. And he'd beaten the man down from fifteen, so it was a bargain. A big Negro he was, speaking a nautical form of English heavily adulterated with some kind of French. He had made his brief entry into Ted's life while the latter was in the Gate and Goat soothing his hard-worked throat after the evening's toil. Ted had not been greatly interested. He had, in his time, refused to buy all manner of things in bars, from bootlaces to ferrets. But the Negro had been quietly persistent. Somehow he had got himself into the position of standing Ted a drink, and after that he had the advantage. Ted's protests that he had nothing to do with the circus proper, and that he was utterly indifferent to its fauna, save for such rats as occasionally ventured into the trailer, made no impression at all. The man's conviction that every person connected with the showground must have an encyclopedic knowledge of the whole brute creation was unshakable: all protestation was merely a form of sales-resistance. He had then proceeded to talk with such animation across several relays of drinks of the attainments and charming qualities of something he referred to as *ma petite Giselle* that Ted had found it necessary to remind himself from time to time that the subject had not shifted beneath their tongues, and it was still a monkey that was under discussion.

In a way, it was hard luck on the Negro that he should have chosen Ted for his approach, since Ted himself had been spending the earlier part of the evening in persuading the reluctant to part with half-crowns of known qualities in exchange for bottles of merely hypothetical virtue. But Ted was not mean-minded. He followed the technique with the attention of a connoisseur, and was prepared to concede that the Negro wasn't doing too badly, for an amateur. Nevertheless, it was scarcely to be expected that even the utmost perfervor and intensity could win more than his detached, and unprofitable, professional approval. Rosie's crack about mugs had more spite than substance. The matter should have ended there, with the Negro butting at the immovable. Indeed, there it would have ended had not the Negro added a new accomplishment to the list of his Giselle's remarkable qualities.

Ted had smiled. Sooner or later the amateur always overreaches himself. It was safe enough to say that the creature was clean, attractive, intelligent, for these qualities are conveniently relative. It was not dangerous even to say that it was "educated"— there being no public examination to set a standard of simian learning. But in making a definite claim which could be put to the test, the Negro's inexperience was laying him wide open to trouble. At that point Ted had agreed to go to see the prodigy. The concession was almost altruistic: he did not believe a word of it, but neither did he mean trouble. He was the man of experience showing the promising beginner the kind of trouble he *might* have landed himself in by a simple divergence from the debatable to the disprovable.

It had been quite a shock, therefore, to find that the monkey was fully up to specification.

Ted had watched it, first patronizingly, then incredulously, and finally with an excitement which it required all his skill in deadpanning to disguise. Casually he offered five pounds. The Negro asked the ludicrous sum of fifteen. Ted would willingly have given fifty had it been necessary. In the end they compromised on ten and a bottle of whisky that Ted had intended to take home. There had been one or two drinks from the bottle to clinch the deal. After that, nothing was very clear, but evidently he had got back somehow—and with the monkey.

"It's got fleas," said Rosie, wrinkling her nose.

"It's a female," said Ted. "And monkeys don't have fleas. They just do that."

"Well, if it isn't looking for fleas, what is it doing?"

"I read somewhere that it's something to do with perspiration— anyway, they all do it."

"I can't see that that's much better," said Rosie.

The monkey broke away from its interests for a moment, and looked seriously at both of them. Then it gave a kind of snickering noise.

"What's it do that for?" Rosie asked.

"How would I know? They just do."

Ted lay and contemplated the monkey for a while. It was predominantly light brown, shot with occasional silver. Its limbs and tail seemed curiously long for its body. From a black, wrinkled face in a round, low-browed head two large eyes, looking like black glass marbles with sorrowful depths, scrutinized first one and then the other with such directness that one almost expected it to produce some sign of opinion. However, it merely returned to its own interests with an indifference which was in itself vaguely offensive.

Rosie continued to regard it without favor.

"Where are you going to keep it? I'm not going to have it in here."

"Why not?" asked Ted. "She's quite clean."

"How do you know? You were tight when you bought it."

"I got tight *after* I'd bought her. And don't keep on calling her *it*. She's a her. You get annoyed with me when I call a baby it, and it's probably a lot more important to monkeys than it is to babies. And her name's Jizzle."

"Jizzle?" repeated Rosie.

"A French name," Ted explained.

Rosie remained unimpressed. "All the same, I don't hold with keeping her here. It's not decent."

Jizzle was at the moment in a complicated and unornamental attitude. She had disposed her right foot round her neck, and was absorbed in an intense study of the back of her right knee.

"She's no ordinary monkey—she's educated," said Ted.

"Educated she may be, but she's not refined. Look at her now."

"What——? Oh, well, monkeys, you know——" Ted said

vaguely. "But I'll show you how educated she is. Worth a fortune. You watch."

—

There could be no doubt whatever: one demonstration was enough to convince the most prejudiced that Jizzle was a gold mine.

"I wonder why he sold it—her?" said Rosie. "He could have made a fortune."

"I guess he just wasn't a showman—or a businessman," Ted added.

After breakfast he went out of the trailer and looked at his stand. It had an inscription across the front:

DR. STEVEN'S
PSYCHOLOGICAL STIMULATOR

About the rostrum boldly lettered posters asked:

IS HESITATION HINDERING YOUR CAREER?
IS YOUR MIND A FLIP-FLAP?

or stated:

A STEADY MIND IS A READY MIND
PLANNED THINKING PAYS
SNAP BEATS FLAP

and advised:

DIRECT YOUR OWN DESTINY
MOBILIZE MENTALLY AND MAKE MONEY
PLAN YOUR PROSPERITY

For the first time the array failed to please him. Also for the first time he was astonished to think of the number of half-crowns it had helped to draw in exchange for the Omnipotent Famous World-Unique Mental Tonic.

"May as well ditch this lot," he said. "We'll need a tent with benches and a stage."

Then he went back to the trailer, and turned Rosie out.

"I got to think," he explained. "I got to work out the patter and the publicity, and we'll get you a new dress for the act."

———

The tryout took place a couple of days later before a critical audience drawn from the profession. It included Joe Dindell, more widely known as El Magnifico of Magnifico and His Twenty Man-Eating Lions, Dolly Brag or Gipsy Clara, George Haythorpe from the Rifle Range, Pearl Verity (*née* Jedd), the Only Authentic Three-Legged Woman in the World, and a sprinkling of others from both the main and sideshows.

The tent was not as large as Ted would have liked, and incapable of seating more than sixty persons, but better things would come. Meanwhile, he made his appearance before the curtain and delivered the buildup as though he addressed the rising tiers in a super-cinema. It was in the approved style of superlative, and when it ended with the phrase: "—and now, Ladies and Gentlemen, I present to you the greatest—the unbelievable—the supreme wonder of the animal world—JIZZLE!" the applause had a quality of discriminating appreciation.

As Ted concluded he had moved to the left. Now, as the curtains drew away, he turned, left hand extended toward the center of the stage. Rosie, having hurriedly fixed the curtain, tripped a few steps on from the other side, stopped with her knees bent in a species of curtsy, projected charm at the audience, and extended her right hand to the center of the stage. Between them stood an easel bearing a large pad of white paper and beside it, on a square table with a red-fringed top, sat Jizzle. She was clad in a bright yellow dress, and a pillbox hat with a curled red feather: for the moment she had pulled the dress aside, and was searching beneath it with great application.

Both Ted's smile and Rosie's were property affairs which could have deceived no one. A few minutes earlier she had flatly and finally declined to wear the new dress he had designed for her.

"I don't care," she said. "I've told you I won't, and I won't. You can dress your beastly monkey how you like, but you won't make me dress like it. I'm surprised at you asking it. Whoever heard of a man dressing his wife like a monkey?"

It was in vain that Ted protested she had it the wrong way round. Rosie's mind was made up. She would appear in the costume in which she was accustomed to hand out bottles of the Psychological Stimulator, or not at all. To Ted's mind it pettily ruined his whole carefully planned effect. It was unfortunate that her brown hair was of much the same shade as the dominant color of Jizzle's fur, but merely a coincidence.

Ted, after a few more high commendations of his protégée, moved over to the easel and stood beside it, facing the house. Rosie advanced, shifted the table with Jizzle upon it in front of the easel, and handed something to the monkey. Almost before she was able to bob and beam and resume her place, Jizzle was on her feet with her left hand holding onto the side of the pad, her right hand drawing swiftly. An astonished muttering broke out among the spectators. Her technique would not have met with approval in art schools, and it gave a certain simian flavor, hitherto unnoticed in her subject by others, but the final likeness to Ted was indisputable. Sheer amazement made the applause a trifle slow in starting, but when it came it was wholehearted.

Ted tore off the sheet and moved away, graciously waving Rosie into his place. She took it with a smile that was resolutely fixed. Ted pinned his picture to the back of the stage while Jizzle drew again. Once more the likeness was remarkable, though perhaps the simian quality was a shade more to the fore. Ted felt that from the domestic angle it was possibly just as well after all that Rosie had not worn the dress. Even so, the audience's laugh put Rosie's professional expression to a test which it only just survived.

"Now, if any lady or gentleman in the audience——?" suggested Ted.

Joe Dindell was the first to oblige. Powerful and massive, he stalked on to the stage to take up one of his best El Magnifico poses beside the easel.

Ted continued to try out his patter while Jizzle drew. She needed no persuasion. The moment one sheet was torn off she started on the next as if the plain paper were an irresistible invitation to doodle between clients. Once or twice Ted let her finish, making it clear that she was able to repeat from memory as well as draw from direct observation. By the end of the show the stage was decorated with portraits of the whole of the small audience who were clustered round, wringing Ted's hand, predicting overwhelming success, and inspecting Jizzle as if they were even yet not quite convinced of what they had seen. The only person who held a little aloof in the celebration which followed was Rosie. She sat sipping her drink and speaking little. From time to time she turned a gloomy, speculative look on the self-occupied Jizzle.

——

Rosie found it difficult to be clear in her own mind whether she disliked Jizzle because she was unnatural, or because she was too natural. Both were, in her view, sound bases for distaste. Jizzle was abnormal, a freak, and it was natural to feel that way about a freak—except, of course, those like Pearl whom one knew well. On the other hand, certain franknesses which would have been unperturbing in a dog, became embarrassing when displayed by a creature, and particularly a female creature, which providence had privileged to be at least a kind of burlesque of the form divine. There was also Jizzle's attitude. It was true that monkeys often snickered: it was true that by the law of averages some of these snickers must be ill-timed—but still . . .

All the same, Jizzle became the third occupant of the trailer.

"She's going to be worth thousands of pounds to us—and that means she's worth thousands to others, too," Ted pointed out. "We can't risk having her pinched. And we can't risk her getting ill, either. Monkeys need warm places to live in." Which was all quite true; and so Jizzle stayed.

From the first performance of the act, there was not an instant's doubt of its success. Ted raised the admission from one shilling to one-and-six, and then to two shillings, and the price of a Jizzle "original" from half a crown to five shillings without any loss of patronage. He opened negotiations for a larger tent.

Rosie tolerated her position as handmaiden for just one week, and then struck. The audience laughed at each of Jizzle's drawings, but Rosie's sensitive ear detected a different note when they saw the portrait of her. It rankled.

"It—she makes me look more monkey-like every time. I believe she does it on purpose," she said. "I won't stand there and be made a fool of by a monkey."

"Darling, that's sheer imagination. All her drawing is a bit monkeyish—after all, it's only natural," Ted remonstrated.

"It's more so when it's me."

"Now, do be reasonable, darling. What would it matter anyway, even if it were so?"

"So you don't mind your wife being jeered at by a monkey?"

"But that's ridiculous, Rosie. You'll get used to her. She's a nice friendly little thing, really."

"She isn't, not to me. She keeps on watching and spying on me all the time."

"Come now, darling, hang it all——"

"I don't care what you say, she does. She just sits there watching and snickering. I suppose she's got to live in the trailer; I'll have to put up with that, but I've had enough of her in the act. You can do it without me. If you must have someone, get Ireen from the Hoop-La. *She* won't mind."

Ted was genuinely distressed, and more at the troubled state of the larger partnership than the breaking up of the act. It was indisputable that something had happened, and kept on happening, to it since Jizzle's arrival. It took the gilt off a lot of things. He and

Rosie had always got along so well together. He had wanted her to have more pleasures and comforts than the returns from Dr. Steven's Stimulator could provide; and now that the big chance had come, discord had arrived with it. No one acquiring such a valuable property as Jizzle could afford not to exploit her properly. Rosie was perfectly well aware of that—but, well, women got such queer fixed ideas. . . . Upon that, he had an idea himself. He made a discreet search to discover if Rosie had been sewing any small garments in secret—apparently she had not.

Business thrived. Ted's show was promoted to mention on the advance bills. Jizzle also thrived, and settled in. She took to Ted's left shoulder as her favorite perch, which was somehow slightly flattering, and also had publicity value, but domestically things went the other way. Little was to be seen of Rosie during the day. She seemed always to be helping, or drinking cups of tea, in some other caravan. If Ted had to go out on business he had to shut Jizzle up in the trailer alone when he felt that both her safety and well-being demanded someone to look after her. But his single suggestion that Rosie might act as guardian had met with so determined a rebuff that he did not like to repeat it. At night Rosie did her best to ignore Jizzle altogether; the monkey responded with sulky moods which broke on occasion into snickers. At such times Rosie would relinquish indifference, and glare at her angrily. She gave it as her opinion that even lions were more companionable creatures. But Rosie herself was far less companionable than before. Ted was aware of an uninterest and grudgingness in her that had never been there before, and he was puzzled: the money that now rolled in was by no means everything. . . .

Had he not been a reasonable, clear-thinking man, he might have begun to feel some resentment against Jizzle himself. . . .

———

The puzzle was to a great extent resolved on a night when Jizzle had already been an established success for six weeks. Ted came back to the trailer later than usual. He had had several drinks, but he was not drunk. He walked into the trailer with a sheet of paper rolled in his hand, and stood looking down at Rosie, who was already in bed.

"You——!" he said. He leaned over and smacked her face hard.

Rosie, startled out of a half sleep, was as much bewildered as hurt. Ted glared down at her.

"Now I understand quite a lot. Spying on you, you said. God, what a mug I've been! No wonder you didn't want her around."

"What are you talking about?" Rosie demanded, tears in her eyes.

"You know. I expect everyone knows but me."

"But, Ted——"

"You can save your breath. Look at this!"

He unrolled the sheet of paper before her. Rosie stared at it. It was surprising how much obscene suggestion could reside in a few simple lines.

"While I was doing the patter," Ted said. "All sniggering their bloody heads off before I saw what was happening. Damn funny, isn't it?" He looked down at the drawing. There could not be a moment's doubt for any who knew them that the woman and man involved were Rosie and El Magnifico. . . .

Rosie flushed to her hair. She jumped from the bed and made a vicious grab at the top of the cupboard. Jizzle evaded her skillfully.

Ted caught her arm and jerked her back.

"It's too late for that now," he said.

The flush had gone, leaving her face white.

"Ted," she said, "you don't believe . . . ?"

"Spying on you!" he repeated.

"But, Ted, I didn't mean . . ."

He slapped her again across the face.

Rosie caught her breath; her eyes narrowed.

"Damn you! *Damn you!*" she said, and went for him like a fury.

Ted reached one hand behind him and unlatched the door. He turned round with her, and thrust her outside. She stumbled down the three steps, tripped on the hem of her nightdress, and fell to the ground.

He slammed the door shut, and snapped the bolt.

Upon the cupboard Jizzle snickered. Ted threw a saucepan at her. She dodged it, and snickered again.

The next morning an air of concern spread outward from the office where the manager and the ringmaster were considering the problem of finding at short notice a man of presence and intrepid appearance to take charge of the lion act. Quite half the day passed before anyone but Ted knew that Rosie also was missing.

Ted went through the next few days with remorse, putting increasing pressure on righteous anger. He had not realized what Rosie's absence would mean. He had done, as he saw it, the only thing a man could do in the circumstances—but very bitterly was he aware of the craven wish that he had never learnt the circumstances.

Jizzle's confident predilection for his shoulder as a perch became a source of irritation. He took to pushing her off impatiently. But for the damned monkey he never need have known about Rosie. . . . He began to hate the sight of Jizzle. . . .

For a week he continued to give the show, mechanically, but with increasing distaste; then he approached George Haythorpe of the Rifle Range. George reckoned it could be done. Muriel, his wife, could easily manage the Range with a girl to help her; he himself was willing to take over Jizzle and run the act with Ted retaining a twenty percent interest in the gross.

"That is," George added, "if the monkey'll stand for it. She seems mighty attached to you."

For a day or two that appeared to be the most doubtful aspect of the arrangement. Jizzle continued to attach herself to Ted, and to watch him rather than George for instruction. But gradually, by patient and repeated removal, the change in mastery was made plain to her, whereupon she sulked for two days before deciding to accept it.

It was a relief to be free of Jizzle—but it did not bring back Rosie. The trailer seemed emptier than ever. . . . After a few days of morbid inactivity Ted took himself in hand. He pulled out his old stock, unrolled some of the old bills for the Psychological Stimulator, and lettered some new ones:

MODERNIZE YOUR MENTALITY
CONFIDENCE CREATES CASH
A KEEN MIND IS A KEY MIND

In a short while he was back at the old stand and the mugs were putting up their half-crowns with a will—but it still wasn't the same without Rosie handing out the bottles. . . .

Jizzle had now settled in well with George. The act was on its feet again and playing to capacity, but Ted felt no tinge of jealousy or regret as he watched the crowds going in. Even his share of the takings brought him little pleasure; they still linked him with Jizzle. He would have given them all up on the spot just to have Rosie beside him again as he shouted the merits of his elixir. He began to try to trace her, but without success. . . .

A month passed before a night on which Ted was awakened by a knock on the trailer door. His heart thumped. Even at that moment he had been dreaming of Rosie. He jumped out of bed to open the door.

But it was not Rosie. It was George, with Jizzle on his shoulder and one of the Range rifles in his hand.

"What——?" began Ted dazedly. He had been so sure it was Rosie.

"I'll show you what, you bastard," said George. "Just look at that!"

He brought forward his other hand with a sheet of paper in it.

Ted looked. Compromising would have been the severest understatement for the attitude in which George's wife, Muriel, was displayed with Ted.

He raised his horrified eyes. . . .

George was lifting the rifle. On his shoulder Jizzle snickered.

THE CURSE OF THE BURDENS

Chapter 1 · Shadow of the Curse

—

"Why talk about an allowance?" said James Burden coldly. "You know the state of affairs as well as I do. It is quite impossible for me to make you an allowance, Dick. I'm sorry, but we're up against facts."

His brother laughed. He was a good-looking young fellow of thirty, with a bronzed, clean-shaven face and merry gray eyes. But the wrinkles—the tiny wrinkles that only showed about the corners of his mouth when he laughed—spoke of something that had aged him beyond his years. That something had been the Great War, long past, but still written on the faces of thousands of young men. And behind the laughter in the eyes there was always a shadow—not of pain or grief, but of things remembered.

"The facts are these, old son," Dick replied. "You never expected to come into this property until you were an old man. You might never have inherited it at all, for our good cousin Robert was looking round for a wife when he fell into the sea and was drowned. This property was of the nature of a windfall."

"Yes, and rotten, like most windfalls," James said sourly. "It takes me all my time to get anything out of it. Ten thousand acres and a mortgage that swallows up all the rents! And this house thrown in—a white elephant that has to be kept, and eats its head off!"

"I'd like to go into the figures."

"Well, I'm afraid I can't oblige you" said James stiffly, "and you wouldn't understand them if I did. Father left us each two hundred and fifty a year. You can live on that and you can work."

"I've been trying to get work, old son—for three years I've done all I can think of. But no one wants me. I shall get hold of a job later on, but just now—well, I thought you could spare me a trifle—say another two-fifty."

James Burden, seated at a writing table in the library of Shotlander, smiled grimly. He was a dark-haired man of forty with a pale, handsome face. He was stouter than his younger brother, but there was no getting over the fact that they were both members of a very good-looking family. One could trace their resemblance to the portrait of their grandfather over the mantelpiece of the library. But whereas in Dick the face had been refined and hardened by a strenuous, active outdoor life, in the elder it had grown more soft and heavy and almost gross in its outlines.

"Two-fifty," said Dick, "until I get a job."

"Ridiculous! Why should you live in idleness on five hundred a year? Five pounds a week is quite enough for a young chap with no ties or responsibilities."

"I'm taking all that on, old chap. I'm thinking of getting married."

"Married? Oh, this is really too much of a good thing! I cannot afford to get married myself and you have the cheek to ask me to support your wife."

Dick Burden laughed pleasantly and lit a cigarette. He had been standing by the fire but now he strolled to the big writing table and seated himself on the edge of it.

"We're the last two," he said, "and we ought both to marry. You don't seem to like taking it on, but I've been thinking about it a good deal. We don't want to let that old monk get the best of us."

James Burden shrugged his shoulders. He did not say "What old monk?" or pretend that he did not know what his brother was talking about. Shotlander Priory had been given or sold to a certain Sir James Burden by Henry VIII at the dissolution of the monasteries. The old prior, crossing the worn threshold for the last time, had called down the curse of Heaven on those who were to take over the property of the church. "By fire and water," he had said, "your line shall perish." And they had seemed the foolish words of an old and dying man. For nearly four hundred years the descendants of Sir James Burden had held the property, though it had never passed from father to son.

"You see, old son," Dick continued, "we're the only two left now, and it looks as if our friend the prior had the best chance he's ever had of knocking us out. Robert was drowned, and that's getting rather near the point, isn't it? We may be drowned or burnt to death, so far as I can see. It'd be a pity for there to be none of us left."

"Do you think so?" said James dryly. "Well I'm not quite so sure about that. But look here, Dick, you can't get over me with all this rot about the race dying out and that sort of thing. You've fallen in love with a girl as silly as yourself and you want me to keep the two of you. If you asked me for two hundred and fifty pence a year I wouldn't give it to you. I'm sorry. If you want to get married soon you'd better find a girl with money or else rough it with the one you've got."

The words were harsh, but they were spoken quite gently. Dick Burden was not in the least offended. He regarded his brother as a "dry old stick"—very practical and full of wisdom.

"Letty wouldn't mind waiting," he replied, "and she wouldn't object to roughing it. But I'm not going to spoil her life for her."

"Letty, eh?" queried James Burden. "So that's her name."

"Yes—Letty Kingsbury."

James Burden's eyes narrowed to two slits. He placed his hand to his forehead as though he were trying to remember something. His face was like a white mask.

"You've met her," Dick went on, "at Easthill on Sea—at the boardinghouse; they call it a private hotel but I call it a boardinghouse. Don't you remember? We went down there last year. Robert was staying there when—at the time of the accident. A slim, dark-haired girl—father a retired Indian judge—old chap with brown face and white moustache. Surely you remember her?"

"Yes—I remember her," said James, speaking very slowly, and then, after a pause, "Has money I suppose?"

"None. Father's got a pension—that's all."

"H'm, yes. Sir Julius Kingsbury—I remember him. Hardly the sort of man to approve of this marriage, eh?"

"Oh, your memory is improving," laughed Dick.

"Yes. Sir Julius gave evidence at the inquest on poor Robert. Sir Julius, so far as is known, was the last person to see Robert alive."

"That's right."

James Burden leaned his elbows on the table and pressed the tips of his fingers together. His eyes were fixed on the portrait of "Buck" Burden, who had sold nearly everything he could dispose of to pay his gambling debts.

"On the whole," said James after a pause, "it's just as well that you can't afford to marry this girl."

"What d'you mean by that, eh?"

"The evidence the baronet gave at the inquest was very unsatisfactory—in my opinion. In fact, I may say that I have grave suspicions that Sir Julius pushed Robert over the edge of the cliff."

"Look here," Dick said heatedly, "I won't have you talking rot, Jim. You're crazy—that's what it is. Your health's bad and your brain's affected."

"You evidently thought so if you expected me to allow you two hundred and fifty a year." He paused and looked at his watch. "If you start for the station now you'll just have time to do it quietly—without hurrying."

"I'm not going to leave this house or this room until you explain your infamous suggestion."

"I'm going to explain nothing, Dick. You've just said I'm crazy, and mad men say things they cannot possibly explain."

"You're not mad. For some reason or another you want to prevent this marriage."

"Lack of money will do that," James Burton said. "It will not be necessary for me to interfere. You'll miss your train, Dick, if you don't look sharp."

"By Jove," Dick muttered. "If your heart weren't dicky, I'd knock the truth out of you."

"There's nothing to knock out," James sneered. "But I'll tell you this: I mean to get at the truth, and I'm going down to Easthill-on-Sea in a few days' time. And I shall stay at the Warlock Hotel."

"Oh, you're a fool! I've no patience with you."

"Perhaps not. And I doubt if you'll have any patience with the police either."

"You don't mean to tell me that the police——"

"I don't mean to tell you anything more. You can warn Sir Julius if you like. He won't bring an action for libel against me; I can promise you that. I know nothing, but I intend to learn everything."

"This is too funny," Dick laughed. "Why you are the only person who has benefitted by Robert's death."

"Think that if you like. But if anything were to happen to me— and it might happen before a week is over—you would inherit a white elephant and the money that's not enough to keep it in food."

"Oh, I see. You think Sir Julius is going to commit murder wholesale in order to provide his daughter with an eligible husband? Upon my word, Jim, the theory of the curse is dreary common sense compared to this. I'm sorry for you, old chap. I hope you'll be better in the morning. I can catch that train if I run all the way to the station. Good night."

James Burden made no reply, but when he was alone—when the door had closed and he was alone with the portrait of the family spendthrift—the white mask seemed to fall away from his face, and his dull eyes glowed with fire.

His white, rather puffy hands moved toward each other on the table, and he clasped them together with such force that when he drew them apart again, the flesh of his fingers was red and indented.

He looked out of the window and saw his brother running down the drive. Then he thrust his hand into his pocket, and taking out a portrait of a very beautiful young woman, gazed at it with hungry eyes.

It was a photograph of Letty, the only child of Sir Julius Kingsbury.

Chapter II · Love's Enemies

—

In late spring, in the summer, in early autumn there was about as much privacy on the pier at Easthill-on-Sea as one would hope to find in Piccadilly Circus. The band played at the end of it, and there was a concert hall and sideshows and penny-in-the-slot machines of extraordinary variety and fascination.

In the winter, however, when the sea was gray, and either sullen or angry, and the sou'westerly gales blew, and the rain came down in torrents, the pier was deserted by all the residents except the untiring anglers, and it was a place where lovers might meet with as little fear of interruption as in a country lane. And there were innumerable shelters from the wind and rain—shelters of glass and wood, facing all ways, so that one could find protection from every wind that blew.

In one of these shelters Dick Burden stood with his back to the sea. In a corner of the seat that faced him sat Letty Kingsbury, her knees crossed and her gloved hands clasped round them. She was wearing a thick ulster of thick brown fleecy material and a neat little hat. She had the pale olive skin of girls who have lived the best part of their lives in India and the red healthy cheeks of a young woman who has recently spent two years by the sea and put in a good deal of her time out of doors. She was radiantly and splendidly beautiful.

And her dark beauty, almost of an Eastern type, was allied with the strength and vigor and vitality of the English "sporting girl." It was said of her that her life in India had "done her no harm." It might have been more truly said that it had given her something that a life spent entirely in England could never have given.

"It comes to this, Dick," she was saying, "we've got to wait."

"Yes, old girl—of course—of course. We couldn't rub along on two hundred and fifty a year, could we?"

"Oh yes, we could! But you know it isn't that. My father won't hear of our marriage. He has even forbidden me to see you or write to you."

"But you've disobeyed him, eh?"

"Yes—for this once."

"Does that mean you're going to give in to him?"

"I don't know."

"How do you mean, Letty? You don't know?"

"Oh, well," she laughed, "Father has thrown himself on my mercy."

"He put it like that, did he?"

"Yes—just like that. Dick, I'm very worried about my father. Up to a week ago he was just—well he was the ordinary prudent father who doesn't want his daughter to make an imprudent marriage. And then—Dick, I suppose you won't believe me when I tell you he really did implore me to have nothing more to do with you. He didn't command or threaten me. He just—well, he seemed to break down altogether. And he is not that sort of man."

"No, by Jove, he isn't. And he gave you no reason—except that I'm very ineligible?"

"He gave no reason at all. He did not talk about money."

"Just thinks I'm a rotter, eh?"

"Don't be absurd, Dick. You know quite well that Father likes you." Dick Burden asked no more questions. He fancied he knew what had happened. He had his brother to thank for this. James had by some means or other acquired a hold over Sir Julius Kingsbury. It was, of course, ridiculous to suppose that Sir Julius had murdered Robert Burden. But the baronet might have been the victim of very strong circumstantial evidence—known as yet only to one man, but quite sufficient to justify the police in making an arrest. A rather eminent retired judge like Sir Julius might shrink from anything of the nature of a public scandal. Innocent, and yet perhaps unable to prove his guiltlessness, he would be inclined to give way, not to actual blackmail but to strong persuasion.

It was a very awkward situation, for Dick could not take Letty into his confidence. It was quite impossible for him to tell her of his brother's suspicions. Could any young man say to the woman he loved, "My dear old girl, I think I can explain this. My brother told me a fortnight ago that your father," etc., etc.? It would have been not only ridiculous, but the end of everything between them. It would be suicide, and a most contemptible form of suicide. Jim would have to be fought with other weapons than freedom of speech.

Later on he might have to be kicked. But for the present he must be treated as the honest head of an old family, who wished to save his brother from an unfortunate marriage.

"You are very silent," said Letty after a long pause. "Are you weighing your own merits and deciding whether I spoke the truth when I said that Father liked you?"

"No, old girl. I was only wondering what kind of bee he has got in his bonnet and how we can catch it. Put a little salt on its tail, I suppose."

"Don't talk rot, Dick. I'm pretty cheerful as a rule, but this beats me altogether. We're up against something terribly serious, Dick. I am very worried about my father. He went up to London about a fortnight ago, and ever since then he seems to have changed—to have got so much older and more feeble. The other day he burst into tears, and about nothing at all, as far as I could see."

"I expect he's ill. Perhaps he went up to town to see a doctor. But look here, Letty, you're not going to give way to him—about me I mean?"

"Yes, openly I am. You must not come to the hotel. I'll meet you there as often as I can. He generally sleeps after lunch, as you know. And I—oh, well, Dick, I'm supposed to be playing golf."

"I don't like this hole-and-corner sort of business, Letty."

"Nor do I, dear. But—well, it would be different if Father were quite himself. And—oh, it's either this or nothing."

The young man flung himself on the seat beside her and put his arm round her neck. Only the gray sea and the gray sky were looking when he drew her closer to him and kissed her passionately. Just these and the yellow, impassive back of a fisherman, clad in oilskins, who was standing twenty yards away from them. The stranger had been there all the time, forever flinging his weighted line far out into the water and never turning his head. He could not possibly have heard a word of their conversation above the noise of the wind and the rain, for he was on the far side of another shelter and was only to be seen through the glass of it.

"I don't see who's going to get the better of us," whispered Dick, "it's just a question of waiting. I'll soon get a job, old girl, and then——" He kissed her again and again, and she suddenly cried out:

"Oh, Dick, that man is looking at us."

He let go of her and laughed. The disciple of Izaak Walton was no longer gazing at them, but he was standing with his face toward them and was taking a flashing, wriggling fish off the hook.

"The first he's caught," said Letty. "How awkward he should have just landed it at that moment!"

"Dick Burden made no reply. He was fascinated by the extraordinary ugliness of the man's face—by the size of it, the thickness of the lips, the thin straightness of the nose, by the small eyes set so far apart that they seemed to be on the very edges of the cheekbones.

And, above all, Dick Burden's attention was not only caught but held by the ridiculous idea that this hideous face was a caricature of his own—a gross and horrible caricature of the Burden type of face.

There were the full lips, and the thin nose, and the eyes set wide apart, but each feature was so exaggerated that it had become a monstrosity.

"A nice-looking chap, eh?" said Dick. "Enough to frighten all the fish out of the sea."

The man turned and flung his re-baited hook into the water again. Far and straight the lead swung through the air for over a hundred feet.

"Some cast, that, eh?" laughed Dick. "I should say he's a pretty hefty fellow. Does he remind you of anyone, Letty?"

"I'm glad to say he doesn't. I don't think I've ever seen a more repulsive face. She rose to her feet and picked up a bag of golf clubs which stood in the corner. "I must be getting along, Dick."

"I'll walk back with you."

"Oh no, you won't! You'll stay here and give me at least ten minutes' start. I'm not taking any chances. Goodbye, you dear."

"Tomorrow—here—the same time?"

"Yes, yes, Dick."

She darted out of the shelter and vanished from his sight. He sat down and lit a cigarette. He had been happy enough so long as Letty was with him, but now, left alone with his thoughts, a hard look came into his eyes.

"What's Jim driving at?" he kept saying to himself. Well, it would be best to ask his brother that question. Very likely he would deny that he had had an interview with Sir Julius Kingsbury and that he had interfered with their love affair. Well, then, he, Dick Burden, would have to see Sir Julius himself. He wanted to avoid that if possible. But somehow or other he would have to get at the truth.

He smoked his cigarette until the hot ash was close to his lips, flung the end out into the rain, and rose to his feet.

He was buttoning up the collar of his overcoat when he heard the sound of hurried footsteps on the planking of the pier, and his brother suddenly came in sight.

"Hallo!" said Dick. "What are you doing here?"

"I've come to have a talk with you. I thought I should find you here. I've just seen Miss Kingsbury."

"Indeed. And she told you I was here?"

"Oh no, she did not stop to speak to me. But she was just coming out through the turnstile—with her golf clubs, and I rather fancied I should discover you here. I'm sorry you have taken no notice of what I told you."

"We may as well have it out," Dick laughed unpleasantly. "I don't care a hang for your opinions, but apparently Sir Julius does. I suppose I have to thank you for setting him against me."

"Most certainly you have to thank me, Dick. I want to save you from this unfortunate entanglement, and I had to speak very plainly to Sir Julius."

"So I imagined. This crazy idea about Robert, eh?"

"Sir Julius would hardly have listened to my suggestion," James retorted, "if there had been no force in my arguments. There was no scene. The baronet is a very reasonable man."

"Oh, is he? Well, I'm not, Jim. You're a liar—no, worse than that—you're a cunning rogue."

"Steadily Dick, steadily. I can't have you talking to me like that."

"And I'll tell you this," Dick continued. "I only hope there is something in that moth-eaten curse. It's about time the family came to an end if you're the head of it."

"I wouldn't speak so loudly if I were you," James Burden smiled. "There's a man fishing on the other side of that shelter."

And at that moment, as though the fellow heard the remark, he turned and gazed at them—only for a few seconds and then he faced the sea again.

"You might get to look like that," said Dick, "if you live long enough. But I hope you won't, Jim."

"Waiting for dead men's shoes, eh?"

The two men stared at each other. Dick's face was as white as his brother's. Then, with a fiery smolder of hate, the red light began to burn in their eyes.

Chapter III · The Blow Falls

—

There was mutual venom in the brothers' eyes, but whereas in Dick's heart was the swift flame of anger and indignation, the hatred in that of the elder man was calm and steady and undying. They turned away from each other as though the tension were unbearable—as though they could only escape from a scene of physical violence by going their several ways.

Dick strode down the pier in the rain and James walked slowly in the opposite direction until he came to the rail by the landing-stage. Then he stood still, gripping the iron bar with both hands and staring out at the sea.

Two hours in the stuffy gloom of a cinema put Dick Burden in a better temper. When he left the place he had tea at a small café, and then he went for a long walk in the darkness. He wanted exercise, and he had no desire to return to his mean and lonely lodgings until the evening meal.

The rain had ceased, but the wind was still blowing half a gale as he climbed the long, sloping road that led out of the town to the summit of the cliffs. Walking to windward, Dick Burden got all the exercise he needed in an hour. When at last he paused from sheer exhaustion he seemed no longer to feel any bitterness against his brother.

It was possible, after all, that James had really been actuated by a desire to do the best he could for him. Dick remembered that he had first regarded the situation in this more kindly light when Letty had told him about her father. He had most certainly suspected his brother of nothing worse than meddling interference—of an honest wish to save the family from being drawn into an ugly scandal. It was not until he had found himself face-to-face with James, and sharp words had passed between them, that rage and hatred had got the better of Dick. And now they seemed to have vanished.

As he stood there in the windswept darkness, looking back at the lights of the town, he was just a little bit ashamed of himself. Jim had answered him softly until there was no longer any chance of turning away wrath. And then—well, it was not so much what his brother had said—though the remark about waiting for dead men's shoes had been turned away, he would have struck his brother—had struck Jim—an invalid. It was not pleasant to think of that.

But now even the terrible glare of hatred had become something vague and uncertain.

The stars shining in a clear sky, the smell of the rain-soaked earth, the sense of great and lonely spaces, the wind—yes, above everything that clean, wonderful wind—seemed to set him apart from the ugly things of this world.

"Old Jim will soon drop all this nonsense," Dick said to himself. And as he strode down the hill toward the town again he thought of Jim as something rather foolish that did not matter at all, and of Sir Julius Kingsbury as a crotchety old man whose brain was out of order. He saw himself as the kind of chap who could knock down all obstacles or climb over them. Never before in all his life had he felt so strong and capable and self-reliant. And Letty was just such another as himself. The two of them together would be quite invincible. He was sure of that.

Even the dismal sitting room of his lodgings had no power to depress his spirits, and the meal, ill-cooked, ill-served and half-cold, was eaten with contentment. When he had finished, Dick poked the fire into a blaze, lit his pipe, and took off his boots. The rain was coming down in torrents, and even the hideously furnished room seemed snug and warm.

Dick Burden stretched himself lazily in a dilapidated but comfortable armchair. He began to think of Letty Kingsbury, and in a quarter of an hour he was most unromantically asleep.

He awoke with a start as something touched his face—awoke and perceived what seemed like a gigantic hand close to his eyes. He sprang to his feet and saw that it was Letty who had touched him. They were alone in the room together. He glanced at the clock and noticed that it was half past ten. And then he laughed foolishly.

"Letty, is this a dream?" he said, and then, as he saw her eyes and the whiteness of her face, he felt as though someone had flung a bucket of cold water over him.

Something had happened—something terrible. Dick Burden felt certain. Letty stood there before him—unable for a moment to speak, trying no doubt to pick the words that would give utterance to that which was in her mind.

And he knew what it was that had happened. It was not that he had feared this tragedy, but simply that he knew—that the knowledge had come to him during those few seconds of silence.

His dream may have had something to do with it, for he had been dreaming of his brother.

"Jim?" prompted Dick at last.

"Yes, dear," she answered, so faintly that he could scarcely hear the words.

"An accident, eh?"

"Yes—oh, Dick, he's dead—he's dead!"—and she covered her face with her hands.

"Here, you must sit down and rest," he said, laying a hand on her shoulder. "They oughtn't to have sent you to tell me. Someone else ought to have come. Sit down, Letty dear."

"No, Dick, I—I'm alright. And they don't know I've come."

"They don't know? What do you mean, Letty?"

"I mean they don't know at the Warlock—perhaps they haven't heard anything there yet. I was down by the harbor when—when they brought it ashore—a fishing boat; they picked it up as they were coming in. I was in the crowd—I saw the face—oh, Dick—Dick!" She began to sob.

Her lover put his arm around her shoulders.

"You poor little thing," he said. "What a cruel shock for you. Perhaps Jim is not dead after all. They'll try artificial respiration for a long time—oh yes, an hour or more. I'll put on my boots and come round with you to the hotel. Look here, I insist on your sitting down just for a minute."

He took her by the arms and placed her gently in the chair from which he had just risen. She offered no resistance. He kicked off his slippers and put on his boots. Then he slipped on his overcoat and said:

"I'm ready now, old girl. I say, it's not likely to be as bad as you think."

Letty stared at him. There were no traces of tears in her eyes or on her cheeks. James Burden had loved her and he had asked her to marry him. And Dick knew nothing of this—the one fact that made everything so much more horrible to her than he could ever imagine.

"Come, Letty," said Dick, "we must get along at once. I dare say we'll pick up a cab outside."

He held out his hand to her, and she caught hold of it, and from the touch of those strong lean fingers she seemed to gather strength and courage. He pulled her to her feet and kissed her on the cheek.

"Poor old girl!" he said. "What rotten luck for you!"

"Don't think of me!" she exclaimed. "How can you spare a thought for me—when your brother——"

"Oh, Jim's alright," he interrupted harshly. "It would take more than an old monk's curse to hurt Jim."

They went outside, where a taxicab was waiting. Letty herself had come in it. She had forgotten that.

Chapter IV · Before the Coroner

—

The body of James Burden had been found by the fishermen in the sea about a mile west of the pierhead and a quarter of a mile from the shore. It had been seen to starboard by Henry Foskett and he had called out to his father, who was at the tiller. The *Rose-*

mary had been put about, and it had taken the two men nearly half an hour to get the lifeless being on deck.

They reached the harbor in ten minutes, and a doctor was sent for and was soon on the spot. After his examination of the body he said that James Burden had been dead for about three hours. There were no signs of violence; no signs of foul play. James Burden had met his end not by drowning, but by shock acting on a weak heart. His watch and cigarette case were in his pockets, and his watch had stopped at half past six. A letter and some cards in a notebook had established his identity, but had not given his East-hill address, and it was not until an hour later that the police discovered that he had been staying at the Warlock Private Hotel.

This was the sum total of the evidence given at the inquest by the doctor and the fishermen. The police gave some further details, the result of communications made to them by Richard Burden and Miss Cramer, the proprietress of the Warlock Hotel.

Dick was called forward, and he took the oath.

"You met your brother on the pier that afternoon?" queried the coroner.

"Yes."

"By accident?"

"Perhaps not quite. I had been talking to Miss Kingsbury and my brother saw her leave the pier."

"She informed him that you were on the pier?"

"No, but he came to that conclusion. He knew that I was engaged to be married to Miss Kingsbury. He told me himself that he guessed that I was on the pier."

"He wanted to see you—about some matter of importance?"

"No. He just wished to see me. We had a chat together for a few minutes and then I left him."

"Did he seem depressed?"

"Not in the least."

"Had he any troubles that you are aware of?"

"Nothing that I know of. If you are suggesting that he committed suicide I think that is very unlikely. My brother was a man who was not easily upset or worried."

"I suppose, Mr. Burden, that there were not many people on the pier at that time—in that weather?"

"I saw no one anywhere near us but a man fishing."

"You did not see your brother again?"

"I never saw him again alive."

"So far as we know at present," said the coroner, "you were the last person to see him alive. It is possible that he did not leave the pier by the entrance."

"That is so. He may have stood about until after dusk and have fallen into the sea. The tide was on the ebb and he would have been carried westward. There was no one about to save him or give the alarm. And my brother had a weak heart. He can swim, but the cold of the water would have killed him."

"Has he been an invalid for many years?"

"Yes—ever since he had rheumatic fever at the age of twenty."

"And his ill health did not prey on his mind?"

"Not at all."

The coroner looked at his notes and frowned.

"I suppose," he said after a pause, "that your brother was not superstitious? He did not believe in this so-called 'curse' connected with your house?"

"Not in the least. I did not mention it to the inspector. The papers got hold of it somehow and made a good deal of it. Of course, after my cousin's death——"

"You needn't talk about that," the coroner interrupted harshly. "I conducted the inquiry. We are not concerned with that just now. Who first told you of your brother's death?"

The abrupt question was flung at him almost as an accusation. Dick Burden would have liked to conceal the truth. The police had not made any inquiries on this point. The cab which had taken Letty Kingsbury and himself to the Warlock Hotel had been dismissed a few moments before the news came over the telephone.

Ostensibly they had both learnt of James Burden's death from Miss Cramer rushing out into the hall from her private room.

Dick Burden would have liked to say, "I first heard the news from Miss Cramer" but he knew he was standing on dangerous ground. His landlady might have told the police about Letty's visits and—oh, well, it was safer to speak the truth.

"Miss Kingsbury," he replied, and he was quite aware that his hesitation had produced an unfavorable impression on the coroner.

"At the hotel?"

"No—at my rooms. She came straight to me from the harbor—to save time."

The coroner stroked his gray beard, and Dick Burden thought that he had never seen a man with a more unpleasant face. He remembered the inquest on his cousin and how this same coroner had badgered poor Jim about little details that had not seemed to matter.

It was as if the coroner could not get away from some pre-conceived idea of suicide or murder—though ninety-nine cases out of a hundred deaths were due to an accident or natural causes.

Well, perhaps it was the fellow's duty to suspect everyone.

"Do you know anyone living at Cowhurst?" asked the coroner.

"I've never even heard of the place."

"It is a small village some twelve miles north of here and about twenty miles southeast of Shotlander Priory."

"I don't remember the name. I may have passed through it, but I certainly do not know anyone who lives there."

"You have never heard your brother speak of the place?"

"Never—so far as I can remember."

"Thank you, Mr. Burden. There is nothing further that I wish to ask you at present."

Miss Cramer was the next witness. She was a tall, big-boned woman of forty, with a large deeply lined face and bright red hair. She was fashionably dressed, and her furs must have cost a great deal of money. She took the oath in a harsh voice that was almost masculine in its pitch.

"How long have you known the deceased?" queried the coroner.

"Let me see," she replied, "I think he came to stay with me three years ago."

"Before Mr. Robert Burden ever stayed with you?"

"Yes—oh yes. Mr. Robert came on his cousin's recommendation."

"And you have never noticed anything odd about Mr. James Burden's behavior?"

"I have always found him a nice, quiet gentleman."

"He arrived at your hotel at three o'clock on the day of his death?"

"Yes."

"And he did not seem upset about anything? He was quite normal, wasn't he?"

"Quite himself."

"A communication was waiting for him?"

"Yes—a letter from Cowhurst."

"You noticed the postmark. Why?"

"Because I was born at Cowhurst, and know the village very well. I told the police that."

"Yes, and you also told the police that Mr. Burden, on the morning of the day on which he was drowned, received a letter from Cowhurst."

"Yes—that is right—I remember it quite well."

"Why did you not come forward and give this information at the inquest on Mr. Robert Burden?"

"The question of the letters from Cowhurst did not seem to me to be of any importance," said Miss Cramer.

"But now you think that it is of importance?" suggested the coroner.

"Yes, of course. I should be a fool if I couldn't see that it was an extraordinary coincidence."

"Have you any reason to think that it is anything more than a coincidence?"

"Only that such coincidences don't happen as a rule."

"You think that these letters were written by the same person?"

"I think it's very likely."

"You couldn't swear that they were addressed in the same handwriting?"

"I took no notice of the handwriting. And, of course, I couldn't have remembered the writing on Mr. Robert's letter, even if I had examined it. But the postmark did attract my attention on both occasions."

The coroner turned over some pages of manuscript—a copy of his notes at the inquest on Robert Burden. The crowded room seemed to quiver with expectancy. Up to the mention of this letter—of these two missives—no one had regarded the case as anything of more interest than an unfortunate accident which had befallen a visitor of some social position. But the coincidence of these communications was something to arrest the attention and hold it.

Here was a definite link between the two tragedies—the suggestion of a common cause. A couple of men, both owners of the same estate! The receipt of two letters, both posted in the same small village!

Even the most level-headed present could not help thinking of murder or of some horror that would drive a man to take his own life.

"Do you often go to Cowhurst?" queried the coroner, after a pause.

"I have not been there for ten years."

"But you know people who live there?"

"Oh yes, several."

"Relatives?"

"No. My father, who lived there, is dead."

"But you have friends who write to you?"

"Yes—now and then."

"And none of them has ever mentioned Mr. Robert Burden?"

"Never. Nor Mr. James either."

"But after Mr. Robert Burden's death, and after you saw the postmark on the letter Mr. Robert Burden received on the day of his demise, it would surely have been natural for you to have said something to your friends at Cowhurst?"

"I have told you that I attached no importance to the letter whatever. It was not until the second letter came that I——"

"Thank you, Miss Cramer," the coroner interrupted. "We are very much obliged to you for your information."

Letty had been summoned as a witness. She heard her name called out, rose to her feet, and took the oath. The coroner smiled at her as though to give her confidence. He asked her if she had known Robert Burden, and she said that she had only spoken to him twice. Did she know Mr. James Burden as well? Yes, quite well. She had lived in the hotel with her father for some time and had often met the deceased. He had struck her as a quiet, level-headed man—not in the least likely to commit suicide. No, she had not seen him at the pier entrance. If she had done so, she would have stopped to speak to him. He had not arrived at the hotel when she had left it. She had not seen him for a month. But she knew he was coming to stay at the Warlock. Her father had told her.

"You were down at the harbor when the body of the deceased was brought ashore?" the coroner inquired.

"Yes," Letty answered. "I went for a walk after dinner. I often go down to the harbor. I like it better than the parade."

"And when you saw the face of the deceased you went off at once to tell Mr. Richard Burden?"

"Yes—at once."

"It did not occur to you to give the fishermen and the police any information—to tell them Mr. James Burden's name and address?"

"No. I was quite certain that they would find all the information they required. A man generally carries visiting cards in his pocket."

"But the address? Remember, Mr. James Burden had only just arrived at Easthill."

"I'm afraid I did not stop to think of everything. It seemed to me that his brother ought to be informed at once, and I hurried off. I took a cab."

For nearly half a minute there was silence, and Letty's heart beat very quickly. Then she was told that nothing more was wanted of her. She felt as though she had escaped from some danger. "I am free," she said to herself, and the look in her eyes showed her gratitude and relief—too plainly. She realized this as she saw the coroner gazing steadily at her.

"One moment, Miss Kingsbury," he said. "Before you go, is there anything you would like to tell us—any information you would care to give? The duty of a witness in these sad affairs is not only to answer questions truthfully, but to inform the court of anything which may help the jury come to a proper verdict."

The color flamed up in the girl's white face—and then died away again. This was a direct challenge—an insult. No other witness had been asked this question. It was almost as though the coroner had said, "You're keeping something back. Come, out with it."

Letty Kingsbury recovered her self-control.

"I have nothing further to add," she replied coldly. "If I had known of anything that would be of assistance I would have told the police."

"Thank you, Miss Kingsbury. I hope you are not offended. The question was a mere formality. We are much obliged to you for your evidence."

She went back to her seat with those sentences ringing in her ears. It seemed to her that there was a covert sneer in them.

What had she told them already? What had she told this man? More perhaps then she had put into words.

Chapter V · Blackmailer or Madman?

—

The jury returned an open verdict at the inquest, but Dick Burden knew that their decision was by no means the end of the matter. He was, in fact, certain that already he was vaguely and indefinitely suspected of murder, although it would have been ridiculous to arrest him. There was no evidence against him, but also there was no doubt that he was the one person in the world who would benefit from his brother's death. He was now the owner of the Shotlander estates, and in a position to marry the woman he loved.

There was no getting away from that fact. His entire outlook on life had changed. A rather hopeless love affair had given place to a possibility of marriage in the near future.

Of course that in itself would have been nothing. Every heir to an estate benefits by the death of his predecessor. But there were other facts that might make it very awkward for him.

He was the last known person to see his brother alive. And there had been a violent—and indecent—quarrel near the end of the pier. If anyone—that ugly fisherman, for instance—had come forward and told the coroner about the altercation, there might even have been a "case" against him.

His brother had been a real obstacle in his path, not merely because his brother was the owner of the Shotlander estates, but because his brother had definitely forbidden his marriage, and had used his influence with Sir Julius Kingsbury to prevent it. And now—well, the obstacle had been removed.

Dick Burden saw all this very clearly as he sat in the library at Shotlander Priory one evening a fortnight after James Burden had been laid in the family vault. For two weeks he had had but little time to think of anything but business. During that period he had discovered that the estates yielded a clear seven thousand a year, and that Jim could very well have spared that annual allowance of two hundred and fifty pounds. It is not pleasant to discover ugly truths about the dead.

Jim had been mean. There was no doubt about that. Well, he had always been an invalid and peculiar.

"Poor old Jim," thought Dick. "Precious little he got out of life!"

He filled his pipe and lit the tobacco, and stretched out his legs to the warmth of the blazing fire. It was nine o'clock, and he could not possibly go to bed for another hour and a half. He did not care to be alone with his thoughts. He yawned, rose from his chair, and made his way to the billiard room, where he practiced difficult shots at the top of the table.

Half an hour later the old butler, who had known three masters in as many years, entered the room and said:

"A gentleman has called to see you, sir. A Mr. Robertson, sir; he said he had no card with him."

"I don't know him," Dick replied. "Well, you may as well show him in here, Atkins."

The butler retired, and a minute later he ushered a man into the billiard room. Dick Burden recognized the ugly face at once.

It was that of the man who had been fishing on the pier! Not at all a person that Dick Burden desired to see again, though he had been interested in the fellow's ugliness—in the face that was a curious exaggeration of all the Burden features.

"I must apologize for this intrusion," said Robertson, when the butler had left the billiard room. "It is an impertinence for a stranger to call upon you at this hour."

"Not at all," Dick answered cheerily. "Sit down, won't you?"

Robertson took off his overcoat. It was creased and dirty, and suggested poverty. His hat was a greasy old black felt.

"I am glad to rest," he said, flinging himself on one of the long leather-covered seats that were set against the wall of the room. "I have had a very long walk—nearly seven miles, to tell you the truth."

"Great Scott! Seven miles! You must have a drink!"

"No, thank you. I am a teetotaler. But I will smoke a cigar—one of my own, if you don't mind. I stick to a particular brand."

He took a cheroot from a shabby leather case and bit off the end. Dick Burden did not like the look of him at all. Why had the fellow traveled such a distance? And why had he walked? He had certainly come on an errand of importance. Blackmail? Possibly, but a blackmailer of intelligence would have shown his hand before the inquest. After it his evidence would be of little value.

The police would only say to him, "That's all very well, but why didn't you come forward at the inquest?" and there would be no answer to that.

A teetotaler and a smoker of very mild cigars! And the most horrible face in the world! Dick Burden did not like the combination.

There was something inhuman about it—well, perhaps not exactly inhuman, but unnatural.

Dick Burden rested his cue against the paneled wall and put on his old shooting jacket. And then, as he began to refill his pipe, Robertson said:

"Do you mind sitting down here, Mr. Burden? There are occasions on which one does not want to shout. By the by, if you don't mind, I'd feel safer if the door were locked."

Dick Burden smiled, walked to the door, and locked it.

"Now then, Mr. Robertson," he said sternly, "let us get to business. I'm not very fond of mysteries."

"Of course not," replied the visitor, "but you're in the thick of them. You'll excuse my saying that, won't you? You recognize me, of course?"

"Well, I did fancy I'd seen your face before."

"Mine are features a man does not easily forget," Robertson laughed.

"Yes, yes—we have seen each other before—on the pier at Easthill. Are you fond of fishing?"

"Not in the sea, Mr. Robertson."

"Ah, that's a pity—h'm, yes, a great pity; teaches a man to be patient. You'll have to be very patient if you're going to hold on to this delightful old place of yours."

"What do you mean?" queried Dick sharply.

"The curse of the old monk, about which I hear. It's working very well. You're the only one left now."

"The police will deal with that," the young man laughed derisively.

"The police won't save you."

Dick Burden smiled, leaned forward, and knocked out the ashes from his pipe on the floor. His mind was moving quickly, but he wanted time to think. He had a shrewd idea that the danger was very close to him—no further away in fact than this newcomer. Possibly the man was mad, but it was more likely that he wished to get on friendly terms with his victim—that he wished to pose as a comrade in the hour of danger.

"We are both in the same boat," said Robertson after a pause.

"You too, eh?"

"Yes, but not for the same reason. They want to get rid of me because I know too much."

"What do you know?"

"I know who killed your brother."

This astounding statement jerked Dick Burden to his feet. He walked round to the open fireplace, where there was a heavy poker of burnished steel.

"I'm not mad," said Robertson. "I was on the pier when your brother was pushed into the water by Sir Julius Kingsbury."

"Sir Julius Kingsbury!"

"Yes, I saw it all quite plainly, and Sir Julius suspects that I witnessed the deed. Sooner or later he's likely to get me, and that is why I've come round here tonight. It's hard luck on you, but it is better for you to know now than later on—after you're married."

"This is a rotten lie, and you—you're a scoundrel, whoever you are."

"You think it is impossible, eh?"

Dick Burden began to refill his pipe. It would be absurd for him to say even to himself that it was impossible for Sir Julius Kingsbury to have committed this crime after all that his brother had told him. According to Jim, the baronet had murdered Robert

Burden, and there was very good evidence that Sir Julius had been afraid of Jim. It was quite possible that Sir Julius, half mad with terror, had got rid of the man he feared.

But then one had to assume that the baronet had murdered Robert Burden, and he, Dick, had never been willing to admit the possibility of such a tragedy. He had regarded Jim as a liar. And now—well, Jim's death might be the actual proof of Jim's honesty.

It was all very horrible—and most horrible of all was the fact that Robertson, like some hideous devil, had made a statement that, whether true or false, would work like poison in a man's brain.

"Nothing is impossible," said Dick when he was puffing at his tobacco, "but one has to consider probabilities. Why did you make no attempt to save my brother?"

"What could I do? I am a poor swimmer, and in my heavy clothes and oilskins I should have gone to the bottom like a stone."

"You could have given the alarm—have run for help."

"It would have been impossible to save your brother. I saw it all quite clearly, Mr. Burden. There is no boat at the end of the pier. By the time I had got to the parade and we had launched a boat it would have been too late."

"Oh, you can't expect me to believe all this nonsense. At any rate, you could have told the police—as quickly as possible."

Robertson rose from the seat and walked slowly toward Dick Burden. He did not speak until they were within a yard of each other. Then he said:

"You are taking it pretty calmly."

"Yes—one doesn't get excited over fairy tales. What is your game, Mr. Robertson?"

"Self-preservation, first of all. Then a desire to save you. Listen to me," he said. "You think I'm a liar. You don't credit my story. Well, do you fancy the police or the coroner would have believed it—my word against the word of Sir Julius Kingsbury? I have no evidence but that of my own eyes. And you'd scarcely have thanked me for bringing this horrible charge against the father of the girl you want to marry. If only in self-defense we've got to be friends."

"I think you're mad."

"We're up against a big thing," Robertson continued. "Kingsbury has marked both of us down, and he is not alone. Even if I could have persuaded the police to lock up Sir Julius—even if he were in a condemned cell, that wouldn't save us. The matter is not nearly so simple as that. It's something I don't understand as yet. But I'm going to fathom it—if I live long enough. The police can't help us. Kingsbury doesn't know for certain that I saw him push your brother into the sea. He suspects it; but I'm trying to make him think that I saw nothing. That's one reason why I've held my tongue."

Dick Burden smiled incredulously. Without doubt the man was insane.

"I wish you would explain," he said. "It's all like a nightmare. Why have you walked here?"

"If a man has to keep off the roads he must walk," replied Robertson. "I'm known to be lazy and fond of my car. I've no doubt all the roads are watched. I came seven miles across country."

"Where do you live?"

"In London," Robertson replied. "Yes, I think I can say I live in London. But I move around a lot in my car—I have taken a room for the night in the Chequers Inn, at Stilehurst. My motor broke down—conveniently. I'm supposed to be in bed and asleep—not to be called until ten o'clock in the morning."

"And you're going back there, eh?"

"I hope to get back," Robertson answered grimly; "but I'm being watched."

The visitor put on his overcoat and hat, slipped his right hand into his pocket, and took out a heavy automatic.

"I'd keep one of these by you," he said. "It's the sort of thing that might come in useful. I wonder if you'd mind my slipping away by the window?"

Dick Burden was weary of the fellow—of this absurd romancer

who, either from vanity or mania, had made himself out to be a person whose life was in danger.

"You can depart by the chimney if you like," he answered coldly.

"Would you object if I turned out the lights? A man makes a fair mark against the window of an illuminated room."

Dick Burden hesitated. He did not quite fancy being alone in the dark with Robertson. But in the end he nodded assent.

"Perhaps it would be better if you left me in here," the visitor added. "I don't want you to run any risks. I can see what you think of me, Mr. Burden. You can trust me here. I shall not steal anything."

He switched off the lights. Dick closed the door behind him, turned the key in the lock, and stood outside in the hall.

—

Five minutes later Dick Burden entered the billiard room and flooded the apartment with light.

He glanced at the bellying curtains, walked up to them, and then paused. Was there any truth in Robertson's ridiculous story? The visitor had rather insisted on switching off the lights, as though there was someone waiting without, in the hope of getting a good mark for a rifle or pistol.

Of course, that was all rubbish! Dick Burden pushed back the curtains and stood looking out into the darkness. Beneath the window there was a wide flower bed and beyond that a gravel path, and further on a stretch of lawn. His shadow, long and gigantic, reached past the grass.

He thought of the trenches in Flanders and smiled. Out there it had been considered bad form to risk one's life for no reason whatever—except to show that one was not afraid.

"I'd better smooth over the idiot's footprints," he said to himself, "or there'll be talk of burglars."

He closed the casement, turned out the lights, locked up the billiard room, and made his way round to the garden, with an electric torch in one hand and a heavy walking stick in the other.

The stick was a poor substitute for a rake, but one could hardly risk being seen with a gardening implement at that time of night. That would have been too absurd.

When he came to the window—the center of the three—he directed the ray from the torch onto the wide flower bed. At this time of the year there were no plants in it, and the surface was smooth and brown.

There was not a single footprint on the earth. Dick Burden calculated the distance from the ledge of the small casement to the gravel path.

"Fifteen feet if it's an inch," he said to himself. No man on earth could have jumped that space to the path. It would have been impossible to stand upright on the sill. "The fellow has smoothed over the marks."

But there was no sign of the mold having been disturbed. And Robertson would have been in the dark and quite incapable of doing anything of the sort.

Dick Burden returned to the house, and for the first time that evening he was really afraid—not of an unknown enemy, but of this extraordinary Mr. Robertson. It seemed to him that he was standing very near to the borderline of the supernatural.

The hideous face—that gross caricature of the Burden features! Had he been talking with some monstrous creation of the curse—something that had lived on century after century, to achieve the downfall of the race?

The idea was fantastic and absurd! But the fear of something strange and inhuman was real enough. That lasted until Dick Burden was in bed and asleep.

Chapter VI · Sir Julius Utters a Warning
—

"Dick thinks we might be married in about three months from now," said Letty Kingsbury, without turning her head to look at her father. She was standing by the fire in their private sitting room at the Warlock Hotel.

Sir Julius, seated at a small table, paused for a moment, pen in hand, glanced at Letty, and then went on with the writing of a letter.

He was a short, thickset man of fifty-five, with a brown, rugged, weather-beaten face. His hair was white and plentiful, and his iron-gray mustache was clipped very close. There was something grim and austere about him—something often found in men who have held posts of high authority in India. He was not liked in the hotel, where he had lived for two years. But for the charm of his daughter, he would have been barely tolerated, except by Miss Cramer, who could not do enough for him.

It was known—even in England—that he had had the reputation of being a hard and unmerciful judge.

That such a man should have broken down—should have pleaded with his daughter and have even burst into tears—seemed almost incredible.

Certainly, in any difference of opinion, it would be Letty, and not her father, who would plead, and plead in vain.

"You see, Dad," Letty continued, after nearly a minute's silence, "it was only a question of money, wasn't it?"

"Not altogether," Sir Julius replied, without taking his pen from the paper.

"But you always said you liked Dick. And it was only a question of money until that morning—a few days before poor Jim died—and then—well, you would not give your reason; but I knew you were thinking of the money all the time."

Sir Julius rested his elbows on the table and pressed the tips of his fingers together.

"You are of age," he said slowly, "and you can be joined in matrimony to whom you please. But if you marry Dick Burden you will be unhappy all your life."

"Oh, Father, how can you say such a shameful thing?" said Letty indignantly.

"You will be unhappy all your life," Sir Julius continued, "not because Dick Burden is the sort of man to make a woman unhappy—nor yet because you will have to face poverty."

"Why then?"

"Because you will be marrying into an accursed family. It is doomed to extinction."

"Oh, Father, you don't really believe all that nonsense, do you?"

"Facts speak for themselves. First Robert and then James Burden! It will be Dick's turn next, and after Dick—perhaps—your child."

"Do you honestly think, Father, that the curse of the monk—do you imagine God would allow———"

"I know what has happened already," Sir Julius interrupted harshly. "It is not for me to say what God will or will not permit. This family is doomed, and if you marry into it you will suffer horribly. Fear, and the loss of those you love! That will be your life, Letty, and I want to save you from it."

"My life is my own, Father," the girl replied, "and if there is any risk of—of unhappiness I am prepared to take it. The curse is all nonsense; but"—she paused for a few moments—"if there is anything else you know of you ought to tell me."

Sir Julius shrugged his shoulders, picked up his pen, and dipped it into the ink again. Then he continued his writing.

"Is there anything else?" Letty insisted.

Sir Julius made no reply. He finished his letter, blotted it, and placed it in an envelope.

"You know my views on the matter," he said as he sealed the envelope. "I shall do all I can to stop this marriage. I am not going to discuss the matter any further with you."

"Then there is something else—some reason why———"

"I have given you my reasons."

"Father, you can't expect me to believe that you're afraid of this so-called curse. What is the real reason? I must know the truth. I—we can't go on like this, avoiding the truth."

Sir Julius rose from his chair, walked to the window, and stared out of it at the sea. And Letty, watching his face and wondering whether she dare ask him any more questions, suddenly saw it change—saw the stern obstinacy of it vanish; noticed the lower lip droop and a look of terror come into the hard, gray eyes.

"Father dear!" she exclaimed, "what is the matter? Are you ill?"

He stepped back from the window, and the girl perceived that the skin of his face had changed from brown to an ugly, whitish yellow. He caught at the back of a chair with one hand. Letty came to his side.

"You are ill, Father," said she in a gentle voice.

"Yes—yes," he answered hoarsely, "I—I am ill. No, I am alright. Some brandy, Letty. I felt faint—no, stay here, Letty. I will go into my bedroom and lie down. There's brandy in the cupboard. Don't make a fuss—that's a good girl. I'll be myself again in a minute or two."

He walked steadily toward a door that led into his bedroom. On the threshold he said:

"Stay here—don't worry. I am better—already."

He closed the portal in her face and locked it. Letty, utterly bewildered, went to the window. The sitting apartment was on the third floor and overlooked the parade and the sea. This was not the most fashionable end of Easthill, but it was near the harbor and the older part of the town. There were very few people to be seen. There had been no mistaking that sudden start—that quick look of horror on Sir Julius's features. It was fear, and not illness, that had drained his face of blood and caused that drooping of the lower jaw.

And the fear, like a disease, had been infectious. She, too, was trembling and afraid as she stared out of the window. Yet she could see nothing that might not have been witnessed on any day of the week—at almost any hour during the winter at Easthill.

A few people hurrying by in heavy overcoats. Two sailors striding past toward the harbor. A sailor standing by himself with his back against a lamppost, a pipe in his mouth, and his hands thrust in his pockets. A pair of young lovers in a shelter, sitting very close to each other. An old man trying to sell bootlaces and matches to a fat, elderly woman in cheap furs.

And on the gray, cold sea, a single fishing smack putting out from the harbor with a patch of white foam at her bows.

There were other people in the picture, but these individuals seemed to stand out and fix themselves as definite objects that could be retained by the memory.

"Someone who is not there now," said Letty to herself. "Something that has now disappeared."

She was frightened, for it seemed to her that, although the baronet was not ill, his brain might be giving way. She could not forget that once before he had changed into another man, that he had burst into tears and broken down completely. And she remembered that on that occasion, as on this, he had been gazing out of the window—just before he had turned and implored her not to marry Dick Burden.

That had not seemed to her to be of any importance at the time. But now it did! Then, again, his belief in this absurd curse! A man's brain is not necessarily unbalanced because he is superstitious. But her father was not superstitious.

He was a materialist, and believed in nothing he could not see with his own eyes.

It seemed to her that now he was in the habit of seeing things—things that were not there—horrible things indeed if they made a coward of a brave man.

The girl strode across the room to the table. The letter her father had just written was still lying on the pad of pink blotting paper, and she saw that the letter was addressed to Sir Julius's bank in London.

There was a knock on the door, and the Swiss waiter entered.

"Mistaire Burden have called to see you, mees," he said.

Letty hesitated before she replied. She did not wish Dick to meet her father while the latter was in his present strange state of mind.

There might even be an unpleasant scene between the two men. But in any case she did not wish Dick to see her father so ill and peculiar in his behavior.

"I will come downstairs," she said, "in one moment."

The menial left the room, and Letty went to the door of her father's chamber and knocked on it. There was no reply, and she tried the handle. To her surprise the door opened. There was no one to be seen.

Chapter VII · Called to Shotlander

—

"Yes, your father went out just now," said Dick Burden. "I saw him, but he didn't notice me. He seemed to be in a great hurry. I say, can't we go upstairs?"

"No, Dick," replied Letty, "I'd rather you didn't. Father is not very well, and I expect he'll be back in a minute. We can talk here alright, can't we?"

Dick Burden looked round the lounge and shrugged his shoulders. Two old women were sitting by the fire in a couple of large armchairs. A young fellow was reading a newspaper by one of the windows. A coarse-featured man of middle age was lolling on the sofa, his eyes half closed and a cigar between his lips. It was not a suitable place for an interview between two lovers.

"What train did you come down by?"

"Oh, I motored here." Dick answered. "I've just bought a car. I thought perhaps you'd like to come out for a run this afternoon."

"I should love to. Are you staying here?"

"I'm putting up a the 'Majestic,' but only for tonight. Shall I call round at half past two?"

"No; look here, Dick, if you'll wait a minute I'll slip on my things and walk with you to your hotel."

"Right you are," he replied. "But be as quick as you can."

Letty disappeared through some curtains that hung between the lounge and the hall, and Dick Burden sat down and lit a cigarette. His face was very grave, and there were dark rings round his eyes. He had not been sleeping very well during the past week. His interview with the strange and fantastic Robertson had affected him more than he cared to acknowledge. Of course the man was mad, but the conduct of even a lunatic requires some explanation. And there was nothing wild or ridiculous about the horrible charge Robertson had brought against Sir Julius Kingsbury. Richard Burden believed that his brother had had some kind of hold over the baronet, and that Sir Julius had a strong motive for getting rid of him.

And he, Richard Burden, was in love with the daughter of Sir Julius Kingsbury, and there was nothing but this to prevent their marriage—nothing but this, an incredible and yet possible obstacle.

He might marry the daughter of a murderer, but not the daughter of a man who had slain poor old Jim. That would have been a monstrous, an impossible crime against nature.

And then there was Robert Burden. Poor old Jim had believed Sir Julius Kingsbury to be guilty of the murder of Robert Burden.

One murder breeds another. Robertson believed that he went in fear of his own life. Robertson had warned him, Dick Burden— had even suggested that he should carry a loaded pistol about with him.

Well, he had taken Robertson's advice to that extent. But he feared Robertson more than he feared Sir Julius Kingsbury. Were they both mad? Was he living in a world of madmen?

Dick Burden smiled at his own thoughts. He smiled at the absurdity of the whole idea—at the way in which he had allowed himself to believe in murder as a commonplace event.

No one had been murdered, and no one would be murdered unless Robertson were a homicidal maniac. He felt just a little bit ashamed of himself.

Men did not go about killing each other in this melodramatic fashion. No doubt the war had taught him to think cheaply of human life. But he ought to have realized that he had made a fool of himself.

He looked round the room, and the drab reality of life came home to him. This ugly furniture—those dull, uninteresting people—this dreary boardinghouse that called itself a private hotel!

This was the real world after all. And he wondered what the old ladies who were sitting by the fire would say if he suddenly cried out:

"You had better be careful. A murderer is living in this place with you."

He could imagine one of them replying:

"Dear me—how dreadful—fancy that! I always told you, Amelia"—yes, the other one would probably be Amelia—"that the society in these places is dreadfully mixed."

He laughed out loud at this imaginary conversation, and everyone turned and looked at him in shocked amazement.

He was in deep mourning, and no one so attired should have laughed like that. More than ever he realized that he was in a world where it is a ten-million-to-one chance against any man being a murderer.

Suddenly the heavy plushette hangings parted, and Dick saw Miss Cramer, tall and beautifully dressed, and with her hair like flame. She came up to him and said in her masculine voice:

"You are wanted on the telephone, Mr. Burden."

He followed her across the hall into her private room, which was near the entrance to the hotel. To his surprise, instead of retiring and saying "I'm sure you don't want me here, Mr. Burden," she went to her rolltop bureau and, picking up a letter, handed it to him.

"No one has telephoned," she said. "The postman brought this a minute or two ago and I did not put it in the rack. I hope you think I did right."

Dick Burden glanced at the letter and saw that it had been posted in Cowhurst.

"Thank you, Miss Cramer," he remarked quietly. "I'm glad you didn't place it in the rack. One doesn't want a lot of foolish talk here."

He thrust the communication in his pocket, and Miss Cramer said:

"I don't want to meddle with your affairs, Mr. Burden, but I trust you will go straight to the police with that letter. Recent happenings have done my house no good. Perhaps you will be murdered now. I ought never to have given the letter to you."

Dick Burden shook his head.

"I am afraid it wouldn't do to tamper with the post," he said, "even with the kindest of motives. But it was good of you not to leave the letter in the rack. I shall possibly tell the police of my receiving it or send a copy of it to my lawyers. And I should be glad if you'd say nothing about it to Sir Julius or his daughter."

"Not unless anything happens to you, Mr. Burden."

Dick left the room and found Letty waiting for him in the lounge. She walked back to his hotel with him, and she noticed that, in spite of his efforts to be cheerful, he seemed to have something weighing on his mind. They said very little to each other during that quarter of an hour. She had much to tell him—much to discuss; but they would be able to talk over their future plans after lunch, and decide if they would be married without her father's consent.

It was a quarter to one when they parted outside the Majestic Hotel. Just a shake of the hand, and a lifting of the hat, and "Goodbye, dear," and "I'll be round at half past two sharp, and we'll have a jolly little run, even if it snows."

The words were prophetic, for at two o'clock it did begin to snow. Sir Julius had telephoned that he was lunching at the club, and Letty was glad, for it was quite possible that he would have forbidden her to go out with Dick Burden. And she would have disobeyed, and that would have meant an unpleasant scene.

At 2:25 Letty was in the lounge. She was wearing a fur coat. The room was full of people, but she stood by the window and looked out at the falling snow. Already it lay an inch deep on the road and parade, and the sea, by contrast, seemed black as ink. It was not the sort of afternoon for a motor-drive. All around her people were talking about the vileness of the weather. A young man chaffed her and suggested a long walk and a picnic.

A 2:40 Miss Cramer entered the lounge and told Letty that a message had just come through for her from the "Majestic." Dick Burden had been suddenly called back to Shotlander on urgent business. He had not even had time to speak himself on the telephone. The manager had acted in his stead.

"Mr. Burden hopes to be down again tomorrow," said Miss Cramer. "He will send you a telegram."

Letty did not show her disappointment. She laughed and replied:

"Well, it's not much of an afternoon for a motor-ride, is it?"

"No dear, and I think you're best out of it. It'd be sure to mean a bad cold, if nothing worse."

Letty walked slowly up the stairs, and when at last she reached the sitting room she sank into a chair by the fire. Ten minutes elapsed before she rose to her feet and took off her fur coat. The snow was falling so thickly that she could not even get a glimpse of the sea.

Chapter VIII · An Unfortunate Adventure

—

Detective-inspector Linkinghorne turned over a page of a long typewritten statement and said:

"You put things remarkably clearly, Mr. Ivory, and, if I may say so, you have quite a literary style. I believe you could make money by writing for the magazines."

Superintendent Ivory smiled and began to fill his pipe. He was a big man, still on the right side of fifty, and would easily have passed for a butcher or a publican.

"My daughter puts things into shape for me," answered he. "I give her the facts and she makes them read well. She has had a good education."

"So has my son," the detective remarked, turning over another page, "but his taste is for mathematics. He was talking about this case to me last night and trying to get me to believe that two and two don't necessarily make four, and then——" He paused and added abruptly: "This Cowhurst business is probably all a blind."

"Eh, what's that—come, come, Mr. Linkinghorne—two letters."

"Yes, the first may have had something to do with the death of Robert Burden. Now, let us suppose I had wished to get rid of James Burden and that I had nothing whatever to do with the demise of his cousin. Wouldn't I just jump at the Cowhurst idea and post a letter from the village—as I passed through it in a car at night? That would lead everyone to think that the two Burdens had both been killed by the same murderer. And that would confuse the inquiry from the start."

"Oh, I don't think like that, Mr. Linkinghorne. It would be against all experience."

"And then," continued the detective, "look at the curse of Shotlander. What a godsend to any criminal. Your daughter had a very pretty little passage about that."

"You mustn't throw my daughter in my face," said Ivory sharply. "I am responsible for all the facts in that statement. My girl——"

"Yes, yes, I know," put in the detective soothingly, "but was it your idea that the working out of the curse might be due to natural laws? Did you tell her to write something to this effect——"

Linkinghorne turned back a few pages and read: "'That which the ignorant ascribe to miraculous agencies may be only due to the hidden forces of nature. It is conceivable that the Burden family may be doomed to perish by their own weakness or some criminal instinct in their own beings.' Was that your idea?"

"No, I'll confess it was not. It was my daughter who suggested that the motive for the crime was the possession of the estate—

that James Burden slew his cousin and was in turn killed by his brother. I tell you this between ourselves, Mr. Linkinghorne. I did not dare put it down on paper."

The sleuth leaned back in his chair and closed his eyes. The two men were sitting on either side of the fire in the dining room of the Linkinghornes' flat. It was a cozy, well-furnished apartment within a quarter of a mile of Scotland Yard.

Superintendent Ivory, of Easthill, was his guest for the night. It was thought desirable that they should first meet in London for an informal talk.

So here they were, smoking on either side of the cheerful fire, and paying no attention to the clock which had just struck two in the morning.

In another eight hours Ivory would be on his way to Easthill, and Linkinghorne would certainly not be in London. But they were men who had often been obliged to take a very short rest between two long spells of toil.

"H'mm, yes," resumed the detective after a silence that had lasted for two minutes. And then he opened his eyes and said: "By Jove! That's a smart little daughter of yours—working the curse into a practical theory. Well, if there's anything in the idea Richard Burden is safe enough, for he's the last of his line."

"Rose—that's my little girl—thought Richard Burden would probably commit suicide, and there'd be an end of the lot," said Ivory.

"Rose Ivory," Linkinghorne laughed. "What a pretty name, and what ugly ideas she has in her head!"

"One must have ugly ideas about ugly things," the superintendent retorted hotly, "even if one is a young girl."

"Ah, the pity of it," sighed the detective—"the pity of it. Well, Mr. Ivory, we've got to find that fisherman."

"We've tried hard."

"Have you advertised?"

"No. It was thought best not to do so. We don't want to draw attention to the fact that he's wanted."

The detective nodded his head in agreement.

"Quite right—for a time. You'll have to advertise though. You have a description of him?"

"Yes, both from Richard Burden and Miss Kingsbury."

"Well, get busy, and then, if he doesn't turn up, we shall know that he has reasons for wanting to keep clear of us. He seems to be a remarkably ugly fellow, and someone ought to answer your inquiries. A man like that would be noticeable anywhere."

"We inquired at every boardinghouse, hotel, and lodging house in Easthill but could not hear of him."

"And at Cowhurst, eh?"

"Yes, of course. My own opinion is that we must concentrate on Cowhurst. But now that you are taking over the case———"

He paused as the telephone bell cut into his conversation. Linkinghorne seated himself at a table near the window and picked up the receiver.

"Yes, Linkinghorne speaking," he said. "Oh, that's you, is it, Jones? . . . You don't say so! Well, upon my word! I'll motor down at once . . . No, I'll take my own little car. Mr. Ivory is here and I dare say he'll come with me. I won't lose time in talk. Good night."

He hung up the receiver, and Ivory said:

"Where are you going to take me?"

"Shotlander Priory, or what's left of it. The place has been burning for two hours, and it's doubtful if a single room of it will be saved."

The superintendent began to ask questions, but the detective cut him short:

"Put your coat on and come along to the garage. I've no chauffeur. It'll be a cold drive in the snow."

Three minutes later the two men set off. The sturdy little car took them across Surrey and over the Sussex border before it climbed halfway up a long, steep hill and came to rest in an impenetrable drift.

Linkinghorne was annoyed. It was impossible to get through. He pulled out a map and studied it carefully. But, as a matter of fact, he did not quite know his position. In the daytime there would have been familiar landmarks, and it would have been easy to read the signposts. The speedometer told him that they were not very far from the Chequers Inn at Stilehurst, where he would have turned to the right on the road that would have taken him to Shotlander Priory. But he was not aware just how far he was from the hostelry, and in the dark one has to be very accurate in taking one's bearings.

He folded up the map, backed the car out of the obstruction, and tried to turn her. He was an experienced driver, but the snow got the better of him. It had filled a wide and deep ditch, and made it level with the turf by the side of the road. The rear wheels of the little vehicle sank suddenly and the two men found themselves lying at a very comfortable angle of forty-five degrees. The bonnet pointed to distant stars in the clear sky. Linkinghorne switched off, and the plucky little engine was silent.

"That's done it," said the sleuth. "We'll have to walk the rest of the way."

"Walk? You're mad!"

"We shall only get wet, and there'll be a nice fire to dry ourselves."

"Can't we find a horse to pull us out?"

Linkinghorne looked at his watch, holding it close to a small electric lamp on the dashboard.

"It is half past four," he said. "You can stay here if you like. Perhaps you had better do so. I'm going to walk."

"The car might get stolen, mightn't it?"

"Yes," laughed Linkinghorne. "Anyone with a horse to pull it out of this ditch might steal it."

"If another car came along—a big car?"

"Yes, yes, if they had a stout tow-rope; but there are not many cars driving about on a night like this."

"True," said Ivory savagely. "Well, do you mind if I do stay here?"

"Not in the least."

"After all, I don't know why we ever started. What use is there in watching a bonfire?"

"We won't discuss that now, Mr. Ivory. I will leave you the flask and the biscuits. You'll be snug enough in here. You'll probably fall asleep with the car tilted back. Like lying on a bed, isn't it? Got plenty of tobacco?"

"Oh, heaps, thank you, Mr. Linkinghorne; but look here, if you get lost in the snow you'll want that flask."

The detective laughed as he climbed out of the car. A hill, not so very far away, stood out black against a red glow in the sky— a glow like the swift coming of dawn in some tropical country.

"Look at that," he said. "Now won't you change your mind and come along with me?"

Ivory shook his head. He was tired and sleepy. Who could tell how far away that hill might really be. And who could say for certain that that glow in the sky was the reflection of the burning house?

"I'll stay here," he yawned.

Linkinghorne did not press the matter. On the whole he was rather glad to be rid of the lethargic Ivory. And, after all, it was an advantage to leave someone in charge of the car.

Chapter IX · A Tragic Discovery

—

Linkinghorne reached Shotlander Priory without adventure and with no greater hardships than a very stiff walk of seven miles and a wetting up to the knees. The fire, as a fine spectacle, was over. The roof had fallen in two hours before his arrival, and it was that which had sent the glow of light into the sky. From the crest of a hill the detective himself had looked down on the last great tragedy of an ancient house. Beyond a wood of tall trees he had seen the black shell of the building spouting flames from every window.

As he had hurried toward it the light had diminished in intensity, and by the time he stood on the lawn, strewn with pictures and furniture, there was nothing more picturesque than great volumes of black smoke and white steam as the fire engines poured their jets of water on the debris.

"You should have been here an hour ago," said a policeman. "She did burn just beautiful, that she did."

Linkinghorne sought out those who could tell him the facts. Representing himself as a reporter on a great London paper, he found many willing to recount all they knew. One by one he discarded them until he came across the butler.

Old Atkins was sitting on one of the plate chests with a pistol in his right hand to protect the valuables. His face was cut and blackened with smoke.

A curious, moth-eaten fur cap covered his head. His thick overcoat was torn and charred.

Linkinghorne was irresistibly reminded of a pirate guarding a hoard of treasure, and thought that the pistol ought to be taken away from that shaking hand.

There was a strange wild look in the old man's eyes, and, of course, no one was likely to carry off chests that might easily weigh two hundredweight apiece.

"A bad job, this," said Linkinghorne, who had been told that this queer figure was Burden's butler. "A cruel job. Do you know how the fire started?"

The old man made no reply, but his fingers seemed to tighten on the butt of the firearm.

"Silver, I suppose, in those chests," the sleuth continued in his gentle voice. "If you could give me any particulars about the fire I'd be grateful to you."

"I answer no questions until I know who's asking them, and I don't reply to them then unless I think I'm helping the law."

"H'm!" said the detective, wondering whether it would not be better to take Atkins into his confidence. Here was an old servant—

the local policeman had told this to Linkinghorne—who had known the last four owners of Shotlander Priory. And the old fellow had spoken of helping the law.

"Idle questions I will not answer," Atkins continued, "nor will I talk with fools. Who are you, sir?"

Linkinghorne said that he was a police officer in plain clothes, and added that he did not wish anyone else to know it, and that he had not even disclosed his identity to the local police.

"You are from London?" queried the butler, "or would it be from Easthill?"

"From London, and I want to hear all about this fire. When did it start?"

"Before midnight, sir; but they'll have told you that."

"Where is Mr. Richard Burden?"

"At Easthill, sir, I believe. He left for that place yesterday morning."

"Of course an attempt has been made to communicate with him?"

"Yes, sir. But the wires are down between Redfield—that's our nearest town—and Easthill. A car was sent off, but it has not returned."

"Only the servants in the house, eh?"

"Only the servants, sir."

Further inquiries elicited the following particulars. The fire had started in the library. Smoke and flames had been seen emerging therefrom by a gamekeeper at midnight. The conflagration had spread rapidly. The more valuable contents of the rooms had been saved, but everything in the library had been destroyed. The local fire brigade and the Redfield outfit had been on the spot in twenty-five minutes.

"But," said Atkins in conclusion, "all the engines in London would not have saved the Priory, for it was doomed to perish."

"You believe in the curse, eh?"

"Do I not believe in God, sir?"

"Working through the hands of men, eh?"

"It might be so, sir."

"You spoke of helping the law, Mr. Atkins. That, I take it, would mean you think someone set the house on fire."

"I do think that, sir. The library was locked up, the master being away—no fire in it, nor anyone smoking there."

"Were any of the windows open?"

"I couldn't say, sir. When Mountain—that's the gamekeeper, sir—first saw the place burning he was a mile away. By the time he reached the house no one could have told whether there was a window open or not. There was none left. But I don't see how the fire could have started if no one did it on purpose."

Linkinghorne asked if the door of the library had been found locked.

"Yes, sir—a heavy oak door it was—studded with nails, and the fire hadn't burnt through it. It was locked, for we inserted the key, and I burnt my fingers as I turned it."

"You opened the door, eh?"

"No, sir. We couldn't open the door. There's a bolt on the in-side, and that was fastened—and that, sir, is the queer part of the business."

"Everyone knows it, of course?"

"No, sir. I kept that to myself. The others thought the heat had jammed the ironwork. I decided to say nothing until I saw Mr. Richard or some responsible person like yourself."

Linkinghorne commended this discretion, and asked the old butler to point out the windows of the library.

"Those three on the extreme left," Atkins replied, "but you couldn't go near them now, sir."

That was obvious. So tremendous had been the heat from the burning house that even where they were sitting, a hundred yards away from the nearest point of it, the snow had melted into slush. Linkinghorne put more questions—he asked for information about James Burden his cousin Robert, and even Robert's father;

chatted pleasantly about the family, seeking in his gentle, disarming fashion for something that would fit in with the strange theory of that child Rose Ivory.

It was a long time since he had paid so much attention to a fantastic idea. But this appealed to him—the possibility that the curse might work through natural laws to its appointed end.

And then, quite casually, as though it were of no importance, old Atkins mentioned the visit of Robertson, and in an instant the detective had thrust aside all strange theories and had grasped the essential clue—so tremendous in its possibilities that it almost took his breath away. But he did not betray his interest in Robertson. And when Atkins had given a description of the man, Linkinghorne asked no more questions. He would wait until he saw Dick Burden.

There were many interrogations to be asked, but Dick Burden was the person to answer them.

"That pistol!" he said, changing the subject with a laugh. "You don't think anyone is likely to run away with the plate chests?"

"Who knows what will happen, sir, in these days, when all connected with this house go in fear of their lives?" replied the old man.

"Oh, well, it is not you, but your master who will have to be careful," said Linkinghorne. "If I were you I should get the police to look after the silver and then go to bed. It's not a night for an old man to be sitting about."

Atkins refused to let anyone else guard the chests, and the sleuth, whose mind was now entirely occupied with the tracing of Robertson, decided not to pursue the matter.

He realized that it would serve no purpose for him to remain longer at Shotlander, and he asked the old fellow where he could obtain a decent bed and breakfast; for by now it was getting rather late, and he was anxious to turn in after his arduous night's experiences on the snow-clad country roads.

"There's the Chequers Inn at Stilehurst," replied the butler. "It's a matter of seven miles from here."

"At Stilehurst? That'll suit me very well. I've heard of the hostelry—quite a well-known place, full of old oak and all that sort of thing. Good night. I'll come over tomorrow, Mr. Atkins, and thank you very much for your information. And look here—don't you tell anyone about that bolted door until you see me again."

After some trouble, Linkinghorne found a vehicle that would take him to Stilehurst. And so it was that the sleuth had another stroke of good luck. It seemed as though Fate were destined to help him in his search for Robertson.

Linkinghorne allowed himself precisely two hours in bed, and after a hearty breakfast he made cautious inquiries about the man he was so anxious to be acquainted with. Of course, the detective did not know that Robertson was supposed to have stayed the night at the "Chequers," but Linkinghorne was aware that Robertson had arrived at the Priory on foot, and it was just possible that he had walked from Stilehurst.

"Oh yes, sir," said the landlord, "I remember the gentleman well—a very ugly person he was, sir, meaning no offense if he's a friend of yours. His car broke down here, and I've every reason to recollect that, because the gentleman went to bed early and we never saw him again."

"Never saw him again? What do you mean? Did he go off without paying his bill?"

"Oh no, sir. The chauffeur paid that—even for the breakfast that the gentleman did not eat."

"Look here," said Linkinghorne sharply. "This sounds like nonsense. You'd better tell the truth. The police are looking for this Mr. Robertson."

"I'm telling you the truth, sir," the landlord replied sharply. "This Mr. Robertson went to bed very early and gave orders that he was not to be disturbed until nine o'clock in the morning. The maid found the room empty and a note pinned to the pillow. It just said that he couldn't sleep and that he was going to walk on to Easthill. He wrote that the chauffeur was to settle the bill and pick him up on the road as soon as the car was repaired."

"Didn't you think that very odd?"

"Yes, sir, but people who can't sleep at night are odd. They do want to get out in the air and walk."

"And you never told the police?"

"No, sir. Why should I have done that? My bill was paid, and the chauffeur said that his master was a 'queer fellow.' Yes, those are the words he used—a queer fellow."

"Did the chauffeur give you any address?"

"No, sir, and I didn't ask for it. It was nothing to do with me."

"Nothing. Still, perhaps—out of curiosity——"

"Oh no sir. I'm not that sort. My bill was paid."

Linkinghorne laughed.

"The ideal host," he said. "Well, this chauffeur? I'd like a description of him."

"A small, dark, clean-shaven fellow, sir, with a scar on his forehead and well-spoken—not a common chap by any means."

"A sort of a gentleman, eh? What time did he leave?"

"About eleven o'clock, sir."

"Not much wrong with the car then?"

"I suppose not, sir. I don't know what was wrong with the car, but the chauffeur put it right himself."

"Have you got that note?"

"Yes, sir, I have."

"Why did you keep it? Looks as if you thought something was wrong," Linkinghorne suggested.

"Not wrong, sir, but queer, if you take my meaning. As a matter of fact, I thought Mr. Robertson might be wanted by the keepers of a lunatic asylum."

"Very likely you're right," the detective laughed. "Well, I'd like to see that note."

"You can have it, sir, and keep it. I'll get it for you now."

"Thanks, and I want a car to take me over to Shotlander."

"Very good, sir."

Elkinson, the landlord, left the private room in which this interview had taken place.

Linkinghorne filled his pipe and lit the tobacco. It seemed to him that he was having the most extraordinary luck.

Within twenty-four hours he had not only obtained an important clue that might enable him to track down this Robertson, but he was going to see a specimen of Robertson's handwriting.

Instinct had led him to Shotlander, but sheer luck had brought him to the Chequers Inn.

But Linkinghorne was a man who was suspicious of good fortune—an ungrateful sort of fellow who was apt to look gift horses long and steadily in the mouth.

"Robertson may never have written this note at all," he said to himself; "the chauffeur may have done so, or even our friend the landlord. And Atkins may have sent me here on purpose."

None of these things was probable, but they were all possible. And Linkinghorne had to consider possibilities. He was still considering them when the landlord, a short fat man with a red face, returned with the letter.

Linkinghorne read it through, and said that he was very greatly obliged to the boniface. The latter also produced a signature-book, in which the late guest had inscribed his name and address— "Mr. Robertson—London."

"Vague, that," commented the detective. "Thank you ever so much. What a lovely morning! Good to see the sun, eh? Snow melting already. I may stay another night here, if I can find my luggage—a long night's rest. I want that."

A few minutes later he departed in the hired car and told the driver to go along the road to London. He thought that he ought to find out what had happened to Ivory before he went to the Priory.

He was in no particular hurry to get to the latter. He wanted to meet Dick Burden there, and it was not likely that Dick would arrive before noon.

The snow was melting, but the roads were very heavy, and there would be drifts. And no doubt the wires were still useless. But in any case, Ivory must be found, and the little car dragged out of the ditch.

Linkinghorne was very fond of his vehicle. He had studied the map, and he knew now, in the broad daylight, exactly where it had come to rest.

He smiled as he thought of Ivory. A good, earnest, painstaking fellow without doubt, but not fond of getting his feet wet.

Well, no doubt Ivory had chosen the easiest way of getting a night's rest. The car, high-backed and tilted at that angle, would have made a very comfortable bed. And there were biscuits, and whisky in the flask. And no more snow had fallen.

He would not find Ivory buried in the snow. And perhaps he would not find Ivory at all. The lazy fellow might have ventured forth in the sunlight in search of a good breakfast. There would be a farmhouse or cottage somewhere near at hand.

On the top of a hill he caught sight of his car. It was still in the ditch. A little further on, the big drift barred the way. On the other side of it Linkinghorne could see the wheelmarks of his vehicle.

"Sorry, sir," said the driver, "but we can't get through this. I reckon that bus ran into it last night and backed out of it again. Hallo, there! Anyone on board?"

No one answered, and Linkinghorne shouted: "Hallo! Hallo! Hallo!" Then he explained that it was his own car and that he had left a friend in it.

"I'd like to get her out of that ditch," he said. "My friend has evidently abandoned her."

"And no blame to him either, sir."

"Well, I'll go and have a look. Can't you get round by some by-road?"

"Oh yes, sir, but it will take twenty minutes or half an hour."

"That doesn't matter," said Linkinghorne, and, alighting from the hired conveyance, he walked back along the road and stopped by a gate that opened into a field sloping upward from the highway.

And from this new position he saw something lying in the field—something that had been hidden from him before by the hedge. It was the body, not of Ivory, but of a stranger, a very small man indeed.

"You'd better turn the car," instructed Linkinghorne, "but draw up by the gate here."

Then he climbed over into the field and made his way toward that dark and ominous blot on the whiteness of the snow.

There were no drifts on this steep bank. In places it had been swept almost bare, and one could see the green of the grass.

The wind of the previous night had taken the snow from it and lifted it into the hollow of the roadway.

Only near the hedge did the snow lie deep, mounting to the top if it and pouring like a cataract over the low barrier of thorn.

The man was lying face downward, arms flung out in front of him and legs slightly drawn up. He was slight of build. A thick-belted black overcoat of some fine smooth cloth, boots and leggings, a peaked cap lying a few inches away from his head—all these proclaimed a kind of livery. When Mr. Linkinghorne turned the body over he was not surprised to see brass buttons on the coat. But he was astonished when he found himself looking into the white face of a dark, clean-shaven man with a long scar across his forehead.

Linkinghorne was angry with Fate for having robbed this man of life. A brief examination was enough to satisfy him that the chauffeur had been dead for some hours. So far as the detective could judge at present, there was no sign of any violence—no wound of any sort. But most certainly the man was dead, and the one person who could have given valuable evidence about Robertson and could have explained precisely what happened on the night the latter failed to return to the "Chequers" would now be silent forever.

But perhaps there was something to be learnt, even from the dead. Linkinghorne searched the man's pockets and transferred various articles to his own. Then he discovered a silver watch and chain, a silver cigarette case, a driver's license, bearing the name of Albert Honeyman and an address in London.

The sleuth went back to the gate and called out to the driver of the hired car. It was no difficult task for the two men to carry that slight burden and place it on the back seat.

"Yes, Honeyman—that's his name," said the driver. "Stayed at Mr. Elkinson's place for one evening. Better drive straight to the nearest doctor, sir, I suppose?"

"That's it, but I'm afraid a doctor will be of no use. It would only be a matter of form. I think I'll go and have a look at my car. I can keep to the high ground of the field and get round the drift. Cover that poor chap up with the rug."

Linkinghorne hurried back along the slope of the field, broke his way through the hedge, and reached his vehicle without difficulty. There was no one in it, but he found a message scribbled on the inside of an old envelope:

I've had a very good night, thank you, and am off to find some breakfast. I hope to get someone to haul the car out of the ditch, but write this in case you should turn up before I come back—

WILFRED IVORY.

Linkinghorne closed the door of the car again, and his keen eyes noted certain matters of interest. On the road there were tracks of a very much larger vehicle than his own—of a car that had stopped close to the edge of the drift, reversed, and then gone down the hill again. And there were footprints—the marks of narrow-pointed boots that had not belonged either to himself or Ivory. So far as he could judge from a cursory inspection, they were the footprints of two men. They could be traced up to his own car and back again, and then to a place in the hedge a little above the spot where he had come through from the field in to the road. Someone had penetrated the bushes themselves, for several twigs were broken, but there were no footprints on the far side of it. This did not puzzle Linkinghorne because long after the snow ceased to fall, the wind must have shifted it. Indeed, there was a bare patch of green on the slope above.

It was only natural to suppose that some of the footmarks had been made by the unfortunate chauffeur. The sleuth took some thin white paper from his pocket and cut out four patterns with a small pair of scissors. Then he went back and fitted a couple of them to the boot soles of the dead man. The other two were much too large.

"The feet of Robertson," he said to himself.

Then he sighed. He would have dearly loved to make further investigations and await Ivory's return. But he owed some duty to the dead, and, in any case, he had to get into touch with London, by telephone or telegram, as soon as possible.

Chapter X · Dick Vanishes

—

Sir Julius Kingsbury brought the news of the fire to his daughter—about 12:30 on the morning of Letty's interview with Dick Burden.

"Most of the furniture and pictures have been saved," the baronet said, speaking very slowly and with a hard, unsympathetic note in his voice. "But the place is completely gutted—only the shell of it left. No lives have been lost, so far as is known."

"Oh, how terrible! Dick was so fond of the place. Who told you?"

"I went round to the 'Majestic' to see Dick. He was not there——"

"Oh, I knew that. He returned to Shotlander yesterday afternoon."

"Why didn't you tell me so—yesterday?"

"I don't know. It did not matter. He was coming back here today. I suppose he wired to the manager of the hotel?!"

"No. The wires broke down last night in the storm. The message came by car. Dick did not visit Shotlander after all. He told the people at the hotel he was going home for the evening. But he did not carry out his intention. At any rate, he failed to arrive."

This information neither puzzled nor alarmed Letty. She was only thankful that Dick had changed his mind. He might so easily have been injured in the fire—might even have lost his life.

Certainly it was a stroke of luck that he had not carried on his original intention of spending the night at the priory.

"Then the folk there don't know where he is?" the girl queried.

"They did not know when the car left Shotlander at four o'clock this morning." Sir Julius paused and stroked his mustache. "I've no doubt," he continued, "that Dick went up to London. Very likely he's at Shotlander by now. Letty, you don't seem to realize what has happened."

"I realize that Dick has lost his home and that he'll never rebuild it."

"Don't you understand that the curse is still nearer fulfillment? It was said that by fire and water the line should perish."

"The house was not alive," Letty retorted. "What is the Priory after all?"

"It is one with those who live in it, Letty. An old place like that is almost flesh and blood. And it has perished. And now—only Dick is left alive. The enemies of Shotlander are relentless. Spiritual or material, they are very near to victory. Letty, my dear child—surely now you will understand——"

"I am not afraid," the girl interrupted. "If there are enemies, I'll help Dick to fight them—even if they are devils. I have that much of you in me, Father."

Sir Julius shrugged his shoulders, walked to the window, looked out of it for a few moments, and then seated himself at his writing-table. There was a knock on the door, and Miss Cramer entered the room.

"I've just heard about the fire," she said breathlessly. "Where is Mr. Richard Burden? Do you know, Sir Julius?"

"I do not," he answered coldly.

"Was he at Shotlander Priory?"

"He was not."

"But he intended to go there," said Letty. "He sent a message to me over the 'phone to say that he was going to motor to the priory, and so he could not take me out for a drive in the afternoon. What is the matter, Miss Cramer? Do you know anything about Mr. Burden?"

"Yes—he had a letter yesterday from Cowhurst; I gave it to him myself. He told me that he would send a copy of it to his lawyers, and he begged me not to speak about it to you and frighten you. But now that no one knows where Mr. Burden is I feel that it is my duty to inform the police."

"You think something has happened to Mr. Burden?" queried Sir Julius.

"Of course I do," said Miss Cramer. "Who wouldn't?"

"I, for one," Sir Julius replied. "A lot of nonsense has been talked about these letters. Still, the police must know. You had better telephone to them at once."

"You should have told us this before," said Letty.

"Oh no. Miss Kingsbury—I promised I would say nothing until it was necessary—until something happened to Mr. Burden."

"Nothing has happened to Mr. Burden," said Sir Julius firmly. "I've no doubt he is now at Shotlander."

"Please telephone at once to the police," exclaimed Letty. "There's no time to be wasted in talking."

Miss Cramer left the room, and Sir Julius dipped his pen in the ink and began to write a letter. For a few moments Letty did not speak, and then she said: "I am going to Shotlander, and I think you had better come with me."

"Certainly not, Letty. And don't forget that if anything has happened to Dick, it has occurred here, in Easthill."

"Why do you say that?"

"Because it was in Easthill that Robert and James Burden died, and it was at Easthill that they received the letters from Cowhurst."

"I am going to Shotlander," reiterated Letty. "I shall be back tonight."

"If you mean to carry out your proposal," said Sir Julius, "you had better not return. I am not going to plead with you. But we can't live together—after this—with any respect for each other. You know I am accustomed to be obeyed."

"Yes, Father dear, but——"

"Oh, this is just an incident," he broke in. "But it means you intend to marry Dick Burden, that my wishes do not count, and that for the rest of my life we are going to be nothing to each other. Well, it is your choice, not mine, Letty."

She looked at him for a few moments without speaking. And she was sorry for him—more sorry than she had ever been for anyone in all her life.

Her pride and stubbornness gave way to pity. For she remembered her father, not as she saw him then, but as she had seen him on the previous morning, haggard and piteous and broken.

And it seemed to her that he might be like that, when she had left him. She pictured him like that—alone.

He almost seemed to her like a child. And yet—he was a man who could not possibly be humored like a child.

"If I did visit Shotlander," the girl said, "I don't suppose I could do any good. Father, you used to like Dick."

"I still like him, but I care most for your happiness. I do not want you to marry into a doomed family, to lose husband and perhaps child—to live a life of constant fear and misery."

The words were spoken in a deliberate manner.

Letty sighed. They were going over all the old ground again. She decided it would be better to give way. After all, she could do no good by going to Shotlander. Dick was not there.

The door opened and Miss Cramer entered the room this time without knocking.

"The car has been found," she exclaimed in her deep, masculine voice. "Oh, Miss Kingsbury, I startled you. There's been no accident. The vehicle never left Easthill. It broke down by a garage in the North part of the town. Mr. Burden left it there to be put right, and said he would call for it in the morning. The proprietor of the garage telephoned to the 'Majestic,' and the manager got in touch with the police. They had just heard when I rang them up."

"There is no news of poor Mr. Burden."

"Don't talk of him like that," Letty exclaimed angrily—"as if he were dead! Of course he went by train! He changed his mind, and was close to the station and perhaps he had only just time to catch the express, so he couldn't take the car back to the hotel."

"Oh, I wish I had your way of looking at things, Miss Kingsbury. Well, I mustn't stop—or you won't any of you get any lunch."

She bounced out of the room, and slammed the door behind her. Sir Julius went up to his daughter and took her face between his hands and kissed it.

"My dear child," he said—"my poor little daughter."

Letty broke down—burst into tears and clung to her father as if she would never let him go.

Chapter XI · Arrival of the Quarry

—

There was no mystery whatever about the cause of Albert Honeyman's death. The post-mortem showed that the man was suffering from a severe form of heart disease, and that it had proved fatal under the strain of some sudden exertion. The starting of a car would have been quite sufficient to kill him, and it was odd that an individual in such a condition should have been a chauffeur.

The mystery lay rather in the circumstances attending the poor fellow's death. Why had he been found in that field? Where was the car? Who was the other man? Apart from the evidence of the footprints, there must have been another person or more, or the vehicle could not have been driven away. It was conceivable that the latter might have gone for help, but why had no more been heard of him, and why had he not put Honeyman in the car and driven to the nearest village?

All these were questions that were still unanswered three days after the fire at Shotlander Priory. Nothing was known about the mysterious car except that it had arrived on the scene, after four o'clock in the morning, at which time Linkinghorne had set out on his walk to Shotlander, and had left before 8:30, at which hour Ivory had crawled out of the little coupe, had seen the marks of the footprints and wheels, and, being hungry, had postponed further investigation until he had found some breakfast. This meal he had been able to obtain at a farmhouse a mile from the snowdrift and a little off the main road. He had made inquiries about the big car, thinking it "caddish" for the owner to have left him in the ditch, but no one had been able to give him any information. On his return he had found a message from Linkinghorne, and later on in the day a mechanic had arrived with a lorry, had pulled the coupe out of the ditch, and towed it along some byroads into Redfield.

The only evidence, therefore, that Ivory could offer was that of time, but there was something suspicious in the fact that he had not been disturbed from his slumbers. This suggested that the man or men in the car were either in a great hurry or did not wish to meet anyone who could identify them afterward.

But the greatest mystery of all was the identity of Albert Honeyman himself. His antecedents had got to be traced. The address found in his pocket proved to be only that of a small tobacconist who received the letters of other people and charged a small fee for this courtesy. The name of Albert Honeyman had been on his books for three weeks, and during that time Honeyman had only called twice for his letters.

"Albert Honeyman himself does not matter," said Linkinghorne to Ivory after the inquest. "That unfortunate fellow is only a clue to this Robertson. I must leave others to find out as much as possible about Albert Honeyman. You and your assistants will have your work cut out in tracing Richard Burden. I shall have to devote my time entirely to Robertson. And then there's Cowhurst and the burning of Shotlander Priory. Upon my word, Ivory, they're going to keep us busy."

Ivory nodded. The two men were in a private sitting room at the Chequers Inn. Linkinghorne was going to stay the night, but Ivory intended to catch an evening train to Easthill.

"One man couldn't keep us as busy as all this," the detective continued after a pause. "We don't know what the game is yet, but there's more than one in it——"

"And perhaps more than one game," Ivory interrupted.

"Yes—possibly. This disappearance of Mr. Richard Burden is most unfortunate, because it is only he who can tell us why Mr. Robertson called to see him."

"My theory," said Ivory, "is that Robertson saw Richard Burden push his big brother off the pier and that Robertson is out for blackmail. And I shouldn't wonder if Richard Burden has committed suicide."

"Ah, you make events fit in with your original theory. That is a common mistake," replied the sleuth.

"And a common cause of success, Mr. Linkinghorne. But theories don't matter just now. We're going to find out what has happened to Burden and Robertson, and who wrote the letters from Cowhurst, and who set fire to the Priory. As you say, we are going to be busy."

"But not too busy to keep our eyes on the trail, Ivory. I shouldn't wonder if they are drawing red herrings across our path. That's an old trick, but it cuts both ways, for if one can find the man with the red herring, it's as good as finding the criminal."

A few minutes later Ivory left to catch his train, and Linkinghorne lay back in his armchair and closed his eyes. For a quarter of an hour he did not move. Then there was a knock on the door and the landlord entered the room.

"A young man to see you, sir," said Elkinson; "name of Jones."

"Jones, eh?" laughed Linkinghorne. "A good name. Show him up."

The landlord retired, and a minute later ushered a tall, dark-haired young fellow into the room. He bore the trademark of police officer and had a rather fleshy red face.

"Well, Jones?" queried Linkinghorne when the door was closed.

"We've found the car, sir."

"Mr. Robertson's car, eh? Well, that's not bad work, seeing that you didn't know the number of it."

"It's outside, sir, and a very nice car it is, too. We found it on Wimbledon Common this afternoon—just standing there—no one in it—engine cold. It was reported to us a derelict that might turn out to be what we were looking for. Anyhow, it's a landaulet."

"Dark blue?"

"No, gray."

"The landlord here distinctly said it was a dark blue car, and we've other evidence to that effect."

"Yes, sir, but it has been repainted."

"Impossible—in the time."

"Oh, it's been very roughly done, sir, and the blue paint is underneath."

"Oh, well, then it is the car. Any information about it?"

"None at present, sir. It was found on a part of the common where hardly anyone would go at this time of year—at the bottom of a steep road that runs down to Queen's Mere."

"Very strange."

"Yes, sir."

"Are they dragging the mere?"

"No, sir, I don't think so."

"Well, they'd better. They may find Robertson's body. He must have come pretty well to the end of his tether if he's had to abandon the car. Any number-plates on her?"

"None, sir, and——"

The door opened without ceremony, and the landlord burst into the room.

"Mr. Robertson, sir," he cried—"Mr. Robertson! He's here, and asking to see you."

Jones looked astonished. Linkinghorne smiled, and nodded, as though he had been expecting a visit from Robertson.

"I will see him in a minute or two," he replied. "Just close the door, Mr. Elkinson—no, stay this side of it."

The landlord did as he was bidden.

"Have you seen the car?" questioned the sleuth.

"Yes, sir," replied the boniface.

"Can you identify her?"

"Yes, sir. A bit of her leather upholstery was torn at the back of the driver's seat, and I remember asking the chauffeur if he'd like one of my maids to stitch it up. It still wants mending."

"Thank you. Well, send up Mr. Robertson when I ring the bell. That'll be in about a minute or two."

The landlord left the room, and Linkinghorne began to fill his pipe.

"You can wait in the next apartment, Jones," he said. "It is my bedroom. You will take a full report of the interview in shorthand. Close the door; then put your ear to the keyhole and write as best you can. No doubt Robertson knows you are here, so you'd better leave this room after he is shown into it. Ring the bell, will you?"

Jones obeyed. Twenty seconds later the door opened and the landlord stood aside to let Robertson enter. Linkinghorne, who had never seen the newcomer before, was astounded at the ugliness of the man's face.

"Well, so long, Jones," said the detective. "I'll see you later on. Good evening, Mr. Robertson. Please take a seat."

"The typical murderer," said the detective to himself; and then allowed: "I've been waiting to see you for some little time, Mr. Robertson."

"Yes, I must apologize for giving you so much trouble. I only landed this afternoon at Ramsgate, and I should have gone away again if I had not come across one of your advertisements in the newspaper. It was most fortunate for both of us."

Yes, indeed," said Linkinghorne grimly. "Please sit down and I'll order drinks."

"Thank you. I don't drink."

"How did you know I was here?" queried Linkinghorne abruptly.

"I did not know. I only suspected. Where the carcass is, you remember, there will the eagles be gathered together."

"You are referring to——"

"The fire at Shotlander. I also read about that in the newspaper."

"And the death of Honeyman?"

"Yes, and a good many other things I knew nothing about—so I came straight here."

"Expecting to find me at this inn?"

"Why, certainly. What spot could be more convenient for you? Besides, Mr. Linkinghorne—I got your name from the paper—I stayed at this hotel and it would naturally interest you. I came here on the chance of discovering you, and I have found you. Now, what is it you want?"

Robertson now accepted the sleuth's invitation to be seated. He lit a cigar, and Linkinghorne proceeded to put his questions.

"On the afternoon of January the 17th," said he, "you were fishing on the pier at Easthill?"

"Was I? Let me see. The 17th, you say? Yes—that's right."

"Why didn't you come forward at the inquest?"

"What inquest?"

"On James Burden."

"I had no evidence to give."

"You were fishing on the Easthill pier. Both James and his brother were there at that time."

"I do not know Mr. James Burden by sight."

"You know none of the Burden family?" queried Linkinghorne after a pause. This was a trap, but Robertson did not fall into it.

"Yes, I know Mr. Richard Burden," was the quiet reply. "I called to see him on—let me see—it would be on February the 9th or the 10th."

Linkinghorne was not astonished at this candor. The man would realize that the butler had already given this information.

"Why did you call at Shotlander Priory?"

Robertson shrugged his shoulders.

"It was not an ordinary visit," Linkinghorne continued. "You must have walked all the way from this inn and back again. There was something wrong with your car."

"Am I on my trial?" queried Robertson.

"No, but you'd better answer my questions."

"Have you a warrant for my arrest?"

"Not yet," Linkinghorne laughed. "If I'd been going to arrest you I should have warned you that anything you might say would be used in evidence against you."

"That's only a formality."

"I want to make things easier for you. You need not answer any more of my questions."

Robertson leaned forward, resting his arms on the table.

"Have a good look at my face," he said, "and tell me if it reminds you of anyone."

Linkinghorne stared hard at the hideous features, and then he smiled. He could not fail to notice that which Richard Burden had seen at a glance. He took three photographs from his pocket—the portraits of Robert and James and Richard Burden—laid them in a row, and studied Robertson's face again.

"You are some relation of the Burdens," he said. "You are—you'll pardon my saying so—a caricature of the Burden family."

"Yes, I am Richard Burden's cousin—the son of his aunt. That fact has been kept a secret for a very long time, and I only tell you now because I want you to understand that, so far from being concerned in the deaths of the Burdens, I am one of the family and myself in danger. I called to see Richard Burden that night to talk over the best method of dealing with this unknown enemy. I know no more than you do about the murders."

"Where did you go that night—after you left Shotlander Priory?"

"I told Honeyman that he could pick me up on the road between Stilehurst and Easthill. I suppose you have my note."

"Yes—here in my pocket."

"Well, then, I did exactly what I said I was going to do. I struck the road to Easthill and walked and walked—resting a bit every now and then."

"And Honeyman picked you up?"

"No. I gave him until noon, and then I took a train to Easthill."

"And what happened to your chauffeur?"

"I don't know. I never saw him again."

"Oh come, come, Mr. Robertson—you never saw your car and chauffeur again?"

"It was not my car," Robertson remarked very slowly, "and Honeyman was not my chauffeur. I know nothing about him. I may tell you that I have no residence in England. I live in a little village called Sarre, near Boulogne. I am well known there. I have a small yacht, and am very fond of fishing. I often cross to the English coast. All this you can prove for yourself, and you can also satisfy yourself that I was back in Sarre on February 12th, and that I have been there ever since—until this morning. In fact, when I crossed to Ramsgate. There is no mystery about me whatever, Mr. Linkinghorne."

"Oh yes, there is," said the detective to himself; but aloud he said: "We seem to have made a mistake, Mr. Robertson."

"Not at all. You naturally wanted my evidence about James Burden, and—and this fellow Honeyman. I'm afraid I cannot help you. I picked Honeyman up in London that night—or rather, in the afternoon. He stopped close to me in Knightsbridge, and asked me if I wanted to be driven anywhere——"

"But the car was not licensed for hire."

"I know that. I took him to be some gentleman's chauffeur who wanted to make a bit. I asked him if he'd drive me to Easthill, and he said he would, and that he'd do it cheaply, as he had to be in Easthill on the following day. He told me his master lived there. Of course, I pretended, when we broke down by the inn, that he was my servant and that it was my car. I know nothing whatever about him."

The interview was over. This story would have to be examined and tested. The main assertions were capable of proof, if they were true. But there was little to be gained by further questions. The man's face was a mask, and no one could read his thoughts.

Linkinghorne went to the fire, lit his pipe with a spill, and then, glancing at a picture which hung over the mantelpiece, saw something dimly reflected in the glass—something that made him turn abruptly on his heel.

Robertson's great arms lay on the table, and his head was bowed between them. His massive shoulders rose and fell as though he was shaken by deep sobs. No sound came from his throat or lips.

"Are you ill, Mr. Robertson?" queried Linkinghorne.

The man raised his head and, leaning back, gripped the edge of the table with his hands. His face was distorted with agony.

"Yes," he muttered hoarsely, "I—I am ill. My nerves have gone to pieces. I cannot sleep, my health is breaking down. I cannot go without rest night after night. I'll stay here at the 'Chequers' for a day or two until you're satisfied with my bona-fides."

—

It was only an attack of influenza after all, but it laid Robertson by the heels for a while as surely as though a prison door had closed on him.

Chapter XII · What Was It He Saw?

—

To the pedestrian or the cyclist or the motorist, Cowhurst is chiefly remarkable for its very beautiful old church, of which the Saxon tower is the principal feature, and the number of its inns in proportion to its population.

As a lover of Sussex aptly puts it in a little poem:

In little Cowhurst
You can drink till you burst

In its one street—a delightful thoroughfare that climbs the hill—there are no fewer than five public houses, and each of them is of a respectable antiquity. But the oldest and noblest is the "Silver Buckle."

This ancient cognizance of the Pelhams is painted on the signboard, carved on the stone, and cut on the paneling over the big fireplace in the hall.

The inn, which still retains its old fretted barge boards and its curiously carved corner posts, is well known to antiquarians, but not much frequented by tourists, except for lunch, for though the food is good, the beds are uncomfortable and it is rather behindhand in the matter of bathrooms and sanitation. To this hostelry, on a cold winter evening, two days after Robertson's arrival at the "Chequers" at Stilehurst, came a young and remarkably pretty girl. She arrived in an ancient cab from a station five miles distant, and she had no more luggage than an old and shabby little suitcase. Mrs. Woodgate, the landlady, a fat and heavy-featured old woman, regarded her with disapproval.

"A bed for the night?" she echoed sharply. "Yes, I daresay we can oblige you."

"For several nights perhaps," said the girl sweetly. "I just love this place. I'd like to live here all the rest of my life."

The landlady sniffed contemptuously and rang a bell. An untidy servant appeared and took the girls suitcase.

"Number six," said the landlady, and then to the guest: "You'll be having dinner, I suppose?"

"Oh, anything will do for me—anything."

"None of your boiled eggs, miss. We don't serve that kind of meal here. It's the full dinner for seven and sixpence or none at all."

"Oh, everything you've got," laughed the girl. "I'm very hungry."

She followed the servant up the broad oak staircase, and was shown into a large, low-ceilinged room with a small bed in it.

"This is your best room?" she queried.

"No, miss. Our best apartments are already taken by Sir Julius Kingsbury and his daughter."

"Miss Kingsbury? Is that the Miss Kingsbury who———"

"I think so, miss," the servant interposed. "They come from Easthill—and I read in the Sunday paper that———"

"Yes, yes. That'll do. Oh, I never thought that I'd have such a thrilling holiday!"

The servant lit two candles and retired. Presently she returned and said:

"The missus told me to ask what name?"

"Name? Oh, Miss Black—Miss Rose Black."

"Miss Rose Black. That do sound funny, miss."

The servant vanished, giggling. Rose Ivory—for she it was— stood before a large cracked mirror and regarded herself as though she were an object of interest. She had every reason to be satisfied with the picture. Soft brown hair, gray eyes set rather far apart, a mouth with a most delightful smile, a small tip-tilted nose—a thin lithe figure! All this would have pleased a man, but it did not please Rose Ivory, who all her life had longed to be tall and dark and stately. She did not wish to look like a butterfly, for she was a very serious young person indeed.

"But perhaps on this occasion," she said to herself, "it will be useful."

She had been sent to Cowhurst on a mission, and she already saw herself as someone of importance. She had had an interview with the great Linkinghorne, and as a result she had been dispatched to the "Silver Buckle" and had been given money to spend.

She had purchased a new evening frock for the occasion, and— well, as she saw herself in the mirror, she could not resist the temptation of putting on her finery.

This made her late for dinner, and when she entered the oak-paneled dining room Sir Julius Kingsbury and his daughter had just seated themselves at a table in the corner. Sir Julius was facing the entrance and she knew him quite well by sight. Miss Kingsbury had her back to the room. Of course it was Miss Kingsbury, but Rose Ivory could not see her face.

The girl seated herself at a table as far away from the Kingsburys as possible, but in a position from which she could watch them.

The dinner was only "full" in the sense that it was long. For the most part it consisted of scraps left over from lunch.

The "Silver Buckle" was famous for its lunches, but few people ever dined there.

To Rose Ivory, however, unused to luxury, it was a very good meal indeed. But she would have enjoyed it better if she had not known that it would be her duty, as soon as possible, to thrust her acquaintance on the Kingsburys. She was well aware of the difference in their social position, and she did not look forward to being snubbed.

"Find out why Sir Julius Kingsbury has gone to Cowhurst," Linkinghorne had said to her, "and make friends with him. Keep an eye on him. You're a pretty girl, and I dare say he'll take a fancy to you."

At the end of the third course Miss Ivory became aware of the fact that she was attracting attention. The baronet's daughter turned in her seat and looked at her. Sir Julius smiled. Oh, yes, they were certainly talking of her and wondering what she was doing by herself at the "Silver Buckle." For several minutes Rose kept her eyes fixed on her empty plate.

"Miss Rose Black," she said to herself—"a young artist suffering from a nervous breakdown." All that sounded very simple. She was an amateur painter, and she had brought her brushes and her sketch-blocks with her. As for the nervous breakdown, that was to excite sympathy and friendliness. She did not like her job at all. The grim reality was that stern-eyed elderly man. She was afraid of him. She could well believe, as she had heard at Easthill, that he had shown no mercy to criminals.

And now—well, if he were not a criminal himself, he had at any rate been placed under observation by the police.

A plate containing two oranges and twelve Brazils was placed before her. She cracked a nut, and a little cloud of dust flew out of it. And then, looking up from her plate, she saw Miss Kingsbury walking toward her. Sir Julius was still in his seat. He had lit a cigar, and was leaning back in his chair.

Letty Kingsbury came straight up to Rose and said:

"Surely I have met you somewhere. Don't you live at Easthill?"

"Oh no," laughed Rose. "I live in London, and I've come down here for a rest and to do a bit of painting."

"I beg your pardon," said Letty. "I was certain I'd seen you at Easthill," and she turned to go from the room.

"Oh, please don't apologize," faltered Miss Ivory. "It's so lonely here, and I'd like to be able to speak to someone. My name is Rose Black."

"And mine is Letty Kingsbury. I'm here with my father—for a day or two. He has been ill and it's quite quiet here, isn't it?"

"Kingsbury?" queried Rose. "Sir Julius Kingsbury?" and then suddenly sprang to her feet. "Your father!" she cried. "What is the matter?"

Letty turned. The baronet was leaning forward and sitting quite motionless, his eyes were open, his face contorted with fear or pain. The cigar had dropped from his mouth onto the table and lay there smoldering. He was staring at the open door.

Sir Julius Kingsbury sat motionless, staring at the doorway as though Death was standing there and he was afraid to die. But there was no one in the doorway.

Letty hastened to her father, but Rose Ivory, who was certain that Sir Julius was looking at someone, walked straight to the door.

There was not even anyone in the paneled hall. After the serving of the dessert the waiter—an ostler between mealtimes—had vanished.

The door of the landlady's private room was open, and Rose

Ivory poked her head round the corner and saw that the room was empty.

Down a passage came the sound of laughter—probably from the kitchen.

Rose Ivory, suddenly aware that she might be on the threshold of a great discovery, cared nothing for appearances. She went out of the hall door and looked up and down a deserted street. And then she ran up the broad staircase.

There was no one on the landing. The inn seemed to be quite empty and silent save for the sounds from the servants' quarters.

No doubt the staff, including the landlady, were at supper.

To Rose Ivory there was something curious and even sinister about the emptiness of the "Silver Buckle."

To her vivid imagination is was as though something very horrible had appeared and that everyone had fled from the sight of it.

Even the laughter did not reassure her.

Women, and men too for that matter, so often laugh at their own fears—inanely, hysterically.

She stood on the landing for a few moments, and then realized that she had been acting in such a way as to attract the greatest possible amount of attention.

She went quickly to her bedroom, took a bottle of smelling salts from her bag, and ran downstairs to the dining room.

She found Sir James Kingsbury sipping some brown-colored liquid from a wineglass. His face was flushed.

"I've brought my smelling salts," said Rose. "I had to turn out my suitcase to find them."

"It was very kind of you," Letty replied stiffly, but Sir Julius held out his hand, took the green glass bottle, and put it to his nose.

"Excellent!" he exclaimed with a laugh. "Better than all the brandy in the world. You are a kind and sensible young lady."

He set down the bottle close to his plate and drained the contents of the wineglass at a single gulp.

"Rotten stuff," he said, "except when one is ill. I have these attacks—at times. They pass very quickly. Let us forget all about it. Do you know this place well, Miss—Miss———"

"Black," said Rose promptly. "No, I've never been here before."

"Then you can't tell us what to do in the evenings, eh?"

Rose laughed. She had imagined that Sir Julius might steal out by himself after dinner, and that she would follow him—"track him down," as she had phrased it to herself.

"Oh, I expect we sit here," she replied, "until we go to bed."

"Rest," said Sir Julius. "I suppose you've come to Cowhurst for peace. Nerves? No, you don't look like a neurotic person. What are you really here for?"

Rose explained that she was an artist. The conversation turned to matters of art, and it was not long before Miss Ivory got out of her depth. But she only floundered for a moment, and then Sir Julius, with a kindly smile, began to talk of Cowhurst, leading up to the subject quite naturally, by discussing the possibilities of the place as a hunting ground for artists.

"At present," he said, "it seems to be quite neglected."

Later on he remarked that he was tired, and asked Letty to go and see the landlady about filling a hot-water bottle.

"The beds in these inns are often damp," he said to Rose when his daughter had left the dining room; and then, after a slight pause: "Well, did you find the ghost?"

"I—I'm afraid I don't understand you, Sir Julius," said Rose, who understood him only too well.

"The ghost I saw in the doorway. You went to work very quickly, and I fancy you're a sharp young lady."

"Oh, please explain, Sir Julius."

"You saw me staring," the baronet continued, "as though I were gazing at someone in a doorway. And then I was ill. My daughter, knowing the cause of my complaint, hurried at once to my side. But you peered into the hall. There was no one there, of course?"

"No one," said Rose, "but I went to get my smelling salts, Sir Julius."

"You didn't think there was anyone there in the doorway?"

"Well, yes, I did. I couldn't help thinking that, could I? You were looking at the door—just as if someone had suddenly appeared."

"There was someone there," said Sir Julius in a low voice. "But it was not a creature of flesh and blood."

"How do you know that?"

"Because it was a man who is dead, my dear child. Of course, you don't believe in ghosts?"

"I don't think I do, Sir Julius."

"Oh well, if you'd been sitting by my side tonight you'd have seen one—or possibly you would not have done so. I have alluded to this matter because I do not wish you to tell my daughter that you thought someone was standing there and that you saw no one. It would frighten her. She is anxious about my health, and I don't want her to imagine that I'm subject to delusions."

"As if I should be likely to say anything to Miss Kingsbury!" Rose exclaimed.

"Well, that's a bargain," the baronet said gently. "I like your honest, pretty face, and I don't think you are really a little busybody that meddles with other people's business. We are going to hire a car tomorrow and go for a drive. I hope you'll come with us."

"I'd like to," said Rose—"most awfully."

Chapter XIII · Linkinghorne Is Puzzled

—

To the police and also to the public the disappearance of Richard Burden was the one thing that mattered. It was conceivable that both Robert and James Burden had met with accidents. Two juries had given separate verdicts to that effect, and but for the curious coincidence of that letter from Cowhurst there might have been no further inquiries. But the total disappearance of a strong, sane young man was a matter that called for a quick and thorough investigation. All the police of England—all the police of the United Kingdom were on the lookout for Richard Burden.

A description of him had gone over telephone and cable to the Continent, and even the American and Canadian liners were watched and searched.

Now, the disappearance of a young man is not in itself a sensation of the first magnitude.

Scarcely a week goes by without some young man or woman vanishing, and in ninety-nine cases out of a hundred the missing person turns up again, for it is easy enough to disappear and hide oneself for a considerable period.

But the disappearance of Richard Burden, following on the deaths of his brother and his cousin, and coinciding with the destruction of Shotlander Priory, seemed to form so exact a fulfillment of the curse upon the family that a blaze of romantic glamour poured upon it.

So far as the public was concerned, the material aspect of the case was almost lost in the psychical and even religious questions involved.

Serious papers dealt very solemnly with the questions. There was a boom in spiritualism. Mediums and fortune-tellers and crystal-gazers had the time of their lives.

The police, however, were not concerned with the fulfillment of curses.

Linkinghorne, in the selection of Rose Ivory as an agent, had not for one moment chosen her because he believed in her ingenious theory that the curse of the monk had been fulfilled by some inherent taint in the family itself. But had realized that any young girl who had been capable of inventing such a theory was a person of more than ordinary ability.

A letter from Rose lay now before the detective on the table of his private sitting room at the Chequers Inn. Five days had elapsed since Robertson's arrival and he was still confined to his bed. All that individual's previous statements had been confirmed.

He was an honored resident in the village of Sarre. Many had testified to his worth and kindliness.

His boat had been in Easthill harbor at the times of the deaths of James and Robert Burden, but it was equally certain that Robertson had been at Sarre and that his boat had been in Boulogne harbor at the time of Richard Burden's disappearance. The trip to London, which had occurred between these incidents, had been satisfactorily explained, and the incidents of the return journey in Honeyman's car had been verified.

Save for the rather eccentric behavior of Robertson on the night of his stay at the Chequers Inn, there had been nothing out of the ordinary in his conduct.

He had gone to London to see his mother, who was living with an old servant in a flat in South Kensington.

Linkinghorne had personally interviewed both these old women, and he had been quite satisfied with their replies.

And now there was this disturbing letter from that very original young lady, the superintendent's daughter.

The communication from Miss Ivory had arrived by an afternoon post, and Linkinghorne's tea was set out before him.

"Dear Mr. Linkinghorne," the girl had written, "there was an adventure on the first night," and she described the illness of Sir Julius Kingsbury and the supposed cause of it. And then she went on to say that she had gone to bed at ten o'clock and had left the Kingsburys still sitting in the dining room.

"I was just a little bit excited," the letter continued, "and I could not sleep. I had a magazine with me, and I had been trying to read it, but I found myself unable to fix my attention on a short story. It neither interested me nor did it lull me to rest. A clock on the landing had just struck one when I heard a door open sharply further down the passage. There were loud steps along the corridor. They turned out afterward to be those of Sir Julius Kingsbury. My door was locked, and when he had passed it I heard a crash and the sound of a struggle.

"I suppose under ordinary circumstances, I should have kept

on the safe side of the door, but I could not forget that you sent me here to take note of anything out of the common, and this was certainly something that does not usually happen in a quiet country inn. I opened my door very quietly, peeped out, and saw Sir Julius kneeling on the floor. His face was toward me, and though his head was bent I recognized him plainly enough in the light of a small oil lamp that was burning in the passage. He was still in the same clothes he had worn at dinner.

"His shoulders were hunched together, his arms stretched out straight down toward the floor, and his fingers curved as though they were gripping something. His two hands were a little distance apart, and the circle made by the curved fingers would just have gone round a man's throat. And they were a few inches off the floor. It was a horrible sight, Mr. Linkinghorne, but the most uncanny part of it was that Sir Julius was still fighting as though he had pinned his man down, but had not yet strangled him. The hands rose as though they had been jerked upwards, and then went down again. The grip of the fingers tightened. Then they moved sideways. He raised his head once, but he did not appear to see me.

"This has taken a long time to write, but the scene did not, I suppose, last for more than half a minute. Then Sir Julius gave a loud cry and suddenly collapsed, rolling over onto his side. And at that moment another door opened and Miss Kingsbury came running down the passage with a lighted candle in her hand. And then two other people appeared—the fat landlady, looking most grotesque in a flannel dressing gown, and a maidservant. Sir Julius came to his senses, and told them that a man had entered his bedroom and, finding that the occupant was still up and dressed, had bolted. He, Sir Julius, had followed him, caught him, and thrown him down on the floor of the corridor. But, after a tremendous struggle, the intruder had got away, and he, the baronet, had collapsed.

"That was Sir Julius's story, and I said nothing. I did not tell them I had witnessed this struggle with an imaginary burglar. I pretended that I had only come out of my room when the man had escaped. I thought you'd wish me to do this.

"Of course, poor old Sir Julius is quite mad. That he saw a ghost and had a supposed burglar on the same day is abundant and sure proof of that."

The description of the imaginary man, as given by the baronet, did interest Linkinghorne very much. It was a fairly accurate likeness of Robertson. This fact was known to Miss Ivory.

"You will understand," she wrote, "that Sir Julius detailed particulars of the burglar before he became normal. This morning he had a talk with me, and he seemed anxious to find out what he had said. He did not ask me in so many words, but he fished very carefully for information. And then he remarked that a blow on the head must have made him foolish, and he gave me an entirely different description of the burglar, making out the latter to be, in fact, as unlike Robertson as possible. I gather from this——"

The detective, reading the letter again for the third time, folded it up and placed it in his pocket. And he registered a mental vow that if he employed Rose Ivory again he would give her a few instructions.

"Keep to the facts," he would tell her, "and only supply the facts. A letter should be very concise and to the point."

Linkinghorne drank two cups of strong tea and ate two cold muffins and several slices of cake. Then he lit his pipe and stretched out his legs to the warm glow of the fire.

He was puzzled and disturbed by the letter, but, above all, he was vastly interested. Robertson had brought forward almost absolute proof that he was an innocent man, and it was very interesting to learn that he had been in the mind of the crazy Sir Julius when he had run out of the bedroom and grappled with an imaginary enemy on the floor of the passage. And this became of more importance when the baronet afterward gave an entirely different description of the burglar. It was quite evident that Sir Julius, for some reason or other, hated Robertson and desired to take his life, and equally evident that the baronet wished to keep his enmity a secret.

Sir Julius was the father of Letty, who was in love with Richard Burden. And the baronet was already a marked man. It was now known to the police that Sir Julius had been seen on the Easthill cliffs near the place where Robert Burden was supposed to have fallen into the sea, in the same day and about the same hour when the tragedy had occurred. The baronet had not yet been questioned on this matter, as the police were waiting to get further evidence. But Sir Julius was being watched.

"It's one of the two," said Linkinghorne to himself, "and perhaps both of them are in it. Sir Julius Kingsbury and Robertson! Well, a queer pair, anyway."

Chapter XIV · Atkins Shows Loyalty

—

Letty Kingsbury firmly believed that her father had seen someone standing at the door of the dining room of the inn and that he had had a fight with the same man in the corridor outside his bedroom. Most certainly the fellow was not a burglar, but it did not occur to her to question his existence. Her father had insisted on paying a visit to this inn at Cowhurst, ostensibly for a change of air, but really, she had no doubt, to find out something about this man—perhaps to meet him. His courage had failed him in the dining room, but later on he had met this mysterious someone face-to-face. And there had been a struggle. That her father had altered his description of his opponent on the following morning did not change her opinion. When he had come to his senses he had drawn an imaginary portrait. He had something to conceal, and he had concealed it to the best of his ability.

Rose maintained a discreet silence. She allowed everyone to form theories.

To Linkinghorne she wrote a good deal, and posted her letter in another village. We know what was in Miss Ivory's communication to the detective; but she said nothing to Letty Kingsbury.

And Letty Kingsbury, indeed, had little time to think of anything her father might say or do. Her mind groped in a great darkness for some ray of light that would show her the face of her lover. She did not believe that he was dead. There were even times when she wished that he might be dead.

That which might be the truth was gradually being forced in upon her reason. Richard Burden was the last man who had seen his brother alive.

James Burden had been in love with her, had done all in his power to prevent their marriage.

There had been a quarrel on the pier—blows—an accident—it would be no more than an accident.

That was how she was being forced to see what had happened. And she fancied that her father knew the truth, and that perhaps Robertson also knew.

Robertson and her father! Well, perhaps it was Robertson after all, who had visited the inn. But that did not matter—at present.

She wanted news of Richard Burden, and she had accompanied her father in the faint hope that she might come across someone at Cowhurst who would give her information that perhaps he would not give to the police.

Sir Julius looked very ill on the day following his adventure, but he would not hear of the drive being postponed.

"It will do me good," he said to Letty when they were discussing the matter in his bedroom before lunch, "and, besides, I hope to combine business with pleasure. I think we will visit Shotlander."

"Shotlander?" the girl queried. Then, suddenly: "Father, you know something about what has happened to Dick! Oh, for pity's sake tell me!"

"You will not see him again," said Sir Julius after a pause. "So far as you are concerned, Letty, he is dead. You can never marry him."

"Is he in England?"

"I don't know where he is, Letty."

"Does Mr. Robertson know?"

"Mr. Robertson? Have you taken leave of your senses? Mr. Robertson?"

The girl looked straight into the baronet's eyes. He was haggard and gray, and of late had been aging visibly. "Mr. Robertson," she said, "was on the pier that afternoon. He saw Dick and me. He may have seen Jim Burden. Mr. Robertson is aware of something and he has told you what he knows. Father, do you understand that my heart is breaking—not because I think Dick is dead—but because—I'm afraid of something that would be worse than his death."

"I know nothing," Sir Julius muttered. "I am seeking enlightenment."

"You think Dick killed his brother?"

"That is very likely."

"They fought—and there was an accident?"

"Yes, yes, of course—an accident. The police do not know that Jim wanted to marry you Letty, that he did all he could to prevent you from marrying Dick. Letty, my dear child, I—I am fighting for your happiness. I cannot say anything more now than that until—until tomorrow. We are caught in a terribly strong net, the two of us. We may not be able to break out of it——"

"I can't understand all this kind of talk," Letty interrupted harshly. "But if we're both enmeshed in the same net we'll have a better chance of getting out of it if I know something about the nature of the entanglement."

"You shall know," Sir Julius answered wearily, "ere very long—oh yes, perhaps before this time tomorrow."

"And you are going to take this Miss Black with us to Shotlander?" Letty queried after a pause. "Miss Black—a stranger?"

"Oh, she's not a stranger, Letty," he laughed. "I know all about that young lady."

"You've met her before, Father?"

"I've seen her often in Easthill. Her name isn't Black. It's Ivory. She's the daughter of Superintendent Ivory at Easthill. Bless her little heart, I know all about her."

"The daughter of Mr. Ivory?" Letty echoed.

"Yes, yes. Linkinghorne has sent her here, I expect—to spy out the land. You didn't believe that story about the smelling salts, did you?"

"Yes, I did," replied Letty.

Sir Julius shrugged his shoulders.

"You must let me deal with these people, Letty. I'm a match for them. Linkinghorne and a silly child are not likely to worry me. We are all in the hands of God, and it's not death that men fear so much as dishonor. Please leave me, Letty. I wish to be alone—for a few minutes."

Letty made her way down the stairs to the dining room, and there she found Rose Ivory. The two girls smiled at each other.

—

Shotlander Priory looked grim and terrible in the pale winter sunlight. Most of the outer shell remained, but all the inner walls, built of timber and plaster, had perished.

To Letty the ruins were the very emblems of death. They stood for the fulfillment of the curse, for the end of an old and honored family.

Sir Julius Kingsbury, however, had not come to Shotlander to gaze on desolation and to moralize. He and the two girls walked round the blackened shell, and only paused by the windows of the library.

"It was in this room," said the baronet, "that the fire started. I think I shall climb in through the window and have a good look round."

"Oh, it is dreadful to leave the place like this," exclaimed Rose. "Why don't they come and clear away the rubbish and——"

"My dear young lady," Sir Julius interrupted, "at present there is no one to give orders, for it is not known whether Richard Burden is alive or dead. And as for clearing away the debris, no one would trouble to do that unless they were starting to rebuild the house. Everything of value was saved, except the contents of this one room, which were burnt to ashes."

He crossed the broad flower bed, and scrambled through the gaping hole where there had once been a window—the way by which Robertson had taken his departure on the night of his visit to Richard Burden.

"I shall go for a walk," said Letty decisively. "I want to get out of sight of this place. Will you accompany me, Miss Black."

"Oh, I think I'll stay here," Rose replied. "I have never seen anything like this before. I'll remain with Sir Julius."

"Right you are. I'll be back in half an hour, Father. What time do we leave?"

The baronet was indefinite in his reply. He might be busy for a while. But most certainly he would not be ready to go in half an hour.

Letty walked across the broad stretch of lawn and made her way past the stables to the kitchen garden—three acres of ground enclosed by a high mellow brick wall. Not a soul to be seen!

After a time she wandered into a private road which ran under the overhanging boughs of trees—the road, so she supposed, to one of the lodges. When she had walked a quarter of a mile she encountered a path that branched off to the left. She followed this for a little way, and came suddenly upon a very old man sitting upon the trunk of a fallen elm. He was looking at something that lay on the open palm of his hand. He did not raise his head at her approach, but his fingers closed on what he held. She recognized him from a portrait that had appeared in one of the illustrated daily papers. It was Atkins, the old butler—the faithful servant who had lived under the rule of four successive owners of Shotlander Priory.

"I am Letty Kingsbury," she said gently. "I was engaged to be married to Mr. Dick Burden. May I sit down here for a little while and talk to you?"

The old man took off his hat and rose to his feet, standing bareheaded. Tears came into his eyes.

"I am not too old to stand, miss," he said in a quavering voice. "I would not dream of taking the liberty——"

"Nonsense," replied Letty sharply. "I want to talk to you—I want you to tell me everything."

The old man unclosed the fingers of his left hand and Letty saw a worn and dented cigarette case.

"His cigarette case!" she cried. "Where did you get it? He had it with him the last time I ever saw him."

"Is that true, miss? Are you sure that you've not made a mistake?"

"I am quite certain. I saw him that morning—the day he disappeared. Where did you find it?"

"In this wood, and not more than half an hour ago, miss. I kicked aside some leaves while I was walking, and there it lay. I knew it at once."

She took the cigarette case from his hand and stared at its blackened surface.

"The fire!" she cried. "No, of course it was not the fire. How silly I am! But Mr. Dick must have been here—no, how foolish I am!—it may have been stolen from him." She caught the old man by his arm.

"Where did you find it?" she exclaimed. "Please show me the exact spot."

The old butler walked along through the trees for a hundred yards, and then came to a wide clearing in the wood. Here there was a pool about a quarter of an acre in extent, and on the far side was a small Grecian temple. It was partly in ruins, and almost hidden with enormous masses of ivy. And beyond this shrine there was only a narrow belt of trees between the building and the road.

As they walked round the edge of the pool, Letty Kingsbury shuddered at the dark stillness of its waters.

"It was just here that I found the cigarette case, miss," said the old butler, pointing with his stick at the decaying leaves.

"We must tell the police at once!" Letty exclaimed. "It will acquaint them with the fact that Mr. Dick has been here since I last saw him at Easthill."

"Aye, and that his house was burnt to the ground that night and that he took no notice."

For a few moments they looked at each other in silence, and then the old man shook his head.

"And if he is dead," he continued, "we cannot bring him to life again. But if he is alive there are reasons why he would not wish us to tell the police."

"You think—you dare to think that——"

"I think no ill of Mr. Dick," the old man interrupted harshly. "But if he has reasons for keeping silence it is not for those who love him to interfere. If he can get the better of his enemies by pretending to be dead, is it for us to inform the police that perhaps he is alive? Mr. Dick, he plays his own game."

His right hand swung out and the cigarette case fell into the center of the pool.

"That will not prevent me from telling Mr. Linkinghorne," said the girl coldly.

"Nor me from saying that you were dreaming, miss. But if you love Mr. Dick you'll hold your tongue—for a little while."

He walked away along the path until he was lost to sight. Letty Kingsbury stood motionless for a little while. And then she was suddenly seized with a desire for action. She went on her knees and began to search among the dead leaves. But she found nothing.

Chapter XV · Rose on the Trail

—

On the following day Sir Julius Kingsbury suggested that he and his daughter should leave Cowhurst and stay for a day or two at

"Chequers" at Stilehurst. Letty offered no opposition to this change in her father's plans. Indeed, it fitted in with her own wishes. After the old butler's discovery of Dick Burden's cigarette case in the woods at Shotlander, the possibilities of Cowhurst seemed of little importance.

On their return from the Priory, and through part of the night, Letty lay awake for several hours, and even in her dreams the girl was conscious of some force that drew her back to the gaunt ruins of Dick's house, and the woods that lay round it, and the dark, silent pool, and the Grecian temple that was almost hidden with the growth of ivy. It was not that she expected to find anything there that would throw light on the mystery of her lover's disappearance. There was only a vague longing to be near Shotlander.

And there were other reasons why she was glad her father had decided to go to the "Chequers."

Both Linkinghorne, the great detective, and Robertson, the man for whom the police had advertised, were staying at the inn. She was curious to see Linkinghorne, but she particularly wanted to see Robertson.

They reached the Stilehurst hotel at seven o'clock in the evening, not so very long after the detective had perused the letter from Rose Ivory. Linkinghorne was informed of their arrival by the landlord.

"I thought you ought to know, sir," said Elkinson. "They never wrote about rooms, or I'd have told you."

"Thank you," said Linkinghorne with a smile. "You are quite right to report their arrival but it is of no importance whatsoever. If Sir Julius should ask to see me, will you please tell him that I am ill and cannot possibly meet him until tomorrow. I will have my dinner up here. Has Mr. Jones come in yet?"

"Yes, sir. He's in the billiard room."

"Would you ask him to come up here?"

"Certainly, sir."

"Oh, and by the by, Mr. Elkinson, I am so unwell that I am not to be disturbed tomorrow morning until noon. I shall put a notice on my bedroom door to that effect. You will call me yourself, and if you get no answer you will understand that I am not in my room. I may have to leave here suddenly, but I do not wish anyone to know that I have gone. Don't forget to send Jones."

———

Rose Ivory said goodbye to the Kingsburys, and went upstairs to her bedroom. She had been told that they were going to the Chequers Inn, but she had no intention of following them. Linkinghorne was there on the spot, and he could deal quite effectively with the situation. She had other matters to attend to, and she was going to do her work well and thoroughly.

She dined by herself in the old paneled room, and was served with a remarkably good dinner. She ate with her hat on and her coat flung over a chair by the side of her. She had paid her bill and was going to leave the inn at nine o'clock. Long before the departure of the Kingsburys she had made her plans, and had dispatched a telegram to a garage at Easthill, asking the proprietor to send a car for her—to take her home. She intended to find Richard Burden—alive and in hiding. Rose Ivory had always believed that Dick had killed his brother and that he had vanished in such a way as to lead the police to think he had been murdered. Her theory—and she had put it into so many words—was that the Burden family was rotten to the core, and that thus it had been doomed to perish. James had murdered Robert for the sake of the inheritance, and the latter had been killed by Richard. No doubt in time Dick would turn up with a wonderful story of captivity and an attempt on his life.

So far—up to the previous day—this had been only a theory. But now there were facts to support it. She had only remained a few minutes with Sir Julius Kingsbury in the ruins of the Priory. Then, making some excuse, she had wandered off to investigate. She had taken the same road as Letty, but instead of turning down the path into the wood, she had kept straight on, had seen the Grecian temple through the trees, and had actually been inside it when Letty and the old butler had appeared on the further side of the pool. She had concealed herself in the great masses of ivy and had overheard the conversation between Letty and Atkins and she had seen the butler fling the cigarette case into the pool. She had managed to slip away unobserved and rejoin Sir Julius several minutes before Letty's return.

And now she was quite certain that Richard Burden was in hiding, and that Atkins knew where he was. She intended to watch the old butler, who would of course have to keep his master supplied with food and water. That Atkins had shown the cigarette case to Letty Kingsbury did not trouble her at all. Atkins had doubtless reasons of his own for suggesting to Letty Kingsbury that Richard Burden might not be dead.

At nine o'clock the car arrived, and Rose was pleased to see that Prince, the proprietor, was driving it.

"I am not going straight home," she explained when she had seated herself beside him and the vehicle was running through the village.

"Do you know the road to Shotlander Priory?"

"Yes, Miss Ivory, but you're not going there at this time of night, are you?"

"I am, Mr. Prince."

"But your father will be expecting you home tonight, Miss Ivory, won't he?"

"No. Look here, Mr. Prince, I'm engaged on very important and secret business for the police. I may have to keep you out all night. Do you mind?"

"Not at all, Miss Ivory—so long as I am paid for it."

"Well, I may keep you waiting for me at Shotlander. On the other hand, I may find someone there who will drive me over to Stilehurst to see Mr. Linkinghorne."

Mile after mile they drove on through the darkness. When at last they reached one of the lodges in the park there was a yellow glow of light in a window, and the gates were closed. They skirted the park wall until they came to another lodge. This was in darkness, and there were no gates at all. Rose had already ascertained that this cottage was uninhabited, and that the entrance was no more than a quarter of a mile from the kitchen garden. The road, in fact, was the continuation of the road that ran past the Grecian temple.

Rose Ivory asked Prince to back his car onto the grass, put out the lights, and leave it there under the shadow of some tall ilex trees.

"You must stay here," she whispered, "and look after the car."

He protested and vowed he would accompany her.

They were still arguing in low tones when they heard the hum of a motor in the distance, and they shrank close to the wall. The high-pitched note came closer and closer, and then it dropped several tones with the falling speed of the engine. Fierce lights blazed between the gateless pillars and a big car swung round the corner into the park and quickened its pace again. The lights dimmed to a mere yellow glow, and in a few seconds they vanished altogether among the trees.

"They have come for Richard Burden," said Rose to herself. "He is going to escape tonight."

"Now, what might they be doing here?" queried Prince. "No one living in the park but the servants and gamekeepers and so on."

"Why, these are my friends," Rose said—"the people I'm expecting to meet here."

"You're sure of that, eh?"

"Quite certain. I recognize the car. I told them I'd meet them further on by the house. I must go at once. I shall be alright. I have a little pistol in the pocket of my coat. You must stop here."

"For how long, Miss Ivory?"

"For an hour—no, perhaps for two. If I'm not back then you can come and look for me."

Rose Ivory walked away across the road, a very faint white streak in the darkness. Her hands were thrust into the pockets of her thick warm coat, and her fingers closed on the butt of an automatic. The weapon gave her no confidence, for she knew that she could not fire at Dick Burden if he tried to escape, or at old Atkins, or the driver of the strange car if they interfered with her. She could threaten them, but she could not take a man's life.

She realized now that she had acted like a little fool. She ought to have gone to Linkinghorne, and he would have done the job properly. But she had desired the sole honor and glory of this capture. For years she had dreamed of an occasion like this—an occasion in which she would do something really striking and remarkable. Somehow or other the reality was not as picturesque as the dream. There was not even a glimmer of romance in the darkness and the sighing of the wind among the leafless trees.

Chapter XVI · Gripping Moments

Sir Julius Kingsbury extinguished the lights of the big car, stopped the engine fifty yards further on, and stepped down from the driver's seat. He knew well enough that he had gone on his final journey, and that never again would he see the light of day. Robertson had made that quite plain to him when they had that last terrible interview at the Chequers Inn—when the baronet had caught Robertson stealing out of the house and had followed him and made him return.

Robertson had accounted for Linkinghorne and Jones. He had drugged the whiskies and sodas, and had left the two detectives in a deep sleep. He had locked the door on them and had smiled at the notice Linkinghorne himself had written: "Please do not call me until noon." Oh yes, Robertson had dealt very effectively with Linkinghorne and Jones. But Robertson had not taken him, Sir Julius Kingsbury, the wretched slave of Robertson, into account. Robertson had forgotten the old proverb that even a worm will turn, and he certainly had not imagined that a man would take his own life to see justice done in the world.

"I must go tonight," Robertson had said. "Every day since my return I have waited for an opportunity. I cannot wait any longer. If I do, Richard Burden will be dead."

Then he, Sir Julius, had asked questions, and Robertson had said:

"You understand what it means if I answer these interrogations or if you stop me from going?" And the baronet had replied: "Yes, Robertson, I know. But there is a way out for me. I can kill you and take my own life—here and now. I ought to have done that long ago."

"Here and now?" Robertson had laughed. "Oh yes, of course! But then poor Dick Burden will die. And you don't want that, do you—for your daughter's sake? And I certainly don't. For here I am, ready to sacrifice myself in an attempt to save the life of one man and the soul of another. Let us first see if we can find Dick Burden, and then discuss what we shall do with our miserable lives."

And they had left it at that, saying little, for they knew each other's secrets, and they were not to be spoken of, nor was there any need to utter them—unless, perhaps, at the very last, when they were so near to eternal silence that they would grasp eagerly at the few minutes of speech left to them.

The door of the closed car opened and Robertson stepped out upon the grass by the side of the road. A shaft of light flashed on Kingsbury's face, and again there was darkness. It was significant that the two men had not been seated side by side, that Robertson had been in the closed part of the car, where he could not talk to Kingsbury. It was as though they most certainly had nothing further to say to each other.

Kingsbury followed Robertson along the road in silence, not seeing him in the intense darkness under the trees, but only hearing the sound of his footsteps. The light flashed out again, and Robertson's hand closed over it. The crimson glow of the flesh of the latter's hand showed like a smear of blood. Kingsbury followed the gleam as they left the road and turned aside through the trees. Robertson stopped, and the light flashed out again on a wet, tangled mass of ivy, falling like a great green cascade from the roof of the building to the ground.

"It is here," said Robertson, speaking in a low voice, "that I must ask you for any weapon that you have brought."

"I have none," Kingsbury replied.

"You will allow me to search you while you hold your hands above your head?"

"Most certainly."

Robertson sought and found nothing, for the very good reason that Kingsbury had quietly dropped his pistol on the ground two yards from where he was standing and had swept a few dead leaves over it. He had not pitted his wits against the cunning of the East for twenty years without learning a few tricks of that sort.

"Thank you," said Robertson, and then he gripped Kingsbury by the arm, so hard, as a matter of fact, that Kingsbury gave a sharp moan of pain.

"You know my strength," said Robertson. "I could kill you with these two bare hands of mine as easily as you could destroy a rabbit."

The light flashed on the ivy again, and Kingsbury, stepping softly back a couple of paces, picked up the pistol and placed it in his pocket. He did not intend to murder Robertson. He only intended to see that Robertson went through with this job.

———

Rose Ivory, creeping softly through the trees, saw a light gleaming from the inside of the Grecian temple. It vanished, and she stood still, scarcely daring to breathe. It seemed to her that someone had heard her approach and that she would have to be very careful. For five minutes she did not move. There was not a sound but the sighing of the wind in the trees. She still hesitated, and then she did as brave a thing as any man or woman could do. She walked boldly forward and switched on her own electric torch. It showed her the great mass of ivy, and—as she went further on the pillars of the temple and the inside of it—the stone walls and seats and more tangled growth.

The place was empty, but there was a door at the back of it, half hidden by the ivy. The woodwork had once been painted white, but now was stained green and brown with age.

She stared at it for a few seconds. She was disappointed, for she remembered that she had seen the other side of this door, from the back of the temple. She could not forget the curious pattern of it. No doubt it had been placed there by the architect to suggest an entrance to further apartments, but it obviously only opened to the wood behind.

Great trails of greenery hung down over the door. Rose Ivory brushed them aside and caught hold of a brass handle, dark and slimy. And then she saw the marks of violence on the door—a battered lock and dented jamb.

"But leading out into the wood again?" she asked herself. And then she pulled at the handle and the door opened a few inches, and beyond it, in the light of her electric torch, she saw, not the carpet of dead leaves and the black trunks of trees, but a similar door—a door of precisely the same pattern, closed and barely eighteen inches away from its fellow.

Moving aside the ivy and opening the door still further, she noticed a narrow passage, running to the right. The thickness of the wall was a mere sham. There were two thin walls and two doors. It was a very ingenious device.

"A hiding-place," she said to herself, "and only known, perhaps, to members of the family."

She handled the ivy very carefully and squeezed herself through the narrow opening. Then she closed the door and walked along the passage, only to find herself facing a blank wall of painted deal paneling. The ingenuity of the builder was not yet exhausted. The girl sought for some exit, and several minutes elapsed before she found it—not in the paneling, but in the boarded floor. Two boards lifted up and disclosed a flight of stone steps. She descended twelve of them and found herself in another passage. She switched off the light and groped her way in the darkness, treading very carefully, and making sure of her foothold.

The passage was broad, and she could only just touch the walls by stretching out both her arms. The atmosphere was stifling at first, but grew more pleasant as she proceeded on her way. Being a very careful young woman, she counted her steps, so that she could measure distances. When she had traveled about three hundred yards, according to her own reckoning, she heard the sound of voices, and saw a gleam of light. After that she moved more slowly and carefully, and gripped her pistol in her right hand.

Chapter XVII · Life and Death

—

"You, Mr. Robertson?" said Dick Burden, as the bolt shot back and the heavy door opened. "Well, you've just come in time. I finished the last of the food this morning, and though there's plenty of water left it's getting a bit stale. And there's only another quart of oil for the lamp. Somehow I always thought you were in this."

Robertson looked round the cellar.

"A sofa," he said, "a chair and a table, food and drink, and an oil lamp. Not so bad. A good many men have less. We've come to set you free."

"Well, that's jolly nice of you," laughed Dick Burden. "I thought you'd come to murder me. But you are alone and you say 'we.' Oh, perhaps you were once an editor."

Robertson shrugged his shoulders. He was scrutinizing the face of the young man. Dick Burden, haggard, dirty, and unshaven, was not a very pleasant picture.

"We'll talk things over," he said after a pause. "Have a cigar?" and he held out his open case.

"Yes, a cigar would be just like heaven to me," replied Dick. "Not drugged, eh?"

"Oh no—quite alright."

Dick Burden lit up, and for a few moments he did not speak for sheer rapture at the taste of tobacco. Robertson kept his eyes fixed on the half-open door. I'd just like to know how you left my library that night," said Dick after a pause. "This way, I suppose."

"Yes—there was a sliding panel in the library. Of course, when the house was burnt down and the roof fell in, all traces of the secret entrance to this cellar were buried in the debris."

"I see—yes, I suspected that from the methods of the chap you paid to kill me. He must have gone through here to the library and set fire to the place, and then returned this way. So the house is burnt down, eh? I did not know that. I could not open the other door. Well, what's it all about, Mr. Robertson?"

The half-open door swung back, and Sir Julius Kingsbury entered the cellar.

"You, Sir Julius?" queried Dick Burden. "Oh, of course, this is just a nightmare. Where do you come in?"

The baronet made no reply. His face was ghastly in the light of the small oil lamp that burned steadily on the table.

"He forced his society on me," Robertson answered after a pause. "Of course, I need not have come here, but that would have been very bad for you, Mr. Burden. I did not know for certain that you were here. I had not even heard of your disappearance and the fire at Shotlander until I landed in England a few days ago. Then I went to the police, and I was taken ill—and I had no chance until tonight. You see, the police cannot be told the truth, and I had to come here without their knowledge. It has been difficult, but, thank Heaven, I am in time."

"I don't understand what you're talking about," said Dick Burden, but I'm jolly glad to see you. And I swear I won't get you into trouble if you'll let me out of this. That'll be alright, won't it, Sir Julius?"

"No. All the guilty shall suffer—all the murderers! Not one of them shall escape the wrath of God."

"Honeyman has escaped," said Robertson quietly. "Honeyman is dead."

"The little dark fellow with a scar on his forehead?"

"Yes," Sir Julius replied. "I suppose he trapped you, Burden."

"He did. I got a letter from Cowhurst asking me to be near this imitation Greek temple at five o'clock that evening. Now, I knew what a letter from Cowhurst meant, and I should have gone to the police with it. But I thought I was man enough to see the job through by myself. I dare say you know the contents of the letter, Mr. Robertson?"

"I do not."

"Well, it spoke of a treasure in gold and jewels—a treasure hidden away in some part of the house and grounds. This belonged to the Burden family, and the writer promised to show me where it was if I would give him half of it."

"Ah, greed!" exclaimed Robertson. "That has always been the real curse of the family! Greed and the love of gambling to satisfy greed! Thus Buck Burden ruined himself. Yes, that was the bait to catch any Burden."

"I was armed," Dick Burden continued, "and I thought I'd get the better of anyone who wanted to do me in. I set out in my car, but it broke down and I had to leave it in a garage. I was just going to take a train when a big Daimler came up and the driver—our friend Honeyman—called out to me and he asked me if he could take me anywhere. It was snowing at the time, as you remember——"

"I don't remember," Robertson interrupted, "for I was not in England."

"Well, Sir Julius will remember. I said to the man, 'What'll you charge to drive me to Shotlander Priory, near Stilehurst?' and the man replied, 'Seven pounds on a night like this, guv'nor.' I jumped into the vehicle. I thought the fellow might come in useful if there was a row." He paused and laughed, looking into their two grim faces.

"Honeyman was too smart for me," he went on. "It was not until he entered the park that he told me he had written me the letter. We'd had a breakdown on the way, I did not arrive until nearly eleven and by that time I'd rather got to like the chap. And when he showed me the entrance to this little trap I thought that he knew a thing or two, and perhaps there was a hidden treasure after all, and that the fact of the letter having been posted in Cowhurst was only a coincidence. Well, we reached this place, and, catching me off my guard, he hit me over the head. When I came to my senses I felt myself imprisoned but I haven't the faintest idea what good he got out of it."

"He was a maniac," said Sir Julius harshly—"a religious maniac. He fancied he had a mission to perform before he died, which was to be the instrument of the vengeance of God. The curse of the monk was unfulfilled, and he swore to fulfill it. He murdered your cousin and your brother; he flung one over the cliff and the other off the pier into the sea. For you he reserved the death by fire instead of water."

"You know this?"

"Yes, Mr. Robertson told me."

Robertson's hideous face wrinkled in a grin.

"Tell him all the truth, Sir Julius," he snarled—"that you saw the murder of Robert Burden."

Dick looked inquiringly at Sir Julius. And the old man bowed his head.

"Yes," he answered after a pause, "I saw that. So did Mr. Robertson. And—and—Dick, I would not let my daughter marry you."

"Tell him all the truth," reiterated Robertson—"everything."

"Mr. Robertson put pressure on me," said Sir Julius in a choking voice. "You see, Dick, this Honeyman was Robertson's son, and Robertson fought for him—used a very ugly weapon."

"Tell him all the truth!" shrieked Robertson. "Yes, Honeyman was my son, and he is dead; and there's nothing to fight for now. But say what weapon I used, Sir Julius. Come, this is the day when everything must be known."

Sir Julius Kingsbury was silent.

"Must I tell him?" queried Robertson. "I kept silence because Honeyman was my son. But why did you say nothing, Sir Julius Kingsbury?"

"It doesn't matter," Dick interposed. "I don't want to hear anything about it."

"But you should hear!" cried Robertson. "This is the day of judgment, and the secrets of all hearts shall be revealed. I was in India with Sir Julius, and——" He paused as he saw that Dick Burden was pressing his fingers to his ears. And then, looking round, he caught sight of Sir Julius pointing a pistol at his head.

"Not another murder, Sir Julius," he said with a laugh. "It is enough for a man to have one on his soul."

Dick Burden sprang to his feet.

"I'm going to get out of this," he exclaimed.

"No," Robertson replied. "You shall not leave here until you've heard what I've got to say."

"Oh, there are two of us against you, and one is armed."

Robertson picked up the table, swung it round, and hit Burden with such a terrific force that the young man was flung against the wall ten feet away from where he stood, and dropped in a crumpled heap on the floor. Sir Julius fired, but his hand was unsteady, and the bullet glanced off the leg of the uplifted table. And then the mass of wood came flying at him as he pulled the trigger again, and he sank down under the weight of it as it caught his shoulder and flung him round like a top. The next moment Robertson's gigantic hands were at his throat, crushing the life out of him.

And Sir Julius Kingsbury saw things in a red mist—the face of a dead man in India, and then the features of Robertson, as he had witnessed them from the window at Easthill, bringing fear and terror into his life, and again as he had viewed them in the dream at the Cowhurst inn.

And then there was the face of Honeyman—seen first on the cliffs and then, later on, from the window at Easthill on the day Dick Burden had vanished, and, for the last time—the face of a dead man that mocked him.

"Let go of him or I'll kill you," shrieked a ridiculously small voice. Robertson did not seem to hear it. He did not even look up from the blackened face of his enemy or perceive the pretty white face of Rose Ivory.

She fired, intending to wound him. But her hand was trembling, and she was not even a tolerable shot with the weapon. The pistol threw high. A small purple stain suddenly appeared on Robertson's temple. That was all, but Robertson lurched sideways and fell on his back. The grip of his terrible hands seemed to tighten in the brief agony of death.

Chapter XVIII · Golden Daydreams

—

Dick Burden and his wife sat on the grass under the trees on the far side of the great lawn at Shotlander. The house had been fully insured, and already the builders were at work on a new residence—a less palatial home, but one that was going to do credit to the foremost architect of the day.

It was late autumn, and they had just returned from their honeymoon in Norway. They were staying at the "Chequers" at Stilehurst, and every day they drove over to Shotlander. The woods were gorgeous with gold and crimson and brown, and the leaves had commenced to fall. The autumn sunlight was warm, and not a breath of air stirred the trees.

"Today is Father's birthday," said Letty after a long silence. "If he had been alive he would have been sixty today."

"He died fighting," said Dick gently. He saved my life."

This was a lie, but Dick Burden never tired of repeating it. He had lain for a month between life and death, and he had not been able to give any evidence until six weeks after the tragedy. Then he had made a simple but entirely false statement to the effect that Robertson had tried to kill him, and that Sir Julius had saved his life—first Sir Julius, by "drawing the enemy's fire," as Dick had put it, and then Miss Rose Ivory, who had finished the job.

That was true enough—that he owed his life to those two. His lie had been merely a suppression of the truth—a silence in regard to material facts. Locked in his own heart was the secret which had given Robertson power to demand the silence of Sir

Julius. Indeed, he knew nothing of this secret, save that Sir Julius had killed someone in India, and that Robertson had proof of the judge's guilt.

No shadow of this unknown crime rested on Letty. Dick Burden was not one who believed in the sins of the fathers being visited on the children. For himself he would not have cared if all the world had known of Sir Julius Kingsbury's crime. But he thanked God that Letty, his dear wife, had been spared all knowledge of her father's guilt. She was not even aware of Robertson's vague accusation—vague, but real enough, or Sir Julius would not have been made an accessory after the fact to the murder of Robert Burden.

Nor did the police know. It was possible that Rose Ivory was cognizant—that she had been outside the door for some little time before she entered the cellar. But, if so, the girl had decided to hold her tongue. In her evidence at the inquest she had distinctly stated that she had heard the first crash of the battle before she reached the end of the passage, and that she knew nothing of what had happened except that which she had seen with her own eyes. He, Dick Burden, had been the sole witness up to this point.

And Linkinghorne and the police had been far too busy over other matters to devote any time to a side issue. They had traced all Honeyman's movements and proved that he was really Robertson's son. They had discovered that he must have used the passage and the cellar as a hiding place during his "religious" war against the Burden family. They had found out that he had run away from home at the age of sixteen, that he had fought in the French Army in the war, that he had been wounded, and that his injuries had probably been the cause of his insanity.

Piece by piece, the history of his life had evolved itself, and even the mystery of his death had come to light. He had been alone in the car, flying down from the scene of his crime. Then for some reason or other he had turned back, and found the way blocked by the snowdrift. He had obviously left the car in order to find out the extent of the drift, and had died of heart failure.

The empty car had been found by a certain Edward Finlay, a professional thief. Finlay had seen a chance of stealing the vehicle, and had driven it back to London. Then, realizing that all the police of England were looking for this car, Finlay had abandoned it.

Subsequently Finlay had been sentenced for a series of car thefts, and had confessed to this one, after his footprints had been compared with the pattern of those left in the snow. But long before Finlay's arrest the police had ascertained that the vehicle had never belonged to Albert Honeyman at all, and that he himself had stolen it.

Oh yes, the police had been very busy and Linkinghorne had not worried himself about Sir Julius Kingsbury. The baronet was dead, and it was not the custom of the sleuth to waste his time on those who had shifted off this mortal coil. And besides, it was clear that Sir Julius was not quite in his right mind a few days before his end. Sir Julius had seen ghosts at the "Silver Buckle" in Cowhurst.

Nor had Dick Burden himself any time to waste on the deceased baronet. The horror of the past lay behind him, and he could only think of the future and the present. The blackened ruins of Shotlander Priory has been cleared away, and a new house was rising on the old site. His hand sought Letty's and found it, and his fingers gripped it hard.

"Your father was afraid of the curse," he said. "That was why he did not wish you to marry me. Well, then, if there ever was any evil in the race I think it must all have been concentrated in Robertson. Do you know, Letty, that when I first saw that fellow I fancied that he was some monstrous creation of the curse—something that had lived on century after century, to achieve the downfall of the race."

"But he only came to warn you."

"No, Letty, he came to accuse your father of having murdered poor old Jim."

"Oh, how horrible!" cried Letty. "My father, the most upright judge who ever lived—a man of honor—a really good man."

"Well, my idea was alright," Dick continued after a pause.

"Robertson's son—with Burden blood in him—very nearly did make an end of the family."

"Yet even in Robertson there was good," said Letty. "He could have left you to die, and he risked the discovery of everything by setting out that night to save you. Oh, dear Dick, need we talk of such terrible things?"

He took her in his arms and kissed her passionately.

"I'd go through it all again, sweetheart," he whispered. "With you as the prize."

—

THE END.

ABOUT THE AUTHOR

John Wyndham Parkes Lucas Beynon Harris (1903–1969) was the son of a barrister, who started writing short stories in 1925. During World War II he was in the civil service and then the army. In 1946 he went back to writing stories for publication in the United States and decided to try a modified form of science fiction, which he called "logical fantasy." As John Wyndham, he is best known as the author of *The Day of the Triffids,* but he wrote many other successful novels, including *The Kraken Wakes, The Chrysalids,* and *The Midwich Cuckoos* (adapted as the film *Village of the Damned*).

ABOUT THE TYPE

The principal text of this Modern Library edition was set in a digitized version of Janson, a typeface that dates from about 1690 and was cut by Nicholas Kis (1650–1702), a Hungarian working in Amsterdam. The original matrices have survived and are held by the Stempel foundry in Germany. Hermann Zapf (1918–2015) redesigned some of the weights and sizes for Stempel, basing his revisions on the original design.